Praise for Julie Klassen Novels

"Christy and RITA nominee Klassen creates a wonderful cast of engaging characters while neatly stirring in a generous dash of mystery and danger into the plot of her latest, charmingly romantic inspirational romance."

Booklist
about *The Girl in the Gatehouse*

"This story captured me in the very first pages and there was absolutely no putting it down. I highly recommend *The Girl in the Gatehouse* as well as Klassen's other three novels."

Author Vicki Tiede

"Klassen expertly infuses her Regency-set inspirational tale with a gothic atmosphere, resulting in a sweetly intriguing romance worthy of Victoria Holt."

Booklist
about *The Silent Governess*

"This book has scandal, mystery, secrets and a budding romance. The characters are written in such detail the reader will forget they are fictional! Klassen has outdone herself with this latest novel. Her writing is comparable to Jane Austen's. She writes with passion and readers will not be able to put this book down."

Romantic Times
about *The Girl in the Gatehouse*,
4.5 stars and Top Pick

"This was one story I wasn't able to put down at all from beginning to end. Full of intrigue and romance, *The Silent Governess* is steeped in gothic atmosphere and fascinating research. I have been a fan of Ms. Klassen's since reading her debut book, *Lady of Milkweed Manor*, and her books just keep getting better and better. She is a must read author!"

CK2S Kwips and Kritiques

"This is an inspired and well-told story of mystery, intrigue and the politics of upstairs and downstairs folk in 19th-century England. The author takes the reader back in time effortlessly. If you enjoy Jane Austen or the Regency period, you will love this book."

Romantic Times
about *The Silent Governess*

"Klassen blends her tale well; each ingredient—romance, friendship, healing arts, mystery—is measured to produce a lively, lengthy tale that will satisfy Regency aficionados and general readers, too."

Publishers Weekly
about *The Apothecary's Daughter*

"Once again, author Julie Klassen delivers a satisfying historical account with plenty of twists to make you want to read just one more chapter. Her characters carry a Dickens' flavor. *The Apothecary's Daughter* is a five-star read."

Novel Reviews

"Klassen has written an amazing historical novel and she handles a 19th-century taboo with grace, style and respect."

Romantic Times
about *Lady of Milkweed Manor*

"Julie Klassen weaves a compelling story . . . fully imagined. I loved it!"

Beverly Lewis, *New York Times* bestselling author
about *Lady of Milkweed Manor*

"This is truly one of the most emotionally gripping novels I've ever read. . . . This story is so full of passion that it will make your heart sing."

Author Michelle Sutton
about *Lady of Milkweed Manor*

The Maid of
Fairbourne Hall

Books by Julie Klassen

FROM BETHANY HOUSE PUBLISHERS

Lady of Milkweed Manor

The Apothecary's Daughter

The Silent Governess

The Girl in the Gatehouse

The Maid of Fairbourne Hall

The Maid of Fairbourne Hall

JULIE KLASSEN

BETHANY HOUSE PUBLISHERS
a division of Baker Publishing Group
Minneapolis, Minnesota

Published by Bethany House Publishers
11400 Hampshire Avenue South
Bloomington, Minnesota 55438
www.bethanyhouse.com

Bethany House Publishers is a division of
Baker Publishing Group, Grand Rapids, Michigan

Printed in the United States of America

Library of Congress Cataloging-in-Publication Data
Klassen, Julie, 1964–
    The maid of Fairbourne Hall / Julie Klassen.
        p. cm.
    ISBN 978-0-7642-0709-9 (pbk.)
    I. Title.
PS3611.L37M35 2011
813'.6—dc23   2011036843

Unless otherwise identified, Scripture quotations are from the King James Version of the Bible.

Cover design by Jennifer Parker

Cover photography by Mike Habermann Photography, LLC

11 12 13 14 15 16 17   7 6 5 4 3 2 1

In each of my four previous novels,
I've included, as a character,
a kind or helpful aunt.
Perhaps this is because I've been blessed
with such outstanding aunts in my own life.
And so, I dedicate this book to my aunts—

Carol, Madeline, Barbara, Sharon, and Lou.

And to Lila, wherever you are.

"Judge not according to the appearance. . . ."

—Jesus Christ

*The only aristocrat known to have
disguised herself as a servant is Georgiana,
Duchess of Devonshire, in 1786.*

—Giles Waterfield and Anne French, *Below Stairs*

Chapter 1

LONDON
AUGUST 1815

He is reading my letters now too....
Margaret Elinor Macy sat at her dressing table, heart
pounding. Her face in the looking glass shone pale beneath
curly dark hair, her light blue eyes anxious. She glanced from her
reflection to the letter in her hand. The seal had been pried open and
unsuccessfully re-pressed. Her mother's new husband had obviously
begun checking her post—perhaps fearful the next invitation she
received would not be to a ball but rather to take refuge in another
house, out of reach and out from under his power.

It was bad enough when the footman began following her every-
where she went, whether the occasion warranted a servant's escort
or not. Then an hour ago she had asked to wear her aunt's pearl
necklace, only to be refused.

"Too many footpads on the streets at night," Sterling Benton had said. Though she and her mother had always worn their better jewelry before.

Sterling had locked in his safe almost all the Macy family valuables "for safekeeping." Privately Margaret guessed he'd sold some pieces and locked the rest away so she couldn't barter them for passage somewhere far away.

He had long since ceased granting her any allowance, claiming strained finances. That might be true, but Margaret knew Sterling had other motives for keeping her dependent on him for every shilling. Though soon to inherit a large sum from her great-aunt, at the moment Margaret was unable to buy herself a hairpin, let alone passage anywhere.

She regarded her wan reflection once more. She was not looking forward to the ball at the Valmores', though in the past masquerades had been her favorite. She loved the disguises, the mystery, the chance to flirt behind a mask, to pretend she was someone she was not. For weeks she had planned to appear as a milkmaid, a costume the Duchess of Queensberry had donned for a formal portrait, sparking a rage of paintings of gentlewomen in servants' attire. Margaret guessed she would not be the only "milkmaid" in attendance that evening.

Her coiffeur was a concoction of dark hair piled high with a long spiral curl gracing each side of her neck. But she was having second thoughts about it. She had relished the notion of fooling the other guests until masks were removed halfway through the ball. At the moment, however, the very idea of costumes seemed frivolous. Besides, the dark hair did not flatter her complexion.

Reaching up, she yanked the wig from her head.

"Joan!" she called sharply.

The second housemaid had doubled as young lady's maid ever since Sterling had dismissed Margaret's abigail. The experienced lady's maid, Miss Durand, was busy arranging Mother's hair. Margaret sniffed. As if it mattered how well a married woman looked. *Her* future did not depend on appearing her prettiest that night.

Joan, a thin, practical housemaid in her midtwenties, hurried in carrying a lace cap and the cape she had been pressing. She tripped over Margaret's dressing gown, bunched on the carpet where Margaret had let it fall. Why had Joan not picked it up?

"Do be careful," Margaret snapped. "I don't want my cape ruined or the cap crushed."

"Yes, miss." As Joan righted herself, irritation flashed in her eyes.

Well, she had only herself to blame. After all, it was Joan's job to tidy the room and care for Margaret's clothes.

"I need you to dress my hair," Margaret said. "I have decided not to wear the wig after all."

"But . . ." The maid bit her lip, then sighed. "Yes, miss."

Joan had secured Margaret's blond hair in a tight knot to accommodate the wig, but now she would need to unpin, curl, arrange, and re-pin her hair with soft height and curls at her temples to flatter Margaret's somewhat round face. She hoped a simple housemaid was up to the task. Margaret guessed she would have to talk her through the process.

Margaret herself had become quite adept at arranging her sister's hair. Enjoyed it, actually. Fortunately, Caroline had not yet "come out" and was not attending the ball, otherwise three Macy women would never be ready in time.

Joan unpinned the knot and began brushing out Margaret's fair locks, using, Margaret thought, a bit more force than necessary.

"Gentle, Joan. I have no wish to be bald."

"Yes, miss."

Margaret had often been told her fair golden hair was her best feature. She could not, on this night of nights, cover it up. She would need all the appeal she could muster if her plan had any hope of succeeding.

Margaret entered wearing the simple blue gown, apron, and mask, with a small lace cap atop her glorious hair and a milk pail in hand. Studiously ignoring the young man beside her, she surveyed the ballroom.

The goddess Diana laughed with a sultan in turban and flowing robes. Egyptians in headdresses, jewels spangling their foreheads, danced with gypsies. Punch's wife mingled with beggars. Some people sacrificed anonymity for attractiveness. Others, especially those wearing the ubiquitous dominoes—masks over their faces and hooded capes—were unrecognizable. The gay music, colorful costumes, laughter, and jesting created a carnival-like atmosphere. But the jovial feeling did not reach Margaret and did nothing to ease her anxiety.

She saw him across the ballroom, and her muscles tensed—a lithe cat fixing upon her prey. Yet she feared she would be the one left injured.

Lewis Upchurch wore a rakish patch over one eye, but was otherwise perfectly turned out in fine evening attire of black tailcoat, pristine white waistcoat and cravat, knee-length pantaloons, and polished shoes. He stood talking to a man and woman. The man she recognized as Lewis's friend Piers Saxby. He wore a tricorn hat and kerchief, looking very like engravings she had seen of Blackbeard and other pirates of old. Margaret was acquainted with Saxby's sister, Lavinia. The two girls had been at school together. Perhaps she might inquire after Lavinia as an excuse to approach the trio.

But she would need to tread carefully. Lewis Upchurch might be a good catch, but he would not be an easy one, and she was by no means certain of her ability to snare him. For a moment she stood where she was, shocked by her mercenary thoughts.

A few years ago, when she learned of the inheritance coming to her upon her twenty-fifth birthday, she'd thought she had no need to marry. Great Aunt Josephine, a spinster herself, had seen to that. Margaret had planned to take her time, marry for love or not at all. But with the odious man beside her determined to spoil that plan, she was willing to compromise. She would never marry a man she loathed, but she could marry charming, handsome Lewis Upchurch. She had been quite infatuated with him once. Had even rejected his brother in hopes of winning him. And Lewis, she believed, had admired her. He had certainly flirted with her.

But then her beloved father had died, and Margaret had lost interest in Lewis Upchurch and society at large. She had remained home in mourning for more than a year. When she had reentered society earlier this season, Lewis had shown renewed if sporadic interest in her, but nothing had come of it. Was she too late?

Pushing back her shoulders, Margaret removed her mask and steeled her resolve. Enticing a proposal from Lewis Upchurch was her best hope, her only plan for escaping the Benton house and the vile snare set for her by Sterling and his nephew.

As if her thoughts, her intentions, had been declared aloud, the young man beside her stiffened. She risked a glance at Marcus Benton and found him following the direction of her gaze across the room. His wide-set catlike eyes narrowed. He looked at her, smile smug beneath his pug nose. He was not a tall man, only an inch or so taller than she. Dark tousled hair fell over his forehead in imitation of casual ease, yet she knew his valet had spent half an hour arranging it. She had once thought Marcus handsome, but no longer.

He took her arm, but she shrugged it off. Inhaling deeply, Margaret strode across the ballroom, empty now between dances. At the head of the room, musicians relaxed over punch and ale, laughing amongst themselves. Directly ahead of her, Lewis Upchurch faced Mr. Saxby and the woman she did not recognize. Like Margaret, her face was exposed. She wore the clingy Grecian robes of a Diana. Margaret would have liked to speak to Lewis alone, but she dared not wait or her courage would fail her. Perhaps the other couple would excuse themselves.

Margaret bolstered herself by remembering that Lewis had shown particular interest in her in the past, seeking her out for dancing, escorting her in to supper on several occasions, calling the next morning as etiquette required. Lewis had been pleasant and attentive, not to mention heartbreakingly handsome. But he had never proposed. Perhaps she had not encouraged him properly. After all, she had been in no hurry to marry.

Until now.

Besides Marcus Benton, only one man had ever proposed marriage to her, and that had been two years ago, before Lewis returned from the West Indies and turned her head. The memory of the way she had coldly and abruptly rejected Nathaniel Upchurch, Lewis's younger brother, still brought a stab of guilt. Nathaniel would have married her once, but she had certainly crushed any feelings he held for her. At all events, Nathaniel was far away in Barbados, and had been for nearly two years, managing the family's sugar interests in Lewis's stead. Even Nathaniel—meek, pale, studious, bespectacled younger son that he was—would have been a better fate than Marcus Benton.

Margaret smiled as she neared the trio, hoping no one noticed her brazen approach. She willed Lewis to look her way, hoping his face would light up when he saw her. She paused before them and Lewis glanced over, but her appearance brought no light to his countenance. If anything, caution shadowed his dark eyes, at least that was how her insecure soul read his expression. *Don't appear too eager,* she reminded herself. A man like Lewis Upchurch was accustomed to desperate women and their desperate mammas throwing themselves at him. She must be careful.

"Miss Macy," he acknowledged politely.

She nodded at him, then turned her most beguiling smile—she hoped—on his friend instead. "Mr. Saxby. You may not remember me, but I was at school with your sister, Lavinia."

Piers Saxby was a few years older than Lewis, his features somewhat ordinary. But he invariably embellished his appearance with all the trappings of a dandy: fine clothes, quizzing glass, and snuffbox.

The man's dull grey eyes lit with recognition if not interest. "Ah, Miss Macy, of course. Indeed, I recall Lavinia mentioning your name." He bowed, and Margaret dipped a curtsy sure to show off her feminine curves. She hoped Lewis was watching.

But when she glanced back up, her heart fell. For Lewis had already returned his attention to the woman beside him. The very beautiful woman, Margaret now saw at closer range.

Sensing her gaze, Lewis Upchurch cleared his throat and said dutifully, "Miss Macy. Have you met the lovely Miss Lyons?"

Margaret turned to the striking brunette. "I have not had that pleasure."

"Then allow me. Miss Barbara Lyons, may I present Miss Margaret Macy. I believe you are acquainted with her stepfather, Sterling Benton?"

The woman's dark eyes sparkled. "Indeed I am. An exceedingly handsome man and most charming too. Do you not find him so, Miss Macy? Why, if he were my stepfather I should never leave home."

Margaret swallowed the hot retort burning her throat and pasted on a false smile. "I don't actually think of Mr. Benton as a stepfather, as I was already grown when he married my mother."

"Quite right, Miss Macy." Barbara Lyons grinned. "If I were you I should not care to think of such a man as my stepfather either."

Margaret shuddered at the woman's innuendo.

"How you must enjoy living in Mr. Benton's fine house in Berkeley Square," the woman added.

Margaret noticed neither she nor Saxby showed any sign of leaving Lewis's side.

"I miss the country, actually," Margaret replied. "And from where do you hail, Miss Lyons?"

"Ah, you must excuse us, Miss Macy," Lewis Upchurch interrupted. "For Miss Lyons here has promised me the next dance, and the musicians are even now preparing to play."

"Oh . . . of course," Margaret faltered, observing with chagrin that as yet only one musician had returned to his place. "Em . . . enjoy your dance." She again curtsied and turned away.

It hadn't been the *cut direct*, but close to it. Cheeks flaming, she walked toward the door, trying not to hurry, hoping her mortification was not obvious to the milling throngs. Nor to Marcus Benton.

She escaped the ballroom and hastened across the hall to the salon designated as the ladies' dressing room for the evening. Inside, her friend Emily Lathrop tied a cloak about her shoulders and replaced her reticule over gloved wrist.

"Emily! How glad I am to see you. Are you leaving already?"

"Yes. Mamma has a headache and wants to go home."

"So do I, as it happens. Might I beg a ride?"

"Of course. But surely your family would—?"

"Oh . . ." Margaret feigned a casual air. "The Bentons are not ready to leave, and I do hate to spoil their evening."

Emily touched her arm, eyes concerned. "They cannot force you to marry him, you know."

Margaret arched one brow. "Can they not? I shall hold you to it." She gathered her shawl and followed her friend into the hall.

There, raised voices from the ballroom drew them back to its doors. *Bang. Squeal*—wood against wood. An overturned chair slid across the floor. The music stopped, one violin shrieking in protest as the musicians lowered their instruments one after the other, and dancers scattered.

Emily grasped Margaret's wrist and pulled her into the ballroom. Margaret resisted, not wanting anyone to see her dressed to depart, but Emily ignored her and stepped closer. Both young women craned their necks to see past taller gentlemen and ladies' feathers to identify the cause of the commotion.

Ringed by the cautious but curious crowd, two men stood, chests out, hands fisted. Both were tall and dark-haired. Lewis Upchurch stood facing their direction, his handsome features sparking with shock and irritation. For one moment, Margaret thought the other man was Piers Saxby, offended at the attention Lewis paid Miss Lyons. But in the next she remembered that Saxby wore evening dress beneath his tricorn hat, while the man facing Lewis wore trim buckskin breeches, tall boots, and a riding coat.

"You are needed at home," the man growled.

Lewis smirked. "And hello to you too."

"Now."

The man's profile came into view—a black beard obscured his features, making him look twice the pirate Saxby had appeared.

"Temper, temper, Nate. Are these the manners you learnt in the West Indies?"

16

Margaret gasped. It couldn't be.

"And what of your manners?" the second man challenged. "Did Father not write and ask you to return home and do your duty?"

Nathaniel Upchurch. Margaret couldn't believe it. Gone were the pale features, the thin frame, the hesitant posture, the spectacles. Now broad shoulders strained against his cutaway coat. Form-fitting leather breeches outlined muscular legs. The unfashionable dark beard emphasized his sharp cheekbones and long nose. His skin was golden brown. His hair unruly, some escaping its queue. Even his voice sounded different—lower, harsher, yet still familiar.

Lewis grinned. "I am doing my duty. I am representing our other-wise dull family during the important social season."

Nathaniel glanced around as if suddenly aware of their audience. "Will you step outside to speak with me in private or shall I drag you?"

"You might try."

Nathaniel grabbed Lewis's arm, and Lewis lurched forward, caught off guard by the strength of the pull.

Beside her Emily whispered, "Is that Nathaniel Upchurch?"

Margaret nodded.

"But he is so changed. Had he not been arguing with his brother, I should not have recognized him. He looks, well, nearly savage, does he not?"

Again, Margaret managed a wooden nod.

"If I did not know better, I would think him a pirate." Emily drew in a sharp breath. "Perhaps he is! Perhaps *he* is the Poet Pirate the papers are full of!"

Margaret barely heard her fanciful friend. Her mind was clouded with a vision of Nathaniel Upchurch as she had last seen him. Eyes wide, pained, and misty green behind smudged spectacles. His thin mouth downturned. Dejected.

Regaining his balance, Lewis shook his arm free. "Unhand me, ape."

At the insult, Nathaniel slammed his fist into his brother's jaw. Gasps and cries rose among the frozen guests, heating them to agitated life.

Margaret did not realize she had cried out as well, until Nathaniel's head snapped in her direction.

For a second he stood there, stilled, one hand grasping his brother's cravat, his other fisted. Across the distance, his gaze met hers. Margaret sucked in a breath at the intensity in those eyes. Intense not with love or longing, but with undisguised disgust. His thin lips twisted into a scowl, making his long nose hawklike.

If she had thought Lewis's recent snub painful, Nathaniel's reaction felt far more cutting, though not a single word had been exchanged. It was as she had feared. He had never forgiven her and could not stand the sight of her.

Margaret turned, snagging Emily's hand and pulling her away.

"What a brute!" Emily panted behind her. "Are you not glad you rejected him when you did?"

Margaret *was* relieved. How fierce he looked. She had never before been frightened of him, nor had she imagined him capable of violence.

Margaret paused only long enough to whisper in her mother's ear that the Lathrops were taking her home, then hurried away before she might object. Distracted as she was by the fight, her mother vaguely nodded. Sterling stood several yards away, his gaze trained on four guests in regimentals escorting the Upchurch brothers from the room.

*A married woman could not own
property, sign legal documents or enter into
a contract, or keep a salary for herself.*

—the legal doctrine of Coverture,
English Common Law

Chapter 2

O n the short ride to Berkeley Square, Margaret remained quiet
as Emily described the fight to her parents. Her mind was
preoccupied, reviewing the disturbing images, the disturbing memories, and her utter failure to achieve her ends.

The stately coach halted before Sterling Benton's tall, terraced town
house, and Margaret thanked the Lathrops and bid them good-night.
The groom handed her down, and she walked the few steps to the
front door. When the liveried footman opened it for her, she did not
miss the crease in his brow at seeing her arrive alone. Perhaps he feared
Sterling might somehow blame him for failing in his watchdog duty.

Margaret sailed past the lackey without so much as a nod of
acknowledgment. Crossing the hall, she lifted her skirt to avoid tripping as she climbed the many stairs.

Reaching the third level, she tiptoed first to Gilbert's bedchamber.
She peeked through the open door, getting a little lump in her throat
to see her brother sprawled across the bed, hand under his cheek and

hair askew, looking very much like the little boy she still thought him. She crept inside and pulled the bedclothes to his chin. Margaret prayed Sterling would not pull Gilbert from Eton as he threatened to do. Gil needed to learn all he could if he was to go on to Oxford and into the church, as their father had always hoped.

Next she stopped at her sister's room. More modest than her brother, Caroline's door was closed. Margaret inched it open and peered in, finding her asleep as well. At sixteen, Caroline would be attending balls very soon. Leaning over the bed, Margaret stroked the caramel-colored hair from her sister's brow. How innocent she looked. How sweet. A swell of love bordering on the maternal filled Margaret's breast.

Caroline's eyes fluttered open before drifting shut again. She murmured sleepily, "How was the ball?"

"Lovely," Margaret whispered, having no wish to worry her. "Sweet dreams, sweetness." *Sweetness*—her father's nickname for her. How long had it been since Margaret deserved the moniker?

She slipped from her sister's room and, taking advantage of their absence, crept down to the adjoining bedchambers Sterling and her mother shared. In Mamma's dressing room, she was surprised not to see the miniature of Stephen Macy displayed anywhere. It had been on the dressing table not long ago, she was sure. Margaret could understand not wanting it in the bedchamber, where Sterling would have to see it. But here in Mamma's private dressing room? Margaret opened the top drawer, and there it was, face down. How disloyal it seemed. She turned over the portrait and studied it, shaking her head in wonder. How much Gil was beginning to look like their father. "We have not forgotten you," she whispered to the handsome, youthful image. "At least, I have not."

Returning the small portrait to its place, she wandered through Sterling's dressing room. How impeccably neat everything was. She hoped his fastidious valet wouldn't catch her in there.

On Sterling's dressing table, she saw a handful of coins—guineas, crowns, and shillings.

Dared she?

As it was, she didn't even have coach fare, let alone money for lodgings, should the situation continue to escalate . . . or rather, deteriorate. She ought to have something put by, just in case. She should not be completely at Sterling's mercy until her inheritance came.

Yet Margaret was a vicar's daughter. She knew stealing was wrong. But was this really stealing, she asked herself, when he had taken her jewelry?

It was a loan, she decided. She would pay him back when she had money of her own. A few coins would seem a trifle then—but now? They might make the difference between escape and a trap. She selected several, but did not take them all—that would be too obvious. How cold the coins seemed against her fingertips, as she tucked them into the pocket of her "milkmaid" apron. She felt their weight all the way back to her room.

Once there, she slid the coins into her reticule. A few minutes later, Joan came in and helped her change into her nightclothes. As Margaret climbed into bed, the distant sound of the front door shutting surprised her.

They were home early.

She quickly blew out her bedside candle as Joan gathered the discarded clothing and backed from the room, closing the door behind her.

A few moments later, someone tapped lightly on her bedchamber door. Her stomach lurched. Was it her mother, or Sterling?

"Margaret?" someone whispered.

Marcus! At her bedchamber door, at night? Margaret's heart thumped in her breast. Surely he would not dare enter.

Candlelight flickered from under the door. Hushed voices echoed in the corridor—Marcus's and a woman's.

Nerves quaking, Margaret rose and tiptoed to the door.

"Yes, sir. Miss Macy's home," Joan said. "She's gone to bed."

Margaret knelt down and peered through the keyhole.

"Well then, Joan, there's nothing to keep *you* from . . ." Marcus's voice grew muffled. As Margaret's eyes adjusted to the flickering light, she saw Marcus pressing his face into Joan's neck, as though to whisper in her ear . . . or kiss her. Margaret's stomach roiled. She couldn't see Joan's face, but she saw Marcus capture the maid's hand and begin to tug her down the corridor.

"There you are, Mr. Benton." The low voice of Murdoch, their butler, interrupted the scene. "Your uncle requests your presence in the study."

Joan pulled her hand free. Marcus muttered an oath and disappeared.

Releasing a breath she had not realized she was holding, Margaret climbed back into bed. Yet long after Marcus's footsteps faded and the house was quiet, Margaret lay awake, unsettling images circling through her mind: Sterling and Marcus. Marcus and Joan. Miss Lyons and Lewis. Lewis and Nathaniel . . .

The last image she saw before sleep finally overtook her was Nathaniel Upchurch's look of disgust shooting across the ballroom and scorching her skin.

In the morning, Margaret entered the breakfast room, startled to find Sterling Benton eating alone. She'd hoped to avoid him, waiting until he, an early riser, would normally have departed, while his wastrel nephew would no doubt still be abed.

Sterling sat stirring a cup of coffee, although she knew he added neither sugar nor milk. With his thick silver hair, chiseled features, and confident sophistication, she understood what women like Miss Lyons, like her mother, saw in him. Still, how stunned and nearly sickened she had been when her mother announced her engagement to the man a mere twelvemonth after Stephen Macy's death.

Margaret forced a civil tone. "Good morning."

He looked up, piercing her with his icy blue eyes. "Is it? You tell me."

Margaret helped herself to a plate at the sideboard, more as an excuse to turn her back on him than eagerness for food. Finding herself alone with him, her appetite had fled.

"I take it you did not enjoy yourself last night," he said. "I did not approve of your leaving alone."

"I was not alone. I left with Emily Lathrop and her parents."

"And you did not dance once, although I am certain Marcus must have asked you."

Margaret knew any offer Marcus made—whether for a dance or marriage—was made at his uncle's behest.

"I was not in the mood for dancing," she said, thinking, *since Lewis Upchurch never asked.*

Sterling sipped his coffee. "You left before the most interesting part of the evening."

"Oh?"

"Nathaniel Upchurch returned from the West Indies as wild as a heathen. He struck his brother, Lewis, without provocation in front of the entire assembly."

Margaret had heard snatches of the argument and surmised there had been some provocation—at least in Nathaniel's mind—but she remained silent.

So Sterling had not seen her come back into the ballroom. The thought that Sterling's eagle eyes were less than perfect felt somehow comforting.

"Your mother tells me he once courted you," Sterling continued.

Margaret blindly placed a muffin on her plate. "That was years ago, before he left England."

"And you rejected his suit?"

"I did."

"Very wise, my girl. Very wise."

It certainly had seemed wise—then and more so now, after last night's violent demonstration. Still the smug tone irked. "And why is that?"

"Because you are free to marry Marcus. As it was meant to be. You cannot fight destiny, my girl."

He rose and stood beside her, his long manicured fingers pressing into her arm. "I would not advise fighting destiny, Margaret. Destiny always wins. And so, my dear, do I."

Margaret shivered but made no reply.

With a last warning look, Sterling left her.

Sighing, Margaret sat down to a solitary breakfast of tea, egg, and muffin. Her stomach churned, and she pushed away the food, sipping the tea instead.

It would not do her any harm to miss a few meals. She always put on a bit of weight during the season, with all the rich food and midnight suppers. Did Lewis Upchurch prefer willowy women like Miss Lyons? Apparently so.

Leaving her breakfast untouched, Margaret returned to her bed-chamber. From the bottom of her dressing chest, she lifted out the mahogany writing box where she kept mementos of her father. She raised the beautifully carved lid and breathed deeply. The aroma from a sachet she had made of her father's pipe tobacco enveloped her in its earthy, spicy familiarity. *Oh, Papa. How I miss you. . . .* She fingered her father's things—his New Testament, two letters he had written to her, his spectacles, and an old pair of his gloves. She gripped the limp leather fingers. What she wouldn't give to hold his hand once more.

That afternoon, Margaret bid a poignant farewell to her sister as her mother and Sterling looked on.

Caroline was returning to Miss Hightower's Seminary for Girls, where Margaret herself had attended years before. Loath to stay in the town house alone with the Benton men, Margaret offered to ride along.

Her mother hesitated. Joanna Macy Benton was a tall, handsome woman, though her once fair hair had darkened to a mousy brown and fine lines marred her face. She was a few years older than her dashing new husband, and all the complexion creams in London could not disguise that fact. Nor could her thin smile belie her deep unhappiness. For though Sterling Benton had pursued her with determined admiration and charm, both had quickly faded after the wedding, leaving the new bride confused and desperate to right whatever it was she had done wrong.

Her mother's eyes, wide and vulnerable, shifted to Sterling before returning to Margaret. "My dear, you know I would enjoy your company, but the barouche would be far too crowded with Caroline and her school friend. Not to mention their many belongings."

She glanced again at Sterling, eager for a look of approval. The two of them clearly had other reasons for wanting Margaret to remain in Berkeley Square.

A few hours later, her brother was packed and ready to leave as well. Gilbert had plans to spend the final few weeks of his term break at a friend's country estate, riding and shooting, until both boys had to return to Eton in early September. Margaret was happy for him, knowing he missed country life as much as she did, but sad for herself. How lonely she would be.

Blinking back tears, she embraced him and kissed his cheek.

"What's all this then, ey?" Gilbert protested her tight hold and grimaced at her tears. "Come on, Mags. I'm not going away forever. I shall see you at the end of next term."

She forced a smile. "Of course you will. I am only being silly."

He winked at her. "Well, nothing new there."

Although they did not speak of it, Margaret knew her young brother was aware of the tension in the house. She did not want him to worry, so she socked him on the shoulder on his way out the door, as any good sister would.

Afterward, Margaret went back upstairs to dress for dinner. She dreaded the thought of dining with only Sterling and Marcus. How uncomfortable that would be. She perused her wardrobe, apathetic about what to wear. Where was Joan? She pulled the bell cord to summon the maid to help her dress. Several moments passed, but no one came. Finally she heard the telltale *clitter-clat* of Joan's worn-to-the-nail half boots in the passage outside. But the footsteps hurried right past Margaret's room.

She pushed open her door. "Joan?"

Joan, rushing toward the stairs, turned back at her call.

"Did you not hear the bell?"

Joan looked pale. "Can't stop now, miss. Theo says Mr. Murdoch wants to see me without delay."

It was clear from her stricken expression that Joan feared she was in trouble. Margaret wondered idly what the girl had done but dismissed the thought. She had enough problems of her own. "But it is time to dress for dinner."

At the opposite end of the passage a door opened, and Marcus Benton stepped from his room, already dressed in evening attire. Joan stiffened and hurried away. Marcus flicked a frown at the maid, before turning a speculative gaze to Margaret. It was the first time she had seen him all day.

He sauntered toward her. "Don't think I didn't know what you were about last night."

Not wanting to be alone with him, or risk his following her into her room, Margaret turned and walked toward the stairway, pretending she had not heard him. She would not bother to change for dinner. What did it matter?

He trotted down the stairs beside her. "Throwing yourself at Lewis Upchurch like that—tsk, tsk."

Margaret bristled. "I did no such thing."

At the landing, he stepped in front of her and blocked her way, cornering her against the wall. "I cannot say I am sorry he rebuffed you, my sweet. For he could never feel for you the way I do." He ran a finger down her arm, and she jerked away.

"Did you really think that if he had not offered marriage before, he would do so last night, for all your batting of lashes and flaunting of décolletage?"

Anger and mortification singed her ears, but she could not refute the charge.

"My dear Margaret. I am not the blind fool Upchurch is. *I* am not immune to your charms. Why do you insist on putting me off? I have been patient these many months, but I grow weary of waiting."

The warm, sweet words soothed her injured pride. His finger

tickled her arm once more, sending shivers not altogether unpleasant down her spine. Like his uncle, Marcus embodied a masculine persistence and confidence she had always found appealing. Was her own confidence so lacking? Would she always be malleable in such hands—lose sight of her scruples and self-worth?

"Oh, Margaret . . ." He kissed the back of her hand, and for a moment she allowed him to hold it. Would it really be so bad to marry Marcus Benton? He was a good-looking young man, though more than a year her junior. He had an elegant bearing even for his slight height and was admired by many girls. And Marcus wanted *her*, wanted to wed *her*. How happy Sterling would be. Even her mother would approve—not because she liked Marcus, but because she was desperate to please Sterling, who seemed determined not to be pleased with her on any account. Margaret could buy peace for the household. Blessed peace.

But at what price?

She squeezed her eyes shut and shook herself mentally awake. What was she thinking? Any interest Marcus had in her was purely mercenary, manufactured for his uncle's sake. Oh, that her mother had never told Sterling of her pending inheritance!

Marcus must have mistaken her stillness for acquiescence, for he suddenly grasped her shoulders and pressed his mouth to hers.

She jerked away. "I have never given you leave to use my Christian name, Mr. Benton," she said coldly. "Much less to kiss me. Please remember that in future."

She hurried down the remaining stairs, but not before she heard him swear under his breath.

After enduring a strained dinner with only the three of them at the table, Margaret retired to her room early, wanting to avoid the men and weary after tossing and turning the night before. She pulled the bedside bell cord to summon Joan to help her undress and bring her some warm milk. Five minutes later, she pulled again. Still, no one came.

Grumbling to herself in irritation, Margaret stalked to her door. If no one would come to her, then she would go down herself and stretch her restless limbs in the process. She had never ventured belowstairs here in Sterling Benton's house. But as a girl, she had spent many an hour in the warm kitchen and stillroom of Lime Tree Lodge, enjoying a snug afternoon baking biscuits with Mrs. Haines or listening to the housekeeper and nurse swap stories of their lives before entering service.

Margaret descended two flights of stairs. Then, passing silently along the ground floor on her way to the basement steps, she heard muffled voices coming from the study and paused outside its door, which was slightly ajar. She sidled closer and pressed her ear to the crack.

"I have tried." Marcus's voice.

"Then try harder." Sterling.

"What would you have me do? I have been as charming and attentive as I know how. She does not like me."

"She once did. When you first came."

"Well, apparently she has revised her opinion. She is cold to me now."

"Then warm her. Have I not placed you here under my very roof? Given you every opportunity?"

Marcus grumbled something Margaret did not hear.

"And last night I saw her talking with Lewis Upchurch. A man who paid her every attention earlier this season. I fear she will stir his interest again, and we shall lose her."

"Lose her money, you mean."

"Need I remind you that whoever marries the chit will control her inheritance?"

"But if she does not marry, she will control it herself."

"And no doubt spend it on gewgaws and falderals and I know not what." A glass clinked against the table. Sterling's voice had risen, but he moderated it once more. "I shall instruct Murdoch not to allow Upchurch to call—nor any other gentlemen, for that matter."

"And I tell you, Uncle, Lewis Upchurch is no longer interested in Margaret."

"Let us hope you are right. Even so, if you have botched things as badly as you say, we can't have her eloping with some opportunistic buck while we're not paying heed."

Marcus said, "A good thing the inheritance is a well-kept secret. If everyone knew, men would be beating down our doors." Sarcasm curled his voice. "If only *you* had known, Uncle."

"You forget yourself, Marcus." Sterling's cool voice held an undercurrent of warning. "Now," he gritted out, "I don't care how you do it, just get her to marry you."

"What do you suggest?"

"Did I not pay for your education, Marcus? Can you really be such a simpleton?"

"What do you mean?"

"Come now. Charm and flattery never fail, at least where Macy women are concerned. Woo her, flatter her, make love to her. And if all else fails . . . compromise."

"You are not suggesting . . . ?"

"Why not. You have done the like before."

Marcus hissed, "But she is a *lady*."

"And will be restored to respectability as soon as she weds you."

Margaret pressed a hand over her mouth, stifling a cry of outrage and swallowing the acid climbing her throat.

Milk forgotten, she stole back upstairs. *The vile lechers!*

Reaching her room, Margaret pushed a chair against the door, doubting it would slow a man for long. She paced back and forth across her bedchamber. She was no match for Marcus physically. If he forced himself into her room, she would be a caged bird, a cornered hare.

One of her father's sermons came to mind, the one about how everyone might take advice from young Joseph. When Potiphar's lascivious wife tried to seduce him, he did not bar himself in his room.

He fled.

She needed to do the same. She would not stay in Sterling Benton's home another night.

But where could she go? She had only the few coins she had found on his dressing table. Those wouldn't take her far. If only her mother were home. For though she had clearly taken Sterling's side to this point, she would never stand for her daughter's ruination!

Margaret heard something and stood still, straining her ears. Had Marcus come to her door already?

Muffled sobbing. What in the world? She crossed to her dressing room and opened the door. Joan slumped against the wall, her pale face blotchy beneath auburn fringe and white cap, her light eyes streaming tears.

"What is it?" Margaret asked, but dread prickled through her, as if she already knew the answer. Had Marcus . . . ?

"It's Mr. Benton. He accused me of taking money from his dressing room. But I never did, miss. I never!"

Margaret's mouth went dry. Her stomach knotted. "I am sorry, Joan. I don't know what to say."

Joan's round eyes beseeched hers. "You believe me, don't you?"

Margaret pressed her lips together. "Yes."

Something in Joan's expression shifted. Her brows lowered and she stared at Margaret with disconcerting directness.

Margaret looked away first.

Joan said, "He told me to leave straightaway, but I snuck up here to see you. I hoped you might believe me and write me a character. I won't get another post without one."

Margaret's mind spun. She had no time to be writing letters. Not now. "I know nothing of character references, Joan. Though I would be happy to vouch for you . . . sometime."

Joan frowned. "It was you what took the money, wasn't it?"

Margaret swallowed back the guilt churning her innards like spoilt cod. How had Joan guessed? She was usually a better actress than that. "It was only a few coins. I never intended for you to take the blame."

The tears in Joan's eyes sparked into anger. "And who else would be blamed when the money turned up missing? It's always the maid."

"I thought . . . I hoped he would not notice."

"A man like him?"

"It was foolish. I see that now."

"But you won't go and tell him it wasn't me who took it, will you?"

Margaret hesitated, then shook her head. "I am afraid not. Not yet. I cannot let him know I have any money."

Joan's face mottled red and white. "Of all the bacon-brained lies . . ."

Margaret reeled. "How dare you? How ungrateful—"

"Me ungrateful?" The cords in Joan's throat stuck out. "What have you ever done for me? It's me what's done for you all these months, up working before you rise and after you're in bed. And for what? To get the sack for taking money you stole!"

The venom in her maid's voice shocked her. She had never known Joan felt this way about her.

An idea struck Margaret and she changed tack. "Where will you go?"

Joan sniffed. "To my sister's. Not that you care."

"I do care. I . . . I want to come with you."

Joan's brow puckered. "With *me*? Have you any idea where I'm going?"

"Your sister's, I believe you said."

"My sister, who lives in a run-down tenement in Billingsgate? You've never ventured into such a neighborhood, I'd wager. And with good reason."

"Let me go with you. I need to leave. Now. But I cannot go anywhere alone at night. It is not safe."

"It's not safe where I'm going either."

"We shall be safer together," Margaret insisted. "Look, I only took that money because I needed it to escape."

"Escape? Why should you need to escape?" Joan's lip curled. "Mr. Benton won't buy the new silk stockings you set your heart on?"

Goodness. Now that Joan had no post to protect, she allowed her tongue free rein. Margaret bit back an angry retort of her own and said earnestly, "No, I need to escape because I fear for my virtue."

Joan's eyebrows rose. "Young Mr. Benton?"

Margaret nodded.

"If it's unwanted attention he's giving you, tell his uncle."

"Who do you think put him up to it?"

The maid's eyes widened. "But, why . . . ?"

"I will explain later. I expect any minute for him to come through that door, and I don't want to be here when he does."

Joan crossed her arms and asked sullenly, "Why should I help you?"

Obviously not out of affection or loyalty, Margaret thought wryly. "Because I will write you the most flattering character reference you've ever read. Why, when I'm through, St. Thomas himself wouldn't doubt your abilities."

Joan's wary expression softened. "Very well. It's a bargain. But I only plan to stay with my sister until I find another place. You'll have to leave when I do."

"Agreed."

Joan surveyed her head to toe. "And you're not going anywhere with me dressed like that."

Margaret glanced down at the flounced day dress of white cambric muslin she'd yet to change out of, her mind quickly skipping to the other gowns in her wardrobe.

But Joan had other ideas. "There's some old clothes of poor Mrs. Poole's up in the attic." She was referring to the belongings of an ancient housemaid who'd died, bent over her pail and scrub brush, a few months before. "I'll fetch you a frock and cap from there."

"What is wrong with my gowns?"

"Nothing. If you want Theo to follow us and every pickpocket in London to harass us."

That was true. If the footman saw her coming downstairs dressed to go out, he would be on her trail before they reached the street.

"I shall be back directly," Joan said. "Meanwhile, cover up that hair."

Her hair. Margaret stared at her troubled reflection in the looking glass. Yes, her blond hair would be a beacon in the night. She thought suddenly of the dark wig she had planned to wear for the masquerade ball. She hurried to her dressing table and lifted the wig from its stand, examining it by lamplight. Decisively, she pawed through the drawer until she came upon a pair of scissors. With them, she lopped off the long curls meant to cascade down each shoulder, leaving only a simple curly wig with dark fringe across the forehead. It would do.

Joan had yet to return. Increasingly anxious to leave, Margaret decided she had better begin changing without her. She slipped her arms from her gown, twisted it back to front, undid the ribbon ties, and let the dress fall to the floor. She stood there in shift and stays. *Heaven help me if Marcus comes in now.* She slipped a petticoat over her head, then sat on the edge of the bed and pulled on two pair of stockings, then her half boots. She went to her wardrobe and found the blue dress and white apron she had worn as a milkmaid and laid them across her bed. Surely they would suffice if Joan failed to find something in the attic. Perhaps anyone who saw her would mistake her for a second housemaid, a friend of Joan's come to call.

She pulled forth her plainest reticule and a carpetbag, and began stuffing in a few necessities. Her mind raced, panicked and muddled. *Think*, she told herself. *Think!* But it was difficult to plan when she had little idea of where she was going or for how long.

Still Joan had yet to return. What had happened to forestall her?

Nervously, Margaret tied her dressing gown over her underclothes and slipped out into the corridor, ears alert for the sound of anyone approaching—friend or foe.

Which was Joan?

Margaret tiptoed toward the stairway and paused. Hearing voices from around the corner, she pressed herself against the wall.

Sterling challenged, "Were you not dismissed earlier this evening?"

"Yes, sir," Joan replied.

"Then why are you still here?"

"I was only packing my belongings, sir." Joan's voice quavered, unnaturally high.

"Packing *only* your belongings, I trust. Let me see what you have in that valise."

"'Tis only clothes and the like, sir."

Margaret heard shuffling and a clasp being unsnapped and snapped. "Be sure that is all you take or I shall hire a thief-taker to hunt you down."

"Yes, sir."

"Mr. Benton?" Murdoch called from the landing below. "Sorry to disturb you, sir. But that man from Bow Street is here."

What man from Bow Street? Margaret wondered.

"Thank you, Murdoch. I shall be down directly."

Margaret risked a glance around the corner in time to see Sterling turn his icy blue eyes on the quaking maid. "I trust you will see yourself out and do no mischief on your way."

Joan nodded.

"Be out in ten minutes or I shall have Murdoch toss you out."

I won't be a cook; I hate cooking. I won't be a nursery maid, nor a lady's maid, far less a lady's companion. . . . I won't be anything but a housemaid.

—Charlotte Brontë, in a letter to her sister Emily

Chapter 3

Ten minutes later, Margaret turned from her dressing table mirror to face Joan.

"Well?"

She wore an old grey frock Joan had unearthed from the attic, the apron she had worn as a milkmaid, and the dark wig pinned securely over her hair.

Seated on the bed, the maid studied her. "It changes you a great deal, miss. But I still think you need a cap."

The only cap Joan had found had yellowed beyond wearing. Margaret lifted the small lace cap she had worn to the masquerade.

Joan shook her head. "Too fine." She pulled something from her own valise. "You may borrow my spare. But if you keep it, it'll cost you one of those shillings."

"Very well." Margaret pulled the floppy mobcap over her wig and looked at Joan for her reaction. "Now will anyone recognize me?"

Joan tilted her head to one side. "If they look close they will."

Margaret looked back into the mirror. She lifted a stubby kohl pencil and darkened her eyebrows, as she had meant to do for the masquerade before abandoning plans to wear the wig. She then pulled open the mahogany writing box and from it extracted her father's small round spectacles. She placed them on her nose and hooked the arms over her ears. Again she faced Joan.

"What about now?"

"Much better, miss. As long as you don't talk, I think your brother could pass you in the street and not know you."

Margaret thought of the accents she had heard daily as a girl, spending hours with first her nurse and then the housekeeper while her mother was busy with this society event or that charity. Nanny Booker was from the north somewhere and Mrs. Haines from Bristol, she believed. Margaret had made a game of mimicking their accents, though now she wondered how charming they had really thought it. "An' wha' if I changed m'voice? Would ya know me then?"

Joan's eyes narrowed. "I don't talk like that."

Margaret quickly reverted to her normal way of speaking. "I know. And I am not trying to ridicule anyone. Only to disguise myself in every possible manner."

Joan lifted her chin in understanding, then dubiously eyed the narrow carpetbag. "Is that all you're taking?"

"Well, I cannot take a trunk, can I? Nor do I wish to arouse suspicion when we leave by the servants' entrance." Margaret riffled through the crammed bag. "I have an extra shift and the milkmaid frock as a spare—it doesn't weigh a thing. A nightdress and wrapper, slippers, comb, tooth powder, and the kohl." She did not mention her father's New Testament, nor the cameo he had given her, wrapped in a handkerchief. She slipped a shawl over her shoulders and looped bonnet ribbons over her wrist. "What else do I need?"

"Don't forget some of that nice paper for my character," Joan said.

When Margaret had slid a piece into her bag, Joan blew out a deep breath. "Well, it's time." She slapped her legs and stood.

Telling Margaret to wait in the room, Joan picked up her valise and crept down the corridor to listen at the top of the stairs. She waved Margaret forward. Margaret slipped from the room, quietly closing the door behind her. She followed Joan down the stairs on tiptoe, barely allowing herself to breathe. They descended one pair of stairs and then another without encountering anyone coming up. At the top of the basement steps, Joan motioned her to wait while she checked the passage below.

The maid's head soon popped back into view and again she waved Margaret down. Together they hurried along the narrow basement passageway, past the kitchen, to the service door at its far end. Joan opened it for her.

Margaret had just stepped through when a voice called from the kitchen behind them.

"Joan? Who's that with you?"

Margaret hesitated, unsure if she should run or turn around. Joan's firm hand on her arm kept her from doing either.

"'Tis only my sister, come to collect me," Joan said. "You heard I got the push?"

"Oh, Joan. I did," the female voice commiserated. "And sorry I was to hear it."

"I didn't steal anything, for the record."

"Of course you didn't. I'd wager he mislaid the money or spent it hisself. Or that nephew of his pinched it. Not fair is it?"

"No, Mary, it's not fair."

"Going to your sister's, then, are you?"

"Until I find another place." Joan gave Margaret a little shove, and she lurched forward, tripping on the bottom step before starting up the outside stairs.

"Good-bye, Joan, and Godspeed."

Margaret reached street level as Joan trotted up the stairs behind her.

"Let's go," the maid whispered, without a backward glance.

Margaret, however, looked over her shoulder several times as they crossed the square, fearing any moment the hovering footman or

Sterling himself would appear behind them. But all was quiet save for the clicking of their bootheels and the distant *clip-clop-clatter* of horse hooves on cobblestones.

They had made it.

What now? She'd known only that she had to get out of Benton's house that very night. In her panicked hurry she had not even left her mother a note. Even if she had, she knew very well Sterling would have read it. And lost no time in following any unintentional clues it held to find Margaret and drag her back. What would she have written at any rate? She didn't know where she was going beyond Billingsgate. And Joan had made it clear this would only be a brief stay until she found other employment. Margaret hoped it would buy her enough time to figure out her next step. She would write to her mother then.

Ahead of her, Joan strode briskly on, and Margaret strained and panted to keep up. On the next street, a man leaning in a shadowed doorway leered at them. Two militiamen whistled as they passed. Margaret decided she did not like walking London streets at night. "Joan? Joan, wait!" Her voice shook. "How far did you say it was?"

Joan glanced over her shoulder. "Three or four miles, I'd reckon."

Margaret swallowed. Perhaps she ought to risk going to Emily Lathrop's house instead. It could be no more than a mile or two away.

She recalled the last time she had gone to the Lathrops' in Red Lion Square. She had been vexed with Marcus and Sterling both, and hoped to beg an invitation to stay with Emily for a time. But she had not been in the Lathrops' drawing room an hour when she heard Sterling Benton's name announced and had to sit there while he lamented that her mother had taken ill and needed her at home.

It had all been a ruse. Her mother was in perfect health, although she had been "sick with worry," and quite put out with Margaret for leaving the house alone—though she had never minded when Margaret spent time with friends before.

At the end of the block, Joan waited for a post chaise to pass, allowing Margaret to catch up with her. "Do you know where Red Lion Square is?"

Joan looked wary. "Yes. My cousin has a post near there. Why?"

"Could you please walk there with me? My friend Emily lives there, and perhaps she might help me."

Joan shrugged an apathetic reply. "I suppose. 'Tisn't far out of my way."

Margaret was surprised she agreed so readily. Joan was apparently eager to be rid of her.

As she trudged behind Joan along busy Oxford Street, Margaret rehearsed how to explain her predicament to Emily, mortifying though it was. Emily would be happy to have her, once she quit laughing over her costume. But could she talk her parents into allowing her to stay? They were unlikely to believe her word over Sterling Benton's. Sterling could be so convincing, so persuasive. He would have them believing his nephew the soul of propriety and her a deluded ninny with an overinflated view of her "irresistible" charms. Mr. Lathrop would gently admonish her to be sensible and send her home with Sterling without a second thought.

She shuddered. Perhaps instead of asking to stay, she would ask Emily to loan her enough money to see her out of town and somewhere safe. Margaret would pay her back with interest as soon as she received her inheritance. She loathed the thought of borrowing money from friends. But she would have to set aside her pride. Pulling the mobcap down more snugly over her black wig and spectacles, she realized she already had.

They walked north and then turned into quiet and pretty Red Lion Square. There, Margaret led the way across the square's central garden. She paused behind one of the trees to survey the Lathrop town house across the street. Joan stood behind her. All was still, save for the flicking tail of a horse harnessed to a carriage waiting several houses away.

Margaret was about to cross the cobbles when she realized with a start that she recognized the landau with its brass candle lamps, as well as the coachman at the reins. Margaret retreated behind the tree once more. As she peered around it, the Lathrops' front door opened and Sterling Benton appeared, framed by lamplight at its threshold, speaking in earnest confidence with Emily's father. Sterling shook his head somberly, appearing the perfect image of concerned stepfather. Mr. Lathrop nodded and the two men shook hands.

Sterling had certainly gotten there quickly. She and Joan had left perhaps only thirty or forty minutes before. Of course they had walked, while Sterling had a horse and carriage at his disposal. He—or Marcus, more likely—must have come to her room soon after she'd left and discovered her gone. Thank heaven she left when she did.

Clattering horse hooves galloped into the square, and Margaret peered around the other side of the tree. A man in a chimney-pot hat and cropped coat rode up, quickly dismounted, and tied his reins to a post. The man's hurry sounded an alarm in Margaret's mind. Was this the man from Bow Street Murdoch had announced before Margaret left? Had Sterling planned to hire a watchman but now commissioned the same man to find and apprehend her?

The newcomer trotted up the walkway toward Sterling and Mr. Lathrop. There on the stoop, the three men spoke, Sterling gesturing and frowning. He pulled something from his pocket and handed it to the officious-looking man. She could not see the object clearly from that distance, but based on the way the man studied it, she guessed it might be a framed miniature portrait. The one commissioned by her father for her eighteenth birthday?

Evidently, Sterling had arranged for the runner to meet him at the place he expected to find Margaret. Where he *would* have found her had she arrived even five minutes earlier. Sterling Benton knew her better than she realized, and that thought riddled her with anxiety. Where could she go, where could she hide, where Sterling Benton would never think to look for her?

A few minutes later, Sterling departed in the carriage and Mr. Lathrop retreated inside, yet the runner remained, leaning against the outside stair rail.

"Well?" Joan whispered.

"The watchman, or whatever he is, is making himself comfortable. I don't think he is going anywhere soon."

"Well, I *must* be going soon," Joan said. "Are you coming with me or not?"

There was no point in staying. Sterling had gotten there first. Even if she managed to sneak inside and speak with Emily, her father would insist on sending her home. It was no good.

Margaret sighed. "Looks like I am."

Joan echoed her sigh. "Well, come on, then."

Staying to the shadows, they crossed the square and returned to the thoroughfare. Joan urged her to hurry, and soon Margaret's thoughts were consumed with dodging flower carts, barrels, carriages, and horse droppings. And with trying to keep sight of Joan's blue frock as she scurried ahead. Soon, Margaret's feet were aching and her side cramping.

Joan turned only long enough to hiss, "Hurry! We've got a long way to go, and it's getting late."

Margaret eyed the passing hackney carriages with longing but knew she should not spend the little money she had. She bit back a groan and kept trotting along, the carpetbag swinging against her leg. Ahead, Joan strode smartly on, ever eastward, her heavier valise apparently no burden at all. Thirty or forty minutes later, they turned south onto Grace Church Street.

The street narrowed and darkened. The cobbles gave way to uneven paving, refuse-filled gutters, and smells that compelled Margaret to breathe from her mouth.

Finally, Joan turned down a lane signposted Fish Street Hill. There, they passed several old tenement buildings before Joan pushed open a narrow door. Margaret breathed a sigh of relief. Her next inhale brought salt air and the rank odor of rotting fish. They were close to the river here, she guessed. And the docks.

Too tired to care, she followed Joan inside and up two rickety flights of stairs. She stood, numb and mute, as Joan knocked softly on the door of number 23.

While they waited, Joan turned and whispered, "I've had all the trouble I care to from your Mr. Benton. I think it best we don't tell my sister your name or who you really are. Peg has never been good at keeping secrets."

Margaret nodded.

A few moments later, shuffling and grumbling came from the other side of the door. Then a woman's hoarse whisper. "Who's there?"

"Peg, it's Joan."

The lock clicked, and the door was opened by a frowzy woman very like Joan in appearance, though several years older and a stone heavier. She might have been pretty once, but her skin was rough, her face too careworn for her years.

"Good heavens, Joan. What's happened?"

Joan answered calmly, "I've lost my place."

Her sister's face crumpled. "Oh no. What did you do?"

"Nothing. Look, it's late. We'll talk in the morning, all right?"

The woman nodded over Joan's shoulder. "Who's this, then?"

Joan flicked Margaret a glance. "She's with me. She just needs a place a sleep for a night or two. Come on, Peg, let us in. We'll help with the children and give the place a good cleaning—whatever you like."

The woman frowned. "Oh, very well. But keep it down. The children are already asleep."

They stepped inside the dark room, which smelled of cabbage and soiled nappies. Margaret could see little, as their reluctant hostess spared no candle for them to get settled by.

"Candles are dear, they are," Peg explained as if reading her thoughts. "There's a bit of light from the window, if you need it. And embers in the stove."

Joan disappeared into the apartment's only separate room. She returned a moment later and tossed something onto the floor. Margaret realized with sinking dread that she was meant to sleep on an old blanket on the floor.

Margaret stood there, waiting for Joan to help her undress. But Joan followed her sister back into the bedchamber.

Margaret whispered after her, "Joan?"

"You're on your own now, miss," Joan said. "I am a maid no longer."
She shut the door behind her.

Well. She needn't be so snippy, Margaret thought, oddly chastised
as well as annoyed. She decided she was too tired to undress in any
case and settled down atop the thin scratchy blanket on the floor,
hoping no mice or rats decided to join her there.

Margaret awoke on her side, stiff. Her hip bone ached from
being pressed against the hard floor. Sunlight, filtering through
sooty windows, shone on the grey wool blanket she had pulled
over herself in the night. Likely it had once been the golden hue
of boiled wool. As she pushed it away, something furry brushed
her hand. She gasped and bolted to her feet. A dark, hairy form
fell from her shoulder to the floor. She shrieked, only to realize it
was not a rat, but her wig. She quickly bent and pulled it on. Another creature appeared before her and she reared back and nearly
shrieked again. This creature had a small pale face, curtained by
stringy ginger hair.

"Hello," the little girl said, staring at her. "Who are you?"

"I am . . ." *Who am I?* Margaret's brain was a fog. She remembered
Joan saying she ought not give her real name. Probably wise. If Sterling
came here to question Joan's sister, Peg might say Joan had been there
with someone, but not that a Margaret had been there.

"I am a . . . friend . . . of Joan's."

"Is Aunt Joan here, too?"

"Yes. In your mamma's room, I believe." She made no effort to
disguise her voice with the child.

The little girl tilted her head to one side. "What's wrong with
your hair?"

Margaret reached up and realized her wig was askew. She righted
the wig and muttered lamely, "Always a mess in the morning. You, on
the other hand, have very pretty hair." She said it hoping to distract

the girl. She did not want her reporting to Sterling or a runner that a blond lady wearing a wig had been there. That would give away her disguise and make Sterling's search all the easier.

She eyed the girl's stringy hair again. "Or you could have. When was the last time you combed it?"

The little girl shrugged.

Margaret looked away from the girl to survey her surroundings. One end of the room housed a small stove, cupboards, and table and chairs. The other end held a pallet bed complete with sleeping boy and baskets heaped with fabric. Apparently Joan's sister was a seamstress of sorts. Margaret spied a piece of broken mirror hanging on the wall by a ribbon and walked over to it, checking her wig and cap and wiping a smear of kohl from between her eyes.

"I want breakfast," the little girl pouted.

"And I want to be a thousand miles from here," Margaret whispered to the stranger in the mirror.

Peg stepped out of the bedchamber, tying on an apron and stifling a yawn. She said, "Light the fire, will you?"

Margaret looked at the little girl. She seemed awfully young to be trusted with fire. It took Margaret a few seconds to realize Peg had asked *her*.

Margaret had poked at many a drawing room fire but had never actually laid one. She eyed the small stove. A bucket with a few pieces of coal sat at the ready.

Joan came out of the room, a toddler on her hip. She glanced at Margaret, then smiled down at the boy. "This is little Henry."

"Named for his father, he is." Peg pulled a sack of oats from the cupboard.

"Papa is gone to sea," a boy of seven or eight piped up. Margaret had not seen him rise from the pallet bed. "I am going to sea one day too."

"Not for a few more years, Michael. Don't be in a hurry," Joan said, an indulgent dimple in her cheek.

Margaret caught Joan's eye, and nodded her head toward the stove. Joan frowned at her, uncomprehending.

"Haven't you got that fire lit yet?" Peg asked, not looking up as she pulled a pot from the cupboard.

"Um. . . . no. I am not certain . . ."

"I'll do it," Joan said in a long-suffering manner, placing the child in Margaret's arms.

At least this was something Margaret could do. Having two siblings many years younger than herself, she knew how to hold a child.

Margaret settled the child against her and soon felt dampness seep into her gown. *Ugh.* She wondered if she could manage to change him. At Lime Tree Lodge, they had employed a nursery maid to deal with soiled nappies.

"What's your name?" the older boy asked her.

"My name?" Margaret echoed stupidly. "Ah . . ." Her mind whirled. "Elinor," she said, choosing her middle name.

"But she goes by Nora," Joan added, perhaps finding the name too grand—or too close to her real name.

"Make the porridge, will you, Nora?" Peg said. "I've got six orders of piecework to finish today." Peg glanced up. "You do know how to make porridge, I trust?"

"'Course she does," Joan said. "You go about your work, Peg, and we'll manage breakfast."

Peg nodded and crossed the room to the waiting baskets.

When her back was turned, Joan whispered, "Peg makes thin gruel for the children. It's better for their little stomachs."

And cheaper, Margaret thought, but did not say so.

"Six parts water to one part groats. Can you manage that? Unless you'd rather change Henry?"

"No thank you. I shall give gruel a go."

Later, after they had eaten thin, lumpy, mildly scorched gruel with neither milk nor sugar, Margaret fumbled her way through drying the pot, spoons, and basins as Joan washed. As she did so, she thought about something Joan had said—that Peg's name and address were recorded in Benton's staff records as Joan's next of kin.

Sterling might very well put two and two together and knock on Peg's door any moment looking for her. Margaret shuddered. She could not stay there long.

After the dishes were put away, Joan sat down with a wrinkled copy of a newspaper a few days old, reading through the advertisements. Not knowing what else to do, Margaret pulled her comb from her bag and went to work on the little girl's hair, untangling then plaiting the ginger strands.

Peg glanced from her sewing to Joan, still bent over the newspaper. "Any luck, Joan?"

Joan shook her head. "It seems everyone wants maids-of-all-work here in town. That's one fate I should like to avoid."

Reaching the end of the girl's hair, Margaret looked around for a ribbon or something else to secure it.

Peg tossed her a thin scrap of muslin. "Here."

Margaret tied the end of the plait, and the girl stroked her coppery braid, smiling coyly up at Joan. "Am I pretty, Aunt Joan?"

Joan looked from her niece to Margaret, then back again. "Pretty is as pretty does, little miss. You remember that."

The jab was intended for her, Margaret realized. At the moment, being pretty seemed of little use. What should she *do*?

*The "Gentleman Pirate" . . . a retired British
army major with a large sugar plantation in Barbados,
abandoned his wife, children, land and fortune; bought
a ship; and turned to piracy on the high seas.*

—Amy Crawford, *Smithsonian* magazine

Chapter 4

Nathaniel Aaron Upchurch spent two restless nights in his family's London residence after his appearance at the ball. He did not see his brother at all the first day. Lewis slept in very late and then had left for his club while Nathaniel met with the family's London banker. He supposed his brother was avoiding him after their fight.

In Lewis's absence, Nathaniel began taking stock of the situation—gathering unpaid bills and paying the permanent staff as well as the valet and coachman who had come up from Maidstone to help run the place. All the while his sister remained in Fairbourne Hall, necessitating the upkeep of both houses simultaneously, further compounding their expenses.

Lewis sauntered down for breakfast late the second morning, sporting a black eye and bruised cheek. "I say, Nate ol' boy, you made quite an entrance the other night."

Nathaniel regarded his brother warily, but Lewis's tone held no rancor. Nathaniel regretted losing his temper, overtired from the journey as he was. He was determined not to do so again.

Lewis sized him up, surveying him from head to toe. Nathaniel became conscious of the fact that he had yet to shave his beard or cut his hair.

"My, my," Lewis drawled. "Who, I wonder, is this rogue before me and what has happened to my young pup of a brother?"

"Two years in Barbados happened."

"The island did not have such an effect on me."

Unfortunately, Nathaniel thought. But he said, "I am sorry we came to blows at the ball."

"I am not." Lewis smirked. "We shall be the talk of town for a week."

Nathaniel said dryly, "Or until the next scandal erupts."

Lewis helped himself to coffee with several lumps of sugar—sugar grown in Barbados, though refined there in England. Nathaniel took his coffee—without sugar—and settled himself at the small desk in the breakfast room. He placed his spectacles on his nose and continued inscribing the outstanding debts into a ledger. He ought to have brought Hudson to do this, but the man had insisted on staying aboard the *Ecclesia* to keep watch, since Nathaniel had given the crew three-days leave.

Lewis turned from the sideboard and laughed. "Now *there* is the brother I remember. Nose in a book and wearing unfashionable spectacles."

Nathaniel ignored the jab. "Were you ever going to pay these bills?"

"Me? Is that not why we have staff?"

Nathaniel clenched his jaw. "You tell me. I see that you have hired another French chef but no clerk or secretary."

Lewis popped a hunk of sausage into his mouth and spoke around the bite. "Monsieur Fournier preferred to stay at Fairbourne Hall, and I could not leave Helen in the lurch, could I?"

"That is exactly what you have done."

"The season is almost over, ol' boy," Lewis soothed. "Then I shall tuck tail and go home like a dutiful spaniel, ey? But to insist I leave

London now? Especially now that you are returned? You cannot be so cruel." Lewis rubbed his bruised jaw. "Though after meeting with your fists, I am not so certain."

Nathaniel noticed that Lewis did not bring up the reasons for his return. He knew their father had written to Lewis about it, but he was relieved not to have to rehash it all again.

After breakfast Nathaniel spent several more hours meeting with tradesmen and bringing accounts up to snuff. Then he allowed Lewis's valet to cut his hair and give him a better shave than he'd had in months. Finally, Nathaniel felt ready to return to his ship, collect Hudson and the rest of his belongings, and set off for Maidstone.

Nathaniel left the coachman and fashionable barouche with Lewis and insisted on driving the old traveling chariot himself—to the coachman's horror. Nathaniel would have settled for horseback or a small curricle, but he had quite a bit of cargo to unload and trans-port to Fairbourne Hall before the captain and crew departed for Barbados without him.

He enjoyed handling the reins, though the boxy enclosed carriage and team did not handle as well as the small trap and spirited mare he had driven around the island.

He pulled up the collar of his greatcoat and pulled down his hat, ignoring the disapproving look of an old dowager-neighbor, stunned to see him playing coachman. No doubt he had just given the gossips more reason to denounce him as uncivilized.

He drove his customary route to the Port of London and, when he arrived, hopped down and tied the horses near the Legal Quays. He turned toward the river and stopped, staring in disbelief. Flames shot up from the *Ecclesia* and smoke billowed. *God have mercy. What next?*

He began running while these thoughts still echoed in his mind, his boots thumping against the wooden planking in time with his heart. Beside the three-masted merchantman, a dinghy floated. Several men waited at the oars, ready to make their escape. This was no accident, then, but an intentional attack. Where was Hudson? *Almighty God, please spare Hudson.*

Nathaniel ran up the gangplank, heedless of the flames and smoke. If only he had retained a skeleton crew. Where were the river police? They were supposed to patrol against cargo theft and vandalism. Had a port worker—or even a member of the river police—been bribed to look the other way?

Fire licked up the mizzenmast. Nathaniel ran to the larboard rail and looked down at the dinghy. Still there. Nate was torn between the desire for revenge and the desire to try to save his ship. The ragged crew smirked up at him. What were they waiting for?

He had his answer soon enough, for a man leapt down from the quarter deck and sprinted across the main. He wore the clothes of a gentleman. His face was tanned, distinguished, and . . . familiar. Nathaniel's gut clenched. *Thunder and turf. Not him. Not here.*

Nathaniel drew his pistol.

Abel Preston skidded to a halt, an infuriating grin on his handsome face. "A pistol? Not very sportsmanlike." He glanced down at the fine sword sheathed at his side.

"But effective," Nathaniel said. "Where is Hudson?"

Preston jerked his head toward the stern. "Fast asleep, poor lamb. Better drag him off before he's overcome with smoke."

Nathaniel gestured with the gun tip. "You lead the way."

"Very well." Preston stepped forward as though to comply but then whirled and slashed out with his sword, knocking Nathaniel's gun to the deck, where it went skidding beneath a pallet of sugar-syrup casks.

Nathaniel drew his sword and struck. The former army major coolly met him thrust for thrust for several minutes. Then Preston stepped back and the two men circled each other warily.

Struggling to catch his breath, Nathaniel scoffed, "This is the career you left Barbados to pursue?"

Preston smiled. "Yes, and I am making quite a name for myself."

"I must have missed it. For I've not heard your name mentioned since you left."

"That is because I've acquired a new name." Preston gave a mock bow and recited, "They call me the Pirate Poet. And some the Poet Pirate. How fickle is Lady Fame, when she cannot settle upon a name."

Nathaniel cringed, remembering several island socials this man had attended—without his wife—during which he had attempted to impress the ladies with his long-winded recitations. Nathaniel *had* heard tales of a poetry-spouting "pirate" but assumed them mere legend. He had never imagined Preston might be that man. He supposed it made sense. The fop always did love poetry. Preston had spent more time composing rhymes than overseeing his plantation—when he wasn't tormenting his slaves. No wonder he'd failed as a planter.

But the man had always been good at one thing—he was highly skilled with the blade. Once again Preston advanced, striking with startling speed. Nathaniel countered, but his every strike was parried with ease. He fought back hard but with the growing realization that he was the inferior swordsman. Barring aid from Hudson, or heaven, he would be beaten. Sweat ran down Nathaniel's face. Fear threatened, but he refused to cower before this man. *Almighty God, help me.*

Preston knocked Nathaniel's sword from his grasp and kicked his feet out from under him in a blinding blur of motion. Nathaniel landed on the deck with a thump, his breath knocked out of him, his sword out of reach. Preston pinned him to the deck with a sword tip to his throat.

I commit my soul into your care, Nathaniel thought. *Please forgive my many sins, for Jesus' sake.* He said, "Take what you want and kill me if you will, but let Hudson go. This is my ship. He only works for me."

Preston's lip curled. "Do you suppose I'd forgotten how you lured Hudson away—stole my best clerk? Not to mention the other problems you caused me."

Nathaniel's calls for reform had not made him many friends in Barbados. Preston had been chief among his detractors, especially after Nathaniel reported his continuing involvement in the slave trade after it was outlawed.

Still pinning Nathaniel to the deck, Preston called over his shoulder, "Turtle, bring me the master's chest." He looked down at Nate once more. "This year's profits, I assume?"

"As well you know," Nathaniel snapped, though he'd taken half the money to their London town house to begin paying bills. The remainder was even now hidden in the coach's lockbox. "I see how it is. Why live off the meager profits from your own ill-managed plantation, when you can live off the profits of others?"

"Exactly so." Preston's eyes gleamed. "I hear your father bragged about this season's yield—the highest in several years, I understand." The man lowered his sword tip to the chain around Nathaniel's neck. "The key?" With a flick of his wrist, he severed the chain, speared the key through its hole and tossed it into the air, catching it handily.

"I've got it, sir!" the man called Turtle shouted, lifting the two-foot-square padlocked chest in the air. His scar, from mouth to ear, looked like a gruesome leer.

"Take it down to the others. I shall join you directly."

Here it comes, Nathaniel thought, his whole body tensing. *He has everything he wants from me. This is the end.* He found himself thinking of Helen. More alone than ever now. And his father. Would he think him a failure? And then he thought of Margaret Macy. Perhaps it was just as well she hadn't married him. He wouldn't want to leave her such a young widow.

Preston lifted his sword once more—to bring down the death blow, Nathaniel knew. Instead the man rose with a jerk. "Away with us, me lads! Take our bounty and be gay. Let these good men live, to see another day!" He leapt from the burning deck and swung from a mooring line with impressive agility.

Nathaniel jumped up and dashed to the rail in time to see the man land in the dinghy with practiced ease. Preston smiled up at him and tipped his tricorn.

Nathaniel called down, "Running away? For all your skill and supposed renown, you are a coward, sir."

Preston's smile faded. "You risk my sword, saying that."

"Name the time and place."

An eerie gleam shone in the man's eyes. "Your place. When you least expect it."

The crew began rowing, and the dinghy pulled away, no doubt on course for a waiting ship.

Nate considered jumping in after him, but that would be suicide. He debated rousing the tardy river police, but there was no time. The stern of the ship was burning rapidly now. His ship. The one he had convinced his father to add to their small fleet. The one he had invested in with his own share of the profits.

He ran to where Hudson lay, insensible but alive, and bodily dragged the man away from the burning master's cabin. A flaming yard clubbed his arm, nearly felling him. Ignoring the bone-deep pain, he lugged Hudson across the main deck and down the gangplank, hearing the alarm being raised at last. Too late. The dinghy was already fading into a dim shape and disappearing behind a row of moored frigates.

Nathaniel ran up the gangplank once more, vaguely hearing Hudson's groggy voice calling after him to stop but not heeding him. He ran into what was left of the master's cabin, grabbing what he could of value—monetary or sentimental. A roar surrounded him. The deck below him buckled. He grabbed one last thing. The only thing he had of hers. He ran from the cabin as it caved in, a section of the wall crashing into his left side, searing his temple.

But he did not let it go.

That evening, Margaret sat thinking at Peg Kittelson's open window, elbows on the sill, her back to the depressing room crammed with toppling piles of piecework, childish babbling and wailing, and meager food. Margaret inhaled the outside air, fresher than the stale apartment, though carrying the smell of the nearby river. She tried in vain to reach an itch through the wig and wished she'd thought to bring a wig scratcher. The narrow lane below, littered with tumbling wads of newspaper and horse droppings, was relatively quiet compared to the clamor of the room behind her.

She wondered if she should try again to contact Emily. Perhaps wait a day or two and knock at the servants' entrance in disguise. Or would the runner still be on guard, questioning everyone who came to call?

On the distant street corner, three young men sat on the stoop of an ale house. A hulking black-haired man tossed pebbles into the gutter, while his thin comrade whittled and spit seed hulls into the street. The third sat, limbs sprawled, head lolling against the wall behind him in an ale-induced doze.

"Come away from the window, girl," Peg whispered. "You don't want that lot to notice you. Blackguards they are."

Margaret was about to comply when clattering hooves and wheels sounded below. From around the corner came a black coach pulled by two horses. As it passed the ale house, the enclosed carriage all but filled the narrow lane, its brass lamps blazing like beacons in the night.

Joan said from her shoulder, "Might as well light a sign asking to be robbed."

Joan and Peg receded into the room, but Margaret remained at the window. The equipage and horses were too fine for the neighborhood. The man at the reins, a sturdy man in his midthirties, did not look the part of traditional coachman. No top hat graced his head. No many-caped greatcoat fluttered in the wind.

The carriage stopped on the street below for no apparent reason, and the driver tied off the reins and clambered down none too nimbly. He opened the carriage door and leaned in. "Are you all right, sir?"

She heard no reply.

Margaret looked past the coach to the ale house on the corner. As she'd feared, the ne'er-do-wells on the stoop had taken notice of the carriage as well. The thin man stopped whittling. The black-haired hulk stilled, his gaze focused on the coach, nose high like a hound on the scent. He slowly rose, gesturing to the second fellow to follow and kicking the foot of the dozing youth.

Dread prickled through Margaret's stomach and along her limbs.

She glanced back down at the driver standing with his head and shoulders in the coach, completely unaware of the danger he had steered into.

"Hello?" she called in a terse whisper, trying to make herself heard. Vaguely she heard Peg shush her in the background. "Excuse me, you there!" she hissed, not daring to shout. She did not want to draw the ruffians' attention to poor Peg's window. Only belatedly did she realize she had not bothered to disguise her voice. No matter, for the man had not heard her.

Margaret closed the window and stepped back, retreating into the relative safety of the room. Well, she told herself, she had tried.

Then in her mind's eye she saw her beloved father calling "Whoa" to his old driving horse, pulling the gig to the side of the road to help a farmer with a broken wagon wheel, mucking his breeches and gloves without complaint. Just diving in to help a fellow traveler in need. How often he had done so.

She turned to the door and yanked it open. "I shall return directly." Without awaiting a reply, Margaret drummed down the stairs. She was halfway to street level before the second thought followed. . . . It had been in the midst of just such a good deed that her father had been killed.

Reaching the front door, she cracked it open. The driver still had his head and shoulders inside the carriage, and she could see that he was repositioning a pillow under a man's bandaged head. A pillow was not going to help either of them if they did not get out of there in the next few seconds!

She peered around the edge of the door. The large man had paused down the street, bending to remove something from his boot. A knife? His thin crony cinched up his baggy breeches as the third man yawned and sized up the unguarded coach. Margaret wondered why the travelers had neither guard nor groom.

She inched open the tenement door a bit farther, glad that it acted as a shield between her and the approaching cutthroats.

Dredging up her best imitation of Nanny Booker, she called sharply, "You there. Best drive off . . . and sharp-like."

The driver swiveled around to frown at her. "What do you want?"

Only then did she see that one of his hands was bandaged. She pointed beyond the open door. "Are ya blind? Get out of 'ere. Go."

55

The man looked in the direction she'd pointed and the skin around his eyes tightened. His mouth followed suit.

"Hold on," he urged the man inside. He slammed the coach door and leapt back up into the coachman's seat far more adroitly than he'd climbed down. He slapped the reins, yelled a command, and snapped the whip in the air. The horses tossed their heads, whinnied and pulled, and the coach began to move away. Too slowly.

She braved one more glance around the door. The black-haired man was running up the lane. He shouted, "Let's get 'em, lads!"

His cronies followed more cautiously.

In a flash she gauged the hulk's gait against the coach's slowly increasing speed. Not accelerating quickly enough. Looking up, she saw the driver glance back, his face grim.

She heard the pounding of the boots just beyond the door she held slightly ajar. At the last moment, she shoved the door wide open with all her strength.

Slam. Umph. The heavy wooden door reverberated violently and came slamming toward her. She leapt back. The door smacked her shoulder, barely missing her face. She heard a shout, a *thud-slap*, as knees and limbs hit the cobbles, followed by a sharp curse.

The door hit the jamb and bounced outward. Through the opening, a pair of black eyes locked on hers. She snagged the latch and pulled the door closed. Hands shaking, she slid the bar home.

Margaret bolted up the stairs as fast as her feet could carry her. She tripped at the first landing and felt her stocking tear. Her ankle and knee screamed complaint as she rounded the first newel-post and shot up the second pair of stairs. Below, the bar splintered and the door crashed open. Footfalls, threats, and curses gained on her as she hoofed it up the remaining stairs and down the passage. She ran into number 23 and shut and barred the door behind her, hoping the men had not seen which of the many doors she had disappeared into.

"What is it?" Joan asked.

"Shh." Trembling all over, Margaret picked up a cumbersome oak chair and propped it against the door.

Peg asked, "Is it those ruffians?"

Margaret nodded.

Peg's eyes grew wide, and she wrapped a protective arm around the child nearest her.

Running footsteps raced past their door.

The women looked from one to the other as they waited, listening.

The footsteps clomped back, more slowly. A man shouted, "I'll find you. And when I do, I'll kill you."

That night, Margaret shared the narrow pallet bed with Peg's son. She didn't sleep well. She was reminded of the days Gilbert would climb into her bed for a story, fall asleep, and then rob all the bedclothes.

In the morning, Margaret sat at the small table with Peg's family, sharing a meager breakfast and strained silence. Even the children were unnaturally quiet. From across the table, sisters Joan and Peg exchanged a pained, meaningful look, which Margaret had no trouble interpreting. She had worn out her welcome already.

She opened her mouth, but Joan beat her to it. "I am afraid, mi— Nora. That after last night, it would be best if you took your leave. If those men see you and figure out whose place . . ."

Margaret nodded, though fear ran through her veins. "I understand."

"And as soon as possible," Peg added. "While that lot is still sleeping it off."

"I know you meant well," Joan allowed. "But I can't have you bringin' danger to my sister's door."

Again Margaret nodded and woodenly repeated, "I understand." She rose, her legs weak and trembling. Where was she to go? And what if those men were out there right now, lying in wait?

She plucked her Oldenburg bonnet from the peg near the door, and tied it securely under her chin. She picked up her bag and bid farewell to each of the children and pressed one of her few coins into Peg's palm. "For your hospitality," she murmured and opened the door.

"Wait," Joan called after her. "I'm going with you."

Peg began to protest, but Joan insisted she needed to find work. "There aren't any positions hereabouts anyway."

Margaret swallowed a bitter pill of pride and humbling gratitude. She guessed Joan was making excuses. But Margaret was not brave enough to insist Joan remain, to bluster that she would be fine on her own. She would not be. And after the near-miss with those men, she was frightened of venturing out alone.

"Very well," Margaret said, the words *thank you* sticking in her throat.

Joan embraced her niece and nephews, and quietly warned Peg not to say anything about them being there. Peg no doubt believed the warning due to the three would-be thieves alone.

Taking valise and carpetbag in hand once more, Joan and Margaret went quietly downstairs. They peered from behind the splintered door, and seeing no one about, stepped outside. They walked quickly down Fish Street Hill, turning from the lane as soon as possible to avoid being seen by any early riser glancing from his window.

Once they were several blocks away, Joan moderated their pace, leading the way toward the Thames and across London Bridge. The wide river teemed with boats—fishing boats moored midriver or docked to unload the morning's catch—while sailing vessels of every size slipped between them.

On the other side of the bridge, they passed the Southwark Cathedral before turning left into the Borough High Street. There, Margaret glimpsed a three-story galleried coaching inn. Joan explained that many stagecoaches as well as a Royal Mail coach departed from The George each day.

From behind the railing of the first gallery above, a swarthy porter carried a bolt of fabric over one shoulder, and a well-dressed gentleman smiled down at them and tipped his hat. On the upper gallery, a woman in a low-cut nightdress blew kisses to a sailor trotting down the outer stairs.

The inn's courtyard swarmed with activity. Dogs barked. Horses snorted and pranced in their braces. A large stagecoach with red wheels prepared to depart. Hostellers checked the horses' harnesses. An official-looking man in red greatcoat and top hat opened the coach door and handed in a matron and her young charge. Once the door was closed, a brawny dark-skinned man strapped barrels to the side of the carriage.

The body of the yellow stagecoach was emblazoned with its final destination in bold and stopping points along the way in smaller lettering. Four passengers sat on its roof, and another shared the coachman's bench. The guard climbed to his position at the rear and blew his long horn.

Joan led Margaret to the front of the clapboard inn, to a protruding half-circle structure with the words *Coach Office* painted above its sash window. Boards listing routes and departure times lined its outer walls.

"Where to, miss?" Joan asked, studying the boards.

Margaret frowned in thought. "I don't know . . ."

"How much money do you have?"

Margaret recounted the coins in her reticule, bit her lip, and pronounced the paltry sum.

Joan stepped to the office window and addressed the booking clerk within.

"Hello. There are two of us traveling together." She laid the coins before him. "How far can we go?"

The clerk stared at her a moment without speaking. Margaret noticed one of his eyes was milky white. With no change of expression, he drew a chalk circle on a map on the counter. Margaret glanced over Joan's shoulder at the circle of modest diameter around London. Not very far at all.

"Stage rates are tuppence to four pence per double mile. Royal Mail is faster, but costs a bit more, and don't leave till tonight."

Joan said, "We prefer to get out of . . . that is, to be on our way as soon as possible."

He turned his milky gaze from Joan to Margaret. "The Northampton line will take you as far as Dunstable for a crown—if you take an outside seat, which is cheaper. It leaves in twenty minutes. Or, the Maidstone Times leaves in thirty."

Joan glanced at her. "Which shall it be, miss? North or south?"

Margaret thought quickly. Her old home, the village of Summerfield, lay to the south, though outside the chalk circle. Would Sterling look for her there? "South, I think." She hesitated. "Unless you prefer north?"

"Maidstone has a hiring fair, I understand," Joan said. "So that would suit me." She lowered her voice. "But remember, it's you what has to get out of town. Once we are safely out of London, you shall go your way and I mine. Understand?"

Margaret felt chastened by the cutting words of her once-docile maid. But she nodded without retort. She needed Joan too much to risk complaining.

Joan turned back to the man. "Two for Maidstone, please."

He took the money, gave them their change, and directed them inside. "Marsh is the coachman you want."

They would go south. Not as far as Summerfield, but as far as their meager coin would take them.

Half an hour later, Margaret found herself, for the first time in her life, sitting on a bench atop the roof of a stagecoach, in an outside seat no less. She gripped the metal handrail so hard her knuckles ached, and they had yet to set off. In front of her, the coachman sat at the ready in his many-caped coat and top hat. Beside her sat a soldier, Joan on his other side.

The soldier turned his cheek toward first Joan, then Margaret, pointing out a long scar. "See that. Not from the war, no. From being struck by a coachman's wild whip."

Margaret swallowed and inched back on her perch as far as the low leather backrest and the baggage behind would allow.

When the guard had assisted the last passenger, he climbed up to his box at the rear and blew his yard of tin—first the "start," then the "clear the road," signal. Margaret cringed. The horn had never seemed so loud from inside a coach.

The coachman called to his horses, "Get on lads. Walk on."

Soon, they were trotting down Southwark streets, gaining speed as they left the metropolis behind. The roads worsened, but this seemed no deterrent to the coachman, snapping his whip and urging his horses faster. Margaret sent up a prayer and held on tight. The careening coach rocked to and fro over the rutted road, and Margaret feared she would lose what little breakfast she had eaten. A man's hat flew off, and the gusting wind pulled at her bonnet and wig. She could not imagine how the wind must bite and torture in winter. She risked loosing her handhold only long enough to tie the ribbons tighter before gripping the rail once more. At every turn, the coach pitched and the soldier's body pressed against her side. He needed a bath.

The stage stopped to pay tolls at several tollgates. The polite soldier leaned near and said, "I prefer traveling by Royal Mail when I can. They don't have to stop and pay tolls."

Margaret nodded her understanding but did not mind the brief stops. They gave her a few moments to rub her aching hand and check her wig and spectacles. Joan, she noticed, bore the journey without complaint.

Margaret leaned forward, mustered a smile, and said to her, "Could be worse. At least it is not raining."

*Maids attending [hiring] fairs carried distinctive
insignia to indicate their particular skills. Cooks,
for instance, wore a red ribbon and carried a basting
spoon, while housemaids wore blue and held a broom.*

—Pamela Horn, introduction to *The Complete Servant*

Chapter 5

Several hours later, the stagecoach approached Maidstone, the county town of Kent, passing hop fields and cherry orchards as it neared. From across the river Medway, Margaret saw many stone and timber-framed buildings, paper mills, and an impressive church with great arched windows and a castle-like tower.

The stage rattled over the bridge, and Margaret spied a boat moored along the riverbank and grain sacks being unloaded onto a wagon. The horses then trotted down a street lined with shops, a bluecoat school, and inns. Margaret read the signs as they passed: Gegan, Carver & Gilder, Miss Sarah Stranger, Ladies' Boarding and Day School, The Queen's Arms.

The guard played "home" on his horn and the coach halted before the red brick Star Hotel. Hostellers rushed out to tend the horses, and the guard hopped from his perch. Taking his offered hand, Margaret climbed gingerly from the roof, knuckles aching, legs shaking. The soldier handed down the carpetbag and Joan's valise, then hopped down himself, tipped his hat, and wished them well.

Margaret looked around. Maidstone. Only thirty-five or forty miles from London. Not far enough away to Margaret's way of thinking. And why did the town's name ring a distant bell in her mind? She had never been there before, and she didn't think she had any family nearby. If only she did have some kind relative, whom Sterling would not think to search down, who might take her in and hide her away. But she could think of no one.

Margaret adjusted her windblown bonnet and glanced at Joan. "What is the plan?"

"My plan is to find work," Joan said flatly. "I'd advise you to do the same."

Inwardly Margaret cringed. She would have to find some way to pay for lodgings, but she had no idea what sort of work she was equipped to do, unless one counted ornamental needlework. She had been an only child until Caroline and then Gilbert came along years later, and her father had treated her more as a prized son than a housebound female.

The second son of wealthy parents, Stephen Macy had gone into the church after his elder brother inherited the estate. He had raised Margaret to enjoy everything he did—well-bred horses and well-trained dogs, serious discussions, and helping people in need. Her mother had drawn the line at cigars. While at girls' seminary, Margaret had learned to enjoy a few typically feminine pursuits, like watercolors and fashion. But when she was home, her father continued to take her riding and on parish calls. But no one would pay her to paint or ride, she guessed, nor to visit the sick with food baskets.

At the thought of food her stomach growled. How Margaret wished she might walk into the Star Hotel, pay for a meal and room, and sleep for days. She sighed. "I suppose finding work is the only option."

Joan pointed down the busy street. "I'm guessing the hiring fair lies in that direction." Joan turned and walked away.

Margaret matched the maid's brisk stride as they followed the flow of the crowd. In the midst of the wide, cobbled High Street, a cupola-topped town hall stood like an island between two rows of facing storefronts. The open marketplace between was filled with milling shoppers, stalls and carts of every description, and noisy fishmongers and hawkers touting the superiority of their goods and services.

"White turnips and fine carrots, ho!" chanted a lad, his donkey laden with baskets on each side.

A man straddled a grinding wheel. "I'll grind your knives for three ha'pence a blade. Knives and scissors to grind, oh!"

The shops on the High Street had opened wide their doors, merchandise spilling forth to add to the color and variety of the marketplace. A baker's shop brought out baskets of aromatic golden buns, spicy-sweet gingerbread, and loaves of every description.

The window of Betts', the butchers, displayed hanging geese, hogs, and sausages. An aproned lad stood out front, selling meat pies to passersby.

The front of the chandler's shop was lined with crates of cabbages, gooseberries, and early apples.

Margaret's stomach growled again.

Her head swiveling from side to side to take it all in, Margaret nearly collided with a man with a barrel on his shoulder, begged his pardon, and realized she had become separated from her maid. She quickened her pace.

At the top end of the High Street, she once again caught up with Joan, who gave her the merest glance and pointed to an open area ahead, cordoned off by ropes hung between barrels. Several people stood within. Two ginger-haired girls leaned against broom handles, talking together and giggling behind their hands. An older woman stood stiffly, a red ribbon pinned to her bosom and carrying a spoon, staring stoically ahead. An old man sat on one of the upturned barrels, whittling. Beside him on the ground sat a scrawny lad of no more than eight or nine, in need of a haircut and a good meal.

"What are they doing?" Margaret whispered.

"Waiting to be hired. Have you never seen a hiring fair before?"

Margaret shook her head. The scene vaguely reminded her of the slave markets she had read about in abolitionist pamphlets. She said,

"I thought you would search the newspaper advertisements, or . . . I don't know, knock at the doors of fine houses and ask if they need another maid."

"At every door in town? Not terribly effective. And have you money for a newspaper?"

The old man must have overheard their conversation, for he rose from the barrel and pulled something from his pocket. Reaching over the rope, he handed Margaret a stained and folded copy of the *Maidstone Journal*. "Ain't many listings, but you might give a look."

Margaret thanked him and unfolded the broadsheet, and together she and Joan studied the employment column.

After a few moments, Joan sighed. "Nothing. Nothing suitable." She lifted the skirt of her blue dress and stepped gracefully over the rope and into the cordoned square. Looking back over her shoulder, she said, "Well? Are you coming or not?"

Margaret hesitated. "I don't think any employer would allow you to bring me along."

"Of course not. You shall have to find your own place."

It felt like a slap. "But . . . I am only suited to be a governess or perhaps a companion. What are the chances of someone coming here to fill such a post?"

"Very slim indeed."

Margaret knew this. These positions—the only acceptable ones for gently bred females, were most often acquired through acquaintances or poor relations, and occasionally through agencies or advertisements.

"What else am I fit for?"

Joan rolled her eyes. "I wouldn't know." Then she added begrudgingly, "But you are clever, I grant you, and could learn most anything you put your mind to."

Joan opened her valise and from within withdrew a large utility brush of some sort. Margaret glanced from it to the spoon and brooms held by the other hopeful hirelings. What had she to announce her abilities, whatever they were? Margaret was fairly well educated, but beyond her father's New Testament had no book to announce that fact in hopes of catching the eye of some parent in need of a governess. What would a lady's companion carry? In her current state of dress, she doubted she would convince anyone she was a gentlewoman fit to educate their children or accompany their elderly relation.

"What about a lady's maid?" she asked Joan.

Joan slanted her a sidelong glace. "Know anything about arranging hair?"

"I have dressed my sister's many times. And I sew and am well read. And I am familiar with the latest fashions."

Joan slowly shook her head. "You have as much chance of finding work here as a lady's maid as a governess or companion. Especially looking as you do now."

But Margaret hesitated to shed her disguise. Beyond being too close to London for comfort, and in a well-traveled county town in the bargain, how exposed she would feel standing there as herself. Margaret Macy at a hiring fair, looking for *work*? Inconceivable.

She opened her reticule and once again counted the few coins within. Her heart sank. She had no money to spend the night in a hotel. No money to travel farther, nor even to travel back to London in defeat. She set her carpetbag on a nearby bench and opened it, reviewing its meager contents once more. She picked up the only item one might deem a symbol of what she was good for: a hairbrush.

She shut the bag and stepped over the rope.

The two ginger-haired maids were hired first. They had been engaged by men who seemed more interested in their fawning manners and the jiggling flesh displayed in low necklines than their qualifications. The old cook stood there still, grimly staring straight ahead. Margaret began to feel sorry for her.

An innkeeper hired the scrawny lad to haul and carry. The boy's resigned nod at the slave-like terms chafed Margaret's heart. Perhaps she only imagined the quiver of his lip amid his raised-chin bravado. She could not help but imagine her brother, Gilbert, having to go out to work at such a tender age. The thought pricked her, and she found herself whispering a prayer for the unknown boy.

Around them the noise of the market—the hawkers, the bargaining, the *cluck-chuck* of hens and squeals of pigs—diminished as the sun began its descent.

Margaret glanced at Joan. "How long does the market last?"

"Not much longer now, I shouldn't think."

The old man said, "Usually breaks up just after four. Looks like we shall have to try again next week."

Next *week*?

A matronly looking woman in a severe black dress, high white-lace collar, and an old-fashioned bonnet came striding purposely across the High Street in their direction, keys dangling at her waist. From the corner of her eye, Margaret noticed both the old cook and Joan straighten their shoulders. Margaret followed suit.

The matron stopped before the rope, her gaze skimming past the cook's spoon and landing on Joan's cleaning brush. She introduced herself as the housekeeper at Hayfield and began drilling Joan with one terse question after another—how long she had been in service, where she had last been employed and in what capacity, why she had left, was she a good Church of England member, was she in good health . . .

Joan answered each question calmly, faltered slightly over why she had left her last place, and offered a letter of character by way of explanation—the reference Margaret had written for her before they left Peg's.

"I prefer to write for my own references." The woman eyed the folded letter with suspicion. "I warn you that I can spy a forged character a mile off. Are you certain you wish to put that letter into my hands?" One steel-grey brow rose. "I cannot promise to return it to you."

Joan's hand trembled slightly, but her expression remained placid. "This letter was written by my own mistress, mum. I trust you will find everything in order."

The housekeeper held Joan's gaze before snatching the letter from her. Margaret had never written a character before. Their housekeeper, or maybe her mother, must have taken care of such things. Perhaps there were certain requirements or customary phrases of which she knew nothing. Would the woman denounce Joan as a fraud and have her hauled in for questioning? What more trouble would Margaret bring down on Joan's head?

The woman unfolded the letter, took in the quality of paper, and began to read. She frowned once or twice as she did so, and Joan sent Margaret a beseeching look.

Finally, the woman looked up. "It is written in a fine hand and by an educated person to be sure. I may yet write to this lady to verify the reference, you understand, but this will suit for now."

Joan nodded.

"Well—" the woman consulted the letter briefly once more— "Joan Hurdle. The pay is eight pounds per annum and you'll be expected to attend church once a month in a rotation with the other servants."

She waited for Joan's response, but Joan did not immediately accept. She glanced quickly at Margaret and then away. "I am very grateful for the offer, mum. And I wonder . . . might you need a lady's maid or companion? I worked with this young woman in a former post, and she is in need of a place as well."

The woman's sharp eyes shot to Margaret, took in the hairbrush, the spectacles, and the ill-fitting dress with apparent disapprobation. "I think not."

Margaret managed a tremulous smile. "A second housemaid, then," she suggested hopefully. Joan was on the verge of leaving her, alone, in a strange town with only a few farthings to rub together.

"I don't need anybody else," the woman insisted. "Nor are you allowed to have any followers, Hurdle—male or female. Now, will you take the post or not?"

Joan pressed her lips together, shooting an apologetic look in Margaret's direction. She opened her mouth to answer, then hesitated, shoulders wilting. "Perhaps you would take her in my stead, mum? She has a fine reading voice and could read to you of an evening when her other work is done."

It was on the tip of Margaret's tongue to toss in a desperate *"I can even arrange hair. And I'm very good with a needle."* But she refrained.

The woman narrowed her eyes at Joan. "Don't you want to work at Hayfield? What have you heard?" She jerked her head toward Margaret. "Or is there something wrong with her beyond her weak eyes and you're trying to foist her off on me? Is she your sister or something?"

"No, we're not sisters. And it's not that I don't wish to work for you. I just thought . . ."

"No, Joan, you take it." The words were out of Margaret's mouth before she could think them through or change her mind. The frightened, selfish child within her wanted to grasp Joan's hand and beg her not to leave her alone, or to beg the matronly housekeeper to take them both, to confess the whole sordid situation and beseech her to help them. But she knew the woman would not care, and would likely not hire either of them if she knew why they were there. Margaret had already gotten Joan dismissed and had forced her to leave her sister's before she'd found another place. She could not, as much as she was tempted to, take this position from her now.

Joan looked at her, eyes searching. She whispered, "Are you sure, miss?"

Margaret's knees were turning liquid beneath her baggy frock. Doubts and anxiety were rising by the minute, but she nodded and pulled back her lips in a semblance of a smile.

"Come along, Hurdle," the woman said. "I have to stop at the chandler's before we drive home. You may carry the sack of rice we need."

Joan followed dutifully behind the woman, valise swinging against her leg. She looked back only once, her lips forming a silent *I'm sorry.*

Margaret's heart twisted in self-pity followed by a pinch of guilt. She had never apologized to Joan for getting her into this situation in the first place and now *she* was apologizing to *her*? If she ever saw Joan again, she decided, she would make things right.

Young persons, on their first entering into service, should endeavor to divest themselves of former habits, and devote themselves to the control of those whom they engage to serve.

—Samuel and Sarah Adams, *The Complete Servant*, 1825

Chapter 6

❧

Finally, the stoic cook heaved a sigh, lifted a beefy ankle over the rope and slogged down the cobbled street. The old man sheathed his whittling knife and rose.

"Best head on home, lass," he said.

Home. Margaret could not return even if she wanted to. And truly, she did not think of Sterling Benton's house as her home. The real home of her heart was still the home of her childhood. Even the name—*Lime Tree Lodge*—brought waves of wistful longing, conjured up memories of good smells and warm embraces, of laughter and horse rides and love. Would she never have a real home again? She felt tears prick her eyes but blinked them away. She would. She would find a way to survive the next three months and then claim her inheritance. She would buy a house of her own—perhaps even Lime Tree Lodge, were it ever offered for sale—and invite her sister and brother to live with her, once they were of age.

Even as the thoughts spun through her mind, she knew deep in her heart they were unrealistic. Her sister would marry. Her brother would have a career and eventually a wife and want a home of his own—perhaps a vicarage if he went into the church. Even so, thoughts of her future independence bolstered her courage and Margaret dried her tears.

Around her, farmers loaded remaining produce back into their wagons. The last of the shoppers hauled baskets toward waiting carts and carriages. Margaret's stomach gurgled a rude complaint. Perhaps a farmer would be willing to give her a bruised apple or the butcher's lad might part with an unsold pie. The notion of asking was tantamount to begging and caused her stomach to churn, nearly overpowering the hunger. What should she do—take her own advice and go door-to-door seeking a place? Or find some almshouse or church that might allow her to sleep under its roof? *Oh, merciful God. I know I have neglected you. I know I have no right to ask you to help me. But I do. Please help me.*

"Hello . . ."

Margaret looked up, startled, into the face of a man standing a few feet away. She had not even noticed him approach. He was a sturdy man in his midthirties, with broad, sloping shoulders and a slightly protruding middle. His hair was light brown, as were his eyes. His features were rounded, pleasant, and for some reason, familiar.

He studied her closely, which discomfited her. She hoped he was not one of *those* men, looking for one of *those* women. He did not look the part and, hopefully, neither did she, but she no longer trusted her first impressions of men.

Perhaps noticing how she dodged his too-direct eye contact, he glanced down. She followed his gaze and realized he was looking at the hairbrush hanging limp in her hand.

"Are you . . . ?" he began, with a quizzical lift of his brows.

She cut him off, eager in the presence of a prospective employer. "Oh! I was hoping to find a place." She reminded herself to disguise her voice—but only a little. After all she didn't wish to be hired as a scullery maid. "As a companion or governess, ideally. Have you any children?"

He ducked his head. "I haven't any children, no. But—"

"Or perhaps a lady's maid—hence the brush." She gave the hairbrush a vague lift. "Or even a housemaid," Margaret added, hating how desperate she sounded.

He looked at her, head cocked to the side. "You are seeking a place here in Maidstone?"

It seemed an obvious question. "Well . . . yes."

A crease formed between his brows. "You don't remember me."

She frowned, faltering as she looked at him. "I . . ."

"Are you not the young woman who helped me avoid a run-in with ne'er-do-wells only last night?"

Her mouth fell open. "Oh! I thought you looked familiar."

"I confess myself stunned to see you here when I imagined our guardian angel still snug in London. I hope you did not have to leave on our account. Did that lot threaten you as well?"

"Well, yes . . ." It seemed the simplest explanation. "And as I was only a guest there. . ." She let her words trail away.

"Well then. How fortunate that you were on hand when we wandered off course. Allow me to thank you."

"It was nothing. I was happy to help."

He inhaled through wide nostrils. "So . . . you are seeking a post?"

"Yes, it seems that I am."

Dimples appeared in his round cheeks and amusement shone in his eyes. "Have you ever been in service before?"

"No . . . That is, well, in my last . . . place, I had the care of a young lady, helping her dress, arranging her hair, reading to her, escorting her on calls, hearing her prayers . . ." She was rambling, she realized. She had done all these things with Caroline. Still she hated to lie. Her father had taught her to prize honesty and shun falsehood. For one dark second she was almost relieved he was not alive to see her at that moment.

The man said, "The mistress isn't convinced she needs another lady's maid, though the last one has retired. So I cannot offer you a chance to put that fine hairbrush of yours to use. Still, one good turn deserves another. I can offer you a position as under housemaid, assuming you're willing to learn."

Margaret Macy—a housemaid? The thought was both mortifying and frightening. She would have no idea what to do.

But neither could she afford to pass up this opportunity, assuming the offer was legitimate and the man offering it trustworthy.

Tentatively she began, "May I ask why your wife doesn't want a lady's maid?"

His face colored. "She is not my wife. Nor I the master. You misunderstand me. I am the house steward. As to why the lady of the house wishes no maid of her own, it is not for me to say. I understand the upper housemaid helps her"—he colored all the more and faltered—"dress . . . and whatnot."

"I see."

He offered her ten pounds per annum—more, she realized with chagrin, than Joan had been offered, and she an experienced maid.

"Does that sound fair?" he asked.

She forced a smile. "Yes."

"When can you start?"

"Right now, I suppose."

"Do you need to let someone know, or gather your things, or . . . ?"

"I have everything here." She lifted her bag, thinking, *And nowhere else to sleep.*

"Very well. This way."

She stepped over the rope and followed him down the High Street to a line of waiting carriages. She felt ill at ease, putting herself in the hands of this stranger, kind though he seemed on the surface.

As they walked, he said, "I forgot to introduce myself. I am Mr. Hudson. And may I know your name?"

She gave the name she and Joan had decided upon—*Nora Garret*. *Nora* from her middle name, Elinor. And *Garret* from Margaret.

"A pleasure to meet you, Nora."

He paused before a stately old carriage, and she recognized it as the one she had seen from Peg's window back in London. She was still stunned he had recognized her, stunned he should hire her because he did. This knowledge soothed the nagging worry that he had hired her with dishonorable intentions. He had not even asked for a character reference and could not in truth have hired her based on her qualifications. If he had hired her out of gratitude, she could live with that.

She hoped the other servants would be as understanding.

"Allow me to give you a hand up."

Only belatedly did she realize he referred not to helping her inside the coach but rather to the coachman's bench outside.

"The master is within, you understand."

After Mr. Hudson had helped her up, he paused to open the coach door and exchange a few words with the man inside. Then he untied the reins and climbed up himself, the coach lurching, then righting itself under his weight.

Margaret had ridden beside her father countless times in his gig, but sitting beside a strange man was far less comfortable. She wondered where the coachman was and why the steward took the reins.

"Have we far to go?" Margaret asked as they rattled down the cobbled street, quickly leaving the busy town center behind.

"Not far. Fairbourne Hall is a mile or so southeast of town."

Fairbourne Hall? The name rang in her memory, and a queasy feeling stirred her stomach, not entirely caused by the swaying of the coach. It could not be. She must be mistaken. She had never been to the Upchurch country estate, only to the town house they kept in London. Still she believed she remembered both Nathaniel and Lewis Upchurch mentioning their family home. How had she forgotten it was near Maidstone?

And now the master was "within." Perhaps Mr. Hudson referred to Mr. Upchurch senior. But Margaret was certain James Upchurch was still in Barbados. Of course, she had thought Nathaniel still there as well until the night of the masquerade ball.

She licked dry lips. "May I ask about the man I saw in the coach? Is he all right?"

"He was injured last night when his ship was set on fire."

"How dreadful."

He nodded. "I took him to a surgeon after it happened. I didn't like the looks of the fellow, so after we left you, we spent the night at an inn and saw a physician this morning before we left town. Says he'll be all right. In fact, I had only stopped in Maidstone to fill the physician's order for salve when I happened to see you."

She looked at his bandaged hand. "You were injured as well?"

He shook his head dismissively. "It's nothing."

"But you were on the ship too?"

"Yes, though regrettably of no help to him. Mr. Upchurch had to drag me from the burning ship."

Mr. Upchurch. Her heart thudded. Then it was true. She had just been hired as a maid in the home of two former suitors. . . .

"Good heavens," she murmured. She could barely take it in. She had planned only a few days ago to seek out Lewis Upchurch privately, perhaps even to brazenly hint they marry. Of course, seeing him so enthralled with another woman had dashed those plans. But she would never want him to see her like this, so bedraggled looking and in such mortifying circumstances.

She very much wanted to ask which Mr. Upchurch he referred to, but knew revealing she was acquainted with the family would put her at risk of discovery. As far as she knew, Lewis was no longer involved in the family business and would not have been the one dealing with Upchurch sugar ships.

Instead she asked, "Had you been overtaken by the smoke?"

"No. Wasn't the smoke that overtook me, but a crafty scoundrel with a club to my head."

"No!"

"Yes. You've heard of the thief folks call the Poet Pirate?"

"Yes. But I thought he was only a legend."

"A legend with flesh and bones. And a grudge. Now, I best say no more. Mr. Upchurch would not want me spreading his troubles."

Margaret remembered what Emily had said at the Valmores' ball—that Nathaniel looked like a pirate and might be the so-called Poet Pirate himself. Clearly, Emily had been wrong.

Still, Mr. Hudson *might* be speaking of their father, Margaret thought, somewhat desperately. Perhaps he had returned with Nathaniel and was the man inside the coach. Maybe Lewis and Nathaniel had remained in London. She ventured, "Is this Mr. Upchurch an older man?"

"No. Not unless you call nine-and-twenty old, and I don't."

"Oh. You called him master, so I thought . . ."

"The father lives in Barbados, so his son is master of the place for all intents and purposes. He has an elder brother, but Lewis Upchurch spends most of his time in London. We'll not likely be seeing much of him."

"Surely he shall come home now," she said, thinking of Nathaniel's demands at the ball.

Mr. Hudson gave her a sharp look.

"I mean . . . now that his brother is home."

He studied her a moment longer, then returned his eyes to the road. Had she already given herself away?

"Perhaps." The steward cleared his throat. "But you, Nora, being a housemaid, will not see much of the family. Maids are to be all but invisible, I understand."

Vaguely, Margaret nodded, but she wasn't really thinking of invisible maids. She was thinking of handsome Lewis Upchurch.

If Lewis did come home, what should she do? Sneak off to find him, reveal herself and her situation? Even if his interest had cooled toward her in recent months, surely he might help her.

A few minutes later, Mr. Hudson turned the horses down a curved drive and reined them in with a "Whoa." The coach came to a halt in front of a stately red brick manor house with a white front door. Tall, white-framed windows lined the first two levels, while the top floor was punctuated by smaller dormer windows. Broad chimneys crowned its roof, while a manicured lawn, shaped hedges, and flower gardens added color and warmth.

Had she not spurned Nathaniel Upchurch years ago, might this now be her home? The irony left a sour taste in her mouth.

A liveried footman rushed out to meet the coach. Margaret twisted on the bench to descend, but Mr. Hudson laid a staying hand on her arm.

"Not here, Nora. After we get Mr. Upchurch inside, I'll drive you around to the servants' entrance."

Her cheeks burned. "Of course." She could hardly believe Nathaniel Upchurch was in the very coach she sat atop. She shivered at the thought of what he might do if he saw her there.

The footman opened the door and let down the step.

Hudson called down, "Mr. Upchurch has been injured. Please assist him inside."

The footman offered a hand to the occupant. The coach swayed as the passenger alighted. Margaret sat stiffly, staring ahead, face averted. She was afraid Nathaniel Upchurch might look up and recognize her and send her away before she'd even begun.

"There you go, sir. Easy does it," the footman soothed.

"I am not an invalid, man. Let off."

"Only trying to help."

Margaret risked a glance and saw a tall dark-haired man in rumpled clothing shake off the footman's hand. A bandage swathed his head, and one arm hung in a sling. A second footman ran forward to help, concern evident in his expression.

Mr. Hudson addressed the servants. "Please see Mr. Upchurch to his room and draw him a bath."

"Yes, sir."

Margaret watched Nathaniel Upchurch hobble to the door, shaking off the second footman's hand as he had the first's. He was certainly not the mild-tempered fellow she remembered from years gone by. She recalled the searing look of disgust he had shot her across the ballroom only a few nights before. It had sent a clear message— *I loathe you.* He would probably relish an opportunity to revenge himself for her cold refusal of his offer.

She could definitely not risk revealing herself to him.

Mr. Hudson drove to the back of the house. There, a groom came forward and took charge of the horses and carriage. Hudson helped Margaret alight, then escorted her down the outside stairs to the basement. Inside, he led her along a passage to a closed door. It took several seconds for her eyes to adjust to the dimmer light. Then he asked her to wait while he went alone into the housekeeper's parlor.

He knocked, was admitted by a faint "Come," and disappeared within, closing the door behind him.

Seeing no one about, Margaret allowed herself to lean against the wall beside the door. She was fatigued from the long, stressful day. Through the closed door she overheard the low rumble of Mr. Hudson's voice, followed by a silence, then expressions of surprise and concern in a female voice. Unable to resist, Margaret tilted her head nearer the door.

A woman said, "I realize, Mr. Hudson, that as house steward, you have the right to hire whom you please, but I would have thought, considering you have just come into your position, that you might at least have consulted me."

He made some placating reply, but his words were not as distinct as the woman's, so Margaret made out only a few words, "London . . . help . . . trial."

A trial, as in it would be a trial to have her there, or a trial period of employment? A heavy sigh followed. Whichever it was, the house-keeper was clearly not pleased by the prospect.

The door opened and Mr. Hudson appeared, grim-faced. "Mrs. Budgeon will see you now." He added on a whisper, "Mind your p's and q's."

The woman within was not what Margaret had expected. She supposed she'd imagined someone like the woman who had hired Joan—a gloomy-faced matron in a decorous high-necked gown and outmoded cap. The woman before her was only in her midforties. Her dress was black but fashionable, striped with grey and brightened by a pretty lace collar. No dowdy cap crowned her thick dark hair, which was neatly pinned back. Her eyes were brown, her face pleasant if a touch long, her complexion fair, her jawline just beginning to soften. She had been a beauty in her youth, Margaret thought. She was attractive still, except for the stern tightening of her mouth and wary light in her eyes.

"Nora, is it?"

"Yes, ma'am. Nora Garret."

"Under servants use only Christian names here at Fairbourne Hall. Except when we have more than one Mary, for example."

Margaret nodded.

"Mr. Hudson tells me you worked previously as a young lady's maid. And that was where?"

"Lime Tree Lodge, in Summerfield."

"And your employer?"

Margaret swallowed. "A Mrs. Haines."

"Normally, I would write to your past employer to request a character reference be sent directly to me. But as Mr. Hudson has taken it upon himself to engage you, I have agreed to give you a month's trial. Employment after that time will depend upon how well you perform your duties, follow house rules, and get on with other members of staff. Do I make myself clear?"

"Yes, ma'am."

"Well. We shall see." The woman rose. "From the looks of you, you've had a long day already. Let's go up and get you settled."

Taking a candlestick, Mrs. Budgeon led the way along the basement passage. Handing Margaret the lit candle, the woman unlocked a storeroom with one of the many keys hanging from her waist and extracted a set of bed linens and a hand towel. Carrying the candle in one hand and her carpetbag in the other, Margaret followed Mrs. Budgeon up a pair of narrow stairs, through a servery on the ground floor, then up two more flights of back stairs. Margaret was accustomed to climbing stairs in the Berkeley Square town house, but not at such a pace!

"You are to use the back stairs for all your comings and goings," the housekeeper said. "You are only allowed on the main stairs for staff assemblies or if you are sweeping or polishing the railings."

Margaret nodded, breathing too hard to answer.

Finally they reached the attic. "The servants' rooms along this corridor are occupied or used for storage. But there is one small chamber you might use beyond the old schoolroom." She turned the corner and added with pride, "Each of the female servants here at Fairbourne Hall

79

has her own bedchamber. That is something you won't find every-where."

Had Joan shared a room, perhaps even a bed, with one of the other maids in the Berkeley Square attic? Margaret had no idea.

Mrs. Budgeon opened the last door, and the musty chalk smell of disuse met Margaret's nose. The chamber was small, narrow, and paneled in white. A cloudy window offered the faint glow of evening sunlight. A cast-iron bed with a bare mattress stood against one wall, a dressing chest and wooden slat chair against the other. Shifting the linens to one arm, Mrs. Budgeon laid the hand towel on the dressing chest, frowning at the empty basin where a pitcher should have been. "I shall send someone up with water."

Margaret's stomach grumbled a noisy complaint, and she felt her cheeks heat.

Mrs. Budgeon glanced at her. "When did you last eat?"

Margaret set down the candle and her carpetbag. "This morning."

"You've missed dinner, and supper isn't until nine." She sighed. "I shall have something sent up to you. But don't get used to being waited upon."

Too late, Margaret thought.

The woman handed Margaret the armload of bed linens. "You are capable of making your own bed, I trust?"

"Of course," Margaret murmured. But the truth was, she had never made a bed in her life.

"In the morning, Betty will show you what is expected here at Fairbourne Hall. I'll hear no excuses of 'but in my last situation things were done differently.' Understood?"

"Yes, ma'am," Margaret said. *No fear of that from me.*

When the housekeeper left, Margaret hung her bonnet on the peg behind the door, and set about trying to make the bed. The sheets and pillowcase were of coarse cotton—nothing as fine as she was used to but clean and sweet smelling. She spread the sheets and tucked them under the tick, too tired to care about the wrinkles. Then she covered it with a blanket of summer-weight wool and a spread of white tufted cotton.

A single rap sounded, and her door was butted open before Margaret could reply. A thin dark-haired woman in cap and apron pushed her way inside, pitcher in one hand, plate in the other.

"Oh." Margaret surveyed the tiny room, and directed the maid toward the dressing chest.

The woman's mouth tightened. "Yes, m'lady," she murmured acidly. She dropped the plate onto the chest with a clunk, then shoved the pitcher into Margaret's arms, some of the water sloshing onto Margaret's bodice. Cold water.

"I'm not yar servant, am I?" she said, her voice lilting Irish. "I've already carried that up three flights of stairs; don't be commandin' me to do more."

"I wasn't." Margaret bit her lip and set the heavy pitcher into the basin herself. She glanced back to find the maid smirking at the bed.

"I hope ya make beds better than that . . . or ya won't last here a week."

Margaret turned to regard the creased bedclothes.

"Well, don't stay up too late. Five thirty comes early." The maid turned on her heel and swept from the room as regally as any highborn miss giving the cut direct.

Margaret sat on the hard chair and ate the bread, cheese, and sliced pickles the maid had brought up. She looked once more at the wrinkled bed and thought it appeared inviting indeed. She was heavy with weariness. Emotionally drained. It was probably only six or seven in the evening, but the escape of sleep beckoned her with its intoxicating pull. Setting down the plate, she rose and stepped toward the bed, and then stiffened.

How would she undress on her own? She ought to have thought of that before the sharp-nosed, sharp-tongued maid left, though she would have been reluctant to ask the cheeky woman for any favor.

Well, she would make do. How hard could it be? Margaret stripped off her apron and hung it on the peg. She pulled the cap and wig from her head and set them beside the bed, near at hand. The gown, loose and wide necked, posed little problem. Margaret peeled it off one shoulder, then the other, then twisted the gown so that the few ribbon ties at the back were easily undone, then she slid the gown over her hips and stepped out. *Nothing to it*, she thought. And Joan had hinted that Margaret was helpless. *Ha!*

She stood there in her stays and shift. Trying the same method, she tugged at the shoulder straps of the linen stays. The very snug straps. She succeeding in wiggling one strap partway down, but the other would not give, taut as it was from being pulled in the opposite direction. She tried to reach around herself to grasp the laces up her back, but the stays limited her movement, and even if they had not, she was not contortionist enough to manage the feat. She reached around with her comb, hoping to snag the lacing, but her shoulder ached from being bent so unnaturally.

Giving up, she sat on the bed to remove her stockings. It was difficult to bend at the waist with the stays in place, the rigid ivory busk running from between her breasts to her lower belly. She managed to untie the ribbons that held the stockings above her knees, then had to lift her leg to roll the stockings from her feet. She sat back, oddly winded from the constriction of bending over in her stays.

She cleaned her teeth perfunctorily with the supplies she'd brought. Then she rinsed her hands and face in the cold water and dried off with the towel the housekeeper had provided. Transferring the candle to the small bedside table, Margaret pulled back the bedclothes and climbed in, still wearing her stays and a fine cotton shift beneath. She glanced down at the wig in a curly heap on the floor. What if someone came in? There was no lock on the door. She hated the thought of sleeping with the warm, itchy wig. Instead, she pulled on the cap alone and tucked all of her blond hair into it. That should do. She blew out the candle.

Though mentally fatigued, Margaret tossed and turned, worried about her future, wondering how her mother was reacting, and what was happening in Berkeley Square . . . until finally, finally, sweet sleep lured her away.

*The first thing a Housekeeper should teach a new servant
is to carry her candle upright. The next thing is those general
directions that belong to "her" place, such as not setting the
brooms and brushes where they will make a mark.*

—The Housekeeping Book of Susanna Whatman, Maidstone, 1776

Chapter 7

The pounding. Who in the world would be pounding at this
hour? London was such a noisy place. Margaret felt she would
never get used to living in such a sprawling, bustling city. She
had not slept well since coming to live in Sterling Benton's house.
She had barely fallen asleep and already the rapping had awoken her.
She rolled over, and began drifting off once more. The pounding
resumed, louder. She pulled the limp pillow from under her cheek
and covered her head with it. *Need sleep . . .*

"You need to get up, lazy lay-a-bed."

Why was Joan pestering her? It could not be morning yet, and
Margaret often slept in until quite late, especially when she had been
out the night before.

The door creaked open.

"Leave me be," she murmured.

The bedclothes were yanked from her body, the cool morning
air prickling her skin. She rolled over to face her tormentor, ready
to give Joan a tongue lashing. "What do you think you are doing?"

She froze. Candlelight illuminated not Joan's face, but that of a stranger. The bed, the room, were not her own. Her mind whirled. *What? Where . . . ?*

A woman stared at her, stunned no doubt at the haughty reception. With a wave of dread, Margaret remembered. She was in London no longer.

Suddenly London seemed the far friendlier fate.

"I . . . I was dreamin'," Margaret mumbled, trying to find the accent of her dear old housekeeper. "I thought you were my . . . someone else."

"I am the upper housemaid here at Fairbourne Hall," the woman said, lifting her offended nose high. "And I am not accustomed to being addressed so rudely."

"I . . ." Margaret could eke out no apology. She sat up on the edge of the bed, carefully nudging the wig under the bed with her toes. "How shall I address you, then?"

The upper housemaid was a short, stocky middle-aged woman. In the flickering light her coloring was uncertain, but the whites of her eyes lingered on Margaret's stays and shift. Likely too fine for a housemaid. But apparently the woman had not noticed the wig. Nor, hopefully, any stray blond hairs.

"My name is Betty Tidy, but you may use my Christian name."

"Betty *Tidy*?"

"Is there something you find amusing about that, Nora?"

That's right, she thought, *I'm Nora.* "Only the name Tidy. For a housemaid."

Betty frowned. "There are many Tidys in these parts. It's a perfectly respectable family name."

"I meant no disrespect, Betty." Margaret bit back a smirk. "In fact I think it the perfect name. The name every housemaid should have."

Betty sniffed and stepped to the door. "I shall give you five minutes to dress."

Five minutes? Perhaps, then, it was fortunate Margaret had not managed to remove her stays, for she would certainly not have gotten them on by herself given five hours, let alone five minutes. She quickly washed her face, then wiped the damp cloth beneath each capped sleeve to remove the previous day's perspiration. She stepped into her dress, tied the ribbons, and wiggled it back to front and up over her shoulders. Then she tied on the apron, pinned her hair, and put on her father's spectacles. Finally, she settled the wig snugly against her head, checking in the small mirror over the dressing chest to be sure all the blond hairs were covered before donning her cap once more. She was glad the generous cap disguised the lump beneath the wig caused by her twist of hair.

She met Betty in the passage and followed her down one flight of stairs to the housemaids' closet, where they retrieved two handled wooden boxes of cleaning supplies. Palms damp, she trotted after Betty down to the ground floor, through a conservatory, and into the drawing room. Would she really be able to manage a maid's chores?

"First, we open the shutters . . ."

That she could do. Margaret made her way to a second window and unlatched and folded back the shutters. In the advancing morning light, she saw that the upper housemaid had faded auburn hair, blue eyes, and the freckles of a girl.

She followed Betty through each room, learning what would become her morning rounds—cleaning the grates, sweeping the carpets, dusting, and generally straightening the public rooms: conservatory and drawing room at the rear of the house. Salon and library on one side of the front entry hall, morning room and dining room on the other. All before breakfast.

Margaret noticed the elegant high-ceilinged rooms and fine furniture but was too busy observing Betty to admire them. Betty worked with brisk efficiency, without wasted motion or apparent strain. Margaret wished she had a notebook. She doubted she would remember everything.

A stout, grave man in a gentleman's black coat and trousers stepped into the library, his dark hair slicked back. Betty introduced him as Mr. Arnold, the under butler. He welcomed Nora and checked their progress, running a white glove over furniture as he went.

At eight o'clock, Margaret and Betty made their way down to the basement and along the dim passage to the servants' hall for breakfast. And not a moment too soon. Last night's bread and cheese were long gone. Margaret pressed a hand to her unhappy midriff. The gnawing discomfort had, until recently, been a foreign sensation to Margaret Macy, one she recognized as hunger, though it was a feeling she had rarely experienced in her routine of late breakfasts, nuncheons, teas, early family dinners, and late suppers.

The servants' hall was a narrow, rectangular room dominated by a long table with a chair at each end and benches along its sides. To the right of the door, pegs held coats and aprons. On one long wall stood an unlit hearth; on the other hung an embroidered plaque, which read,

A good character is valuable to everyone,
but especially to servants.
For it is their bread and butter
and without it they cannot be admitted
into a creditable family,
and happy it is that the best of characters
is in everyone's power to deserve.

At the far end of the room, several high windows emitted cheerful morning sunshine. An oil lamp suspended from the beamed ceiling supplemented their light. In the corner stood an old pianoforte, shrouded and silent. How generous that the Upchurch family allowed its use by the servants. She wondered who played.

She took her place on a bench next to Betty and Fiona, the sharp-nosed housemaid who had brought her water and food the night before. Two kitchen maids introduced themselves, but their names went in one of Margaret's ears and out the other.

On the opposite side of the table, the two handsome young footmen in livery sat sullenly, paying no attention to her or the other maids. It was a strange feeling, being ignored by men. The grave under butler, Mr. Arnold, whom she had met upstairs, moved to sit at the head of the table, but at the last moment he scowled and sat on the bench to the right of the chair. Several servants exchanged wry looks, though no one dared a word.

The table was laid with silverware and china—not the finest, but china just the same. Butter knives crossed bread plates and sturdy mugs sat at the ready. At one corner lay a cutting board of freshly baked bread, a pot of jam, and a jar of butter, as well as a pitcher of milk. A teapot steeped on a trivet. Another maid came in, a plump young woman with a smile as broad as her figure. She set a basin of porridge near the foot of the table before taking her place beside Margaret and introducing herself as Hester, the stillroom maid. A young scullery maid and hall boy scurried in with plates of sausages, sliced tomatoes, and a dish of boiled eggs before disappearing once more.

A tall thin man in a white coat—the chef, apparently—entered with the housekeeper, discussing the day's menu. The man's black hair was still damp—he was just beginning his day, Margaret surmised. The stillroom maid must prepare the servants' breakfast, while the chef reserved his talents for the family's fare.

Mrs. Budgeon, looking neat and rested, took her place at the foot. She glanced around the table. "I trust you have all introduced yourselves to Nora?"

Heads nodded and murmurs agreed.

Mr. Hudson stepped into the room and Betty snagged Margaret's sleeve and all but yanked her to her feet. She belatedly realized that everyone rose when the house steward entered—a sign of respect for the highest-ranking member of staff. Mr. Hudson took his place at the head, sending a sheepish smile toward the under butler, who fastidiously ignored him.

Mr. Hudson gestured for everyone to sit. Then he folded his hands at the edge of the table and bowed his head. The others followed suit.

He prayed simply. "For this food, and this day, and your many blessings, make us truly grateful. Amen."

The chef, sitting next to the under butler, speared a sausage. He passed the basin of porridge with a scowl and instead sawed off a generous hunk of bread and slathered it with butter. Upon this, he laid two slices of tomato, which he salted and peppered heavily. Then he cut the sausage lengthwise and laid the planks across the tomatoes. He set to his creation with knife and fork.

Margaret ate her porridge with creamy milk but without the sugar she indulged in at home. She sipped her tea with relish, again missing the sugar but not commenting. The warm richness of the tea with fresh milk was pleasure enough.

Mr. Hudson cleared his throat and announced, "Mr. Upchurch has decided to reinstitute the practice of morning prayers. So please assemble in the main hall at nine sharp."

Margaret saw Mr. Arnold send a look of surprise to Mrs. Budgeon, who ignored him, even though the surprise in her own expression was evident. Beside Margaret, Fiona grumbled, as did several others. The elder of the two footmen rolled his eyes.

"Well, I think it a splendid idea," Betty said. "We haven't had prayers since Mr. Upchurch senior went off to the Indies."

The grumbling faded as they returned to their meal. The chef was the first to excuse himself, likely having a great deal of work awaiting him in the kitchen. A few minutes later the footmen and under butler departed to lay the family's breakfast upstairs. Mrs. Budgeon glanced at the clock atop the mantel, and that was signal enough that everyone else rose to return to their duties.

Margaret followed after Betty as she stopped in the stillroom to assemble a tray of tea things and a pressed newspaper to take up to Miss Upchurch while Fiona prepared a tray for Mr. Upchurch. Fiona had already taken up cans of hot and cold water and emptied the chamber pots while Betty and Margaret were busy in the public rooms.

Upstairs, Betty gestured for Margaret to wait and then let herself in to Miss Upchurch's bedchamber to deliver the tea and help her dress. Margaret, who had met Helen Upchurch several times, was only too glad to remain in the corridor.

Afterward, Betty and Margaret returned the tray to the stillroom. The kitchen maids passed by, clad in clean aprons, their hair smoothed back under their caps. Taking Betty's cue, Margaret followed them up to the main level.

Betty whispered, "It's the first time these poor girls have been allowed abovestairs."

At nine, servants from every nook and cranny of the house filed into the front hall, with its broad entrance doors, marble floors, carved ceiling, and impressive main stairway. The staff lined up in rows on the floor near the bottom stair, waiting in fidgets and whispers.

Mr. Arnold muttered, "Didn't know he'd become a vicar whilst he was away."

The library door opened, and Nathaniel Upchurch entered the hall, his sister at his side. Stomach knotting, Margaret slipped a little farther behind the tall chef.

Mr. Upchurch carried a black book in one hand, his other arm still cradled in a sling. He wore a bandage above one eye, which reminded her of a pirate's eye patch, askew. She wondered how badly he was hurt and why he was determined to lead prayers when he was recovering from recent injuries. How somber he looked—little like the fierce, wild-haired ruffian who had started a brawl at a Mayfair ball. The beard was gone. His hair groomed. The rough sea-voyage clothes replaced with everyday gentleman's attire: coat, waistcoat, cravat.

Hesitating, Mr. Upchurch handed the book to Hudson, behind him. Then he patted his pockets with his sound hand in vain. Was he searching for his spectacles? He used to wear them, she recalled. He said something in low tones to Mr. Hudson, and Hudson opened the book to a page marked with a square of paper before handing it back.

Mr. Upchurch cast a swift glance at the assembled group. Beside him, Helen Upchurch smiled up at them.

Margaret ducked her head.

"Good morning." Mr. Upchurch cleared his throat, squinted at the book, then read, "From First Peter. 'Honour all men. Love the brotherhood. Fear God. Honour the king.'" He turned the page. "'Servants, be subject to your masters with all fear; not only to the good and gentle, but also to the froward.'"

Around her, Margaret felt bodies stiffen, and a snotty footman muttered something she was probably better spared.

Fiona huffed. "That's convenient."

Margaret shushed the disrespectful maid without thinking, earning herself a glare from the Irishwoman.

Mr. Upchurch tucked the book back under his good arm and bowed his head. "Lord, help us each to serve you well this day, in whatever place you have seen fit to place us. Amen." He nodded to the group in dismissal and turned away.

His sister offered them what seemed an apologetic smile, perhaps hoping to soften his benediction. The others began to grumble or to stonily make their way back to their posts. But Margaret stood where she was.

Had God seen fit to place her in the service of the Upchurch family? Or had she simply made a muddle of her life?

After breakfast, Nathaniel carried a cup of coffee with him from the dining room into the library. Hudson was already inside, ready for their morning meeting, but he said nothing for several moments. Nathaniel surveyed Hudson over his coffee, sipped, then lowered the cup. "What?"

Hudson winced. "Far be it from me to interfere, sir. But that might not have been the best choice of Scriptures for your first shot at morning prayers."

"Oh?"

"Consider, sir. How that Scripture might seem an . . . arrow, more than the gentle admonition you no doubt intended."

Nathaniel opened the book on his desk and reread the passage. "Is that why I received surly looks? It was simply the next verse in my own daily reading. I knew it had not gone well and assumed it my delivery. I shall choose more carefully in future."

"Ah." Hudson nodded his understanding. "Well. I am certain it shall go better next time."

Nathaniel regarded his steward. Robert Hudson was a few years his senior. Although originally from England, he had spent many years living and working aboard ships before settling in Barbados. There, Nathaniel had hired him away from Abel Preston, the neighboring planter neither man could stand. As a clerk, Hudson was forthright and completely trustworthy. The two men had become fast friends, their relationship more partnership than master-servant. Though Hudson never failed to show him respect, neither did he fail to speak his mind.

When Nathaniel's father commissioned him to return and put Fairbourne Hall to rights, he had lost no time in convincing Hudson to return with him as steward. If Mrs. Budgeon and that coxcomb of an under butler did not like it, he did not care. Hudson would lead them with humility and competence. A rare combination of traits, which Nathaniel hoped to learn to emulate.

Nathaniel finished his coffee and set down his cup. "And far be it from me to interfere with the servants, Hudson, but I am curious. Mrs. Budgeon lodged a complaint with my sister about your hiring a housemaid without consulting her." He raised a hand before Hudson could protest. "I trust you to hire whom you like, but not two days ago you avowed your intention to leave the female staff entirely to the housekeeper."

"I know, sir. But I found quite an unexpected gem at market yesterday."

"Oh?"

"Remember the girl I mentioned to you? The one who warned me when I stopped to check on you near the docks?"

Nathaniel frowned at the memory. "Your wild driving knocked me from the seat."

"Be that as it may, I saw that very girl at the hiring fair in Maidstone. Woebegone she looked too, standing there alone after everyone else had gone home."

"You hired her because she shouted at you to move along?" Incredulity and amusement tinged Nathaniel's words.

"You don't remember that night, sir. Laid low with the surgeon's laudanum as you were. You did not see the cutthroats descending to do us a violence and no doubt steal us blind in the bargain. She not only brought them to my attention, but she shoved a door in the leader's face when he would have overtaken us. The last thing I saw before we turned the corner was those three brutes trying to break down the lodging house door. Until I saw her again yesterday, I feared she might have come to harm on our account."

"Is that why she left London?"

"I believe so, yes."

"Hmm . . . Strange that she should come here, do you not think?"

Hudson shrugged. "Not so strange. Maidstone has a regular hiring fair and is not terribly distant from London."

"I suppose."

Hudson grimaced and screwed his lips to one side. "Do you think I have made Mrs. Budgeon *very* angry?"

It was Nathaniel's turn to shrug. "The woman is a professional. She will get over it no doubt. Assuming, that is, your girl is a good worker and knows the difference between a hairbrush and a chimney brush."

Standing in the basement passageway, Margaret watched Betty's stubby fingers and rough, heavily veined hands as she laid out brush after brush on the narrow worktable.

Betty turned to her. "Now, name each brush and describe its proper use, if you please."

Margaret's mouth went dry. Before her were brushes of every imaginable description. Long-haired, short and wiry, feather, miniature brooms, and more. She had little idea what they might be called or how each was to be used.

She began, "Well, this is a feather duster of course, and, um . . ." She licked her lips. "You know, Mrs. Budgeon made it quite clear that I was not to try to do things as I did in my former place. Therefore, perhaps you had better teach me how each of these brushes is to be used here at Fairbourne Hall."

Betty studied her a moment, then sighed. "Very well." She picked up one bristled handle after another. "Picture brush, shoe brush, hearth brush, plate brush, flue brush, library brush, velvet brush, banister brush, carpet brush, wall broom, bed broom . . ."

Very soon, Margaret's head was spinning. She hoped there would be no examination. Miss Hightower's Seminary for Girls had not prepared her for this.

Why, you know, Sir Thomas's means
will be rather straitened if the Antigua estate
is to make such poor returns.

—Jane Austen, *Mansfield Park*

Chapter 8

Nathaniel found Helen ensconced in her favorite chair in the family sitting room—where he suspected she spent the majority of her time. He took in his sister's plain grey frock, her severely pulled-back hair, and the pallor of her cheeks. Helen was only a year his senior, but at the moment she looked older than her thirty years.

She glanced up from her novel. "How are you feeling today?"

Her words struck him as the distant kindness of an acquaintance.

"In body? Better. I cannot claim the same for mind and spirit." He settled himself on the settee across from her.

"What did the river police say? Any hope of catching the vandal?"

He snorted ruefully. "Catch a man most people believe mere legend? How they laughed behind their hands when I admitted Hudson and I had been overtaken by a lone attacker, a man who calls himself the Poet Pirate no less. Of course I told them the man's real name as well, but I don't think they believed me."

"I am sorry, Nathaniel." She shook her head. "At least the ship was not lost. You can make repairs, can you not?"

He had barely returned and didn't want to burden her with the reality of their finances just yet. He exhaled a deep breath. "We shall see. Now, let us talk of something else. How have you been keeping while we have all been away?"

"Well enough. And how was Papa when you left him? In good health, I hope?"

How he abhorred the polite restraint between them. "Yes. The warmer climate seems to agree with him. Says he barely notices his rheumatism anymore."

Helen studied him. "But . . . does he mind being alone there?"

He hesitated, biting back a sarcastic retort about the charming widow from a nearby plantation with whom their father spent an inordinate amount of time. Considering Helen's solitary state, it seemed unkind to mention it. He said instead, "He has lived there a long time now, Helen. He has many friends."

"And you? Were you sorry to return?"

Nathaniel considered. Should he tell her about the escalating arguments between him and their father? He said, "In hindsight, the timing of it all seems God-ordained, receiving that letter from Stephens when we did."

Helen shook her head. "I still cannot believe Stephens wrote to Father. He always insisted servants should know and keep their place. I cannot believe he would say a word against Lewis."

In his mind's eye, Nathaniel saw the somber face of their dignified old butler. He had written to say he felt it his duty to apprise James Upchurch of the state of affairs at Fairbourne Hall, to make him aware of the decline of the great estate it had been his honor to serve for more than twenty years. Stephens apologized but said that he could not in good conscience remain longer. The butler had given his notice, not to Lewis or Nathaniel but to their father—the real master in his eyes, absent or not.

"His tone was very respectful—quite mournful, really."

Helen pursed her lips. "Still, I thought him more loyal."

Nathaniel fought against incredulity. "Helen, the man had not been paid in six months. Stephens paid a quarter's wages to the lower servants out of his own savings. He tried to cover for us to keep the Upchurch reputation from suffering."

She stared at him. "I had no idea it had come to that. Certainly, had Lewis known he would have done something. Stephens should have told him."

Nathaniel hesitated. He knew his sister doted on Lewis. Everyone did and always had. She would not thank him for speaking against their elder brother.

Helen asked, "So Father sent you home to take the place in hand, did he?"

"In a manner of speaking, yes. I own I feared the entire staff would have deserted by the time I reached you."

"You overreacted, the both of you. Things are not so bleak, as you see. You needn't have come."

Did she wish he hadn't? Probably. Nathaniel shrugged. "Father and I had come to an impasse, at all events. I refused to manage the plantation as long as slave labor was used, and he refused to transition to paid laborers."

"Lewis says our profits would suffer greatly."

"They would indeed. But there is more to life than profits."

She lifted her chin. "You held no such compunctions before you left for Barbados."

All too true, and his conscience smote him for it. "I had not seen the institution for myself then, Helen. It was not real to me, merely theoretical. Since then I have seen the cruelty of overseers and masters like Abel Preston. I have heard the cries and seen the scars."

Helen winced. "I tend to agree with you. But certainly Papa and others have seen what you saw and have not come to the same conclusion. How do you account for it?"

He slowly shook his head. "I don't know. Willful blindness. Apathy. Greed. Misinformation or ignorance. I cannot say. All I know is that I am convinced to the core of my soul it is wrong."

She picked at the doily on the arm of her chair. "At least Papa and the other planters did not fight Parliament when it abolished the slave trade."

He nodded. "That was years ago, yet slavery continues. The only reason the planters did not fight the abolishment of the trade itself was because by that time Barbados was no longer dependent on slave importation." His stomach twisted. "They encouraged slave reproduction instead."

Helen looked down at her hands, clearly disconcerted.

It was his turn to wince. "Forgive me."

She cleared her throat and forced her head up. "But do we not live by its profits? Was not your ship purchased by slave-wrought sugar, as well as your Oxford education and the very clothes on your back?"

"You begin to sound like Father," Nathaniel said dryly. "And you are right, of course. To my shame. But we need not go on as we have in the past. Sugar is not our only source of income, Helen. We had a good crop this past season, yes. But the market is not what it once was, and overall profits are declining, slavery or no. I believe we should sell out. If we retrench, invest wisely, and live modestly, we can live off the income from the estate here." He realized he was going on like an excited boy. Or an evangelist. He sighed. "But Father is not ready to give it up."

She asked gently, "Is he very angry with you?"

Nathaniel inhaled deeply. "He is disappointed—there is no denying it. He says he respects my convictions but finds them too inconvenient." His father was honest at least; Nathaniel gave him that. He drew himself up. "All this to say, it was time for me to come home. I can be useful here. Look after things."

"But please don't blame Lewis," Helen said. "If there wasn't any money, what did you expect him to do?"

Nathaniel rubbed a hand over his eyes. Again, he bit his lip to stop himself from saying what he wished to say: *"I expected him to stop spending money we didn't have on new clothes, a new barouche, new horses, lavish dinner parties, improvements to the London house, and I know not what."* His stomach churned anew at the thought of the stacks of bills he'd discovered when he spent a few days there.

When he was silent, Helen continued, "Perhaps we ought to have been more careful, but how was Lewis to raise money to pay the servants? Surely you did not expect him to *work*."

Nathaniel said, "The rents from our tenants have not been collected for the last two quarters. He might have done that. For now, Hudson and I will endeavor to bring the accounts to order. If that dashed Preston had not stolen half our profits we would be closer to bringing finances up to snuff. I am only glad I did not leave the whole in that chest."

"Does *he* know that?" Helen asked.

Nathaniel had wondered the same thing. "I don't know. He said he'd heard Father had boasted about our profits. Hopefully not the specific amount." He sighed. "I pray we've seen the last of him." But somehow Nathaniel doubted it.

Helen regarded him earnestly with hazel eyes very like their mother's, gone these many years. "I am glad you were not injured more seriously."

"Thank you."

How long since he'd heard a kind word spoken by one of his family. The kind words of a woman were salve, even if spoken by his sister. Still, he wished he could rekindle the camaraderie he had shared with Helen in their youth, even if she preferred Lewis.

For a moment, he wondered how Helen could idealize Lewis— as did every other female of their acquaintance, who saw only the handsome exterior and charming, carefree ways. But then Nathaniel realized Helen did not know their elder brother as well as he did. Lewis had gone away to school as a boy, then on to Oxford and his grand tour, then had spent much of his time in London or at this or that friend's country estate.

In his boyhood, Nathaniel had been taught at home by a tutor but then had followed Lewis to Oxford. His first year had overlapped with Lewis's last, and he had spent more time in his brother's company, witnessing his antics away from the restraints and duties of home. But beyond term breaks and holidays, how much time had Helen and Lewis really spent together? Nathaniel didn't like to disparage his brother. He loved him and always would, though he did not always like or respect him. Lewis seemed to save his charm for the fair sex, their sister included, and who could blame him? Many was the time Nathaniel would have traded his higher marks and accomplishments for an ounce of that charm where women—or at least a certain woman—were concerned.

That night, Margaret trudged along after Betty, through the house and down the back stairs once more. She wanted nothing more than to return to her room and sleep. Instead she followed Betty like a weary duckling trailing its parent.

"You're in for a treat tonight, Nora. Monsieur Fournier has prepared quite a feast to welcome Mr. Upchurch home. And we're to have the leavings for our supper."

And feast it was, though Margaret was not accustomed to being served from dishes with portions missing, partial jelly moulds, and congealing sauces. But the other servants beamed at the dishes in anticipation, not minding the secondhand nature of the feast.

Monsieur Fournier waved his long arm and pointed a hairy-knuckled finger as he named each dish: vermicelli soup, trout en Matelote, stewed pigeon, French beans, and vegetable marrows in white sauce. And later, the finale—gooseberry tarts and fresh pineapple.

Everyone *oohed* and *ahhed* over the dessert, for pineapple was a rare luxury.

Mr. Hudson gave thanks, and they began the supper, passing things politely when asked and eating quietly. How unexpectedly formal the meal was. Margaret felt transported back to an uncomfortable evening when her great-aunt had invited her to dine with a crusty dowager countess. This was not how she had imagined servant suppers to be.

Abruptly, a few people began to rise, Betty among them, and Margaret made to follow. But this time, Fiona grabbed her arm and pulled her back down. She hissed in her ear, "What are ya doin'? Only the uppers go."

The upper servants—Mr. Hudson, Mrs. Budgeon, Mr. Arnold, and Betty, as first housemaid—rose and quietly left the room in somber procession.

"Where are they going?" Margaret whispered.

"To the moon—what do ya think? Pug's parlor, o' course."

Mr. Arnold paused in the threshold and looked back. "Fred, I trust you will remember to walk the dog after your supper?"

"I will, sir."

The under butler, Margaret noticed, carried a bottle of port beneath his arm, while the servants were left with small beer.

Margaret had heard of the custom of the "upper ten" partaking of their pudding and of finer dishes and wines separately from the under servants in the housekeeper's parlor. Still, she felt a strange stab at finding herself at the lower end of the social hierarchy. Left out.

The feeling soon evaporated, however, because the stiff atmosphere in the servants' hall melted into relaxed conviviality once the uppers—the bosses—were gone.

Thomas, the dark-haired first footman, raised his glass of small beer. "Here's to the return of Mr. Upchurch."

A female voice to Margaret's right said, "I wish Mr. *Lewis* Upchurch would return."

Margaret snapped her head around in surprise. She took in the wistful expression of the heavyset stillroom maid she had met at breakfast.

"Do you? Why?" Margaret could not help but ask. She found it somehow disconcerting that she was not the only maid awaiting Lewis's appearance.

Hester gazed into the distance but did not answer.

Dark-haired Thomas slanted Margaret a look. "You've never seen him, or you wouldn't ask. All the girls flutter about Mr. Lewis."

"I don't know why." The second footman, Craig, shrugged.

"Come on now," Jenny said. "We all know it isn't Mr. Lewis Hester pines for, but the young man what comes with him."

Margaret turned to the kitchen maid. "Who's that?"

Jenny looked at her, incredulous. "His valet, of course."

"Oh, right," Margaret murmured, noticing how pink Hester's round cheeks had become.

"I don't know what girls see in him either," fair-haired Craig pouted. "What's he got that I haven't got?"

"Class, that's what he's got," Jenny answered. "And genteel ways."

Another kitchen maid answered, "And so handsome in his fine clothes."

Craig frowned. "Well, I've got fine clothes."

Thomas threw down his table napkin. "You call livery fine?" The footman's lip curled. "For trained monkeys, maybe."

Margaret was surprised the first footman despised the very livery he himself wore.

"Oh, now don't listen to Thomas," Jenny soothed. "I think you're both quite handsome in your livery. Very smart."

"Thank you, Jenny." Craig added hopefully, "I don't suppose you have a sister?"

Thomas smirked. "Or a grandmother. Craig isn't fussy."

Craig glared, but the others chuckled, enjoying the teasing nearly as much as their desserts.

The next morning Margaret began her first full round of work. If she had thought the day before taxing, this one promised to be more so. The previous day had been spent in learning and in observing Betty or assisting her. Today, Margaret was on her own. Betty had assigned her the drawing room, conservatory, hall, and steward's office to clean before breakfast, while she would see to the library, salon, morning room, dining room, and servery. Fiona, meanwhile, would take care of the early morning duties abovestairs—taking up water and emptying the slops in the bedchambers as well as cleaning the family sitting room.

In the drawing room, Margaret did as Betty had taught her. First she lugged all the furniture she could move to the center of the room: chairs, settees, tea tables, and end tables. These she covered with cloths to protect them from the dust she was about to raise whilst sweeping the carpet. She grasped a handful of damp tea leaves from a wide-mouth jar, gave them a final squeeze, and sprinkled the leaves over the carpet. This was meant to freshen the carpet and sweeten the air, but to Margaret it seemed illogical to cast debris on something she was meant to clean.

Selecting the carpet sweeper brush from her box, she went to work on her knees, sweeping the scant dirt and occasional pebble toward the hearth, from which she had already removed the fender and polished the grates. Afterwards, she wiped her hands on a cloth. She removed the dust covers and dusted the furniture and then began dragging the pieces back to their places. Perspiration trickled from beneath her wig and down her back, causing the skin beneath her long stays to itch. She was breathing heavily and her back ached by the time she restored the last piece of furniture to its proper—she hoped—place.

Gathering up her tools into the housemaid's box, Margaret paused to wipe a hand across her brow.

One room down. Three to go.

After breakfast, Betty hurried upstairs to help Miss Upchurch dress, leaving Margaret to sweep the main stairs and rub the banister with a little oil.

They attended morning prayers and then Margaret helped Betty clean Miss Upchurch's apartment—Betty still did not trust her with the family bedchambers, nor to make beds alone. She helped Betty tie back the bed curtains and strip the bed to air, emptied the washbasin, and tidied the dressing room.

As the afternoon wore on, Margaret found her knees aching and her hands dry and stiff. She helped Fiona collect the soiled laundry throughout the house and was then assigned to scrub the basement passageway leading from the servants' entrance on one end, all the way to the men's quarters on the other.

On her hands and knees, with a bucket of hot water heated on the stove, Margaret scrubbed a floor for the first time in her life. Her knees throbbed against the hard stone floor, and her hands burned from the harsh soap. She was midway down the passage when hall boy Fred came in the servants' door with a rangy wolfhound, its wiry grey hair slick and wet.

Margaret sat back on her heels. "I've just washed that floor," she grumbled.

"It's all right," Fred said. "Jester's cleaner than either of us. He's just had a swim in the pond."

Suddenly the dog at Fred's heel shook himself mightily, spraying muddy water all over Fred's trouser legs and Margaret's face and bodice.

She squeezed her eyes shut, sputtered, and groaned. "Oh, no . . ."

"Sorry, miss," Fred said.

Mrs. Budgeon appeared in her doorway nearby. "What is the matter?" She looked from Margaret, to Fred, to the dog and back again. Surveying Margaret, her lips thinned and she sighed. "Well, Fred, you've won the honor of finishing that floor. Nora, I would tell you to bathe, but we haven't time for all that now. Go on up to your room and clean up as best you can. You do have another frock, I trust?"

"Yes, ma'am. Well, one."

"Let's hope it suits."

Margaret took herself up to her room and cleaned her face, neck, and hands as best she could at the washstand with her allotted bar of soap. She had peeked inside the servants' bathing room Mrs. Budgeon had referred to. The small room lay at the end of a narrow side passage, past the servants' hall. But she had yet to use the tub it contained. Until she figured out how to remove her stays, she would make do with sponge baths in her room.

She changed into the blue gown, eyeing her bed with longing, but forced herself back downstairs.

After the family ate their dinner, Margaret helped Mrs. Budgeon wash the china in the storeroom adjoining her parlor. The room was fitted with a special wooden sink lined with lead for the purpose. Once dry, the housekeeper meticulously examined each piece for damage before checking it back in.

As evening darkened to night, Margaret began longing for her narrow attic bed with the most ardent zeal—though she wondered if her wobbly legs would carry her up the many stairs even one more time. And to think she had to do it all again tomorrow! Tears filled her eyes from fatigue and self-pity. She would never live through another day of this, let alone three and a half months.

When they finished their duties at last, Betty walked with her up to the attic and followed her all the way to her room. There, Betty closed the door behind them and faced her. Her reddish-brown hair peeked out from under her cap after the long day. Her elfin blue eyes shone with concern. Margaret expected some private reprimand, but instead, Betty said, "I saw you sleeping in your stays that first morning. Are you still?"

Cheeks heated, Margaret nodded sheepishly. "I can't reach the laces."

Betty shook her head and gave a long-suffering sigh. "Very well. Let's get them off you."

She did so, and what blessed relief it was. After wearing the garment around the clock and through unaccustomed exertion, the stays had left their mark. Betty took one look at the welts and insisted she would help her morning and night from then on.

If I live that long, Margaret thought.

Betty squeezed her arm as if reading her mind. "It'll get easier by and by. You'll see."

When Margaret finally climbed into her bed after ten, she lay awake, sheet pulled up to her chin but the blanket folded at the foot, unwelcome on the warm summer night. She had opened the small window, but not a breath of breeze stirred the air. She lowered the sheet to her waist. Even that effort made her wince. Never had she been so physically exhausted. Her arms ached from strenuous effort—pushing brooms, wringing mops, scrubbing floors, brushing grates, flinging sheets and making beds, reaching high to polish windows and clear cobwebs, carrying heavy buckets of water and worse. Her light work with a needle and her watercolors, her hours on the pianoforte, had not prepared her poor spindly arms for such exertion.

She crossed her chest, massaging each forearm with the opposite hand—hands already blistered and dry from hot soapy water, blacking, and lye. Thank heaven she had not ended up as a laundry maid or she would depart Fairbourne Hall with stubs.

Margaret rolled over. Her legs were sore as well, from climbing up and down stairs carrying buckets, piles of laundered bedclothes, baskets of small clothes fresh from the laundry, and her housemaid's box. She would have legs like a pack mule in no time.

So tired . . . And yet she could not keep her eyes closed. In her mind revolved a painted carousel of objects, duties, instructions, and warnings. Shoe brushes, grate brushes, bed brushes. Open shutters by seven, make beds by eleven. Never drip candle wax. Never wax mahogany. Always scrub hands between blacking and bed making, and whatever you do, don't speak to the family unless spoken to. Around and around it went. Margaret groaned. She had never imagined the work of a housemaid could be so taxing.

She still found it difficult to grasp that she was doing such work in the manor of the Upchurch family. How strange to be under Nathaniel's roof. She had seen him at morning prayers, of course, but according to first Mr. Hudson, then Betty, it was unlikely she would see much of the family otherwise, except in passing. What would Nathaniel say to finding her living in his house, eating his food, polishing his floors? He might enjoy the latter, she mused, but resent the former. A good thing, then, that he was unlikely to see her.

Margaret thought about Helen Upchurch, whom she had seen at morning prayers as well. Helen was five years older than Margaret, and the two had had only a passing acquaintance. Still, Margaret had been saddened to hear of her disappointment in love when the man she hoped to marry died a few years before. Apparently she had now resigned herself to life as a spinster.

There was no sign of Lewis Upchurch, the only Upchurch she thought she might turn to—had she the nerve to do so.

Margaret massaged her fingers. She heard a whine, and for a moment feared she had moaned aloud, but then someone scratched at her door. She started up in bed, reaching in a flailing panic for her wig. The door creaked open.

"Just a moment!" she whispered urgently. But it was too late. Whoever it was walked into the room, feet clicking on the floorboards. Margaret's eyes adjusted just as a damp nose nudged her elbow. In the dim room, she reached for the wolfhound's grey head, silvery white in the faint moonlight.

"Jester . . ." she scolded mildly. "What are you doing up here— come to give me another bath?" She stroked the big dog's ears. "Your master would not approve. A beast with your bloodlines, consorting with a servant?"

Saying the word aloud gave Margaret pause. "I am a servant," she whispered to herself, incredulous. She lay there, exhausted and sore, thinking she should just pack up and leave. Sneak out and go . . . somewhere. Anywhere. But at the moment she was too tired to move.

The next afternoon, Nathaniel took himself to the library to write to his father and the family's solicitor, apprising them both of the situation with the ship and with Fairbourne Hall. He'd hoped to use part of the sugar profits to begin repair work on the *Ecclesia*, but knew he must first bring the languishing estate into order. He and Hudson had completed an initial inspection of the place. The manor roof leaked into the old schoolroom, several laborer cottages needed repair, the orchard had grown wild, one of the tenant farms sat vacant, a fence was down, and the list went on. Nathaniel sighed. As much as he wanted to, he could not in good conscience funnel money into his ship. Not yet.

Through the open library door, he glimpsed his brother sweeping through the hall, unannounced. He supposed Lewis felt he needed no announcing in his own home, infrequently though he slept there.

Nathaniel added his signature to the letter, replaced the quill in its stand, and rose to find and greet his brother. He hoped to make peace with him. And to be firm about the family's need to get their affairs in order—and keep spending in line with their reduced income.

Arnold appeared in the threshold. "Excuse me, sir, but your brother has just arrived. He did not wish to be announced, but I thought you would want to know."

Nathaniel found the under butler's ingratiating manners irritating, but forced himself to reply civilly, "Thank you. Where is he now?"

"The sitting room, I believe, with Miss Upchurch."

Nathaniel thanked the man again, crossed the hall, and climbed the stairs. His family had long preferred the upstairs sitting room to the formal drawing room on the main level. As he neared the sitting-room door, he heard his brother's booming voice and his sister's calm happy tones.

"Lewis, you can't know how pleased I am to see you."

"So you've said. Twice. Did Nate tell you what he did to me in London?"

"Ask you to come home?"

"He punched me—right in the midst of the Valmores' ball."

"He never!"

"He did. Of course, I got my licks in too. Man has to stand up for himself, you know."

"Oh, Lewie. Is that where that bruise came from? I was afraid you'd been breaking hearts again."

"Only two or three a week."

"*Lewie . . .*" Helen scolded fondly, "one of these days someone's father, or brother, or sweetheart will do worse than bruise you."

"Then perhaps I ought to swear off women. After all, you are my favorite, Helen, and always shall be."

"Oh, go on. I can tell the difference between charm and a hum, you know."

"And which has old Nate been giving you?"

"Neither. Though he has been a *bit* overbearing since he's been home."

Helen's words stung. Nathaniel crossed the threshold in time to see Lewis rub his jaw.

"As I am painfully aware. Had I known things were so bad here, I would have come sooner."

Helen raised one brow. "I did write to you."

"Yes, but you are always so mincing with your words, so careful not to alarm me, that I had no real idea how bad the situation had become."

"Servants up in arms, shopkeepers at the door, butler gone without notice . . . *that* was mincing words?"

Lewis tweaked her cheek. "Well, I am here now. Do say you forgive me. I cannot abide having both of my siblings vexed with me."

Helen smiled adoringly at their handsome brother. "I could never stay vexed with you, Lewis."

"That's my girl. Now, that's what I like to hear."

Nathaniel cleared his throat and crossed the room. "Hello, Lewis. Glad you could come."

"You made sure of that, didn't you?"

Nathaniel saw the purple bruise on his brother's jaw and grimaced. "Sorry."

"That's all right. I made good use of it, I can tell you. The ladies were full of sympathy and comfort, never doubt it."

"I don't."

"And look at you!" Lewis gestured toward Nathaniel's sling and the bandage on his temple. "Told you I got my licks in, Helen."

Nathaniel and Helen exchanged a look. Deciding not to worry her with more discussions of thieves—pirates or bankers—he asked Lewis, "Would you mind joining me in the library? I would like you to meet our new steward and take a look at the books together."

Helen frowned. "But Lewis has just arrived."

"I am afraid several items simply will not wait."

Helen looked ready to protest further, but Lewis patted her hand, then hauled his tall lanky form to his feet. "Oh, very well, I'm coming. Don't knot your neckcloth."

The whole household assembled in the hall in the morning, before breakfast, for family worship.

—*A Memoir of the Reverend Alexander Waugh*, 1830

Chapter 9

❧

There was a great deal of buzzing and giggling that night as Margaret made her way along the basement passage to the servants' hall for supper. When she entered, she saw Fiona, Betty, and the kitchen maid Jenny standing clustered about Hester, speaking in smiles and whispers.

Curious, Margaret approached the small clutch of women. Fiona's green eyes sliced her way but immediately returned to Hester as though she had not seen her. Betty sent her a quick smile without pause in conversation or invitation to join them. Margaret stood there, a little apart, feeling like a third shoe.

Thomas entered the servants' hall with a young man she had never seen before. He was of middling height—not quite as tall as Thomas, but his shoulders were broader. At least they appeared so, under the well-cut black coat, grey pinstriped waistcoat, and crisp cravat. He held himself with athletic ease, smiling at Thomas as the two men talked. His hair was deep red, thick and slightly wavy, brushed just so across his forehead. His complexion was fair, his nose straight, his eyes a bright blue. Margaret realized she was staring. He returned her gaze, and Margaret looked away, embarrassed. She was sure Fiona would be scowling at her. But all the other maids were staring at the handsome young man as well.

Betty stepped to her side and whispered, "That's Connor. I've known him since a lad. Isn't he a handsome one?"

"Indeed. Who is he?"

"Mr. Lewis's valet," Betty said with evident pride. "They arrived from London this afternoon."

Margaret's heart raced. *Lewis Upchurch is here!* Under the same roof. Perhaps she would see him soon. Might she find a way to speak to him in private?

The valet crossed the room to greet them. "Hello, ladies."

A chorus of grins and good-evenings rose in reply.

Connor kissed Betty's cheek, then his sparkling eyes lingered on the stillroom maid. "And Hester, my girl, how are you?"

Hester smiled, her face glowing in round-cheeked loveliness. "A sight better, now you're here." She turned to Margaret. "And this is Nora. New to us since your last visit."

"How d'you do, Nora? A pleasure to make your acquaintance." His smile was genuine but quickly returned to Hester. "A pleasure to be among you all again."

At nine the following morning, the house servants once again filed into the hall for morning prayers. The valet Connor stood among them, between Hester and second footman Craig, who sent doleful looks his way.

Margaret, as was her habit, found a spot at the back behind someone taller than she, usually Monsieur Fournier. They were all creatures of habit, she had noted, and in general occupied the same places each morning. Connor was upsetting this order. Is that what had Craig looking resentful? Or was it the man's obvious popularity with the ladies? *Poor Craig.*

Margaret surreptitiously peeked out from behind the chef's

white-coated shoulder, keeping an eye on the library door, heart beating hard.

The door opened and her stomach knotted. Nathaniel Upchurch, with his sister at his side, entered from the library. There was no sign of Lewis. Disappointment and relief warred within her. She guessed Lewis was still abed or had gone for a morning ride.

Nathaniel's arm was no longer in a sling, but a small bandage still graced one temple. And this time he wore his spectacles. Ah . . . she remembered him in spectacles. Apparently he only wore them for reading these days. With them, he looked more like a clergyman than a pirate.

Nathaniel found his place in the book and cleared his throat. He hesitated, left his thumb marking the spot and looked up at them, then down once more. "Many of you have been with us for years and remember me as the arrogant youth I no doubt was. Perhaps you think it hypocritical of me to stand before you now, as though I think myself worthy to be your spiritual leader. I do not. I am convinced not of my own worthiness, but of God's. I need to hear the words of this book—its truth, forgiveness, hope—as much as anybody." He looked up with an apologetic smile. "I know I'm no great orator. But I ask you to bear with me as I fumble through this new duty."

Margaret felt it, the easing of tension and resentment. Mr. Hudson grinned, and Mrs. Budgeon and the under butler exchanged impressed glances. At the far end of the front row, Betty nodded, tears in her eyes.

Nathaniel found his place once more and read, " 'The God of peace, that brought again from the dead our Lord Jesus, the great shepherd of the sheep, through the blood of the everlasting covenant, Make you perfect in every good work to do his will, working in you that which is well pleasing in his sight, through Jesus Christ; to whom be glory for ever and ever. Amen.' "

After morning prayers, once the Upchurch family had gone to their own later breakfast, Margaret, Betty, and Fiona went back upstairs and retrieved their boxes from the housemaids' closet. The days previous she and Betty had worked side by side in Helen's and the absent James Upchurch's rooms, Betty demonstrating how all was done. But today Betty was leaving her alone to clean two different rooms—those of the Upchurch brothers.

An unmarried lady in a gentleman's bedchamber? Normally such a thing would mean instant ruination. But there was nothing normal about Margaret's current situation.

As she departed, Betty told her to fetch Fiona when she was ready to remake the beds, as making beds properly was often a two-person job, especially for a new girl.

Margaret sighed, bracing herself. At least the rooms would be unoccupied at this time of day.

Opening the door, she surveyed the first masculine bedchamber, paneled in dark wood with rich burgundy draperies. She tied back the bed curtains, stripped the bedclothes, laid them over a chair, and pushed open the windows to air out the room. Then she steeled herself and reached under the bed, pulling forth the chamber pot with averted eyes and stopped nose, pleased to find its lid in place. Hopefully, Fiona had emptied it during the early morning water delivery.

Margaret carried it into the dressing room, grimacing at the wadded cravat, soiled shirt, and stockings on the floor. She wondered which Upchurch brother slept in this room and guessed Nathaniel, based on his unkempt appearance at the ball. She imagined Lewis to be more fastidious, considering how exquisitely dressed and groomed he always appeared. Though, perhaps his valet, Connor, was due the credit. Setting the pot aside, she tidied the dressing room, wondering why the man's clothes were in disarray. She did not recall any mention of Nathaniel Upchurch having a valet, so perhaps one of the footmen or the under butler performed double duty, though poorly.

She dumped the soapy water from the washbasin into a pail. Wiped clean the vessel, changed the water in the pitcher, and returned both to the washstand. She put off emptying the chamber pot as long as possible. Finally, she resolutely lifted the lid. Breathing only from her mouth, she tipped the pot over the pail, heard the slosh, and then risked a peek. Something had stuck to the bottom. She tapped the pot against the lip of the pail to dislodge the remnant. *Ugh.* She had not spent two years at Miss Highworth's Seminary for this!

Successful at last, she cleaned her hands and returned to her other duties. She swept the floor and carpets, and began dusting. She noticed several coins and wadded receipts on the bedside table. As she picked up the crumpled papers to dust the table beneath, she glanced at them. One was a scrawled note. *Meet me at 11. Our place. —L.* The others were receipts from White's, a men's club in London. With a twinge of guilt, she replaced the papers and the coins.

Reminded of Sterling's money, and of Joan, Margaret asked forgiveness once again and finished straightening the room.

Leaving the bed to air as instructed, Margaret took herself into the second bedchamber and dressing room assigned to her. She glanced at the clock and realized she would need to hurry if she was to finish by eleven. Fortunately, this second pair of rooms was much neater than the first. Lewis's room, she guessed. No clothes lay strewn on the floor. The papers and books on the corner desk were neat and orderly.

She went about her routine, relieved the chamber pot had already been emptied, whether by Fiona or dutiful Connor she did not know but silently thanked them both. She noticed an open book on the bedside table and, curious, glanced beneath her spectacles to read its print. It was the Bible, opened to the gospel of John. This gave her pause, and she began to second-guess the room's occupant. She had not thought Lewis the sort of man who read his Bible in private, though she would be happy to be proven wrong. Her father had been such a man.

She was leaning far over the bed, attempting to pull free the tangled bedclothes to air them, when the door burst open behind her.

She gasped, chagrined to be found hands and knees on the bed, rump in the air. She leapt to her feet, whirling to see who had entered. Was it Fiona come to help her remake the bed?

No.

Nathaniel Upchurch entered the room, barely looking her way. He held up a staying hand when she would flee. "Go about your work. I shall be out of your way in a moment."

Margaret felt as though she had just run up a flight of stairs. She took a deep breath and told herself to calm down. She picked up the pillow and began to plump it, stealing a glance over her shoulder to where Nathaniel was pawing through a desk drawer for something. Nathaniel's room. Nathaniel's Bible. That made sense. Not Lewis's. Lewis was the slovenly one. Well, what did it matter if Lewis was not neat? That was what servants were for. She bit her lip, hard, at the thought.

How strange it felt, to be . . . well, almost embracing Nathaniel Upchurch's pillow. To be running her hands over his bedclothes. The thought made her cheeks heat.

Apparently finding whatever he was looking for, he turned and strode across the room without a second glance.

Of course a man like Nathaniel Upchurch would never notice a housemaid, would never pay her unwanted attention as Marcus Benton might. Would never look at her closely enough to recognize her or to find her attractive. She should be relieved.

She was still standing there beside Nathaniel Upchurch's bed when Fiona strode in. "There you are. Not finished yet? Never knew a maid so slow. Come, come. I'm to help you make up the beds. Heaven knows you cannot manage it alone."

Fiona's stinging reprimand reminded Margaret of Joan. How her former maid would snigger to see her now.

That evening, Nathaniel entered the dining room, dressed for dinner. Helen sat alone at the long table, wearing a dull burgundy evening gown that did little to flatter her complexion.

"Where is Lewis?" he asked, taking his place at the table.

"He won't be joining us tonight. Said he was visiting friends in Maidstone."

Irritation flashed through Nathaniel. Lewis had barely arrived and was already finding reasons to leave Fairbourne Hall. "Which friends?"

"He did not say."

Nathaniel thought of their acquaintance in Maidstone—Lord Romney of Mote Park, the Whatmans of Vinters, the Langleys, the Bishops. For himself he did not care, but why had they not included Helen in their invitation, if invitation it was. He felt offended on his sister's behalf. Or had Lewis simply gone uninvited?

He said carefully, "How are the Whatmans . . . ? Have you seen them lately?"

Helen shook her head. "I believe they've been spending a great deal of time on the coast. Mr. Whatman has taken to sea bathing, I understand. For his health."

She glanced at the footman, who, taking his cue, removed the lid from the soup tureen. Helen served Nathaniel, then herself, in traditional family style.

As Nathaniel spooned his vegetable-marrow soup, he asked, "Tell me, how did you occupy your time while I was away?"

She shrugged and dipped her spoon. "Oh, I read a great deal. And I did what I could as mistress of the place while Lewis was in London."

"How long has it been since you've attended a social event?"

She hesitated, eyes on her bowl.

"I have been gone for two years," Nathaniel pressed. "Tell me you have not remained home the entire time I was away?"

She frowned. "Of course not!"

"And I don't count attending church, nor Christmas and Easter with Uncle Townsend."

Helen's face reddened. "Someone had to stay home to look after the place. And Lewis puts no pressure on me to pay calls. He understands."

As Nathaniel served Helen brills in shrimp sauce, he again surveyed the evening gown he had seen her wear a few times already. He waited until the footman replaced the soup tureen with a platter of lamb cutlets, then said, "And I take it you have had no new gowns recently?"

She took a sip of wine. "What need have I for new gowns? Mamma's lady's maid made over some of my frocks before she retired, to disguise the wear. I would have thought you would be glad of the economy."

"We are not so poor you cannot dress well, Helen. Or attend an occasional entertainment. I guarantee Lewis has not forgone the latest in haberdashery, nor every lavish party of the season."

She shook her head. "Do not speak against Lewis, Nathaniel. I will not hear a word against him."

Nathaniel took a deep breath. "My point was not to disparage Lewis, but to express my concern for you. I hate to see you trapped here. Not living your life."

She slowly shook her head. "Can you not conceive—a least a little—how I might feel? My chance at happiness was denied me."

Yes, I do understand, Nathaniel thought, but he refused to admit it aloud. "I am sorry for your loss, Helen. I am. But that was years ago. Do you mean to go on living as though a widow forever?"

"Why not?" Helen's eyes flashed. "What use have I for frivolous entertainments or to pretend an interest in other men I can never feel? And now . . . now I am a spinster. On the shelf. Do you know how people would talk if I showed up at a ball after all this time? 'Does she not realize she is too old?' they would say. 'Who does she think she is, a debutante?'"

"If you think yourself the topic of conversation after all this time, you overestimate yourself."

Helen's mouth fell ajar. "What an unkind thing to say!"

"I did not mean . . ." He grimaced. "Why is it you seem determined to twist my every word? I only meant you worry too much—the gossips have moved on a hundred times over."

She winced. "You still hope to marry me off, then—get me off your hands?"

"Of course not, Helen. I did not say you ought to cast a net for a husband. But could you not socialize with other women?"

"And do what? Play cards? Gossip? I have no taste for either."

"But it does you no good, living in seclusion like this."

"How do you know? Excuse me, Nathaniel, but how would you know? You have been gone these two years with little thought to my well-being. Why now do you suddenly care?"

"That is not fair, Helen. You know it was Father's decision to summon me to Barbados when Lewis chose to return. I know I was not faithful in writing letters, but my every hour was taken up in plantation affairs."

One eyebrow rose. "Your every hour?" She leaned back, hazel eyes alert. "Did you meet *no* interesting young ladies your entire time there?"

He inhaled deeply. "I did, actually. Well, one."

"Oh?"

"Ava DeSante. Her father owns a neighboring plantation. She is accomplished, intelligent, beautiful . . ."

"But?"

"But she could not understand nor respect my objections to slavery."

Helen blinked. "I am sorry to hear it, but really, were you surprised? From what I understand, slaves are the very lifeblood of plantations. No slaves, no profits—or at least, greatly diminished profits."

Nathaniel slumped back in his chair. "Yes, as Father never tires of reminding me."

His sister studied him over her glass while the footmen removed the entrees and laid the next course. "You have changed, Nathaniel, while you were away."

He paused, his own glass held midair. "For the better or worse? I hate to ask."

"Both, I think. Your new fervor makes me wary, I admit. But I do respect your stance." She tilted her head to one side, regarding him. "But you seem, well, harder somehow. Guarded. Did Barbados do that to you, or did she?"

He swallowed. Did Helen refer to Ava, or to *her*? The truth was, Nathaniel had been illogically relieved when his courtship in Barbados had ended. He shook his head. "If you had seen what I've seen, Helen. The vile things men do to other men for the sake of money. . . ."

She asked quietly, "But is that really all it is?"

He did not answer. What did she want him to say—that he was still hurt over his disappointment with Margaret Macy? After all this time? It was imbecilic. He would not do it.

Helen dabbed her lips with a table napkin. "I support emancipation and the need to retrench." Her mouth rose in a one-sided grin. "Even if it does mean I shall have to curtail my *excessive* visits to the modiste."

Nathaniel grinned in return, thankful for her attempt to lighten the moment. Perhaps his sister might warm to him yet.

His grin faded, and he continued to eat without tasting a thing. As much as he tried to fight it, his mind reeled back to the still-painful day Miss Macy cast him aside.

Nathaniel waited in the drawing room of the Macys' modest town house while the footman went to announce him. His hands shook. His pulse pounded. He paced the room, rehearsing the words that would change their lives forever. Yes, a kernel of insecurity lodged within his heart. He was not blind. He had not missed the attention Lewis had paid Margaret since his return. But surely she realized Lewis was only flirting with her. It was his way. Margaret's feelings, Margaret herself, meant little to his brother and everything to him. She must know that.

A few minutes later, Margaret swept into the room, an expectant smile on her lovely face.

Nathaniel rose, his heart lifting at the sight of her. "Miss Macy."

"Oh . . ." she faltered. "Mr. Upchurch." She glanced toward the mantel clock.

Had she been expecting someone else? Nathaniel remained standing, suddenly ill at ease.

Margaret sat stiffly in an armchair and gestured to the settee across from her. "Please, won't you be seated?"

He considered his options, then sat at the end nearest her chair.

"I wish to speak to you," he began, a drop of perspiration rolling down his hairline. "About Barbados. About . . . you and me. Our future." Why must his voice shake like a schoolboy's?

She stared at him, lips parted.

Nathaniel hurried on, "Because of Lewis's return, my father has asked me to travel to Barbados to take his place."

Still she said nothing.

He swallowed and continued, "I realize it might be difficult for you were we to live in Barbados for a time, but when I spoke with your father, he—"

"Live in Barbados?" she sputtered. "I am not moving to Barbados, Mr. Upchurch. I hope I never gave you that impression. I could never leave my family—live at such a distance to them."

He hesitated, taken aback. He would forgo Barbados for her in a heartbeat, but he hated to disappoint his father. "Ah . . . Well then. I shall write to my father and inform him—"

She rose abruptly. "Don't. Please don't say another word, Mr. Upchurch. I fear a misunderstanding has occurred between us. I have no plans to marry in the near future. No plans to marry anyone. If I have led you to believe otherwise, I apologize. I see how you might have thought—earlier in the season, I mean. But at present, no."

An invisible fist struck him. Pain lanced his chest and his vision blurred. What was happening? He blinked and blinked again.

She clasped her hands before her. "I apologize, Mr. Upchurch, but I cannot marry you. There was a time I thought I could. But things have changed and I am sorry."

He tasted bile. "Because of Lewis?"

Shame colored her cheeks, yet she lifted her chin. "Yes, I do admire your brother. I cannot deny it."

Another blow. A kick in the ribs. He drew a painful, jagged breath and said quietly, "I think it only fair to warn you. Lewis is unlikely to marry you."

Irritation flashed on her face. "And so I should ignore my feelings for him and marry you instead?"

His heart deflated. His hopes . . . crumbled. "Margaret . . . Miss Macy. I . . ." He pressed his eyes shut and cleared his throat. "I had no idea things had gone so far . . . had . . . come to this. I must say, I . . . I am deeply disappointed."

"Can you not be happy for Lewis and me?"

He stared at her, bewildered. "That I cannot do. Nor can I stand by and watch the two of you and pretend . . ." He slowly shook his head. "I think, after all, I shall sail for Barbados without delay."

"Then I wish you safe journey, Mr. Upchurch."

He flinched at her indifference. He shook his head again, stunned and bemused. This was not how he had imagined the events of this day. His gut twisted as he crossed the room. At the door, he turned back. "I wish you never feel as I do at this moment, Miss Macy." He opened the door, then hesitated. "Or, perhaps . . . I hope you do."

"Again, I am sor—"

He held up his palm, anger flaring. "Enough. I don't want your pity. I bid you good-day, madam. And good-bye."

He turned on his heel and left the room, slamming the door behind him.

Nathaniel could still hear it, that door slamming shut in his past . . . and on his fondest dream.

The upper housemaids undertook the lighter jobs,
making the beds in the best bedrooms and
keeping an eye on the lower housemaids. The latter
would lay and light the fires, clean the living rooms,
polish the brass, carry upstairs the water
for washing, and empty the chamber pots.

—Margaret Willes, *Household Management*

Chapter 10

I t isn't fair, Betty, and you know it," Fiona complained as the three of them gathered their boxes from the housemaids' closet the next morning.

"I know, Fiona. But—"

"But what? In every other situation I've had, the lowest-ranking maid has had to deal with the slops. It's what's done. Isn't right I've had to haul water and empty slops for all the family, especially now that Mr. Lewis has come. And Connor, for all his handsome ways, hasn't offered to take it over."

"Now, Fiona. I won't hear a word against Connor. Sends all his wages home to provide for his brothers and sister. Such a high position at so young an age. It's no wonder he leaves the like to us."

"Leaves it to me, you mean. And I've had enough. At least we might share the duty."

Betty sighed. "Very well." She turned wide, expectant eyes on Margaret. "Nora, Fiona makes a good point. She's been carrying up the water cans and emptying the chamber pots every morning while I was training you. But you've got the way of things now. Give or take. It's only right you should take your turn with that duty."

Margaret found herself nodding but inwardly cringed. It had been one thing to go into the gentlemen's bedchambers when they were up, properly dressed, and well out of the rooms. But to go in first thing, while the men were still in their beds? Wearing—or not—who knew what? She shuddered at the thought and prayed no one ever learned she had done so.

A few minutes later, after Fiona and Betty had gone downstairs to clean the public rooms, Margaret stood before Lewis Upchurch's bedchamber door, water cans in hand, heart banging against her ribs. Should she wake him? Use this opportunity to reveal herself and enlist his help? Her stomach clenched at the thought. No, she could not reveal herself as Margaret Macy while Lewis Upchurch lay in his bed. She would have to wait for a better time.

She reminded herself that her goal was to slip in with the water and slip out with the slops without waking the sleeping men. Very soon the weather would turn and she would somehow have to lay and light a fire in each room as well, in perfect quiet. She thought back to her time in Berkeley Square and even before that to her childhood in Lime Tree Lodge. Joan had been excellent, she realized now. For Margaret had awakened to a warm fire in autumn and winter with little thought to how it got there. Among a succession of housemaids at Lime Tree Lodge, there had been one maid—she did not recall her name—who clanged the irons and muttered over the tinder, waking the whole house whilst lighting the morning fires. She had not lasted long.

Taking a steadying breath, Margaret eased open the door, its whining creak sending a snake of dread down her spine. Stepping inside, she surveyed the dim room by meager predawn light. The bed curtains had not been drawn closed. She looked beyond them with an anticipatory wince, but the bed was empty. In fact it was still neatly made. Margaret felt her brow furrow. Lewis remained in residence, she was sure. She would have heard if he and the charming Connor had left Fairbourne Hall already. How strange. Had he stayed the night with some friend? Or fallen asleep downstairs? On one hand she was relieved not to find him there, to not be alone with him in his bedchamber. On the other hand, she was foolishly disappointed. She quickly went about her tasks, leaving the water and checking the chamber pot. Empty. He'd been out all night.

Mulling this over, she left Lewis's room and stepped down the corridor to Helen's. As she was about to lift the latch, footsteps sounded on the stairs. Startled, she looked over her shoulder. A shadowy figure crept up the stairs and around the newel-post. In the light from the candle left burning at the landing, Margaret saw Lewis Upchurch, fully dressed and still wearing an outdoor coat. Was this her chance? Even if he had no interest in marrying her, might he not at least help her arrange a more suitable hiding place?

She stood, quavering, hand on Helen's door latch, as Lewis walked toward her down the corridor. *This is it*, she told herself. *Open your mouth. Say something.*

No sound came.

As Lewis passed behind her, he patted her bottom. Margaret's face flushed hot. She craned to look over her other shoulder. Lewis sauntered on. At his door, he turned, winked at her, and then let himself into his room without a flicker of embarrassment.

What insolence! She reminded herself that he didn't know who she was. But was patting a maid's bottom any better?

Still shaking, Margaret slipped into Helen's room and took a moment to catch her breath. The bed curtains were drawn, but a soft snore told Margaret its occupant slept on undisturbed by her presence. She completed her tasks without incident.

In Nathaniel's room, she was not as fortunate. The bed curtains had been left tied back—leaving a full view of Nathaniel Upchurch lying on his stomach, arms wrapped around his pillow, cheek pressed into its downy depths. A sheet was pulled up to his waist; a nightshirt covered his upper body and arms.

She tiptoed closer, knowing she should avert her eyes and complete her tasks as quickly as possible. Instead she paused several feet away. How peaceful he looked. How much younger with neither stiff cravat, spectacles, nor somber scowl. His fair cheeks were peppered with black stubble. Did he shave himself, she wondered. Or did Mr. Arnold do so for him?

As she regarded him, a thought came, unbidden. *He might have been my husband. I might now be sharing his bed.* She swallowed, her neck heating at the intimate thought pondered in that private place. *Instead I'm emptying his chamber pot.*

With that, she pushed futile thoughts away and returned to her work.

Margaret stood at the railing as Betty demonstrated how to dust the family's collection of vases, displayed on shelves built into a recess at the top of the main staircase. From below came the sound of the front door opening and Mr. Arnold greeting some male guest.

Lewis Upchurch's gregarious voice echoed from the hall below. "Don't bother, Arnold. I'll show him up myself."

Betty shot her a sharp-eyed look, but footsteps were already trotting up the stairs. There was no time to slip down the corridor and into one of the vacant rooms. Betty stepped away from the railing and as far into the corner as she could, presenting her back to the two men mounting the stairs. Feeling foolish and self-conscious, Margaret followed suit.

The men passed without pause or a word, as if finding two grown women standing with their noses to the wall was an everyday occurrence. Margaret realized for the first time that it probably was. Thinking back, she recalled the Berkeley Square housemaids doing something similar when they accidentally crossed paths with Sterling or her mother. She had given it little thought before, but now decided that when she had a house of her own, she would make certain the staff knew such a practice was not necessary.

The men entered the family sitting room, one of them giving the door a shove behind him, but it did not fully close. From inside, voices rose in amiable greeting. Margaret idly wondered who the visitor was.

Keeping a wary eye on the partially opened door, Betty quietly continued her demonstration. "Now, take your dustcloth—no, that's your glass cloth. Right—that one. We have to be prodigious careful, for these pretty things are worth a pretty penny, Mrs. Budgeon says."

They were lovely vases. Margaret could not imagine that the Upchurch men appreciated them. No doubt some female ancestor had collected them and chosen to display them so prominently at the top of the stairs.

Betty gingerly picked up the first vase, holding it as gently as a baby bird. "Now take the thing careful-like in one hand while you run the cloth inside its innards."

From inside the room, a man's voice shouted, *"Margaret Macy?"*

Margaret started violently and let out a shriek. Had Sterling Benton come for her already? Frightened, Betty jerked back, sending the vase crashing to the floor, shattering it to pieces.

Betty cried out, her hand belatedly covering her mouth.

Margaret stood there, uncertain. Should she flee, which would draw attention to herself, or hope her disguise sufficient?

She risked a glance over her shoulder, and quailed as Nathaniel Upchurch strode out of the sitting room, his expression turbulent.

"What is all this?" he asked.

Betty ducked her head, "Sorry, sir. Beggin' your pardon, sir."

Footsteps tattooed up the stairs. Mrs. Budgeon appeared, her mouth a grim line.

Margaret wanted to say, knew she *should* say, *"It was my fault."* Had Mrs. Budgeon been there alone, she would have done so. But with Mr. Upchurch standing there as witness? The words would not come.

Mrs. Budgeon shot Betty a frosty glare, then turned primly to Mr. Upchurch. "I am sorry, sir. Betty has never broken anything before. The cost will be taken from her wages, of course."

Nathaniel exhaled a dry puff of air. "Should we withhold her wages a dozen years, she should never be able to pay for that relic."

Beside her, Betty blanched.

Mrs. Budgeon clasped her hands together. "Again I am sorry, sir. Would you have her dismissed?"

Betty sucked in a sharp breath.

"I don't . . ." He hesitated. "That is for you and Mr. Hudson to decide. Bring the pieces to the study so he may make note in the inventories when he returns."

"Very good, sir."

Helen's concerned face appeared in the threshold behind Nathaniel, but no one else joined her there. No Lewis, no unseen visitor. Whoever had come to call was surely not Sterling Benton, Margaret told herself. How foolish she had been. And now a vase had been broken—and Betty's perfect record with it.

Nathaniel cared little for the antique vase, although he knew his father would be vexed to learn of its demise. His mind was still echoing with the news Lewis's friend had brought with him from London. When Piers Saxby had gleefully announced, *"You shall never guess who has gone missing—not seen nor heard from in more than a week . . . Margaret Macy!"* it had struck Nathaniel like a violent kick to his gut. Shocked, he had forgotten himself, echoing her name more vehemently than he had intended. He did not miss the knowing look his sister and brother exchanged. The crash in the corridor had been a welcome diversion from their too-knowing glances.

When Nathaniel returned to the sitting room, Saxby said, "Good heavens, Nate. Are you all right? You look ghastly."

Nathaniel took a long shaky breath. "I'm fine. A maid broke a family heirloom, that's all."

Saxby blew out a loud exhale. "What a relief. Not about the heirloom, of course, but I was afraid I had blundered in telling you. If you still hold feelings for the girl . . ."

Nathaniel pulled a face. "That was years ago."

"Glad to hear it," Saxby said. "Hate to think of you pining over some chit. Pray take no offense, Miss Upchurch, but I have rarely suffered from sentiment where women are concerned. Although I realize not every man is as fortunate."

Lewis rubbed his chin. "Come to think of it, I did hear an *on dit* before I came down. Apparently Sterling Benton has been calling on all her friends in town, fueling any number of rumors."

Helen reclaimed her seat. "You might have told us before."

Lewis raised a hand in defense. "In all honesty, it slipped my mind. What with Nate here dragging me to the inquisition as soon as I returned and numbing my brain with ledgers and recriminations and I know not what."

Nathaniel pressed his lips tight. *I will not lose my temper. I will not . . .*

Lewis went on, "It is not as though the Macys are closely connected to our family. I am acquainted with the girl, of course—as are we all." Lewis turned to him. "*Do* you still harbor feelings for her?"

"Of course not, but—"

Saxby laid a hand over his heart. "Pray forgive me, Nate. I should not have been so cavalier in breaking the news."

"You did not err in telling us," Nathaniel insisted. "We are acquainted with both the Macy family and the Bentons. Of course we would be interested. And disturbed to think that any lady of our acquaintance might be . . . might have met with some foul fate."

"Oh, I don't imagine it is anything as dramatic as all that," Lewis said.

"Not that the girl doesn't have a flair for theatrics," Helen added. "She does, as I recall."

Lewis shrugged. "More likely she's gone off in a pet over a spat with a new suitor. Or her mamma refused her a trinket or something of that sort. She'll return as soon as her purse is empty, and that shall be that."

"No doubt you are correct," Nathaniel said, wishing to end this conversation. He was surprised at how much he hoped Miss Macy was all right. For all the resentment he had felt toward her—even wishing she might have her own heart broken one day—he would never wish bodily harm to befall her. The very thought of it made him want to charge off to London, sword blazing, and rescue her. What a fool he was. Even now.

Finally, Margaret's heart slowed to a rate approaching normal. What a start she had been given. Several, actually. First hearing her name called, fearing Sterling had come, then the vase shattering, and Nathaniel Upchurch charging out to see what had happened. He had not recognized her, she assured herself and took another deep breath.

She wiped her hands on her apron and swallowed. She had seen the look on Betty's face. Felt the silent terror at the thought of losing her place—for something that wasn't even her fault. Margaret had no intention of making service her life's work, but Betty did, and for her, being dismissed would be catastrophic.

But nor was Margaret ready to lose *her* position—she had barely gotten there, and hated the thought of being put out with barely a shilling to her name. And so she stood there, mute, while Betty picked up the pieces and followed Mrs. Budgeon down to her parlor to discuss the matter.

Twenty minutes or so later, Margaret had just finished dusting the remaining shelves when Betty returned, white faced.

"What did she say?" Margaret whispered.

"She said we was to talk to Mr. Hudson about it, but Mr. Hudson is gone calling on tenants. So I am to see him tomorrow after dinner."

Again the words *I am sorry* stuck in Margaret's throat. Instead she said, "It was an accident. Surely they won't put you out for that."

Betty's brow creased in incredulity. "Maids is put out for a few coins gone missing or a piece of china broke. That was a family heirloom. Worth a great deal of money."

"I . . . I didn't mean to startle you. I—"

Betty's face puckered. "Why *did* you cry out? Did you see a mouse or some-like?"

"No." Margaret slowly shook her head. "Not a mouse. A ghost."

At five thirty the next morning, Margaret slipped her hands through the armholes of her stays and stepped into her frock, expecting any moment to hear Betty's sharp single knock, ready to pragmatically lace up her stays and hurry her along with her brisk "The shutters await, my girl."

No knock came.

When a clock struck six somewhere in the house and Betty still had not come, Margaret left the stays unlaced beneath her frock and hurried down the passage, around the corner, and along the main attic corridor to Betty's room. She knocked softly and the door swung open on its hinges. Glancing in, she saw Betty sitting on her small, neatly made bed, staring down at her hands resting in her lap.

"Betty? Are you all right?"

"Hmm?"

Margaret quipped, "The shutters await, my girl."

No answering grin lifted Betty's mouth. She was no doubt still upset about the vase.

Margaret stepped into the room. When Betty made no move to rise, Margaret sat gingerly on the bed beside her. She noticed then that Betty held something in her hands. A large gilt brooch ornamented with a stag's head and several long chains dangling from it. A chatelaine.

"That's pretty," Margaret said.

Betty nodded. "My mum gave it to me. She was housekeeper at Mote Park for many years. The mistress gave this to her to mark her twentieth year in service. How proud she was, wearing this pinned to her waist, Mote Park keys hangin' from it, and these other usefuls as well." Betty lifted the small pair of candle scissors and ran a finger over three small gilt boxes hanging like appendages from the chatelaine. "This one holds a toothpick, this one a needle and thread, and this one an ear scoop."

"It's very nice," Margaret agreed. She guessed it was made of brass and not gold, though the gilt still shone after all these years. It had obviously been well cared for.

Still Betty stared down at the chatelaine in her lap, tears filling her eyes. "I shall never see twenty years now. . . ."

"Don't say that," Margaret soothed, patting Betty's arm.

The tears settled it—Margaret knew she must say something, do something, before Mrs. Budgeon and the steward reached their verdict about Betty. She hoped kind Mr. Hudson would be lenient.

Finally, Betty laid the chatelaine back in a velvet-lined box on her bedside table and rose with a sigh. "Well. Turn around and let's have a tug on those fancy stays of yours. Then we'd best be on our way. Like I always say—"

"The shutters await," Margaret supplied.

Betty raised one brow. "And the chamber pots besides."

Margaret hurried through her duties, nerves giving her the energy her lack of sleep would normally have drained. There was nothing like the pressure of knowing one had done wrong, and that every minute of putting off doing right might bring more trouble to one-self or another to distract one's focus. Margaret finished her duties quickly. How well, she could not say.

Palms damp, Margaret knocked on the door of Mr. Hudson's office on the ground floor, tucked behind the main stairway.

"Enter," she heard from within and pushed open the door, wiping her palms on her apron.

She hesitated. Mrs. Budgeon was there as well, seated before the man's desk.

"What is it, Nora?" Mr. Hudson asked.

"I . . . never mind, sir. I shall come back when you're not busy."

"You are here now. What is it?"

"I wanted to . . . that is, I needed to tell you that it wasn't Betty's fault about the vase. It was my fault. I startled her and . . ." She felt Mrs. Budgeon's gaze and ducked her head. "Please don't dismiss her for my mistake."

"Why say something now and not at the time?" Mrs. Budgeon asked.

Margaret felt her cheeks heat and kept her head low. "I was afraid, ma'am. That was wrong of me too."

How self-conscious she felt with those two pairs of eyes on her bowed head. She risked a glance and found Mr. Hudson studying her. "Very well, Nora. We had already decided not to dismiss Betty, but thank you for telling us."

Relief filled her. "Thank you, sir."

When Betty emerged from Mr. Hudson's office half an hour later, Margaret expected her to be cheerful and relieved, but Betty's head was bowed and her mouth tight.

"Betty, what is it?" She followed her to the back stairs. "You are not to be dismissed, I understand?"

She shook her head. "No. Not dismissed. But my wages garnished for the quarter."

"Oh no. But I thought—"

"'Twas Mrs. Budgeon's decision, I gather. To remind me to be more careful in future."

"But I told them it was my fault."

"I know you did. Mr. Hudson said as much, and I do appreciate it. But I am the upper housemaid, so it was my responsibility."

Margaret winced. "Will you be all right?"

Betty sighed. "I shall manage. But my . . ." Her sentence trailed away unfinished.

"Your what?" Margaret prompted.

Betty lifted her quivering chin. "Never you mind; I'll sort it somehow."

I am as yet 'wanting a situation,' like a
housemaid out of place. I have lately discovered I
have quite a talent for cleaning, sweeping up hearths,
dusting rooms, making beds, etc.; so, if everything
else fails, I can turn my hand to that.

—Charlotte Brontë, in a letter to her sister Emily

Chapter 11

The next day, Margaret backed from the drawing room, pulling the double doors closed as she went. Thomas, the first footman, appeared out of nowhere and gave her arm a playful pinch. "Fetch me up some German polish, there's a love."

Margaret hesitated. Was that one of her duties as well?

Thomas smiled at her. He had very good teeth, though quite large. And something about those gleaming teeth, hard blue eyes, and dark hair reminded her of a wolf.

He gave her a gentle nudge. "You do know where the stillroom is, I trust?"

"Of course." Chin high, Margaret turned on her heel and padded through the servery and down the basement stairs.

The stillroom. What memories of Lime Tree Lodge it evoked. The snug room with a cheery fire and sunlight from its high windows gleaming off copper kettles and colorful glass bottles. With its own stove, brick baking oven, worktable, basin, shelves displaying pots and jelly moulds, and cupboards containing tea, coffee, and more. Filled with the aromas of spices sweet and savory—ginger and coriander, cloves and rosemary. Where pastries and biscuits were prepared one moment, distilled beverages the next. Vinegars, pickles, and preserves on some days. Soaps, cosmetics, and medicinals on others.

Oh, the hours Margaret had spent perched on a stool in the still-room at Lime Tree Lodge with Mrs. Haines, cutting ginger biscuits with copper cutters or making toffee.

Belowstairs, she passed the butler's pantry, kitchen, and the house-keeper's parlor. The stillroom was next door, the domain of both Mrs. Budgeon and the stillroom maid who carried out her many orders and receipts.

"Hello, Hester." Margaret smiled at the round, sweet-faced maid as she entered.

"Hello, Nora." Hester returned her smile and added a wink. "What brings you down to the dungeons this time of day?"

"The footman needs something called German polish."

"Does he now? And why is that your problem?"

"I don't know. He asked, so I thought it was something I was meant to do."

"Thomas was it?"

Margaret nodded.

"Craig is a lamb, but mind you watch that Thomas. Charmer he may be, but lazy in the bargain. Gettin' the new girl to fetch and carry for him." She shook her head. "Maybe in your last place housemaids was responsible for furniture polish, but here that's the footman's duty. Ah well. You're here now and I'm glad for an excuse to chat."

Hester continued on with her work, crushing rose petals into a jar of salt.

"Um . . . have you any of this polish?" Margaret asked.

Hester looked up. "You've got to make it, love. Have you never?"

"I am afraid not."

"Nothin' to it." Wiping her hands on her apron, Hester led her to the long, low stewing hearth, where several pots were bubbling and simmering already. She picked up an earthen pot with tripod feet and handle.

"First off, you melt a pound of yellow wax and an ounce of black resin in this pipkin." Hester gathered the ingredients from various drawers and shelves in the room. She added the wax and the resin to the pot and handed Margaret a wooden spoon. "Once it's melted, pour in two ounces of spirit of turpentine. Give or take. Now give 'er a good stir."

Margaret stirred, and once the concoction was fully melted, added the spirit of turpentine.

"All there is to it. I believe that's the first thing Mrs. Budgeon taught me to make when I come here. So I could make sure the footmen made it correct-like."

Hester took the covered jar to the stillroom basin, washed it out, then returned to the hearth. "Let's pour it in here. Careful now. Don't want to burn yourself. Tell Thomas he needs to wait until it cools before he uses it. He knows, of course, but he's not above skippin' a step if he can get away with it."

Margaret picked up the jar, but the heat singed her hand and she quickly plunked it back on the worktable.

Hester shook her head, bemused. "Your apron, love. Your apron."

Margaret nodded and took up the jar once more, protected by a corner of her apron. She felt oddly pleased with herself at her small accomplishment, even though she had done little more than stir.

Thomas was waiting in the drawing room when she returned, staring idly out the window. He whirled when she came in, then smiled, relieved not to be caught by a senior servant. Striding over, he gave her nose a cheeky tweak. "There's a love."

He took the pot from her, cursed, and bent to quickly set it down. "Dashed thing's hot!"

She bit back a smile and returned to her own duties.

As arranged, Nathaniel met Hudson outside in the arcade—a long, covered walkway from the house through the rose gardens. It had been a later addition to the original manor. The arcade's open-air walls consisted of a series of arches supported by ornate pillars. It was there the men met for their morning fencing bout with practice swords.

Fencing was Nathaniel's favorite way of taking exercise, with riding second, and rambling with the dog third. He was in far better physical condition now than he had been before sailing to the West Indies. When he met Hudson soon after arriving there, the two men had formed the habit of taking regular exercise together, whether fencing, hunting, riding, or even boxing, though the latter had proved a failure never to be repeated.

Nathaniel was the quicker of the two, and his skills finer, which was no surprise considering the classical training he'd received, while Hudson was primarily self-taught. Still, what the man lacked in finesse, he more than made up for in endurance and sheer determination. And how the man perspired! Nathaniel nearly felt sorry for the laundry maids.

After exchanging good mornings and comments about the fine weather, the bout began. Advance, lunge, retreat, retreat. Strike, parry-riposte. Feint, attack, parry-riposte . . . On and on it went in a rhythmic cycle. Now and again a balestra was thrown in, or a rare flèche, until one man slipped up or tired and gave his opponent an opening to score a hit.

Half an hour into the bout, Hudson struck with impressive speed, but Nathaniel parried. Nathaniel lunged and Hudson countered . . . but too late.

"Touché," Hudson acknowledged.

"Bravo," Lewis drawled.

Nathaniel glanced up and saw his brother leaning against one of the columns. He had not noticed him come out of the house.

Hudson wiped his forehead with a pocket handkerchief, preparing to continue. He addressed Lewis, "Would you like to give it a go, sir? I don't mind bowing out."

Lewis waved away the offer. "Heavens no. Too much dashed work. You two go on."

Nathaniel panted to catch his breath. "Was there something you wanted, Lewis?"

"Just to let you know I return to London tomorrow."

Irritation surged. Lewis had yet to help him prioritize the repairs needed at Fairbourne, nor had he agreed to expense-reducing measures for the London house. "Already? But—"

Lewis held up a hand. "Don't start. I have several things to attend to in town, but I will return soon, I promise."

That afternoon, Margaret stepped from the servants' hall just as the under gardener appeared in the basement passage, carrying a basket of long-stemmed cut flowers.

"Hello there, love. New, are you?"

"Yes. I'm Nora Garret."

"Well, Nora. I would be much obliged if you'd deliver these to Mrs. Budgeon for me. Mr. Sackett's nippin' at my heels to get back to work."

"Of course. They're lovely. For Miss Upchurch's apartment?"

He nodded. "And the hall."

Margaret lifted the basket to her face, inhaling deeply of the sweet aromas of late-summer roses and white clematis, amid other beautiful, though less fragrant varieties.

Betty, she knew, was repairing a torn seam for Miss Upchurch, while Fiona and Mrs. Budgeon were busy taking an inventory of the linen cupboard.

Margaret had already realized no one at Fairbourne Hall had an eye for flower arrangements. What a pleasure it would be after the drudgery of polishing summer-bright grates, sweeping stairs, and emptying chamber pots.

Margaret carried the flowers to the stillroom, knowing Hester would have the containers and implements she would need.

Hester greeted her warmly and welcomed her back into her sunny, warm domain.

For Helen's dressing table, Margaret chose a blue porcelain vase and filled it with a low arrangement of pale roses, pink asters, blue cornflowers, and dainty white clematis with lovely trailing vines. For the hall she used a gilded bowl and made a taller arrangement of golden chrysanthemums, garden phlox, purple coneflowers, verbena, and greenery. She enjoyed every minute of the task.

"You've a gift, Nora!" Hester praised, which pleased her inordinately.

Margaret carried the first vase up to Helen Upchurch's apartment, a bright chamber of white and blues. Placing the flowers on the dressing table, Margaret rearranged the pretty vanity set, Helen's collection of porcelain birds, and a framed miniature on either side of the vase. Stepping back, she admired her work. A great improvement.

Then her attention was drawn to the miniature portrait itself. She picked it up once more and studied the face. Was this the man Helen had hoped to marry? An exceedingly handsome man, if the artist's brush was accurate. How she would like to pick up a brush once again. It had been too long.

Helen's voice startled her. "Beautiful, was he not?"

Margaret quickly set the portrait down, stunned and chagrined not only to be caught poking about, but to be alone with Nathaniel's sister.

Risking a look over her shoulder, she was relieved to find Helen's eyes trained on the portrait.

"Yes, miss," she replied, accent warbling. "I'm sorry, miss. I . . ."

Helen waved away her apology. She walked over and reverently picked up the miniature, staring down at the face with an expression both dreamy and pained.

Margaret bobbed a curtsy and quickly slipped from the room.

Margaret sat beside Hester in the servants' hall that night, lingering together with several others after supper, enjoying the camaraderie and the chance to sit and relax after a long day's work. Around her, everyone listened with fond amusement as Connor regaled them with tales of his five brothers and younger sister.

"All as ginger-haired as he," Hester whispered in Margaret's ear.

Connor said, "The first time I went home in my new clothes after I become a valet, no one would come to the door. My own home and they wouldn't answer my knock. Turns out my little sister had seen 'some fine gentleman' coming up the lane and ran to tell my brothers the bill collector had come to call. I went around the back and found them all huddled in the woodshed, hiding from their own brother!"

Chuckles and grins were exchanged around the room, and Connor beamed a charming smile. Margaret could certainly see why Hester was taken with the young man—as all the maids were.

Lewis had always had that same effect on women, young and old alike.

As Margaret made her way up to her room and prepared for bed, she found herself thinking about him. She recalled the first time she had seen Lewis after his return from Barbados more than two years ago—and the effect he'd had on *her*. . . .

Margaret glimpsed a tall dark-haired man striding across the ballroom with such confidence, such presence, that all paused to look. The fact that he was heart-stoppingly handsome caused those looks to linger.

"Who is that?" a debutante near her breathed.

Margaret's friend, Emily Lathrop, followed the direction of their gazes. "That's Lewis Upchurch. Nathaniel Upchurch's older brother."

Margaret had seen Lewis Upchurch in the past, but he had never taken any notice of her. So while she enjoyed the view, she entertained no thoughts of him beyond surprise at seeing him there.

Margaret turned and looked instead for Nathaniel Upchurch. He saw her at the same moment and crossed the ballroom to meet her, a shy smile on his bespectacled face.

She stepped away from the other young ladies to speak with him. "Good evening, Mr. Upchurch. I see your brother is back. I don't remember your mentioning he planned to return."

Nathaniel grimaced. "That's because I didn't know. Seems Lewis got bored and decided to return to London without my father's approval."

"I am sorry to hear it."

"As was I." He glanced over at the ladies and gentlemen crowding around Lewis, all eager to greet him. "Though we are alone in that sentiment."

Margaret and Nathaniel danced together twice after that and then he led her to the punch table for a glass of ratafia.

Lewis appeared at his elbow. "Hello, Nate. Do introduce me to this lovely creature you're monopolizing."

Nathaniel hesitated, then turned to oblige him. "Of course. Miss Margaret Macy, my brother, Lewis Upchurch."

"But we have met before, Mr. Upchurch," Margaret said. "Though it was more than a year ago. I don't expect you remember—"

"It can't be," Lewis protested. "I would have remembered an exquisite face like yours. Do say you'll dance with me."

Never had Lewis Upchurch looked at her with such admiration, such intensity in his warm brown eyes. It was as though he were seeing her for the first time. Perhaps he was. Perhaps he had never really noticed her amid all the other women forever flocking about him like chattering hens.

Unsettled and bemused by his charming flattery, she faltered, "Oh . . . well, of course. If you like."

It was only a dance, she told herself. Nathaniel did not own her, nor was it even proper for the two of them to dance more than twice together in the same evening. They were not engaged.

Even so, she did not miss the wariness that flashed in Nathaniel's eyes.

Margaret danced with Lewis twice that night, and at the next ball, and by the next week she allowed him to escort her in to supper in Nathaniel's stead.

Lewis is better looking, a better dancer, more confident, and more exciting, she justified to herself, overwhelmed by the astounding fact that the man everyone wanted, wanted her.

With a sigh, Margaret rolled over in her attic bed, wondering yet again why his interest had not lasted.

In the morning, when the staff again assembled for morning prayers, Lewis Upchurch stood in the hall between his brother and sister for the first time. Lewis, Hester had told her, would be returning to London that very afternoon. He had spent only a few days at Fairbourne Hall, but did plan to return soon. This last word had made Hester's eyes sparkle and brought dimples to her cheeks.

Nathaniel opened the book, then hesitated. He turned to his brother and offered it to him. Lewis waved the offer away, indicating Nathaniel should continue.

Nathaniel did so. He read a brief Scripture and prayed. Margaret liked that instead of reading a prayer by rote every morning, he often uttered prayers of his own invention, crafted in the moment evidently, judging by the screwing up of his face, the occasional pauses, and false starts. Mr. Arnold denounced him a poor cleric. But Nathaniel's earnest informality in prayer, though in little else, reminded Margaret of her father, also denounced a poor cleric by many. Though not by her.

When Mr. Upchurch lifted his head to dismiss them, Lewis stepped forward before he could do so.

"Just a brief announcement . . ." Lewis began.

Beside her, Fiona stiffened in anticipation and Thomas quietly groaned.

"You are probably not aware, but today is Miss Upchurch's birthday. She will ask for no gift for herself and tells me she only wishes that everyone would, in her words, 'be happy and get along.'" He shot Nathaniel a telling look, then grinned at his sister. Helen met his glance with a wary one of her own, clearly unsure of his plan.

"In that spirit, and in her honor, I have asked Mr. Hudson to give all of you a half day—this very afternoon, to spend as you please."

Gasps and exclamations of surprise and delight swept through the assembly. Nathaniel and Helen Upchurch, Margaret noticed, looked as surprised as the rest. Did Lewis not realize what he was doing? How was his sister to enjoy even a decent birthday supper if the entire staff was off duty?

But Helen beamed up at her brother. "That is an excellent notion, Lewis. I could ask for nothing better for my birthday."

Mrs. Budgeon looked far less pleased. Concerned no doubt about what would be left undone, who would prepare dinner for the staff, not to mention the family, and a whole host of other tasks. She glanced at Mr. Hudson, perhaps seeking an empathetic grimace, but Mr. Hudson rubbed his hands together like a young boy anticipating a treat. The housekeeper rolled her eyes.

Cheerful chatter arose from the staff as they departed in twos and threes like chirpy robins in springtime, talking among themselves, laughing, joking, and hurrying to finish their remaining duties in record time. Only Hester looked deflated. Margaret glanced at Connor and was surprised to see him glaring at his master. Then she understood. For Connor would be leaving with Lewis and unable to share in the afternoon's pleasure.

At one, the staff hurried to their rooms in various parts of the house or stable loft to divest themselves of the marks of their servitude—the caps, aprons, and tools of their trade. Some were going off to visit family in the nearby hamlet of Weavering Street or in Maidstone proper. Others had no family in the area but were making plans with one or two companions to go into Maidstone for an afternoon of revelry, shopping, or just enjoying the out of doors. It appeared Miss Upchurch had authorized the use of the wagon and horses to transport anybody who wanted to go into Maidstone. The groom warned that the wagon would leave The Queen's Arms at eight sharp and any latecomers would have themselves a long walk back.

Margaret carried her housemaid's box back to the closet, then started up to her room. She paused on the stairs to retie the laces of her half boot. From below, she heard Fiona and Betty talking as they stowed their own supplies. Apparently they, along with the two young kitchen maids—nieces of Betty's—planned to walk together into Weavering Street to enjoy an unexpected afternoon with family.

Margaret overheard Betty say, "I suppose we should ask her to join us."

Fiona hissed, "Why? After what she done to you?"

Betty sighed. "I know. I'm with her day in and day out as it is."

"That's right. You need a respite if anybody does."

The closet door closed. Betty said tentatively, "But she is new and doesn't know anybody else. I doubt she has anywhere to go."

Fiona groaned. "Oh, a pox upon you Betty, for yar fun-killing charity. Very well, you ask her. Though I shan't enjoy my half day half so well as I might."

Ears burning, Margaret hurried upstairs, slipped into her room, and quickly lay on the bed.

A minute later, Betty knocked once and poked her head in the door. "Nora, a few of us are walking into Weavering Street. One of my brothers keeps a little inn there, so there's sure to be plenty of food and foolishness. You're welcome to join us if you like."

"Thank you, but I think I shall just stay here and rest. Maybe do a bit of reading."

"But it's a beautiful day."

Margaret turned on the bed to face her. "Then I shall walk the grounds later. You go on. Have a good time."

Betty shrugged. "All right, then. I'll come by to unlace your stays before I go to bed." She hesitated. "If you change your mind, we'll be in the Fox and Goose. Just a half mile or so up the road."

"Thank you."

Margaret waited until Betty had shut the door and the passage was quiet, then rose and stepped to her open window. She couldn't see anything, but she could hear distant laughter, whoops, and wagon wheels as the revelers departed, each to their own ideal of relaxation and enjoyment.

Margaret sighed.

Why should it sting? Why should she care? She hadn't wanted to spend time with servants since she was a girl. Why should she now? She was only lonely because she missed her own friends and family. That was all. She wished for the hundredth time she could write to her mother or sister. But a Maidstone postal marking would reveal her whereabouts.

Margaret wandered around the corner and down the attic corridor, silent now. Several doors stood ajar. None bore locks. Entering the room of a servant of the same sex was not considered taboo. The rooms weren't theirs, after all—everything belonged to their employers. Betty had told Nora that as the lowest-ranking housemaid, she would likely be assigned to clean the servants' quarters one day soon. Apparently people in service had little privacy. A situation Margaret had not considered when she'd adopted a wig.

Margaret paused in the threshold of Betty's room, neat as a pin as usual, with nothing on the washstand save a hairbrush and her week's allotment of soap. The bedside table was bare as well.

She stepped next into Fiona's room, smaller than Betty's, but just as neat. Beside a worn chair pulled near the window was a basket of knitting wool and needles, and on the arm of the chair, a worn copy of the novel *Pamela*. Margaret grinned. *Pamela* was an old story about a virtuous maid who tirelessly warded off her master's attempts at seduction until he finally married her. It was no wonder someone like Fiona might enjoy it. Though she was somewhat surprised to learn Fiona could read. And did.

Her conscience smarting from snooping, Margaret left the room and wandered down the many pairs of stairs to the kitchen, hoping for something to eat. She found Monsieur Fournier seated at the worktable, quill in hand and inkpot nearby, bent over a letter.

"*Bonjour, monsieur.* I thought everyone had left."

"Nora." He straightened. "Come to steal from my kitchen, ey?"

"Yes, please." She grinned.

He looked at her from under his great bushy black brows. And for a moment she feared he was truly angry. Then he shook his head, one side of his thin mouth quirking. "Ah, very well, *ma petite.* It shall be our secret, *non?*"

He rose and bustled about the kitchen. In a few moments, he

placed before her a ramekin and a spoon. "Now. Today I prepare zis with East India sugar. Made without slave labor, you see. Mr. Upchurch insists, even though it costs more. So. We shall eat zis in ze name of research, *oui*?"

Margaret nodded and pierced her spoon through a layer of burnt sugar, dipping into a creamy custard and, at the bottom, a layer of dark chocolate. She placed the intermingled layers in her mouth, closed her eyes, and savored the rich, bittersweet kiss upon her tongue.

"Oh, monsieur. I think I am in love."

He grinned with satisfaction and picked up his quill once more.

She wondered how he stayed so thin. She took another bite and glanced at him. "What are you writing?"

"I write to my brother. He is a chef as well, but in France. I write to him little improvements to old family recipes. Or to ask him what herbs Mamma put in her *potage aux champignons* . . ." He lifted an expressive hand. "But I never hear back. I hope all is well."

"I am sure it is. But with the war barely over . . ."

"Yes, yes. The mail is *peu fiable*."

She nodded, echoing, "Yes. Unreliable, indeed."

His head snapped up, eyes alight with surprise. "You speak French, *mademoiselle*?"

Too late she realized her error. "Oh . . . no. Not really. My mother has a French lady's—lady friend, and I heard French spoken now and again. That's all."

He studied her, his expression measuring and perhaps even suspicious. Then he seemed to shake it off. "In his last letter, more zan a year ago now, my brother promised to send *Le Cuisiniere Impérial*—the very best book of French cuisine. But . . . well . . ." He lifted both hands and shrugged. *"C'est la guerre."*

Margaret licked her spoon. "Perhaps you should write your own book."

His dark eyes gleamed. "Perhaps I shall."

From down the passage, the tinkling of keys filtered into the kitchen and swelled into melody. The old pianoforte being played in the servants' hall. She looked up in surprise, but monsieur seemed to take it in his stride, listening distantly as he spooned another bite into his mouth.

"Who is that?" Margaret asked, reluctant to leave her sweet dessert to investigate.

"Madame Budgeon."

"Really? I had no idea she played."

"She is a woman of hidden talents, Anna Budgeon."

Anna? Margaret mused, "I wondered if she would take the afternoon off, or do the work of all the missing staff combined."

"She could no doubt, with vigor to spare."

He said it with admiration, and she regretted her sarcastic remark.

"And you?" she asked. "Why are you not off at some inn with the others?"

He pulled a face. "I cannot abide English food, Nora. I make no secret of zis. English ale little better. No. I told Mr. Upchurch I appreciate his offer, but I prefer to stay and prepare something *extraordinaire* for Miss Helen's birthday. *Seulement moi,* in a quiet kitchen. Sweet music in my ears and sweet aromas in my nose."

His last word drew her attention to his abundant nose hairs, and she forced herself to look away. She guessed the scullery maid would not enjoy the mountain of dishes awaiting her return but didn't say so.

Rising, she said, "Then I shall leave you to it."

"If you like. Though you are pleasant company."

"Thank you. And thank you again for the delicious pudding."

He nodded. "Not going out?"

She shook her head. "Betty was kind enough to ask, but . . . I think I shall do a bit of reading instead."

His head tilted to one side. "The new maid reads books and speaks French. *Très intérresant.*"

Leaving the kitchen, Margaret tiptoed down the passage and peeked into the servants' hall. Mrs. Budgeon sat, head bent, hands spread wide, playing with abandon. And though the instrument was not in perfect tune, the housekeeper played very well. Hidden talents, indeed. She wondered who had taught her and guessed Mrs. Budgeon did not often have opportunity to practice and enjoy her skill.

Margaret decided not to disturb her.

She returned to her room but was too restless to read. The warm, sunny afternoon beckoned her out of doors. She tied on her bonnet and retrieved her reticule, which still contained her worldly treasures—her few remaining coins and cameo necklace. Then she trotted down the back stairs and out the servants' door.

The warm late-August air embraced her. She paused to tip her face to the sunshine, the warmth on her skin as sweet as the pudding had been. The wolfhound, Jester, appeared and trotted beside her, tail wagging.

Her half boots crunched over the pebbled drive as she walked between the kitchen garden and one of the flower gardens, surrounding her with the fragrances of comfrey, lavender, and intermingled floral scents. She followed the hedgerow to the front boundary of the estate. Jester shadowed her as far as the road, but there she told him to stay. She was surprised when the dog obeyed, though he watched her depart with mournful eyes.

She would walk into Weavering Street, she decided. Whether or not she would have the courage to enter the Fox and Goose remained to be seen.

The tiny hamlet of Weavering Street was a collection of cottages and shops that had sprouted up during the building of Fairbourne Hall and continued to succor the spouses of several estate workers. Mrs. Budgeon, Margaret had heard, did the majority of the marketing in large and prosperous Maidstone beyond.

Margaret strolled up the walkway fronting the businesses—a combination butcher shop and bakery as well as a chandler's shop which sold a bit of everything, displaying its wares in a many-paned bow window. As she passed, she breathed in the delicious aromas of pies and cakes, pungent cheeses, and savory sausages.

She stopped short at the sight of Joan standing beside a gig, its horse tethered near the chandler's. A jumble of emotions crowded her throat. Nostalgia at seeing a familiar face. Shame at the weakness she had displayed in her former maid's presence. Gratitude. And fear of rejection.

"Hello, Joan," she said tentatively.

Joan looked over and also seemed to hesitate. "Well, well. Never thought I'd see you again." She stepped up to the walkway. "What are you doing here?"

"I have a post nearby."

"You? What as?"

"Housemaid."

Joan shook her head in disbelief, then glanced toward the shop door. "Someone came along and hired you after I left?"

Margaret nodded. "Eventually." Joan didn't appear interested in long explanations, so instead Margaret asked, "So . . . are you out enjoying a half day as well?"

"Half day? Hardly." Joan snorted, again glancing toward the shop. "The Hayfields have been in mourning for nearly a year and are broke in the bargain. So no time off, no servants' ball, no gifts at Christmas, nothing. Several left for better places because of it, which is why I was hired."

"I'm sorry to hear it." Guilt slithered through Margaret. "How is it working there otherwise?"

Joan shrugged. "I've had worse. The housekeeper's a terror, never satisfied. But I've got a roof over my head. The food is decent and the others aren't a bad lot."

It wasn't very convincing. "At least you're not a maid-of-all-work," Margaret suggested weakly.

"Yes, I avoided that fate, at least." Joan smirked. "I suppose your place is a bed of roses?"

"Not bad, though one of the other housemaids barely tolerates me." Margaret almost added, *"She reminds me of you,"* but thought the better of it.

At that moment, the stern Hayfield housekeeper stepped out of the chandler's.

"Let's go, Hurdle. Stop dawdling."

Joan looked once more at Margaret. "Well, good-bye again."

"Good-bye, Joan," Margaret whispered over an unexpected lump in her throat.

She stood there, watching until the two women climbed in and the gig moved on. Then Margaret turned to the chandler's window, idly wondering what the old biddy had found to buy there.

She casually surveyed the hodgepodge of wares—from cheap candlesticks to cookware to bottles of the latest patent medicines for those who did not wish to venture to a Maidstone apothecary. She regarded the collection with some amusement and, if she were honest, condescension. Clearly, the shop did not have the most elite of clientele. She was about to continue on, when something behind the glass reflected a ray of sunlight, shining, winking at her. She frowned and bent nearer, as much as her stays would allow, to view the object more closely.

Her breath caught. There beside a paltry collection of slightly dented pots and kettles lay a gilt chatelaine in a velvet box. It could not be . . . Chatelaines were not uncommon, she told herself—in fact they had become quite ubiquitous. Even fine ladies wore them, inlaid with mother of pearl and even jewels. This one bore no jewels but a distinct engraving of a stag's head on the body of the brooch. Empty key chains and three tiny gilt boxes lay in a tangle beneath. *Oh no . . .*

Before she consciously chose to do so, Margaret stepped inside the shop, only distantly hearing the jingle of the bell announcing her arrival. A diminutive man with thin hair and the bushiest side whiskers she had ever seen stepped forward to greet her, hands clasped before his narrow, vested chest.

"Good afternoon. How may I help you?"

"The chatelaine in the window . . ." She was tempted to ask whose it had been to verify her suspicions. But Betty's brother lived in the hamlet. She did not want to embarrass Betty before her family, or for word to reach Betty that Nora had been snooping into her affairs. "Who . . . that is, I don't recall seeing it there before."

The man shook his head, a sparkle in his eye belying the regretful expression. "No, miss. Just come in today, it did. And a fine piece it is. How lovely it would look pinned to your frock just there."

She did not like the man eyeing her waist. She frowned. Betty would never forgive her if she heard some Fairbourne housemaid was thinking of buying her cherished chatelaine for herself.

"I wasn't thinking of it for myself."

"Oh." Disappointment etched his features, but then his brows rose. "A gift, perhaps? And a fine gift it would be, indeed."

Margaret licked her lips. "I don't know. I . . . How much are you asking?"

"For a fine piece like that? Dear it is, but worth every farthing to the lucky lady who wears it."

A farthing she could manage, but from the gleam in his eye she guessed he was asking far more. "How much?"

"Oh . . ." He screwed up his face, lips protruding, as he took in her reticule, her leather gloves, her bonnet . . .

She knew she would not like his answer.

He named a figure. An astounding figure.

"But . . . it isn't real gold, you know. It's only brass."

"Pinchbeck, actually."

"Which still isn't gold," she insisted.

"I could let it go for a bit less, for a fine young lady like yourself."

She huffed. "I am not a fine lady, sir. I am a housemaid."

"You don't say? Where are you placed? Fairbourne Hall?"

Margaret turned to leave before she said something she regretted. She reached for the door latch.

"Don't be hasty, miss," he called to her. "A pound, two and six. And that's as low as I can go."

"Did you give her a pound, two and six?"

His brows furrowed. "Who?"

"The woman who brought it in." She swallowed and added, "Whoever she was."

"Well, a man has to make a profit, hasn't he?"

"From other people's misfortunes?"

There, she had said too much. She turned and left the shop without another word, ignoring his plaintive calls to reconsider.

She stalked back down the road, back toward Fairbourne Hall. She could not face Betty. Not now. She did not have that much money. Nowhere near it. All she had was the cameo necklace her father had given her. It was likely worth quite a bit more than the chatelaine, but she could never part with it. Not the last gift her dear papa had given her. Perhaps when all this was over and she had her inheritance, she would send Betty a new chatelaine. Or even drive back down in a private carriage and buy back Betty's chatelaine from the greedy little man, as much as it would gall her to do so.

In the back of her mind, a voice asked, "Will it still be there months from now?" But she resolutely ignored it.

The housemaid's folding back her
window-shutters at eight o'clock the next day
was the sound which first roused Catherine.

—Jane Austen, *Northanger Abbey*

Chapter 12

Margaret arose feeling refreshed the next morning. She had gone to bed early the night before, and though she tossed and turned for a time, she had gotten more sleep than usual. Betty had forgotten to come to her room to unlace her stays, so again Margaret had slept in them. Constricting as they were, keeping them on did make dressing in the morning so much the quicker—and possible solo. She hoped Betty had not similarly forgotten to attend to Miss Upchurch. The upper housemaid had been doing what she could to dress her mistress and arrange her hair since the lady's maid retired, but based on Helen Upchurch's appearance at morning prayers, Betty's skills in that department were rudimentary at best.

Margaret thought again of what she had heard about Helen Up-church's great disappointment in love, and the rare sympathy in the gossips' tone as they speculated about her long absence from society. Something about her father refusing his consent to the match and then the man's untimely death soon after. Poor Helen. She recalled the good-looking man in the miniature portrait on Helen's dressing table. No wonder she was disappointed.

Helen Upchurch had never been a ravishing beauty, not with that pointed nose reminiscent of her brother Nathaniel's, nor with her somewhat sallow complexion. But she had been handsome enough and well thought of. It was such a shame, really. Margaret realized that she had done nothing when she'd heard of Helen's loss. She wondered if she should have, could have helped somehow. Would a kind letter or call really have been so taxing?

Margaret pushed thoughts of the past aside—anxious now to see how Betty fared.

She finished dressing, pinned her blond hair back into its tight bun, positioned her wig, cap, and spectacles, and sat on her bed to await Betty's knock. . . . She retrieved her father's New Testament and read for a quarter of an hour. . . . Still the attic was quiet. It was time to go down and open the shutters, but again Betty had failed to show up at her door. Had she gone down without her? Was she so very angry with her?

Margaret once again made her way to Betty's room. The door was closed. She knocked softly, listened, but no one answered.

Gingerly, she pushed open the door. The room was dim, the shutters closed. As her eyes adjusted, Margaret frowned, retracting her head like a turtle encountering an unexpected obstacle. Betty was still in bed. She lay on her stomach, face smashed into her pillow, cheek bunched up, mouth slack. Her arm hung out of the bedclothes, limp, fingers nearly reaching the floor. How strange. Betty never slept late.

"Betty?" she whispered, not wanting to startle her. But Betty did not rouse. "Betty!" Margaret repeated, suddenly fearful the woman was ill . . . or worse.

She hurried to the window and threw back the shutters. Dawn light seeped into the room. Returning to the bed, she grasped Betty's shoulder and gently shook her.

The upper housemaid muttered something unintelligible.

"Betty, you've overslept. What will Mrs. Budgeon say? I don't want you to get into trouble."

"Wha' time is it?" Betty asked, voice thick, as though her mouth were stuffed with cotton wool.

"It's gone six."

"Six?" Betty's eyes popped open. Wincing, she twisted around, sat up, and pressed her hands to her temples. Her complexion greened, and those same hands grasped her mouth in alarm.

Thinking quickly, Margaret grabbed the basin from the washstand and thrust it under Betty's chin. Betty retched. Then retched again.

She groaned. "The room's spinnin', Nora. Just give me a few minutes to gather my wits. The shutters await. . . ." Weakly she fell back in bed, throwing an arm over her eyes.

From the evidence and foul odor, Margaret came to the surprising conclusion that stalwart, dependable, workhorse Betty had been in her cups last night and was paying the devil this morning. On second thought, perhaps not so surprising, considering what she'd had to part with yesterday. But to drink the money away?

Hopefully not all of it.

Again, Betty began to rise, only to moan. "Aw-oh, my head . . ."

"There, there, Betty. Lie back. Sleep is what you need." Margaret gently settled Betty back onto her pillows and pulled up the bedclothes. She drained the basin into the chamber pot, rinsed it with water from the pitcher and drained it again. She left the basin next to Betty's bed. Just in case. She closed the shutters and then took the covered chamber pot out with her to dump it.

Margaret hurried through Betty's early morning routine as well as her own, folding back shutters, polishing grates, and sweeping and dusting the main floor rooms Betty usually handled, trusting Fiona was doing the others. Then she hurried down to the basement for the water cans, perspiration trickling down her back and along her hairline. The dashed wig was hot.

She saw Mr. Arnold entering the servants' hall for breakfast. If she did not scurry in now, she would miss the prayer. Mr. Arnold would not be pleased—Mrs. Budgeon either—but she needed to finish for Betty's sake. Her stomach growled, but she quickly filled the water cans and carried them up to Nathaniel's and Helen's rooms, emptying the slops before returning belowstairs.

When she reached the servants' hall at last, sweaty and weary, the others were already rising, Jenny beginning to clear.

Mrs. Budgeon's lip thinned in disapproval. "If you are late, you don't eat, Nora. Unless you have a valid excuse . . . ?"

Her mild whirled. She was hungry. She would have given her last shilling for one of Hester's muffins. But what could she say that would not get Betty into trouble? "Um . . . no. Duties took longer than usual, that's all."

"Where is Betty?" the housekeeper asked.

"Uh . . . In one of the rooms, I expect. She wasn't hungry."

Someone snorted.

Jenny giggled, then whispered, "Not surprising. After all she drank last night."

If Mrs. Budgeon heard, she ignored the comment. "Your duties, yours and Betty's, are completed I trust?"

"Yes, ma'am."

"Then, see you are not late for dinner."

Margaret looked at the clock above the mantel. It was the time Betty always veered from her housemaid duties and went up to help Miss Upchurch into her clothes and dress her hair. It would not do for Miss Upchurch to be kept waiting. Word would get back to Mrs. Budgeon all too quickly, and such an omission would not easily be forgiven by the exacting housekeeper.

Margaret went upstairs and, gathering her courage, entered Miss Upchurch's room once more. She had been inside the apartment several times to deliver water or flowers, but not to help the mistress of the manor prepare for the day.

She folded back the shutters and heard a stirring in the bed behind her.

"Where is Betty?"

Margaret took a steadying breath, reminding herself to alter her voice. She had not seen Helen Upchurch socially in two years. Still, she would have to be careful not to give herself away.

"Somethin' come up, miss." To herself she added, *Literally.* "Betty asked me to come in 'er place this mornin.'"

Helen regarded her. "You're the new girl."

"Yes, miss." Margaret bobbed a curtsy, glad for any excuse to bow her head.

"What is your name?"

"Nora, miss. Nora Garret."

"Welcome, Nora." Helen gave her a sleepy smile.

With her gentle smile and dark hair tumbling around her shoulders, Helen Upchurch looked younger and prettier than usual, even in the worn, unadorned nightdress.

"I do hope Betty is all right?" she said.

"Oh, she'll be right as a trivet in two shakes, I'd wager. We're all a bit behind after yesterday—that's all."

"I do hope the time off on account of my birthday did not cause problems. . . ."

"No, miss. I didn't mean that. It was right kind of Mr. Upchurch and yourself, ma'am."

"I am glad to hear it. Did everyone enjoy themselves?"

Margaret poured some of the hot water into the basin and laid out a fresh towel. "Yes, miss. Very much." *Some a bit too much*, she thought, then asked, "And did you enjoy your birthday supper?"

"Oh yes. Monsieur Fournier outdid himself. It was a delicious buffet and a lovely evening. Only . . ." She hesitated. "I do wish *both* of my brothers might have shared it with me." Helen looked troubled a moment, but then her expression cleared. "But Lewis had pressing business in town and simply could not stay. How disappointed he was to miss it."

"That's too bad, miss."

While Helen washed, Margaret stepped into the dressing room, opened the wardrobe, and surveyed its contents. She was surprised at the modest selection. Many gowns were several years out of fashion, even more so than Margaret's own gowns had become since Sterling limited their spending.

"What would you like to wear today, miss?" She pulled forth a gown of bishop blue. She had not yet seen Miss Upchurch wear it. It would look so well on her.

Helen sighed. "I don't know . . ."

"If I may, miss. How about this lovely blue?"

Helen glanced over and her lips parted, then she frowned. "Not that one. I don't wear that one."

Then why keep it, Margaret wondered, but knew better than to ask.

"The grey day dress will do fine."

That one she had already seen Miss Upchurch wear. Several times.

Margaret bit her lip and shook the dress to loosen the wrinkles, found a dress brush and gave the skirt and sleeves a quick once-over. She helped Helen on with a freshly laundered shift, then held open a pair of stays without busk or boning. At least this she knew how to do, having helped her sister many times. Helen slipped her arms through the holes and then turned her back toward Margaret, clearly as accustomed to being dressed as Margaret was. Again it was a relief not to be face-to-face with the woman.

"Not so tight, if you please."

"Sorry, miss," Margaret murmured, though she thought it a pity. With a little cinching Helen's feminine figure could be quite attractive.

Finishing the stays, Margaret then helped her into a petticoat and stockings, tying the ribbons above Helen's knees before helping her into the gown itself.

Finally, Helen sat on a small stool before the dressing table, arranging her skirts about her. She picked up an elegant brush and began stroking her long brown hair, judging her progress in the mirror.

Margaret felt a pang of homesickness, not for the Bentons' house, but for her sister and brother, even her mother. How often she had brushed her mother's or sister's hair, even trimmed Gilbert's unruly curls now and again.

"Allow me, miss."

Helen's motions stilled, and Margaret gently took the brush from her hand. She brushed the woman's hair with long strokes, pausing when she hit a snarl to carefully untangle it before continuing. Brushing Helen's hair soothed her and reminded her of Caroline, though her sister's hair was lighter in hue and weight. In the mirror, Margaret noticed Helen had closed her eyes. *Good*, she thought.

At closer range now, Margaret noticed a few strands of grey in with the brown.

"Are you able to dress hair?" Helen asked. "If not, I can manage a simple knot on my own."

How undemanding Helen Upchurch was, Margaret thought, in her loose, bone-free stays, old dress, and easygoing ways.

"It'd be my pleasure, miss, to give it a go."

"Very well."

Margaret soon found herself absorbed in the task. She brushed the hair upwards from Helen's neck and gathered it in one hand, then leaned over to set down the brush. She had seen Helen often enough since arriving to know she wore her hair in a plain, severe knot low at the back of her head. But in Margaret's opinion, it would look much prettier with soft height. She thought of suggesting heating the clay curling rod, but the day was too warm for a fire. So she settled for leaving out two thick strands at either temple, dampening these with water, winding them up, and pinning the curls to the sides of Helen's head. These she allowed to dry while she continued to arrange the remaining hair high on the crown of her head.

Margaret leaned over again, snagged the pins, and secured the coil. When she finished, she removed the pin curls from Helen's temples, pleased when the strands hung in spiraling tendrils on either side of her face. Fortunately, Helen's hair had some natural curl, unlike Caroline's, which would hang limp without help from a hot iron.

So engrossed was Margaret in dressing Helen's hair, that it took her several moments to notice how still, even stiff, Helen had suddenly become.

Margaret glanced up with a start. Helen no longer had her eyes closed, nor was she looking at her own reflection in the mirror. She was staring, eyes wide, at her.

"What are you doing?" Helen breathed.

Margaret's heart pounded. She stared back, then feigned interest in an imaginary stray lock of hair. Had Helen recognized her, or was she merely offended at the liberties a new maid had taken with her hair? Perhaps Margaret was reading too much into the question.

Swallowing, Margaret chose to respond to the latter meaning and exaggerated her accent. "Just tryin' to give your hair a bit of height, miss. But I can do it over if ya like."

She held her breath, feeling Miss Upchurch's scrutinizing stare on her bowed head. The silence was thick. Margaret's palms grew damp. Her voice breathy, she asked, "Which earbobs would ya like to wear, miss?"

Helen swiveled on her dressing stool, and Margaret backed up several steps. The woman's direct gaze was even more intimidating than it had been in reflection. Margaret forced herself to meet that gaze.

Helen asked warily, "Why are you here?"

Margaret was sure Helen must hear her heart *ta-tomb*ing in her ears. "As I say, miss. I'm only helpin' Betty today. I meant no harm."

Helen's eyes narrowed. "I don't know what you are about. But I shall be watching you."

"Yes, miss," Margaret murmured. "Will there be anythin' else, miss?"

Helen slowly shook her head.

Margaret curtsied, turned, and strode to the door, feeling Helen Upchurch's suspicious eyes follow her every step of the way.

In the corridor, she nearly collided with Fiona. The thin Irishwoman was out of breath and grim-faced. She glanced from Margaret to the door she had just exited.

"What were ya about in there?"

"Just helping out. Since Betty's not able."

"I was just going in. Is she angry?"

She thought of Helen's suspicious face. "Not angry, no."

"Did ya tell her Betty was . . . ?"

"I only said we were a bit behind after yesterday and I was filling in this morning. That's all."

"A bit behind? Sure and that's a fine way of sayin' foxed and sick as a dog. Castin' up her accounts was she?"

"Well . . ." Margaret gestured helplessly.

"Are ya sayin' *you* helped the mistress dress?"

"Yes."

"Perhaps I should go in and check . . ."

Margaret touched Fiona's arm. "The mistress is fine. Washed, clothed, hair dressed."

Fiona breathed a sigh of relief, then murmured, "Which is more'n I can say for Betty."

"Have you seen her?"

Fiona nodded. "I was just up lookin' for her and found her sleepin'. Y'ought to have told me."

"You had your own work." Margaret's stomach growled, and she turned away. It was time for morning prayers.

Fortunately for Betty, no one seemed to notice her absence. Afterward, Margaret and Fiona went back upstairs to clean the family bedchambers. When Fiona later rejoined her to help remake the beds, there had still been no sign of Betty.

"Poor lamb," Fiona said, shaking out the aired bedclothes. "She was low indeed last night. Worried about her ma."

"Her ma? I thought she had passed on."

Fiona frowned. "What put that notion into yar head?"

Margaret inhaled. "She showed me her mother's chatelaine. I assumed . . ." Margaret let her words drift away on a shrug.

"She isn't dead, only retired. Ailing." Fiona went to the other side of the bed and helped her spread the sheets. "Mrs. Tidy was a fine housekeeper, until her health failed and she could work no more. Had an apoplexy, poor soul, and needs constant care now.

She lives with a widow in Maidstone, and Betty's wages support them both."

"Is that why she sold her chatelaine . . ." Margaret breathed, stricken at the thought.

Fiona's head snapped toward her. "Did she now? And how might you be knowing that?"

"I saw it in the chandler's window."

"Is that where she went off to? Never said a word to me. I wondered where she come by all that money for drink. Must have fetched enough for her ma with plenty left over to drown her sorrows."

"But surely she might have explained . . ."

"Tell her mother, the sainted housekeeper, what never made a mistake in her life, to hear her tell it. Let on her wages was being garnished? Not Betty. She has her pride, hasn't she?"

Margaret winced. "But not her prized possession."

"And whose fault is that? All yar fine words won't get it back neither, so don't be lookin' down yar nose at her."

"I wasn't."

Fiona gave her a sidelong glance. "So ya came into Weavering Street yesterday, but couldn't be bothered to join us?"

"I meant to, but—"

Mrs. Budgeon popped her head in the door. "Here you are. I have just come from the green bedroom. Why is that bed not yet made? It is nearly eleven."

Margaret glanced at Fiona, but Fiona trained her stony gaze on the pillow in her arms.

"It's my fault, ma'am," Margaret said. "I fell behind today, but I'll soon catch up."

"You had better." She turned to leave, then paused. "Thank you for helping out, Fiona."

Fiona nodded.

Mrs. Budgeon asked, "Have you seen Betty?"

Fiona looked at Margaret.

Margaret faltered, "Um . . . yes. Last I saw her she was in one of the other bedchambers." Well, that was true to a point, though the bedchamber had been her own.

"When you see her, tell her I need to speak with her."

At that moment, Betty appeared in the doorway, looking sheepish. "Here I am, Mrs. Budgeon. I am terribly sorry . . ."

The housekeeper said, "You are responsible for overseeing the duties of the under maids, but Nora is not new any longer and must learn to complete her duties on time herself. You and Fiona cannot continue to cover for her."

Betty's mouth dropped open. "But . . . I—"

Margaret said quickly, "That's what Betty is always telling me, Mrs. Budgeon. I shall do better in future. I promise."

Mrs. Budgeon studied her. "Very well. We shall let it pass this once. I knew yesterday's idleness would exact its price."

"Right you were," Margaret agreed.

In the doorway, Betty nodded, her pale countenance and red-rimmed eyes hinting at just how high a price it was.

Chamber maid wanted who can dress hair,
clear starch, read & write, bear moderate confinement,
work well at her needle, dress a young lady, is sober &
honest & well behaved. Apply Mrs. Lambe, Stall St.

—Bath Chronicle, 1793

Chapter 13

Margaret stood waiting in her room in her wig, shift, and undone stays when Fiona knocked on her door the next morning. She had been expecting Betty.

"Betty's already hard at work. Makin' up for yesterday, no doubt. She asked me to help ya with yar stays this mornin'."

"Thank you, Fiona."

"It's a favor to Betty, mind, not you."

Margaret turned her back to Fiona. But Fiona circled her, surveying the long stays of ivory linen which came down to her hip. The shoulder straps and satiny gusseted cups supported, while pretty stitching decorated the front.

"Well, well. Such finery for a housemaid. A castoff from yar last mistress?"

"Um . . . it belonged to one of the daughters, yes."

Fiona nodded and stepped behind her, pulling the single lace through the many holes with more force than necessary.

"Thank you," Margaret said through gritted teeth, and waited for Fiona to step from the room.

"Let's have the rest, then," Fiona said.

Margaret preferred no audience when she pulled her petticoat and day dress over her head, in case her wig should slip. "Thank you, but I can manage the rest on my own."

Fiona stuck out her lip, as though impressed. "That's somethin,' I suppose."

Two hours later, her first round of duties completed, Margaret went downstairs for breakfast. On her way to the servants' hall, she passed the housekeeper's parlor. From within, Mrs. Budgeon hailed her.

"Nora?"

Margaret veered into her doorway. "Yes, Mrs. Budgeon?"

The housekeeper looked up from the tea she was measuring. "It seems you made quite an impression on Miss Upchurch yesterday when you took it upon yourself to help her dress and arrange her hair." Her tone was not complimentary.

"Betty was busy elsewhere, ma'am. I only meant to help the one time."

"In future, you are to see me before promoting yourself."

"I had no intention of promoting my—"

"Do not interrupt me."

Margaret swallowed.

"Nor will you make any further changes in your assigned duties. Do I make myself clear?"

"Yes, ma'am."

"Very well." Mrs. Budgeon avoided her eyes and took a deep breath. "It seems Miss Upchurch would like you to dress her hair once again. You will attend her immediately after your breakfast."

"But ... I ..."

"It was not a suggestion, Nora."

"No, ma'am. Yes, ma'am."

Heart pounding, Margaret scratched on Miss Helen's door. A proper lady's maid had no need to knock before entering her mistress's bedchamber. But there was nothing proper about the maid trembling at Helen Upchurch's door. She wondered if Helen really wanted "Nora" to dress her hair, or if she had another reason for summoning her.

"Come."

Whispering a prayer, Margaret pushed open the door and stepped inside. Helen was seated at her dressing table, fully clothed. Betty had obviously been there before her.

Helen glanced up at her in the mirror. "Nora, was it?"

Mouth dry, Margaret nodded.

"Kindly dress my hair, please."

Please. Had Margaret ever said the word to Joan?

Margaret walked forward, glad Helen's back was to her but wishing she might throw a shawl over that mirror.

She picked up the brush and again began stroking through Helen's hair. Glancing down, she noticed that the high neck of Miss Upchurch's gown was frayed—the decorative buttons sagging on their threads. The dress was not only worn but outmoded. Helen Upchurch had always dressed quite fashionably when Margaret had seen her during the London seasons. But that was before her heart had been broken and she put herself on the shelf.

As she pinned Helen's hair, she felt the woman's eyes watching her in the mirror. Margaret swallowed and, nervous, stuck the final pin too deep.

Helen winced. "What are you doing?"

Margaret did not like the odd light in Helen's eyes. The light of suspicion . . . or recognition? She said in her acquired accent, "Beg pardon, miss."

Helen blinked. She asked slowly, "Why are you here at Fairbourne Hall?"

That question again. Margaret licked dry lips. She wondered once more if Helen knew. Had she seen through her disguise when her brothers had not? She was probably reading too much into Helen's questions. After all, the woman had not tossed her out on her ear after their last meeting.

Margaret summoned her courage. "I needed the work, miss," she began. "Glad I was when Mr. Hudson offered me a place."

Helen's eyes narrowed. "Why would you want to work *here*?"

"I . . . There was no work in London."

Helen's expression hardened. "There is always work in London."

"I couldn't stay there, miss. I had to get away."

"But *why*?" Helen repeated, her expression perplexed, frustrated.

Margaret swallowed. "Because my . . ." She hated to use the word *father* related to Sterling Benton but didn't want to name the man. "My stepfather was pressurin' me to marry his nephew—a man I can't abide." Margaret shuddered anew at the thought of marrying Marcus Benton.

Helen seemed to consider this, then said slowly, "You cannot be forced to marry against your will, you know. The law prohibits it. You can marry or not as you choose."

"Did *you*?" Margaret's tongue jabbed the words before she could stop them.

A flush of pain and of indignation marred Helen Upchurch's face.

Remorse swamped Margaret. "I am sorry, miss. I shouldn'ta said it. But you know men has their ways of gettin' what they want and there is little women can do to stop 'em."

For a moment, a faraway look misted Helen's hazel eyes. "Yes, I do know." Then she looked up sharply again in the mirror. "What are you playing at in coming *here*? If you have some scheme in mind, I warn you—"

Margaret lifted both hands in her defense. "No scheme, miss. I woulda gone farther than Maidstone, but I hadn't the money. When Mr. Hudson found me at the hiring fair, I didn't even know which family he worked for. Honest I didn't."

For several ticks of the clock, the two women stared at each other in the looking glass.

Then Helen seemed to reach some decision. She rose and turned, saying officiously, "Well then . . . Nora. You had better go about your duties, had you not?"

Knees weak, Margaret bobbed an awkward curtsy. "Yes, miss. Thank you, miss." She backed from the room, not fully certain what had just transpired. Had Helen Upchurch just agreed to allow her to continue her ruse? Or had she imagined all those telling looks and suspicious questions? She would need to tread carefully and follow Helen's lead.

In the corridor, Fiona grasped her arm none too gently. "In there again? What are you about? Waiting on the mistress is Betty's job. And if it wasn't, it'd be mine."

"I only went because she asked for me."

"And why is that? Because ya pushed yar way in, didn't ya? Took advantage of Betty bein' indisposed to wheedle yar way into her place. The mistress would barely know you existed otherwise."

If only Margaret had foreseen that. "I only meant to help."

"Help yarself, ya mean. You know Betty hopes Miss Helen will bring her up as lady's maid, official-like. A step toward becoming housekeeper one day."

Margaret had not thought of that. She was tempted to point out that Betty had no talent for either hairdressing or making over old gowns, nor any of the other beauty tricks a lady's maid was supposed to know. But it would be unkind to say so. And—seeing the anger in Fiona's expression—unwise as well.

"I know you won't believe me, but I have no wish to be Miss Upchurch's personal maid."

Fiona snorted. "And why not? Prefer blacking grates, I suppose?"

"No. It isn't that. In fact I like dressing her hair, but . . ." How could she verbalize her real objections? *I don't like the way Helen Upchurch stares at me. I think she recognizes me but is toying with me.* Besides, Margaret knew many gentlewomen took their personal maids with them on calls, and to house parties, and shopping . . . Margaret had no wish to be out and about and increase her chances of being seen. Recognized. Considering her situation, being an invisible housemaid was better by far.

"But?" Fiona prompted.

"You'll just have to trust me when I tell you that you have nothing to fear from me. I don't want Betty's job—yours either."

After morning prayers, while the family ate their later breakfast, Margaret went upstairs to clean the brothers' bedchambers. She hurried, as usual, dreading being caught in the room should Nathaniel come upstairs. Knowing Lewis had returned to London, Margaret had skipped his room yesterday in her hurry to complete her other duties as well as Betty's. The amiable Connor had left the room in a mess when he'd packed up while the others were off enjoying their half day, and it took her longer than it should have to clean it this morning. She was behind schedule when she hurried into Nathaniel Upchurch's bedchamber and began her work there.

Margaret paused in her dusting to inspect a model ship on the dressing chest. This was no child's toy, but a detailed scale model. A wooden hull, polished and veneered, rigging made of horsehair and silk, masts and spars carved of ivory. How did one dust a ship? She picked up the model in her hands, tipping it back to see the word *Ecclesia* painted on its side.

Snap.

Margaret froze at the sound. The main mast had broken off in her hands, taking a small section of decking with it. She sucked in a breath. "No . . ."

The door opened behind her, and she whirled around. In her panic, she hid the pieces behind her back like a child caught in yet another misdemeanor.

Nathaniel Upchurch strode across the room with barely a glance her way. Did he think servants unworthy of his notice?

He went to his desk, retrieved a book, and turned to go.

Relief—she was not to be caught after all. Once he had gone, she would sneak the ship up to her room and try to repair it herself. But then might she, or Betty or Fiona, be accused of stealing it? A ship such as this would bring a high price in town. No. She could not do it. Besides, she told herself, she was a woman of four and twenty, not a sneaky seven-year-old.

"Sir?" she blurted.

He hesitated at the door, frowning. She supposed he didn't approve of maids speaking first. "Yes?"

"I'm afeared I broke yer ship," she said, laying the accent on thick.

His gaze swiftly flew to the pieces she now held forth in her hands.

"I was dustin' it, sir. I'm dreadful sorry. I shoulda been more careful-like."

He strode swiftly across the room, eyes riveted on the ship, lips pulled tight. He did not look at her, yet she saw irritation or something worse sparking in his eyes.

He tossed the book back onto the desk with such force that it slid off onto the floor. He paid it no heed. He took first the ship from her hand, then the broken mast, assessing the damage and trying to fit the pieces together.

He murmured to himself, "First the real thing, now this."

Guilt pricked and coated her innards with remorse. "I shall have it repaired, shall I? Perhaps someone in town might—"

"Leave it," he snapped. Setting the ship on his desk, he turned on his heel and left the room.

The door slammed behind him, reverberating through her heart. She remembered that look. This feeling. She hated disappointing him yet again.

With a sigh, she returned to her work. Bending to pick up the fallen book, she glanced at it and saw that it was a volume of poetry. Robert Burns. A corner of some paper, a card perhaps, protruded from between its pages like a child sticking out his tongue. It had likely been jarred loose during the fall. Something about the paper snagged her attention. She wondered what poem Nathaniel Upchurch deemed worthy of marking. She slid her fingernail to the spot near the back of the book and opened the pages to see what it was.

She stared. Blinked. Felt her brows furrow. Poem forgotten, she turned the rectangle of thick parchment to right the image upon it.

Studied it through her spectacles, then again beneath the lenses. Yes . . . It was definitely what she thought it was. An intermingled flush and chill ran over her body.

How strange that he had kept this small amateur watercolor. She did not recall giving it to him. Did he not know it was by her hand? Perhaps he had stuck it into the volume to mark some place long ago and had completely forgotten about it, and when he found it later did not remember the artist was the very woman who had spurned him, the woman he despised. Surely he would not have kept it had he remembered.

The painting was one of her better attempts but nothing of any value, monetary or sentimental, surely. It was only a pretty watercolor of Lime Tree Lodge, idealized no doubt, ivy climbing its walls, clematis cascading down its trellis, the garden adrift in honeysuckle blossoms and daffodils, their white cat, Claude, lying across the front steps. The only person in the painting was a young woman in a yellow frock, sitting on a swing at the side of the house, facing away, revealing only a glimpse of profile beneath the white bonnet. She had imagined Caroline as the figure swinging in the side yard, but now that she thought about it, she had owned a yellow frock at some point, whilst Caroline had not.

She was tempted to keep the painting. It was hers, after all. And how she would love to have this reminder of Lime Tree Lodge. Of better days.

But she dared not. She could not risk him missing it, and wondering why this old painting by Margaret Macy had gone missing so soon after the arrival of a new housemaid.

When Nathaniel returned to his room later that evening, he picked up the volume of Burns poetry he'd discarded earlier. From it, he extracted the small watercolor of Lime Tree Lodge—the last thing he had rescued from his burning ship. He wondered why he insisted on torturing himself. Still, he allowed the memory to come.

Nathaniel had met the Reverend Mr. Stephen Macy at a debate

sponsored by the African Institution. The topic was immediate vs. gradual emancipation after slaves were first educated for freedom.

There had been several distinguished speakers on both sides of the debate, but Nathaniel found himself most moved by the simple, heartfelt plea of a clergyman from a neighboring county. Mr. Macy called for immediate freedom, declaring souls had no color, and that everyone was equally important to God, whose son died to purchase freedom for all.

Nathaniel did not agree with everything the man said, but his heart was touched. Looking back now, he realized Mr. Macy had planted a seed in him, which would not come to fruition until after he had lived in Barbados and seen the atrocities of slavery with his own eyes.

After the debate adjourned, Nathaniel introduced himself to Mr. Macy. The reverend accepted his hand, and even his disagreement, gracefully. In fact, he invited Nathaniel to call on him at his home when next he traveled that way.

A ride to his uncle Townsend's took Nathaniel into Sussex later that fall. Nathaniel decided he would take Mr. Macy up on his offer. The village of Summerfield was not large, and by asking the blacksmith, Nathaniel was quickly able to locate Lime Tree Lodge.

What a picture the cottage made. Two stories of golden stone hung with ivy and capped by a slate roof. Beautiful old trees bordered the property and a stone fence surrounded a garden awash in autumn color.

Nathaniel sat astride his horse across the lane, partially hidden by a large willow, taking in the scene and wondering whether or not to intrude. A gig and single grey clattered into view and Nathaniel recognized Stephen Macy at the reins. Beside him sat a young woman with fair hair. Adoration lit her face as she laughed at something Mr. Macy said. She kissed his cheek and leapt from the gig before it came to a complete stop. Loping to the tree swing in the side yard, she began swinging with energetic pleasure more youthful than her years. He felt himself smiling, and his heart lighten at the sight.

A much younger girl and boy ran out from the cottage. The young woman jumped from the swing, landing neatly, and surrendered her seat, pushing first one sibling and then the other.

Stephen Macy appeared beside Nathaniel's horse, mouth quirked and amusement in his eyes. "Do you plan to sit there all afternoon and enjoy the view, or are you coming inside?"

"Ah. Sorry, sir. Wanted to give you time to settle before I knocked."

Stephen Macy looked over the stone fence at his three offspring. "That's my eldest, Margaret. We just returned from parish calls. She's a treasure, as are my younger children. I am a blessed man."

"I see that, sir."

Mr. Macy regarded him. "Nathaniel, wasn't it?"

"Yes, sir."

"My wife is not at home, but do come in and join me for tea."

"I don't wish to intrude."

"Not a bit of it. Come. Arthur will see to your horse."

A few minutes later they sat down together in a cozy parlor. An elderly housekeeper brought in a tray laden with biscuits and tarts and every good thing.

The young blond woman stepped into the room and hesitated at seeing him. "I'm sorry, Father. I did not realize you had a guest."

"Come join us, my dear. This is Nathaniel Upchurch. Mr. Upchurch, my daughter Margaret."

Nathaniel rose and bowed. "Miss Macy."

She curtsied. "Mr. Upchurch."

At closer range, the young woman looked familiar. Nathaniel said, "I believe I have seen you before, Miss Macy. In London, during the season?"

"Have you?" Self-conscious, she touched her windblown hair and dipped her unpowdered face. "I am surprised you recognize me; I must look a fright."

"Not at all."

Her face was still rosy from the carriage ride and exertion of the swing. In his view, this Margaret Macy was far more appealing than the powdered, perfectly coiffed lady of the ballroom. She looked unaffected, spirited, and breathtakingly beautiful. Had her father not been in the room he likely would have said so.

Margaret joined the men for tea, sitting ramrod straight and clearly uncomfortable. But her father's teasing soon cajoled her into laughing at herself and at him. Then he went to work on Nathaniel, regaling his daughter with an exaggerated account of catching Nathaniel "spying" over their garden wall.

Nathaniel could not remember when he had enjoyed a visit more. By the time he departed charming Lime Tree Lodge a few hours later, he had determined to stay in contact with Mr. Macy. And to court his beautiful daughter.

After Easter the following spring, Nathaniel and Helen packed up and moved to London for the social season. They believed their brother Lewis would not be joining them that year. He had sailed to the West Indies at their father's behest the previous summer. James Upchurch found it expedient to live in Barbados the majority of the time for the management of his affairs. He had summoned his elder son to join him there, hoping to detach him from unsavory connections at home.

At the first ball of the new season, Nathaniel saw Miss Macy and immediately requested a dance. She happily agreed, and the two began a courtship that lasted for many weeks. She seemed to enjoy his company, allowed him to escort her in to supper, and received him with pleasure when he paid the requisite call the next morning. All seemed to be going swimmingly.

But then Lewis returned.

Nathaniel slid the watercolor back into the book and closed it with a snap. He had no wish to think about what had happened after that.

In 1770, a British law was proposed to
Parliament granting grounds for annulment if a
bride used cosmetics prior to her wedding day.

—Marjorie Dorfman, "The History of Make-up"

Chapter 14

In Helen Upchurch's room a few days later, Margaret lifted the lid
from a partially used jar of cold cream pomatum and inspected
its contents. The cream had an unusual greyish cast. She took a
tentative sniff and jerked her head back. Rancid. How long had it
been since Helen had any new cosmetics? No wonder she used the
soap made right there in the Fairbourne Hall stillroom, drying to a
lady's complexion though it was.

Hester would know what to do. Margaret let herself from the room
and down the back stairs.

Margaret had tinkered with homemade cosmetics as a girl, when
she had been in a hurry to grow up even though her mother had
deemed her too young for cosmetics. In the stillroom at Lime Tree
Lodge the indulgent Mrs. Haines had allowed her to mix a little vegetable rouge tinted with red carmine. Also a little pot of lip color
made of wax, almond oil, and alkanet. She had helped Mrs. Haines
prepare pearl water to help Margaret combat the blemishes of youth,
and a chamomile hair rinse to brighten her blond hair.

Of course, all this had been years ago, and she did not recall the ingredients or mode. After Margaret's coming out, her mother had approved a few prepared cosmetics, purchased from an apothecary or modiste. So much easier and packaged so prettily: Rose Lip Salve, Pear's Liquid Blooms of Roses, and Gowland's Lotion. But Margaret believed that with a bit of help, she could manage cold cream pomatum and perhaps an oil of rosemary hair tonic for Miss Helen as well. She wondered if she might sneak a bit of walnut juice into the tonic to gently cover Miss Helen's greying strands. Her mother's maid used just such a concoction to keep grey at bay.

Thinking of hair color, Margaret wondered, not for the first time, if she ought to forgo the wig altogether and dye her hair instead. Once done, her day to day life would certainly be easier and more comfortable. Her risk of discovery so much decreased. But for every advertisement in the London newspapers touting the various nostrums available for darkening one's hair or returning it to the glossy shades of youth, there were also warnings about the ill effects of their ingredients—salts of iron or carbonates of lead.

Even without such warnings, Margaret would be loath to dye her hair. It seemed so extreme, so permanent. What if her hair never returned to the fair color she prized? She needed to remain brunette for only a few months, a fortnight of which had passed already. She decided she could put up with the wig a little longer.

When she reached the stillroom, Hester greeted her with her usual cheer. "Hello, love."

"Hello, Hester. The mistress's cold cream pomatum has gone rancid. Help me make more?"

"With pleasure. Why, I can't remember the last time we mixed up somethin' for Miss Upchurch. Long overdue on other things too, I'd wager."

Hester pulled down a thick green leather volume from one of the shelves. "It's been so long, I'd best check the measures. . . ." She flipped the creased, oil-stained pages.

"Here we are. One ounce oil of sweet almonds, half a drachm each of white wax and spermaceti, with a little balm."

Hester began bustling about the stillroom, opening drawers and reaching up to shelves to gather tools and ingredients. She instructed Margaret to melt the almond oil, wax, and whale oil in a glazed pipkin over hot ashes in the hearth. Margaret did so. Then she poured the mixture into a marble mortar. Hester handed her a pestle, and with it, Margaret pressed and stirred the cream until it was smooth and cool.

"Orange flower or rose water, do you think?" Hester asked.

She recalled Helen relishing the scent of the roses she'd put in her room. "Rose, if you have it."

"Indeed I do."

While Margaret continued to stir, Hester drizzled in rose water for fragrance.

Hester returned to her book and read, " 'This cold cream pomatum renders the skin at once supple and smooth. If not meant for immediate use, the gallipot in which it is kept should have a piece of bladder tied over it.' "

Margaret knew apothecaries tied wet pig bladders over their pots of ointments and nostrums, because as the bladders dried they shrunk, forming an airtight seal. Margaret quailed. She didn't relish the thought of touching pig parts.

"I'd like Miss Helen to be able to use it right away."

"Then a parchment cover will do."

Margaret waited until the next morning to carry up the cold cream pomatum to Helen's room. She uncovered the pot and set it on the washstand without comment. She did not want Helen to notice her delivering it and mention it to Mrs. Budgeon, nor to further rouse Fiona's ire if word got around that Nora had usurped yet another of Betty's rightful roles. She walked briskly into the dressing room to set it to rights and find a few more hairpins.

Miss Upchurch stirred in her bed, and Margaret guessed Betty would be in any moment to help her dress. Margaret wished Helen would wear something besides the grey, dull gold, and brown day dresses or the dark burgundy evening gown. She ran her fingers over the garments in Helen's wardrobe, noticing a lovely ivory-and-green walking dress she had never seen Helen wear. On closer inspection she discovered the likely cause: two buttons were missing and the holes themselves were frayed.

Margaret carried the dress into the bedchamber.

Helen, washing her face and hands in the basin, looked up. "Morning, Nora."

"Morning." She hesitated. "Miss Upchurch?"

"Hmm?"

"This walking dress is missing a few buttons. Do you mind if I take it and repair it this afternoon?"

"If you wish to."

"Thank you, I do. Betty and Fiona sew in the afternoons when their other duties are done, and I think I shall join them."

Helen pressed a hand towel to her face. "Very well." She lifted the pot of pomatum. "This cold cream smells wonderful. It must be new."

"Yes." Margaret quickly changed the subject. "Did your lady's maid keep a tin of buttons somewhere about?"

"I don't know. Betty might. If you cannot find any to match, perhaps you might walk into Weavering Street. There is a little shop there where Miss Nash often bought ribbons and buttons and things." Helen pulled a few coins from the reticule on her dressing table and handed them to Margaret. "You may tell Mrs. Budgeon I sent you."

"Thank you. If I find we already have spares to suit, I shall return the money."

Helen waved the assurance away. "I trust you, Nora."

Margaret hesitated at that remark, looking at Helen to see if she'd realized what she'd said, and if she had meant it. "Do you?" she asked softly.

Slowly, Helen lifted her head and for a moment the two women simply looked at one another. Then Helen said, "Yes. Oddly enough, I find that I do."

Margaret's throat tightened. She whispered, "Thank you."

Gown over her arm, Margaret turned and walked to the door. When she reached it, Helen added, "Don't make me regret it."

That afternoon, Margaret found Fiona and Betty already seated in the sunny attic room that had once been the domain of the lady's maid before her retirement. It was a spacious room, larger than Betty's superior room and twice the size of Margaret's, with a dress form in the corner, an ironing board, bolts of cloth in an open cupboard, a worktable in the center, and a bare bed along one wall.

They stopped talking as soon as she entered, which gave Margaret the uneasy sense they'd been talking about her. She forced a smile. "May I join you?"

Fiona eyed her warily, but Betty answered, "Of course, Nora. Always more mending to be done."

Fiona's lip curled. "Looks like she's brought her own work."

"I have. Miss Upchurch's gown is missing a few buttons."

Betty's face puckered wistfully. "Asked you to do it, did she?"

Margaret shook her head. "Actually, Miss Upchurch specifically told me to ask you, Betty, if we have a tin of buttons where replacements might be found. She said if anyone would know, it was Betty."

Betty's round eyes widened. "Did she, now?"

Margaret nodded. She hoped she would be forgiven the slight exaggeration. Judging by Fiona's smirk, that seemed unlikely.

Betty rose and hurried over to the cupboard, pulled open a drawer, and extracted a round tin. "Here are the spare buttons. I don't believe I have seen any what would match those exactly, but . . . let's have a look, shall we?"

"Thank you, Betty. Miss Upchurch was right—you were the person to ask."

Fiona rolled her eyes.

"These might do," Betty said, plucking two buttons from the tin, neither the right size nor shade.

Margaret smiled politely. "I'll keep looking, shall I? You two go on with what you're doing. I know Mrs. Budgeon wants those new tablecloths soon."

Fiona shook her head. "Why she has us making new cloths and table napkins, I'll never know."

Margaret asked, "Do you mean, because the Upchurches don't often entertain?"

"Not for ages. They never even have anyone to dine, save that friend of Mr. Lewis's."

"A handsome devil he is," Betty said.

"Devil is right."

Were they referring to Mr. Saxby or to Lewis himself? Personally she had never thought Piers Saxby handsome. He was too much the dandy for her tastes. Lewis was undoubtedly handsome. But a devil? She didn't think either man deserved that title.

Margaret sat down and sifted through the entire tin without finding a suitable match—or four buttons of any kind to replace the quartet of buttons running from high waist to neck.

Betty tied off her thread and sighed. "Time to fetch the clean sheets from the laundry." She propped her hands on the arms of her chair and levered herself up.

Margaret rose. "Why don't I go? You two are busy, and this gown can wait."

"Would you? That's kind of you, Nora." Betty eased back into her chair.

Fiona's eyes narrowed, no doubt questioning her motives.

The truth was, Margaret simply wanted an excuse to leave the house and walk into Weavering Street without Betty knowing Miss Upchurch had entrusted her with the errand. She dared not, however, go without informing Mrs. Budgeon.

Margaret retrieved the clean sheets from the laundry maid in the washhouse and carried them to the linen cupboard for the house-keeper to check in. Once there, she explained her errand.

"Very well, Nora." Mrs. Budgeon surprised her by agreeing readily. "I take it I can trust you to return directly?"

"Yes, ma'am." Margaret gestured with her hand. "There and back."

The housekeeper nodded.

Margaret asked, "Would you mind keeping this between us?"

The housekeeper frowned. "Why should it be a secret?"

"It's only that I don't want Betty to feel slighted."

Mrs. Budgeon studied her. Margaret was afraid she'd said too much, been too presumptuous—as though an upper housemaid could have anything to fear from a lowly newcomer like her.

"Very well, Nora. I take your meaning. No use in hurt feelings if they can be avoided. But should Miss Upchurch decide to make the situation of your helping her more . . . official . . . some hurt feelings will be inevitable."

"I am not hoping or pushing for anything official . . . or permanent, Mrs. Budgeon. I only want to help where I am able."

One brow quirked. "Well. We shall see."

A few minutes later, reticule over her wrist and bonnet tied beneath her chin, Margaret let herself from the servants' door, up the recessed stairs, and across the drive. She relished the rare bit of freedom, of solitude, of sunshine and fresh air. Of not having her hands in lye or polish or turpentine. Crunching along the gravel path between gardens and lawn, she inhaled deeply of roses and freshly scythed grass and strolled happily up the road. She didn't see Jester and wondered where the dog was.

She had just reached the boardwalk fronting the row of Weavering Street shops when Nathaniel Upchurch stepped from the blacksmith's stall across the road, Jester at his heel. Her stomach gave a little lurch. Nathaniel glanced over and frowned. He looked perplexed, perhaps even disapproving, at seeing one of his housemaids strolling through the hamlet. She ducked her head.

If they met on the street, would he greet her? She doubted it. She was only a servant, after all. He kept his distance from the servants, except for Mr. Hudson. He seemed to treat Mr. Hudson more like a friend than a steward.

Jester had no such reservations. The dog bounded across the road, tail wagging, tongue lolling. She patted his head in greeting and kept walking. As she approached the chandler's, she saw, from the corner of her eye, Mr. Upchurch crossing the road in her direction. Her pulse pounded. She turned away, feigning interest in the display window. For a moment, in her self-conscious awareness of being watched, the contents of the display window remained a blur, but then she blinked them into focus. She scanned the items in the window yet again, heart sinking.

The chatelaine was gone.

Dread filling her, Margaret hurried into the shop, Nathaniel Up-church and his dog forgotten. The thin shopkeeper looked up from his counter as she approached.

"The chatelaine, sir. Is it gone?"

"No, it's right here. Brought it up front to display it proper."

"Oh." She exhaled a sigh of relief. "Good." She hesitated. "May I see what buttons you have?"

"Buttons?" He seemed disappointed but quickly recovered. "Of course." He pulled out a long shallow drawer filled with buttons of every variety and laid it on the counter before her.

She selected two buttons of varying shades of bluish-green. As she held them up to compare them, the image of Betty's grieving blue eyes appeared before her. She blinked the image away. Lying on the counter nearby, the chatelaine beckoned her attention, but Margaret resisted, spending the next quarter hour looking not only at buttons, but ribbon trim, lace, and fabric.

In the end she selected four new buttons, a few yards of ribbon, and a length of sheer lawn from which to fashion a fichu. Again the chatelaine drew her eye. For a fleeting moment, she thought about forgoing the falderals and purchasing the chatelaine with Miss Upchurch's money instead. Would Helen even notice mismatched buttons? But Margaret quickly scolded herself for even considering the idea. She was a vicar's daughter. A lady. A trusted servant. The irony of considering herself both lady and servant in a single thought struck her, and she bit her lip.

She handed over one of Miss Upchurch's guineas and then carefully slid the smaller coins the shopkeeper proffered as change into her reticule. As she did she spied her cameo necklace nestled inside. The gift from her father. Irreplaceable. Dear. She pressed her eyes closed.

What would you have me do, Papa? She silently asked. *What would you have me do, almighty God?* She bit the inside of her cheek, but still tears pricked her eyes.

Heart thudding, Margaret reached in and grasped the cameo necklace by its gold clasp and slowly, reverently extracted it. The hawk-eyed shopkeeper watched every move, his gaze riveted on the gold chain, the fine if modest-sized cameo. She laid the cameo on the counter, its chain spiraling down beside it, her stiff fingers holding firmly to its clasp.

Two mornings later, Helen Upchurch inspected the made-over walking dress in astonishment. "Why, you did more than sew on new buttons, Nora. This is lovely."

"I'm glad you like it, miss."

Margaret was very glad, because she had spent far too much time working on it, staying up into the wee hours the last two nights to finish the stitching. She had added a border of trefoils around its hem, contrasting cuffs, and a wide band of the same material at the waist.

Helen looked up at her. "You did all this with only the few coins I gave you?"

"And odds and ends I found in Miss Nash's old room."

Helen chuckled. "How strange to hear you say her name when you have never met her."

"That's what the others call the room."

"I suppose they think it odd that I have not engaged another maid?"

Margaret shrugged. "A little." She hesitated. "May I ask why you have not?"

Helen sat on the dressing room chair and faced her. "You see, Miss Nash was my mother's maid. Mamma was very fond of her. I was happy to keep her on after Mamma died. But when Miss Nash reached a certain age, she began to slip a little. Mentally and physically. She began doing my hair in little girl ringlets and sewing a great many youthful frills and flounces to my gowns. So I convinced her to retire. She will live out her life in a snug cottage on our estate. She was loath to go, but I assured her she had done her duty by me and I no longer needed a maid dedicated solely to my appearance. I had, after all, given up my social life. My days of balls and routs and flirtations were over. Betty could help me dress and pin my hair when needed. If I hired a new lady's maid, Miss Nash would take it as a slight, I fear. She might come to think it was not that I no longer *needed* her, but that I no longer *wanted* her."

"And did you?"

Helen sighed. "You saw the condition of my frocks? They were not so much better while Miss Nash was still here. She even once scolded me for no longer fitting into my little-girl stays, as though she had only just noticed I had developed a bosom."

"But Miss Helen . . ."

She waved away Margaret's argument before she could voice it. "The truth is, I really don't care. I have no desire to spend a great deal of time on my appearance, or the family's money on fashion. It simply does not matter to me."

Margaret was formulating a suitable reply, but Helen cut her off with uncharacteristic defensiveness. "On second thought, I shall wear my old grey gown again. I have no need to dress especially well today."

"But—"

"That will be all, Nora. You may return to your duties."

That evening, Margaret stood in her room, gently stretching her weary neck, shoulder, and arm muscles as she waited for Betty to come and unlace her stays. Behind her, the bedchamber door banged open.

"How dare you?"

Margaret spun toward the door, thankful her wig stayed in place. Fiona stood there, hands on her hips, clearly in high dudgeon.

"Mrs. Budgeon sent me to the chandler's this afternoon. How surprised I was to find Betty's chatelaine gone." Fiona advanced into the room, expression menacing. "And who bought it, I ask Mr. Johnston. And what does he tell me? A housemaid with spectacles and a great deal of dark hair."

Fiona's eyes narrowed to mere slits. "Ya know how much it means to her. How dare ya buy Betty's chatelaine for yarself?"

"She didn't."

Both women turned. Betty stood in the threshold, cradling the chatelaine in both hands.

"She bought it for me."

Margaret had slipped into Betty's room that morning and left it on her bedside table, wrapped in tissue.

Betty's eyes glistened with tears and fastened on Margaret. "Thank you. I shall pay you back when I can."

Margaret shook her head. "You needn't. It was the least I could do. I hope it makes up for the trouble I've caused you."

Betty winked, a tear spilling over her round cheek. "I wouldn't go that far."

Margaret smiled. The surprise and joy on Betty's face eased her pain over the loss of her cameo. For the moment, at least.

Several mornings later, Fiona knocked on her door. Actually knocked. When Margaret opened the door to her, the maid stepped inside and thrust something into her hands.

"What's this?" Margaret asked, unfolding a stiff white garment.

"Short stays what lace up the front. You can get them on and off yarself."

Margaret pulled her gaze from material to maid. "You made this for me?"

Fiona grimaced. "It isn't a gift, now is it? Those fancy stays of yars aren't suitable for a working girl. And it isn't fair to Betty, always having to be dressing ya morning and night. This—"

"I agree," Margaret interrupted. "Is this the sort you and Betty wear?"

"It is. And if it's good enough for the rest of us, it's good enough for you."

Margaret smiled. "More than good enough, Fiona. Why, I have rarely seen such fine stitching."

Fiona winced and fidgeted. "Go on, that's going it a bit brown. You'd think I'd given ya silk drawers or somethin'." She gestured with both hands. "Now, let's see how it fits."

Over her shift, Margaret slipped her hands through each armhole of the short stays, which were rather like a man's waistcoat, though not as long. The stays were made of sturdy corded cotton with gussets, four or five pair of holes up the front, and even a few embroidered embellishments. Margaret pulled the two sides together over her bosom, effectively lifting and supporting her breasts.

"Now take that string there," Fiona said, "and go back and forth between those holes, like ya was sewing."

Margaret did as instructed, then tied the string.

Fiona surveyed her work. "Fits ya rather well, if I do say so myself."

"It does indeed. Thank you again."

"Mind you, I only did it so ya might dress yarself from now on."

Apparently, the Irishwoman would rather die than to be thought doing Nora a favor. Margaret grinned. "Still, I appreciate it. You might simply have told me to make one myself."

Fiona tilted her head to one side. "Now, why didn't I think of that?"

But Margaret thought she saw the faintest glimmer of humor in Fiona's green eyes.

This hand is surely far too fine,
This foot so dainty and small.
The manner of speaking which I have,
My waist, my bustle,
These would never be found
On a lady's maid!

—André Rieu, "Mein Herr Marquis"

Chapter 15

Horse hooves. The jingle of harnesses. High in the attic, Margaret heard them only distantly.

On that drizzly mid-September afternoon, Margaret had been assigned to clean out the old schoolroom, now used for storage. Beneath the window, pails caught drips from the leaking ceiling. Along the far wall, several trunks lay in a neat row like coffins. In one of these she had found space to stack the primers, slates, and maps which had been left in a dusty, moldering pile in the chimney corner. In another trunk, she found layer upon layer of old ball gowns a decade out of fashion. From Miss Helen's coming-out days, she guessed.

Mrs. Budgeon had also instructed her to clean out the fireplace and flue after years of disuse. Why now? Margaret had wondered but managed to bite her tongue. Apparently the housekeeper wanted to make sure the new maid didn't begin to think too highly of herself.

Margaret was attempting to clean the flue with, yes, the flue brush. She was foolishly proud of herself for identifying the correct tool. Vaguely she heard the sounds of hurrying feet and the ringing of bells but, concentrating on her task, paid them little heed.

The angle for cleaning the flue was awkward. Kneeling before the grate, Margaret leaned in, her head inside the fireplace. For a fleeting second, she thought it fortunate she wore a dark wig, for if she was not careful her hair would be black soon enough. With that thought, she pulled the white cap from her wig and tossed it out of range, not wanting to spoil it. Margaret scraped the inside of the flue with her brush, dislodging a wad of sooty buildup and a cloud of dust. She coughed and squeezed her eyes shut, wondering what coal dust did to one's lungs and vision. She scraped again.

The door behind her burst open and Margaret started, hitting her head on the lintel.

She lowered her head and saw Betty run in, gesturing frantically. "Here you are!" She huffed. "Did you not hear the bells?"

Margaret checked her wig with a black-streaked hand as she backed from the fireplace. "Not really. Not with my head up the chimney. Why?"

"It's a call to assembly. In the main hall." Betty surveyed Margaret's face, wincing. "You've got soot on your spectacles. Your face too. But there's no time. Everyone else is down there already." She bent and extracted a clean cloth from the housemaid's box nearby and handed it to Margaret. "Here."

Taking it, Margaret rose from stinging knees and wiped her hands. "Assembly for what?" she asked. "We've already had prayers."

"Someone's come, and we're to assemble immediately. That's all I know. But that's ten minutes ago now."

She poked a hand into Margaret's back and turned her toward the door. "Let's go!"

Dropping the cloth, Margaret bent quickly and retrieved her cap, settling it back on her wig. "All right?" She angled her face toward Betty as they hurried to the stairway.

Betty grimaced. "Here, take my handkerchief and wipe your spectacles at least."

"But that's your best handkerchief."

"Go on, we haven't time to argue."

Margaret removed her glasses, polishing the lenses as she clambered down the attic stairs, almost tripping and missing a step.

"Better?" she asked, slipping the spectacles on once more.

Betty glanced at her and sighed. "It'll have to do. Stay in the back."

They reached the next floor. When Margaret would have continued down the back stairs to the ground floor, Betty pulled her by the wrist past the family bedchambers toward the main stairway the servants were not to use—except when sweeping and polishing. Margaret wondered why but did not argue.

Then she saw. The staff had gathered in the hall below—outdoor servants and estate workers as well. Gamekeeper, carpenter, grooms, stable boys, gardeners, and others she did not know stood on one side of the hall floor. Behind them stood the laundry maids, the hen woman, the spider brusher, and the dairy maid. When the floor had become too crowded, other servants had lined up in rows behind them on the wide steps, filling the stairs past the first landing. Monsieur Fournier, Hester, the kitchen maids, and scullery maid. Behind them Fiona, the footmen, and hall boy. The estate workers were not obligated to attend morning prayers at Fairbourne Hall, so Margaret had never seen the entire staff assembled before.

Margaret followed Betty down the steps, hoping to join the crowd as quietly and unobtrusively as possible. She found herself ducking her head, as though that would make her invisible or draw less attention to her soiled self.

Margaret stopped on the stair behind the blond second footman. Betty stood beside her.

"What's happening, Craig?" Betty whispered.

He shrugged.

Margaret looked down past the waiting flock of servants to the four people standing on the other side of the hall facing them. Standing a little apart from the men, Mrs. Budgeon surveyed the group, as though mentally counting their ranks. Appearing satisfied, she turned to the three men—Mr. Hudson, Nathaniel Upchurch, and . . .

Margaret froze. *Sterling Benton. Here. Now.* Standing for all intents and purposes in the same room with her. Her heart rate accelerated, thudding hard.

Sterling made an impressive and commanding presence with his silver hair, deep blue frock coat, and ebony walking stick. His hat was carefully held by the under butler, but he had not surrendered his coat. Hopefully that meant he did not intend to stay long.

Mr. Hudson said something to Nathaniel. Nathaniel nodded and took a half step forward, facing them squarely and clearing his throat.

"Good afternoon, everyone. This gentleman is Mr. Sterling Benton of London. I will let him tell you why he is here and ask that you give him your full attention."

Sterling stepped forward, turning something in his hands.

"I am here today because my stepdaughter has been missing for nearly a month. My dear wife, her mother, is beside herself, as you can well imagine."

Margaret could hardly breathe.

"I don't know why she left. She did have a bit of a . . . lover's quarrel . . . with her intended, and may have flown in a fit of pique. She is an impulsive girl, I admit. But whatever the reason, I want to find her and return her safely to her mother, and to her repentant future husband. All will be forgiven. We simply want her home."

He lifted the object in his hands. A miniature portrait. "This is her likeness, painted several years ago. I would like you to pass it one person to the next, so each may see it. Her name is Margaret Macy. She is four and twenty years old. If any of you have seen her, please speak up. Or, if anyone sees her after I leave, tell the steward here and he promises to send word directly."

Margaret's ears buzzed; her chest, neck, and face felt hot and sticky. While each person looked at the portrait, then passed it on, Sterling Benton looked closely at him or her. Looking for a reaction, or for *her*?

The minutes felt like painful hours standing on broken glass. Fearing she might faint, Margaret forced herself to breathe deeply, barely resisting the urge to pant, or duck down, or flee.

Finally the portrait reached the row ahead of them. Craig looked at it quickly, shook his head, and passed it up to Betty. Betty glanced at it, hesitated, looked again, then handed it to Margaret. Margaret swallowed. How strange to see her former image while in her current circumstances. How young the girl in the portrait looked, light yellow hair curled and piled high around her face, fair brows above proud blue eyes, pale cheeks, and pink lips. It didn't seem like her. Not anymore.

"Do you recognize her?" Sterling Benton called up.

Too late, Margaret realized she had held on to the portrait too long and had drawn attention to herself. She quickly handed it back to Betty with a shake of her head. She dug an elbow into Betty's side.

"Uh no, sir," Betty answered for her. "Sorry, sir. She's a pretty thing though."

Mrs. Budgeon called up, "Mr. Benton did not ask for an assessment of her beauty, Betty, but thank you."

The portrait made its way back down more rapidly, passed from hand to hand. Mrs. Budgeon gave it to Mr. Hudson, who glanced at it, looked again, and then murmured, "Betty is correct."

He passed it to Nathaniel Upchurch, who returned it to Sterling Benton without a glance.

Sterling looked around the hall once more before pinning Nathaniel with a look. "And where is your good sister?"

Nathaniel said evenly, "My sister is not much out in society these days, so it is highly unlikely she would have come across Mar . . . your stepdaughter."

Sterling gave a thin smile. "Still, she is a woman, and women can be so much more discerning than men, I find. Don't you?"

Nathaniel stared at the man. Without looking away from him, he said crisply, "Mrs. Budgeon, would you please send for Miss Upchurch?"

"Yes, sir."

But Mrs. Budgeon, looking up at the crowd blocking the stairs, speared Margaret with a look and commanded, "Nora, please ask your mistress to join us."

Margaret did not move, the words barely registering in her frozen brain. It was Betty's turn to elbow her. Coming to life, Nora turned and hurried up the stairs, feeling a pair of eyes scorching her back.

She all but ran down the corridor and into Helen's room without knocking. She rushed straight to the washstand. "Your presence is requested in the hall, miss."

Miss Upchurch looked up expectantly from her writing desk, her brow furrowed. "Oh? Why?"

With nervous energy, Margaret washed her hands, then retrieved the new fichu from a drawer. "A man has come," she said, barely managing an accent. "A Mr. Benton."

Helen cast her a quick look. "Sterling Benton?"

Margaret nodded, arranging the fichu around Helen's shoulders and tucking it into the neckline of her gold day dress.

"What does he want?"

Margaret swallowed. "Says his stepdaughter has gone missing. And he's showing her miniature and asking if anyone has seen her."

"And did anyone recognize . . . the woman in the portrait?"

Margaret repinned a lock of hair that had come loose from Helen's twist. "Only Mr. Upchurch, I think."

"Why does Mr. Benton ask for me?"

"I don't know, miss. To ask if you've seen the girl, I suppose."

For a moment the two women looked at one another face-to-face and eye-to-eye.

Helen asked soberly, "And have I?"

Margaret pressed her lips together to keep them from trembling. Her throat went dry. She whispered, "That's for you to say."

Helen cocked her head to one side. "But?"

In the silence, the mantel clock ticked.

Hoping to give her a way out, Margaret stammered, "But . . . your brother did tell him that, *your* seeing . . . her . . . was highly unlikely. You not being out much in society."

Helen frowned. "Be that as it may, I have eyes, have I not?"

Margaret lowered her gaze. "Yes, miss."

She had said the wrong thing. Now what would Helen say?

Margaret followed Helen back to the stairway, staying a few yards behind her, matching her stately pace. She was reluctant to return to the hall, her every nerve pulsing a warning—*Turn around, run, flee!*

Instead she put one foot in front of the other and followed her mistress. Would Helen expose her? What would happen if she did? She would lose her place to live, her dignity, her freedom. Would she be forced to leave with Sterling? She had nowhere else to go.

The people on the stairs parted like the Red Sea to allow their mistress to pass between them.

Margaret resumed her place beside Betty.

"Ah, Miss Upchurch." Sterling Benton beamed his icy, enigmatic smile. "How good of you to join us. A pleasure to see you again, even though one would wish for happier circumstances."

"Mr. Benton."

He handed her the portrait. "You may recall my stepdaughter, Margaret Macy?"

Helen regarded the framed image. "I recall Miss Macy, though of course she was not your stepdaughter when last I saw her in London. She was the daughter of Mr. Stephen Macy, an exceptional gentleman and clergyman, gone from this world too soon."

Margaret's heart squeezed to hear the words. She had not realized Helen had more than a passing acquaintance with her father.

Mr. Benton's mouth tightened fractionally. "How kind of you to say."

Helen inclined her head.

"You have heard, I trust, that Margaret has gone missing?"

"I did. Mr. Saxby brought the news from town a few weeks ago. Do you fear some harm has befallen her?"

"I pray not. That is why I am doing everything in my power to find her."

"Is it?" she asked archly.

Careful, Miss Helen . . . Margaret thought, worried Miss Upchurch might unintentionally tip her hand.

"Did she leave alone?" Helen asked.

"As far as I know, though she may have taken her maid with her."

"The maid is missing too?"

He shifted his feet. "She was dismissed from our employ the day Margaret disappeared."

"May I ask why you are so concerned? The Margaret Macy I remember was young and foolish. Impulsive even."

Margaret winced. *Ouch* . . .

"I hope you take no offense, Mr. Benton?"

"Not at all."

Nathaniel Upchurch cleared his throat, perhaps aware of the listening ears of many fidgeting servants. He said, "Why do we not continue this discussion in the library. In private?"

Mrs. Budgeon and Mr. Hudson exchanged relieved looks. As Mr. Hudson dismissed the staff to return to their duties, Margaret felt similar relief but also dread, wondering what would be said about her when she was not there to hear.

In the library, Nathaniel leaned against the desk, arms crossed. His brain pounded painfully with Benton's words "*her repentant future husband . . . future husband . . .*"

Helen took a seat and gestured for Benton to do the same, but he refused her offer and continued to stand.

Helen asked, "So how do you know Margaret hasn't simply gone off on a lark? A shopping trip or a visit with friends?"

Benton pulled a face. "For nearly a month?"

"Surely she had the means," Helen said. "A girl like that always has a good deal of money in her purse, has she not?"

Benton looked away. "Actually she did not. We were . . . forced to stop any allowance to her. Her expenditures had become exorbitant."

"Ah. And what of friends or family she might have gone to?"

"I have already been to see her friends and sent a man to call on her few remaining relatives. No one has seen her."

"So you believed they had not seen her but, I take it, question my brother's word, as you insisted on seeing me?"

Benton fidgeted. It was the first time Nathaniel had seen the man look uncomfortable. "Perhaps you are not aware that your brother Lewis danced with Margaret and paid her several calls in the past and again earlier this season."

His sister shot Nathaniel a look. "Did he?"

Nathaniel ignored an irrational stab of jealousy and answered coolly, "Lewis dances with any number of women, as you well know. I can assure you, Benton, your stepdaughter was not alone in receiving his attentions."

"Do you suspect an elopement?" Helen asked, incredulous. "Lewis would never do such a thing. And why would you think Margaret would countenance the notion? I thought you said she was all but engaged to your nephew."

Sterling stilled. "I never mentioned my nephew. Who told you that?"

Helen hesitated only a second. "I . . . suppose Mr. Saxby must have mentioned it with the rest of the town gossip."

Benton studied her face. "Yes, Margaret was on the cusp of being engaged to my nephew, Marcus Benton. They did quarrel, I admit. But nothing serious. He is a very forgiving young man and still has every intention of marrying her."

Another stab of jealousy. Nathaniel clenched a fist and endeavored to keep his expression neutral. "You still haven't explained why you are here. Lewis has gone back to town."

"I have already been to see Lewis. Of course he denies any knowledge of Margaret's whereabouts. I suppose I thought she might have come here to see Lewis and stayed on even after he refused her."

"Why would Margaret hope for a proposal of marriage from my brother if she is as attached as you say to your nephew?" Helen asked.

"Who can understand women? Perhaps she seeks to make him jealous."

Helen frowned.

Sterling ran a hand through his thick silver hair. "I am here because I am running out of ideas of where to look for her. I am growing desperate."

"Why 'desperate'?"

Sterling regarded Helen warily. "Do you not think me capable of concern for my wife's children? If only we could be assured she was all right. Receive some word of her . . ." He handed her the portrait once more. "Are you certain you have not seen or heard from her, Miss Upchurch?"

Helen met his apparently frank gaze a moment longer, then looked at the portrait again. "A woman would not see such a lovely face and not recognize her, Mr. Benton. A man either, not with all that glorious blond hair." She glanced up at Nathaniel. "Would you not agree, Nate?"

Nathaniel stared dumbly at her. "I . . . wouldn't know."

Helen rose and returned the portrait. "Now, will that be all, Mr. Benton? If I were you, I should not worry. I am certain your wife will receive news of her any day now and by her own hand, assuring you of her continuing health and safety."

Slowly shaking her head, Helen gave Sterling a feline smile. "A young woman like Margaret Macy—who can guess what she might do on a whim?"

Margaret studied herself in the small looking glass in her room. How changed she was. It was little wonder no one had linked the Margaret Elinor Macy of the portrait to the Nora Garret staring back at her now. The hair and darkened brows were strikingly different, of course. And the smudged spectacles did mask her eyes to some degree. The Miss Macy of old would never have worn so dowdy a cap or a stained maid's apron. But the changes went deeper than that. Her face was thinner now. After nearly a month of constant hard work, simple meals, and rare sweets, she had lost weight. Her cheekbones were more prominent, with new hollows beneath, and her jawline more defined.

She removed her father's spectacles. She actually saw better with them. She had probably needed spectacles for some time but had been too vain to admit it. Without the lenses, her eyes still seemed different. But how, she could not say for certain. Less noticeable dark circles now that she was sleeping somewhat better? Less world weary?

And even without the spectacles, she was beginning to see herself more clearly than before.

*Housemaids were meant to be invisible, and all
cleaning had to be performed either before the family got up or
while they were absent. As one housemaid later wrote, "It was
assumed, I suppose, that the fairies had been at the rooms."*

—Trevor May, *The Victorian Domestic Servant*

Chapter 16

After breakfast the next morning, Margaret went upstairs to Miss Upchurch's room with some trepidation. She wondered if Helen would tell her what had been said behind closed doors yesterday. What Sterling had said, what Helen had revealed . . . or not revealed. Margaret hoped she would tell her, even as she feared what she might learn.

When Margaret entered, Helen was not sitting at her dressing table as usual. Instead she stood beside her desk, pointing down to a sheet of paper lying atop it.

"Sit."

Margaret hesitated at Helen's stern syllable. "What . . . ?"

"I suppose you haven't paper and ink of your own," Helen said. "So sit and write your letter here."

"Letter?"

Helen's eyes flashed. "To your mother. You do have a mother, I trust? One who might be worrying and wondering where you've gone?"

Margaret swallowed. Realizing there was no longer any point in altering her voice with Helen, she said quietly, "I have wanted to write. But were I to post a letter from Maidstone, would not the postal markings divulge my whereabouts to—"

"To the evil stepfather?" Helen archly supplied. "I have thought of that. Hudson travels to London tomorrow to meet with a shipwright or some such. I will ask him to post the letter while he is there."

Margaret marveled at her kindness. "Thank you."

Helen gave a dismissive wave of her hand. "Your mother deserves to know you are alive and well."

"You are right." Margaret sat down at Helen's desk, picked up the quill, dipped it in the ink, and began her letter home.

My dear Mamma, Caroline, and Gilbert,

I am sorry I have not written sooner. I hope you have not been unduly concerned about me. I am fine and in good health.

Pray do not worry about me or try to find me. I am content where I am and do not wish to return home for reasons you, Mamma, as well as Mr. Benton, understand.

I trust Mr. Marcus Benton will be taking his leave of Berkeley Square very soon. Do bid him farewell for me.

Attend well to your studies, Caroline and Gilbert, know that I miss you, and never forget how much I love you.

Sincerely,
Margaret

Finishing her letter, she blotted the ink, read it over, and then folded it. She fleetingly wondered if the Turkey Mill watermark—paper milled right there in Maidstone—might give her away. Thankfully, it was the most popular paper the country over.

Helen came over and set a lit candle on the desk—Margaret had not even noticed her leave the room for one. Wordlessly, she handed Margaret a stick of sealing wax. Margaret softened the stick over the flame and then applied a circle of wax to the edge of the letter.

Helen gave her a handled seal stamp. "This one is only decorative, not the family crest or anything identifiable."

"You've thought of everything," Margaret murmured, pressing the stamp into the wax and lifting it, checking to make certain the seal held. She was glad Helen had thought of that. For though she had addressed the letter to her mother, she had no doubt Sterling would read it as well—and scour it for clues.

Two days later, on a rainy Sunday afternoon, Margaret found herself bored and with nothing to do. Her work was finished. The mending caught up. She had nothing new to read. She thought to have a chat with Betty, but when she paused outside her door, the sound of soft snoring told her the upper housemaid was enjoying a rare and well-deserved nap.

Feeling lonely, Margaret took herself belowstairs. The stillroom was empty—no sign of sweet Hester. She continued on. Entering the kitchen, she found the large room uncommonly quiet. She was surprised Monsieur Fournier and the kitchen maids were not scurrying about as usual, preparing the family's dinner.

Instead she found the chef alone at the kitchen worktable, feet propped on a crate, eyes closed, listening to . . . ? She paused to listen and heard the faint sound of the pianoforte being played.

"Good afternoon," she whispered.

The man's bushy eyebrows shot up as his eyes opened. "Ah, Nora." He straightened.

She glanced around. "I haven't seen the kitchen this quiet since we were all given a half day for Miss Upchurch's birthday."

He nodded. "The family is dining with an uncle zis evening. So, for a few hours, at least, I am a man of leisure." He lifted a carefree gesture with both hands.

She smiled. "Something tells me you wouldn't like being a man of leisure for long. You enjoy your work too much."

He pursed his lip and pivoted his hand in a gesture of *comme ci, comme ça.*

She cocked her head to the side, listening to the distant music. "Does Mrs. Budgeon play every Sunday?"

"Not every, but now and again."

"Has she no family nearby to visit? I never hear her speak of children or a husband."

He shook his head. "Mrs. Budgeon is not married. It is customary for housekeepers to be called Mrs., whether they are married or no. You know zis, yes?"

"Oh yes. I had heard that." She regarded him a moment, then asked, "Do you ever think about working somewhere more grand? Where your skills might be better appreciated?"

His eyes sparkled. "You hope to be rid of me?"

Margaret felt her cheeks heat. "Not at all."

He shrugged easily. "Mr. Lewis did offer me a post in London. He entertains a great deal, I understand. Many distinguished guests."

"Why did you not accept?"

Monsieur Fournier did not answer for several moments, and she feared she had offended him by prying.

Finally he said, "You know the housekeeper remains at one house—she does not travel for the season. She stays with her maids to keep all ready for the family's return."

It was an odd answer. Or was it? "I see . . ." Margaret murmured. She did see, she thought. Or was beginning to.

He cocked his head, listening almost dreamily as another melody melted through the kitchen door. "That is a Jadin sonata. She plays it well, does she not?"

Nathaniel had remained busier than usual during the last week. He had been obliged to attend a series of commissioners' meetings about local road repairs and to meet with the vicar to devise plans for relief of the parish poor. Because of his responsibilities at home, he'd sent Hudson to London in his stead to meet with a shipwright to discuss repair estimates. During Hudson's absence, Nathaniel was busier yet, taking on his steward's duties as well as his own—overseeing the carpenter and slater repairing the roof and the workmen erecting a new fence.

He had greeted Hudson's return three days later with relief. Hudson reported that the *Ecclesia* had suffered no further vandalism, and that he had published the reward Nathaniel offered for the capture of Abel Preston, the so-called Poet Pirate. Finally, Hudson handed him the repair estimates from the shipwright. The figures stole Nathaniel's breath. So high. Too high. They would have to seek another bid.

Now that Hudson had resumed his normal duties, Nathaniel spent the morning catching up on his own correspondence. In the afternoon, he went upstairs to relax with Helen in the family sitting room over a game of draughts. Helen beat him handily. As usual.

Hudson knocked and entered. Helen, Nathaniel noticed, straightened her already impressive posture. His sister always seemed to stiffen in the new steward's presence.

"Miss Upchurch. Mr. Upchurch."

"Hello, Hudson," Nathaniel said. "Did you need something?"

He hesitated. "Actually, I hoped to have a word with *Miss* Upchurch."

Helen folded her hands primly in her lap. "Of course, Mr. Hudson. What is it?"

"It is your Miss Nash. Your former lady's maid, I understand."

"I know who she is."

"Of course. I wonder . . ."

Helen's expression tightened. "Has something happened to her?" she asked quickly. "Has she taken ill?"

"No, miss, it isn't that. She seems in good health, relatively speaking. But her cottage, on the other hand, is not."

"Well, fix it. Is that not part of your responsibility as steward, Mr. Hudson?"

Nathaniel was surprised at his sister's almost snappish tone.

"That's just it, miss," Hudson said. "She refuses to allow me or the estate carpenter inside to make repairs. I only learned about the leaking roof and moldering floors when Mrs. Sackett—"

Helen's brows furrowed. "Mrs. Sackett?"

"The gardener's wife. She visited the old woman and was appalled at the condition of the place. She convinced her husband to report it to me."

"I see." She pulled a face. "No, I don't see, actually. What has this to do with me?"

Hudson patiently explained, "When I spoke to Miss Nash, at her door, she said she was never allowed men in her rooms at Fairbourne Hall and doesn't mean to begin now. She said you would understand and support her decision."

"Oh dear."

Hudson fidgeted with the coins in his coat pocket. "You see my predicament."

"I do." Helen considered. "Perhaps we might go and speak with her together, Mr. Hudson? See if we might make her see reason?"

Hudson's eyes twinkled. "I'd happily accompany you anywhere, miss. But make Miss Nash see reason . . . ? I shall leave that to you."

An hour or so later, Nathaniel walked across the lawn toward the road, tossing a stick to Jester as he went. He was on his way to meet with the Weavering Street craftsman he'd commissioned to make new cradle scythes for the upcoming harvest.

Hudson and his sister strolled into view, returning from the direction of the estate cottages. They were talking and laughing companionably, apparently successful in their quest. Helen smiled up at Hudson, and he was glad to see his sister warming to their new steward. One look at the man's beaming face, however, and Nathaniel realized Hudson was long past *warm*.

Margaret steeled herself, as she always did, when it was time to enter one of the men's bedchambers—especially the first time of a morning, when the occupant was still in his bed. She had gotten over the initial shock of having to do so but still did not relish the prospect. Her early training was imbedded too deeply within her. Heaven help her if anyone ever found out she had done so not once, but every morning for months.

Margaret took a deep breath and eased open Nathaniel Upchurch's door. Slipping inside, she closed the door behind her so any corridor noises would not disturb the sleeper. It was too late, however, for the sleeper seemed disturbed already. Nathaniel's head thrashed from side to side, though his eyes remained closed. *What in the world?*

One leg, dark with hair, escaped the bedclothes. Cheeks warm, she averted her eyes. She delivered the water, found the chamber pot blessedly empty, and made to leave. But Nathaniel groaned like a man in pain. He was having a bad dream, apparently. A very bad dream. She risked another glance, knowing she ought to slip out before he awoke. How rude an awakening would it be to find a housemaid staring down at him?

He moaned again, a tortured sound. If only he had a valet to rouse him and end his misery. But there was only her. A wave of dark hair fell over his brow, and with those piercing eyes closed, he looked younger, less dangerous. For a moment he reminded her of Gilbert, who had experienced terrible nightmares as a young child. She had never hesitated to wake him, to soothe him, to stroke the hair from his brow.

Margaret took a tentative step forward. From the weak morning light leaking from between shutters and transom, she saw Nathaniel's face contort. Poor man. Of what must he be dreaming?

Perhaps if she whispered to him, the dream would end, or at least shift, without him waking and she could slip out undetected.

She took another step toward the bed and leaned near. "Sir?" she whispered. "Sir?" Gingerly, she reached a hand toward his shoulder. Dared she give him the barest tap?

His hand shot out and he grabbed her arm. She gasped. His eyes flew open, but they were glazed with that vague, unfocused look she recognized from Gilbert's sleepwalking days. His eyes might be open, but Nathaniel Upchurch was still asleep.

She tried to extract her arm, but his grip was too tight. "Sir, you're dreaming. Wake—"

He rolled toward her, grasping her other arm as well. "Margaret?"

Her heart lurched. Was he dreaming of her, or of some other Margaret?

"Cannot save her . . ." The ragged timbre of his voice tore at her heart.

"Sir. You're all right," she soothed. "You're safe." She hesitated, then lifted one of her captured hands and awkwardly patted his arm. "Margaret is safe."

He suddenly pulled her toward him and she lost her balance, falling to her knees beside the bed. He pulled her closer yet, until their faces were very near.

Stunned, Margaret did not move quickly enough to escape his grasp. Was not sure she wanted to escape him. Nathaniel Upchurch was dreaming of her, touching her, perhaps about to kiss her. Was she dreaming as well?

She could feel his hot breath on the sensitive skin of her upper lip.

"Margaret . . ." The name was part groan, part growl.

She was filled with a sweet, aching longing to bridge the lingering space between them. She leaned down and their lips met in a feather touch. Sparks thrilled her every nerve. He angled his head to deepen the kiss, pressing his mouth to hers, fervently, fiercely. Her head felt light, her pulse pounded.

What was she doing? The heady, delicious kiss took her off guard. She had never expected such a passionate, forceful embrace from a man she had once thought timid. *A man who doesn't know what he is doing,* she reminded herself. *Who is dreaming.*

She, on the other hand, knew very well what she was doing. She tried to pull away but, leaning over as she was, fell forward, her elbows spearing his chest. Crying out, she scrambled out of his hold and to her feet.

"What on earth?" His voice was different now. Lucid, though still hoarse. Awake.

She turned away, flying toward the door.

Incredulous, he called, "What in heaven's name . . . ?"
Too shaken to force an accent, she fled without a word.

Heaven help him. What had just happened? In his mind swirled a quagmire of conflicting thoughts, images, sensations. . . . Had he been dreaming? *Merciful Father.* Had some well-meaning servant slipped into his chamber to calm him, only to be pulled into his bed? What had he been thinking? He squeezed his eyes shut, trying to remember. The dark putrid smoke of the dream laid over him like a heavy cloak, making it hard to breathe. He could still feel the shock, the fury, the terror of the fire. His ship. Being destroyed.

Pieces of the dream returned to him. Had he been calling out loud enough to bring down a servant from the floor above? *Good heavens.* He had not had night terrors since boyhood. He supposed with the recent stress it was not surprising they had returned. But the loss of the ship was not the heaviest weight on his chest, not the elusive, nagging thought flitting just out of sight and recall.

When had the dream changed? He had been clashing swords with Preston, both men trying to reach the gangplank and block the other's escape, when he'd heard a female voice, calling to him. *Margaret.* He had recognized her voice with a start. What was she doing aboard his ship? How had she gotten there? He looked wildly this way and that, trying to locate her. Was she trapped among the rapidly amass-ing wreckage of toppled masts and rigging that had once been his prized possession?

He'd tried to call to her, his voice coming as if through a sea of uncarded wool. She would never hear him over the roar of the fire, the crack and bang of falling timber.

Preston took advantage of his distraction and drove his sword deep into Nathaniel's chest. His heart. Breaking. *Oh, Margaret, why?* Though she had destroyed his happiness and dreams, still he must rescue her. He ran across the deck, hand to his wound, and pushed a fallen mizzenmast out of his way. The smoke burned his eyes and seared his throat. So dry.

"Where are you? We must disembark. I cannot save her."

Then suddenly, miraculously, she was in his arms. Safe. Their embrace had felt so real, so sweetly, painfully real. And suddenly the past evaporated. She was there with him, and that was all that mattered. He would not waste one moment. He pulled her close, relishing the feel of her against him. He pressed his mouth to hers, kissing her deeply, as he had long dreamed of doing . . .

Dreamed . . .

Disappointment drenched his soul. It had only been a dream. A delicious, torturous dream. Had there even been a woman in the room? An innocent housemaid come to empty his slops only to be shocked and appalled by his crazed, groping behavior? He had long promised himself he would never trifle with anyone in his employ—that he would respect the female servants as he did the men. Be the benevolent master his heavenly Father was to His servants.

Nathaniel ran a hand over his face. Paused to feel his lips . . . lips he was so certain had been pressed to Margaret Macy's. What had he done—how would he ever explain? He wasn't even sure which girl it was. The poor thing might be gone by breakfast, after telling a shocked and disapproving Mrs. Budgeon how he had molested her. Or might she keep her post in desperation, but avoid him in terror all her days at Fairbourne Hall?

He grimaced again, trying to remember exactly what had happened, to sift out fact from fiction, reality from dream, and wishing to block the whole episode from his mind. Would he never be over Margaret Macy? How did she manage to torment him over the distance of years and miles, wherever she was now?

But the longer he ruminated, the more the dream faded and the events blurred, until he was not certain a maid had been in his arms at all. In the dim dawn light his room seemed undisturbed. If only his heart and mind could claim as much.

He looked toward the door. Shut. Would a maid have bothered to close it were she fleeing in fear? Unlikely. So perhaps no one had even yet been in his room.

He glanced across the bedchamber in the other direction, and glimpsed water cans on his washstand. His heart fell. He rose and crossed the room as though approaching a trap about to spring. He hoped against hope these were the cans from the night before. He dipped in his finger and winced.

Still warm. Very warm.

After that, Nathaniel had climbed back into bed and lay there for a time, praying. He must have fallen asleep, for when he opened his eyes again, the sun was shining through the windows, brightening his mood, as did the cheerful birdsong. Arnold came in with a tray of coffee and the newspaper and went about setting out his clothes. He seemed the same as always. No disapproving looks or news of a housemaid giving notice.

"And will you be riding this morning, sir? Or fencing?"

"Hmm? Oh. Riding, I think."

Everything was as it should be. The same as the day before and the day before that. Perhaps a maid had brought in water as usual but otherwise it had all been a dream. He was really quite sure of it now. What a relief. No apologies to make. No woman in his bed. No ghostly Miss Macy with ethereal blond hair whispering to him in the night that he was safe. That she was safe. Perhaps it was a sign. God was telling him he was finally past it. His heart was safe—Miss Macy fared well wherever she'd gone, and was none of his concern. Everything was fine. It was time for Nathaniel to get on with life in the here and now.

Invigorated at the thought, Nathaniel threw back the bedclothes. He swung his legs over and for a moment sat on the edge of his bed, bowing his head in thanksgiving for a new day. The sunlight splayed over his nightshirt-clad knees. Something shone on the plain white fabric like a thread of a brighter hue. He pinched the errant thread between thumb and forefinger, preparing to toss it in the rubbish basket, but stopped. Instead, he lifted the thread before him and in the shaft of sunlight saw it was not a thread but rather a long hair. A long blond hair.

He frowned. Who among his staff had such hair? None that he could think of, though he made a practice of not looking often nor directly at the young women in his employ. He supposed it might have come in by way of the laundry. He would not recognize the laundry maids if he passed them in the street. Or perhaps Lewis brought home some lady's hair upon his person and it had transferred to Nathaniel via the laundry. Lewis, he knew, had no lack of female admirers of every description. But even as his logical mind tried to reason away the blond remnant, to avoid linking last night's dream with its subject, he could not succeed for long. He had dreamed of blond Margaret Macy, only to awaken with a long blond hair in his bed? Dear God, have pity on a poor sot. What sort of sign was that?

Margaret pressed two fingers to her lips, still tender from Nathaniel's kiss. A pair of fingers was not so much different than a pair of lips, she reasoned, but somehow the pressure of her fingers, once soft, now already beginning to roughen, felt nothing like his lips had—firm, smooth, yet punctuated with scratchy whiskers on chin and cheek. Just thinking of it caused her to experience anew the sweet heady tension, the hammering heart rate, the delirium of thought and emotion. She had never felt that way in her life and wondered why.

Margaret had been kissed before. She thought back to Marcus Benton's forced kiss not so long ago, his fingers biting into the tender skin of her upper arms. But that act had evoked revulsion, anger, fear . . . not the dreamy longing that lingered over her now, that languor of limb and mind. Marcus's had been an act one wished to forget. Nathaniel's a moment to savor and relive. She told herself she was being foolish. For he had not known what he was doing. If he had known it was her, really her, he would never have kissed her, held her with such urgency. But he had been dreaming of kissing her, so did that not mean something . . . something wonderful? She thought she had killed any feelings he'd had for her. But perhaps she had been mistaken.

How different she would feel if she believed Nathaniel Upchurch had tried to kiss Nora, a defenseless housemaid. She thought of Lewis's flirtatious past and Marcus's outright seduction of girls who felt they had little choice. Margaret thought she understood for the first time why Nathaniel Upchurch never really looked at, and certainly never ogled, his servants. It was to her advantage, for he had not looked at her directly enough to recognize her.

She wondered what it would be like to kiss Nathaniel when he was fully awake. She doubted she would ever know. For awake and in his right mind, a gentleman like Nathaniel Upchurch would only kiss his wife with that measure of unguarded passion. She'd had her chance to be his wife and had spurned it, spurned him. A choice she was beginning to truly regret.

Nathaniel asked Hudson to ride with him that morning, and the steward happily obliged. They rode away from the estate and cantered along a country lane, scaring up grouse and pheasant. Then they slowed their mounts to a leisurely walk, enjoying the swish of horsetails against dragonflies, a gentle September breeze, and companionable silence.

Finally, Nathaniel began, "What do you suppose it means, Hudson, when I dream of a beautiful blond lady and awaken to find a long blond hair in my bed?"

Hudson chuckled. "My goodness, sir. What vivid dreams you must have!"

"You have no idea."

Nathaniel was confident Hudson knew he was not suggesting he had actually had a woman in his bed. Since his change of heart on Barbados, he had made every effort to keep his ways pure. He asked, "Have we some blond housemaid I am unaware of?"

"You seem unaware of all the maids, sir, if I may say." Hudson paused to consider, staring up at the blue sky as though a staff roster were written there. "There is a scullery maid with fair hair, but hers is

a rather short mop of curls. The laundry maid's hair might once have
been considered blond, but it's all but grey now. And your sister's
hair is a rich coffee brown."

Nathaniel gave his steward a sharp look, and Hudson turned away,
face reddening. "Not that I have cause to notice." He cleared his throat.
"I can think of any manner of ways a stray hair might have ended in
your bedclothes. I will ask Mrs. Budgeon to speak to the laundry maid
straightaway, and see that she takes more care in future."

Nathaniel waved the notion away. "Never mind, Hudson. I was
only curious."

"Very well, sir." Hudson coughed. "But do let me know if you find
any more . . . em . . . souvenirs."

Nathaniel nodded. He realized he was lost in thought when he
looked over to find Hudson studying him with wry amusement.

"Must have been some dream, sir. Did you eat something unusual
last night, I wonder?"

"Come to think of it, Monsieur Fournier served herrings in some
new garlic sauce, and I ate too many of them."

Hudson's eyes glinted. "Herrings, you say? I shall have to remember
that." He sighed. "What a man wouldn't do to have such dreams."

For the first time since his return, Nathaniel found his eyes traveling to the female servants he had consciously avoided before,
both for their ease of mind and his privacy. He did not stare, only
glanced quickly to gain a general impression of hair and stature.
Had one of them been in his bedchamber early that morning? Was
it her? Or her?

Stop it. None of the women, young or old, seemed unusually uncomfortable in his presence. All turned their backs or heads, feigning
invisibility when he neared and then quietly resuming their work
once he'd passed. He had not ordained the cold, impersonal system,
but it had reigned at Fairbourne Hall since his grandmother's day,
and he had given it little thought before now.

He trotted upstairs, deciding to return to the scene of the morning's strange dream. A middle-aged housemaid with auburn hair passed him in the corridor, eyebrows high, perhaps surprised to see him returning to his bedchamber at such an early hour, but she made no comment. He opened his bedchamber door and saw the rising billow of bedclothes being lofted over the bed, and the apron of the invisible housemaid beyond.

When the bedclothes lowered and settled, the maid glanced up and gave a little gasp. Unless he was imagining it, her face blanched, then mottled red.

Here then was a housemaid who *did* seem alarmed by his presence. Or was she merely startled, unaccustomed to being disturbed at this time of day? He looked at her more closely, but the young woman ducked her head, clearly uncomfortable. He recognized her as the new maid Hudson hired, the one who wore spectacles and had broken his model ship. He blinked, trying to recall his dawn awakening. Had the face above him—whether in dream or reality—worn spectacles? Perhaps . . . He couldn't quite recall. She had turned and fled so quickly.

A fringe of dark hair covered much of the new maid's brow, the rest of her hair hidden beneath a floppy mobcap. Her eyebrows were dark as well. A pretty girl to be sure, but not the woman who'd left behind a loose blond lock.

"Sorry to startle you. Go about your work. I shall be out of your hair in a moment." Why was he chatting away with a housemaid who clearly wanted him gone? *Out of your hair?* He had never uttered such an inane phrase in his life. He had hair on the brain.

Imbecile, he scolded himself. He was harebrained indeed.

Do nothing in your master's house that you feel
obliged to conceal to keep your situation.

—Samuel and Sarah Adams, *The Complete Servant*

Chapter 17

Nathaniel and Helen once again sat talking in the family
sitting room when Hudson entered.

"You wanted to see me, sir?"

"Hello, Hudson. I was just telling Helen about your idea to hold
a servants' ball at harvest time."

Helen gave a small smile. "I think it a marvelous notion." She gripped
her hands in her lap. "Would you mind terribly if I helped you plan it?"

Hudson pursed his lips in surprise. "I wouldn't mind at all, miss.
In fact it would be a pleasure."

Her smile widened. "Good. It is very exciting and far too long since
we have done anything for our people here. Did you do anything like
it for yours in Barbados?"

Hudson knit his brows. "For the slaves, miss?"

She faltered, "Well . . . No, I don't suppose that would be quite
the thing."

Nathaniel and Hudson exchanged a look.

"We had no 'balls,' in the English sense, no," Hudson explained.
"But the slaves celebrate the end of harvest or 'crop over' with dancing and feasting in the plantation yards."

"Oh. I see." Helen brightened. "Then this shall be the inaugural servants' ball for the both of us. I have several ideas, but what have you thought of so far?"

Hudson rocked on his heels. "Well . . . there should be food, of course. A nice buffet supper."

"I wonder if Monsieur Fournier would have any suggestions? Though perhaps we ought to hire a cook and waitstaff for the day so none of the servants have to work."

"I doubt Monsieur Fournier will relish the thought of handing over his kitchen. But day help is an excellent idea."

She beamed, and it did Nathaniel's heart good to see his sister looking so happy.

"We must have music, of course," Helen said. "And dancing."

Hudson agreed. "Mr. Arnold informs me he knows of an excellent fiddler who plays all the country dances."

"Wonderful."

Nathaniel felt like a spectator at a shuttlecock match as the two batted ideas back and forth.

"And perhaps a few games or a contest?" Helen added. "A prize or two?"

"Or a small gift for everyone."

"Very thoughtful," she enthused. "This will be great fun, Mr. Hudson. I for one look forward to it."

Hudson nodded slowly, eyes fastened on her bright, smiling face. "As do I."

The following morning, Margaret entered Miss Upchurch's bedchamber to dress her hair as usual. Helen stood at the window wearing her day dress of Devonshire brown. When she did not turn, Margaret went to join her at the window to see what had captured her attention. The distant clang of steel drew her gaze down to the arcade below.

There, Nathaniel Upchurch and Mr. Hudson were fencing in shirtsleeves. Through the columns, Margaret saw them advancing and retreating, lunging and striking, in an intricate fast-paced dance. Their swords clashed, circled, and struck again, morning sunshine glinting off polished blades.

Without looking away, Helen murmured, "What is it about men and swords?"

Even from a distance, Margaret could not help but admire their grace and agility. Nor could she fail to notice the outline of Nathaniel's broad shoulders against damp shirtsleeves. Nor how his leg muscles strained against snug white pantaloons with each lunge. She hoped Helen could not read her thoughts.

She glanced over and saw a strange light in Helen's eyes as she observed her brother. Or was it Mr. Hudson she watched? Margaret hadn't the courage to ask.

Leaving Helen at the window, Margaret took herself into the dressing room to see if anything needed to be done. A few moments later, Helen came and sat at her dressing table. She eyed the new arrangement of flowers Margaret had delivered earlier that morning—yellow and white chrysanthemums amid vibrant greenery.

Helen turned to smile at her, but her eyes quickly returned to the colorful flowers. "Did you arrange these?"

"I did."

"Exquisite."

The simple compliment pleased Margaret greatly. She was less pleased by Helen's apparel but made no comment. By now, she was resigned to Miss Upchurch's habit of alternating between her day dresses of grey, brown, and a dull gold color that did no favors for her sallow complexion.

Margaret picked up brush and pins to begin, only to be startled when Helen suddenly rose from her seat.

"Do you know, I believe I shall wear the green walking dress you made over for me. Such a pity to waste it. If you would kindly help me change?"

Margaret smiled. "Of course. I should be delighted."

She brought out the dress and a pair of long stays. "The line of the gown would be so much improved by correct underpinnings, Miss Helen. Would you mind terribly?"

Helen's face puckered at the sight of the boned contraption, but she acquiesced. "Oh, very well."

Margaret helped Helen out of the brown dress and unstructured undergarments, then into the long stays. While Margaret worked the lacing, Helen eyed her reflection in the looking glass, tilting her chin from side to side. "And perhaps, just a touch of rouge?"

Another surprise. "With pleasure." Curiosity nipped at Margaret. "May I ask . . . is today some special occasion?"

Helen colored. "Not at all. Why would you ask that? I have nothing scheduled today beyond a meeting with the steward and chef. Nothing special at all."

Margaret and Betty sat companionably together in the servants' hall, polishing silver. The others had long since departed to their own afternoon duties.

Betty glanced over and said, "In my last place, the butler polished the silver."

"Really? I cannot fancy Mr. Arnold mucking his hands with polish and the like."

Betty snorted. "Nor I, and him only an under butler."

As they worked, Margaret noticed Betty's freckled hands and how heavily veined and work-worn they were, more aged than the rest of her. Margaret hoped three months of labor wouldn't do the same to her hands.

Betty was probably almost old enough to be her mother, yet they held nearly the same position. She wondered if Betty minded.

"How long have you been a housemaid, Betty?" she asked.

Betty set down a silver fork and picked up another. "Oh, fifteen years here, give or take. And eleven at the Langleys' before that. Started as a scullery maid when I was just a girl, then moved up to kitchen maid, then housemaid. Never had to work the laundry, thank the Lord."

"Was this your dream, then?"

"Dream?"

"What you wanted out of life."

"*Pfff.*" Betty's hand was in constant motion as she spoke. "Few indeed get what they want in life, and that's a fact. Look at Fiona."

Margaret glanced up quickly. "Fiona? What about Fiona?"

"Never you mind. The point is, I don't think any little girl *dreams*, as you call it, of working as a scullion all her days, does she?"

"But what would you do if you could do anything?"

Betty pursed her lips. "Nora. I don't mind chattin' to pass the time, but it's foolish to hanker after the past or the impossible. I am content enough. I have been in service since I were fourteen. It's all I know and ever will, and that's all right by me."

Even though the words were spoken kindly, Margaret felt chastised. "I am glad to hear it," she murmured, fastening her attention on yet another butter knife.

Betty applied silver polish to several serving spoons with vigor and skill, the topic evidently forgotten.

A few moments later, Betty said abruptly, "There is one thing."

Margaret looked up, not sure what she was referring to.

"One thing I would like." Betty's focus remained on the spoons.

"What's that?"

"I would like to be housekeeper one day. It's the top rung, you know. And, well, if I reach that, I'll know I've done my best and all I could. I would be proud to wear my mum's chatelaine heavy with keys, commanding respect from servant and master alike."

Margaret grinned. "Sending fear into the hearts of all the maids, you mean, when they hear the jingle of your keys."

A small grin dimpled Betty's cheeks. "That too."

"I'm going to tell Mrs. Budgeon to watch her back," Margaret teased.

"Don't you dare!"

"Don't worry, Betty. I won't say a word about you hankering after her job."

Betty slanted her a wry look and moved on to the fish forks.

Margaret said, "Honestly, I think you would be an excellent house-keeper, Betty Tidy."

"Oh, I don't know . . ."

"I for one would be proud to work for you," Margaret insisted.

Betty's eyes sparkled with mischief. "You say that now. But Mrs. Budgeon is a pussycat compared to the housekeeper I'd be." She tucked her chin and gave a decent impression of Mrs. Budgeon in high dudgeon, "Now get about your work, my girl. We're not paying you to chat and idle!"

Margaret hauled yet another kettle of hot water from the kitchen into the servants' bathing room belowstairs. The small, tiled room held a generous double slipper tub, chair, mirror, and a shelf and hooks for clothing and towels. She'd taken a few quick baths since she'd arrived but mostly made do with sponge baths—room temperature water from the basin in her room, a rough towel, and her weekly bar of soap. But she didn't feel really clean, and her scalp was beginning to itch under the wig. She wanted a real bath. She could hardly wait to wash her hair again.

The kitchen had running water, piped in from a cistern outside. This she heated on the stove in large kettles. The house was quiet. Even the scullery maid had scrubbed her last pot and gone to bed. She ought to be sleeping too. But first, a bath.

How long it took to fill the tub! She had never given it a thought all those times she had told Joan to draw her a bath, regardless if she had just had one a day or two before. Baths relaxed her and helped her sleep, she had justified. How much extra work she had caused poor Joan, though the woman never complained. At least, not to Margaret directly.

Margaret carried her kettles back to the kitchen for one more refill. That should bring the water level up past her legs, she hoped. Then perhaps one more can to rinse her hair. Her arms began to tremble from the heavy load, her hand to feel permanently bent in a clutch. Ah, but the warm water would soon soothe her aches and pains.

She lugged the kettles down the long passage, past the housekeeper's room, stillroom, storerooms, and around the corner to its end, only to find the bathroom door closed. She was sure she had left it open. She frowned. Surely not . . .

She knocked experimentally. "Hello? Is someone in there?"

No one answered. The door must have swung itself shut. Relieved, she pushed it open and shrieked. Thomas sat in the bathtub. In her bathwater.

He didn't even have the shame to appear sheepish. In fact, he waggled his eyebrows at her by the light of a candle lamp—the one she had lit. Fortunately the tub hid all but his head and upper torso from her view. She was torn between the desire to flee, shielding her eyes, and the urge to throw him bodily from the tub.

"What do you think you are doing?" she fumed. "I hauled all that hot water for my own bath."

He smirked. "I did wonder who left it. Awfully kind of you."

"It was not kind," she said between clenched teeth. "It was for my own bath. Why would you presume someone filled it for *you*?"

His eyes narrowed. "How high and mighty you speak all of a sudden."

She felt her cheeks burn. "Well, I'm angry!"

He gripped the sides of the tub and made as though to rise. "Then I shall get out straightaway if you like."

"No! Not with me standing here. I shall wait outside."

She stepped out and closed the door. Five or ten minutes later he finally emerged, hair slicked back, skin still glistening. "It's all yours, love."

"I trust you're going to help me refill it?"

"No need. It's perfectly good water. Still warm. I shall even come in and scrub your back, if you like." He winked at her.

"Not on your life. How selfish you are."

He lifted his square chin. "Well, I shall definitely not fetch and tote for you after that." He turned away, whistling to himself as he walked jauntily down the passage, her towel around his neck.

Jackanapes!

The tub, at least, had a drain pipe, or she would have had to haul away the dirty water before she could refill it. While the tub drained, she began the whole process all over again, refusing to bathe in water used by the boorish Thomas. She retrieved a clean towel from the servants' linen cupboard, and laid it over the chair. This time she closed the door when she returned to the kitchen, hoping to mark her territory.

Finally, an hour after she should have, she shut the bathroom door behind her, levered the chair beneath the latch, and disrobed. She removed her spectacles, extracted the anchoring pins, and peeled off the wig. Lifting a foot over the tub edge, she tested the water. Just right. She stepped in and sat down, knees bent. How good the hot steamy water felt on her back and bum. She released a long, satisfied sigh.

Reaching up, Margaret unpinned her hair from its tight knot, then leaned over to pile the pins on the shelf. She combed her fingers through her hair and massaged her scalp. Ahh . . . She sank lower in the tub.

Margaret washed her body and lathered her hair, relishing the relief and pleasure of the scrubbing. Then she poured the remaining water from the kettle over her head to rinse, careful not to spill any onto the floor, which she would have to clean up. She leaned back against the high back of the tub once more. Her eyes began to droop. If she wasn't careful she would fall asleep.

Eventually the water began to cool, and the parts of her above its surface grew chilled. She stood, toweled off her body, and stepped from the tub. She slipped into her night dress, wrapper, and slippers, unplugged the drain, and gathered up her pins. Too exhausted to comb out and repin her hair and replace the tiresome wig, she instead wrapped her head in the towel, careful to be sure all her hair was covered. She rolled the wig and pins into her dress and tucked the bundle under her arm. At the last minute she remembered her spectacles and picked up the foggy lenses from the shelf. Her towel was too tight to allow her to slip the earpieces on, so she simply carried them. The passageway would be dark but for her candle lamp, and she was unlikely to meet anyone this time of night.

Checking to make sure she had gathered all of her belongings and left no blond hairs in the tub, Margaret stepped from the bathroom, hands full with wadded garments and spectacles in one hand, and the candle lamp in the other. She had made it to the foot of the basement stairs when she was startled by footsteps coming down, directly toward her. She looked up in surprise only to quickly wish she had kept her head down. Nathaniel Upchurch was descending the stairs, carrying his own candle.

She was naked. Suddenly naked. Without floppy cap, wig, dark brows, and spectacles to shield her face, her self. What was he doing belowstairs?

"Beg pardon, sir," she mumbled, forgetting she was to be mute unless spoken to. She moved to the other side of the stairs, head ducked, and climbed quickly from view. She didn't risk a look back to see what expression might reside on that strong, haughty face: shock that she had spoken to him, shock at her state of dress, or the shock of recognition? *Heaven help me either way.*

Nathaniel Upchurch had decided to go down to the kitchen himself, though he rarely entered the servants' area these days. He had been too restless to sleep and hungry in the bargain. He thought a bit of bread and cheese might help. Normally, he would ring for a servant. But after his recent encounter with the housemaid, he was reticent to ask anyone to come into his room at such a late hour.

But as he reached the bottom of the stairs, a figure appeared in the shadowy passage below and scurried up the stairs past him. He froze. His mind flashed light and dark. His heart rate accelerated. The woman he had just passed—the voice had belonged to the new housemaid. But the face belonged to the woman who haunted his dreams. Margaret Macy.

It could not be. . . . He sunk to the stairs, sweat pouring from his skin. He was distraught, exhausted, losing his mind. The stress of the fire, the loss of half the year's profits, the debts. These had taken their toll, and he was now imagining, hallucinating the face of Miss Macy on one of the housemaids?

He shook his head to clear his vision and his mind. *Dear God in heaven, help me.* The image seemed burned into his brain, unshakable. The oval face with pointed chin, framed so starkly by the towel. The face so young and innocent, without the powder and paint she had worn at the ball when he had glimpsed her last. The blue eyes, wide at seeing him, fearful.

No! He was imagining things. The new housemaid had come to Hudson's aid near the London docks. Hudson had then recognized her at a hiring fair in Maidstone, and offered her a post out of gratitude. This maid did not speak nor dress like a Macy. Besides, she had dark hair, unless she had dyed it. And she was a maid, for heaven's sake, though not a good one, he gathered. Proud, conceited Margaret Macy would never so demean herself as to enter service. Besides, he would have recognized her immediately.

Or would he have? He had never really looked at the new maid, any of the maids for that matter, until he feared he'd kissed one of them. And they, in turn, did their best to avoid him. If he were honest, as a younger man he had thought himself too far above the servants to give them a second thought. Since his change of heart, he no longer felt himself better than the people working for him. Still, that did not change the ways ingrained in him since youth. Which was obvious in the fact that he had barely looked at this new maidservant before now.

How strange that he had imagined Miss Macy's face on the new housemaid. He needed more sleep. He needed to pray more fervently for God to heal his heart, to help him get over her. He thought he had, for the most part. Returning to London and seeing her, though fleetingly, must have brought her to the forefront of his mind again. *Botheration.*

He rose from the stairs, wishing it were not so late. He was tempted to rouse Hudson from his slumber and demand a rematch of the morning's fencing defeat. A bout with the foils seemed to help. He felt he could go twenty bouts at that very moment.

Nathaniel decided he would not look at her again, not risk another fanciful likeness, until he had fenced with Hudson, bathed, dressed, read from the Scriptures, prayed, and prayed some more. Then he would be ready to face her. To see that she was merely a housemaid from a rough London neighborhood. A fishmonger's daughter, perhaps. Or even a merchant's daughter, for her speech, though accented, carried the vocabulary and syntax of an educated woman. He would see her for what she was and be relieved to find his faculties intact. Might there be some small stab of disappointment that she was not Miss Macy in the flesh? *Ridiculous.*

The clash of steel striking steel echoed against the garden wall as the two men fenced in the long arcade, hemmed in by its columns. Hudson retreated, struggling to parry as Nathaniel advanced, driving him back and back, closer to the arcade's end with every lunge. Finally the practice tip hit its mark, and Hudson touched his chest in acknowledgment.

"Touché," he panted.

Nathaniel stepped back, still bouncing gently on his feet to stay loose.

"Good heavens, sir!" Hudson wiped a sleeve across his brow. "What has got in to you this morning? You're on fire!"

"Determination," Nathaniel gritted, breathing hard.

"To kill me? What have I done since yesterday to so vex you?"

Nathaniel's only answer was to raise his blade once more, and the bout resumed. He advanced, striking again and again. His wrist and fingers began to ache, his thigh muscles to burn from the low stance and grueling pace. Sweat poured down his face and back, shirtsleeves clinging to damp skin. He scored another hit, and the men paused to catch their breaths.

Nathaniel shook the sweaty hair back from his brow. Between pants, he said, "Tell me again why you hired the new housemaid?"

Hudson grimaced in surprise. "I told you, sir. To repay her kindness."

"You said you recognized her."

"Yes, from London, the night of the fire. When we lost our way."

"But had you seen her before that?"

"No, sir. Where should I have seen her before?"

Hudson would not have seen her. He was being illogical again. Miss Macy would have been quite a young girl the last time Hudson was in England.

"Never mind."

"Do you recognize her, sir? From somewhere else, that is?"

"No," he said. "She reminds me of someone, that's all." *But God help me if I'm wrong.*

Nathaniel muddled his way through morning prayers, trying not to stare at her. He would not ogle her in front of the other servants. Not embarrass her or himself. Yet how could he see her more closely? He supposed he could corner her behind closed doors in one of the bedchambers when she was making beds and doing whatever else maids did to tidy the place, but that might stir rumors. Rumors which would make it difficult for her to stay, once he assured himself he was mistaken. Besides, he did not like the thought of sneaking up on her while she worked. He had done so inadvertently once or twice before and had frightened her half to death. But what reason could he give Mrs. Budgeon to summon the girl to the library for a private interview?

When the staff was dismissed, he turned to the housekeeper. "Mrs. Budgeon. I would like a word with the new housemaid, when it's convenient."

Mrs. Budgeon looked stricken. "What has she done now? I know I was her biggest critic in the beginning—girl had not a whit of experience. But she has improved. I'm sorry if you are disappointed, sir."

"Not at all. Nothing of the kind. Mr. Hudson has made me aware of a great kindness she paid us before she came here. It is why Hudson engaged her in the first place. But I have never thanked her myself and wish to do so."

Mrs. Budgeon hesitated. "I would be happy to pass along any message, sir, if you would rather."

"Thank you, but I would prefer to do so myself."

"Very good, sir." She formed an unconvincing smile and backed away, no doubt believing something unsavory afoot. Well, it could not be helped. He could not tell her why he really wanted to see the new housemaid.

Two hours later, he stood in the library, watching the young woman carefully as she entered. She clasped her hands before her and kept her head bowed, not meeting his gaze. Her face, what he could see of it beneath the dark fringe, was quite pale.

She did not speak, and for a moment neither did he. How should he go about this?

She bit her lip, twisting her hands. "You asked to see me, sir?"

Her voice trembled—was it *her* voice? It was difficult to say with that unfamiliar accent.

"You are not in any trouble, Nora. Do not be uneasy."

She darted a look up at him. His heart constricted at that flash of her face. *Lord, please give me clarity of mind.*

"Come closer, please. I mean you no harm."

Her throat convulsed as she swallowed, but she obeyed, taking three steps forward.

His voice was a low rumble in his ears. "Look at me."

She hesitated, then slowly lifted her chin.

His throat went dry.

He was either insane, or there stood Margaret Macy—or some long-lost twin—with black hair instead of blond. Had she dyed it, or was it a wig? She had darkened her brows as well. His heart began to beat hard—fast and irregular. He clenched the hand behind his back and forced his expression to remain impassive.

Why was she here? What on earth was she doing? He thought back to Sterling Benton's visit. Something was wrong there. He had sensed it, even as he tried not to allow her disappearance to concern him. A part of him was relieved at this confirmation that she was alive and well. Another part of him was suspicious of her motives for coming to Fairbourne Hall. Perhaps it had been some ploy to ensnare Lewis into marriage. She wouldn't be the first girl to try. But, he argued with himself, Lewis had returned to London and she remained.

How had he not recognized her before? He remembered what Sterling Benton had said about women being more discerning than men. He also recalled several times in the past when he had commented on how alike two people were in appearance and Helen had scoffed at him. *"Their hair is similar, and perhaps their stature, but otherwise they look nothing alike."* Or, *"How can you confuse Lydia Thompson with Kitty Hawkins? Yes, they are both ginger-haired girls, but beyond that they are completely different. One is freckled, the other pale. One has blue eyes, the other green. And one is clever and the other insipid!"* Yet both he and Lewis continued to confuse the two.

He wondered if Helen had recognized Miss Macy. He was certain Lewis had not or he would have blurted it out like a great joke long ago. But he was not sure what Helen might do.

What should *he* do? Expose her deceit and demand an explanation? Notify her stepfather? Toss her out on the street? Take her in his arms?

He fisted both hands as the wave of contradictory desires swept over him, but he stood stock-still, barely even blinking. What a strange twist of fate this was. That she should be here, under his roof, under his power. With Lewis back in London, he was her master for all intents and purposes, at least as far as her employment and housing were concerned. He rather liked the notion of holding some power over her for once. What a relief after the awful power she had held over him these last few years, whether she knew it or not.

He knew Margaret had an impulsive nature, as Benton and even Helen had allowed. But would she really enter service—would any gentleman's daughter—unless she was truly desperate? And she was actually doing the work, according to Mrs. Budgeon. If it had been some foolish schoolgirl prank to put herself in Lewis's path, that lark would have long since ended with disillusionment and weariness after a few days of drudgery. She must have another reason.

He decided he needed to find out what was really going on. He would not hand her over to Sterling Benton—a man he had never liked at all events.

Margaret's face had gone from pale to blushing red while he stood there staring at her.

With a supreme effort, he schooled his features and moderated his tone of voice. "You need not worry, Nora. I have only asked you here to thank you. Mr. Hudson told me of your brave help the night we were nearly set upon by thieves in London. He has already thanked you, I know. But I had not."

Behind her spectacles, her round eyes blinked. She swallowed and nodded, murmuring, "Yer welcome, sir."

Had she spent time belowstairs with servants in her youth? Where else would she have cultivated that accent?

He said, "Very good. That will be all."

Clearly relieved, she bobbed a curtsy.

For now, he added to himself, watching her go.

Chapter 18

A fter attending the funeral of an old tenant, Nathaniel walked
back into Fairbourne Hall, thinking about the best way to
find an industrious young farmer to take the old bachelor's
place. He needed to increase the profitability of the estate if he had
any hope of repairing his ship.

Reaching the sitting room, Nathaniel paused in the threshold.
Inside, Hudson and Helen stood near one another at the balcony
window, heads together, bent over some papers Helen held—lists of
things to be done for the servants' ball, he imagined. His sister wore
an attractive green-and-ivory striped gown he hadn't seen before,
with a sash that emphasized her narrow waist.

Helen smiled up at him as he approached. "Hello, Nate."

"Why, Helen, do my eyes deceive me, or is that a new dress?"

She lifted her chin. "No, it isn't new. But I own, it has been made
over. Nora did it."

"Nora?" He prayed she could not see his heart suddenly lurch in
his chest.

His sister eyed him carefully. "The new housemaid. I don't imagine you've met her?"

"Um . . . yes," he faltered. "I believe I know who you mean."

Noticing his discomfort, Hudson said smoothly, "Well, you look lovely, Miss Helen, if you don't mind my saying so."

Helen dipped her head, pleased but self-conscious. "Thank you, Mr. Hudson. Now, if the two of you would stop staring at me, we have a ball to plan. . . ."

His sister's face blushed becomingly. How strange to think Robert Hudson had put that blush there. If so, did he mind? It was unexpected and, he admitted to himself, mildly disconcerting to see his ladylike sister on such friendly terms with a man in his employ. He was not quite certain how he felt about it.

But perhaps he was mistaken. Perhaps his sister was merely wearing a bit of rouge. He quickly dismissed the notion. His practical sister would never bother with anything as frivolous as cosmetics.

Margaret trudged up the back stairs to the attic and down the passage to her room. She felt bone weary and hoped to rest for half an hour or so until it was time to help Fiona gather the laundry. She nudged the door closed behind her, then took off her apron and spectacles and sat on the bed, sliding off her slippers. A scratch sounded at her door, and before she could respond, the wolfhound pushed it open with his head, as he had done before. She couldn't think what attracted the dog to her small dim room. Did she still smell of that morning's sausages?

"I'm too exhausted to play with you, Jester."

With a little whine, the hound walked to the small oval rug beside her bed, turned around, around again, then lay down, curling himself on the rug, tail tucked, chin resting on his forelegs.

"That's what I have in mind to do too."

She lay down on her made bed, pulling the little lap robe over her legs. She had a good thirty or forty minutes to rest. What luxury.

She found her mind replaying her meeting with Nathaniel Upchurch, when he'd summoned her to the library to speak with her. He'd told her to "Come closer. . . . Look at me." And her heart had pounded so loudly she was sure he would hear it.

Then he stood there and stared at her. Just stared. How unsettling it had been. She'd begun to fear her masquerade was up, and was torn between wanting to bolt and wanting to confess all. But then he'd surprised her by saying he merely wanted to thank her for her help back in London. Why then, after so much time? But what a relief to know that was all he wanted. That her secret was still safe.

On the floor nearby, the dog gave a little sigh of contentment. Margaret smiled, feeling content as well, and drifted to sleep.

After a long and tedious meeting with the church commissioners, Nathaniel felt like shooting something. He thought he might take himself grouse hunting before September got away from him. He looked about for Jester, who was always eager for a jaunt in the woods, but didn't see the hound anywhere. He asked the footman on door duty, "Have you seen the dog?"

"Yes, sir. Just went up the stairs a bit ago."

Likely on his way to my bedchamber, Nathaniel thought and headed for the stairs.

He had always been fond of the wolfhound and had missed him whilst he was away. He had thought of taking Jester along to Barbados, but it had made little sense to inflict such a long sea journey on an animal who loved nothing better than to run in the woods, chase down a fox, or stir a bevy of game birds. When Nathaniel was busy or away, he knew the hall boy or groom exercised the dog, but he preferred to do it himself.

In the old days, his mother hadn't allowed dogs above the ground floor. But the rules had grown more lax since her death. He found he enjoyed Jester's company and didn't mind him sleeping on his floor near the hearth. Though the dog didn't appear every night.

When Nathaniel reached the top of the main stairs, a thin, dark-haired housemaid staggered around the corner, arms full of linens.

"Have you seen the dog?" he asked.

"Aye, sir. Near about run me over. He's gone up the back stairs."

"Thank you." *That's strange*, Nathaniel thought. *Well, in for a penny, in for a pound.* A bit of exercise would do him good, he decided as he started up the stairs, especially after forgoing a fencing session with Hudson that morning.

Still, he hesitated to enter the attic, the domain of the female servants. He had rarely ventured there since boyhood, when his daily vigil to the schoolroom had brought him up those stairs nearly every day. But he had no real business there now. *What could Jester be doing up here?*

Nathaniel walked along the passage, but all the doors were closed. He turned the corner into a side passage. There, at its end, one door stood ajar.

Walking quietly, Nathaniel reached it and glanced in, surprised to see a figure lying atop the made bed, napping peacefully. Nora, or rather, Margaret. And curled on a rug before her bed and looking quite content, lay his wolfhound. Jester's eyes opened, clearly aware of his presence, but the dog made no move to rise or join him.

Disloyal creature, Nathaniel thought, part amusement, part irritation. Yet he could not blame him for being drawn to that particular door.

Giving up his plans to go shooting, Nathaniel went back downstairs and found Helen in her favorite chair in the family sitting room, needlework on her lap and tea beside her.

"Well, Helen. What do you think of our new housemaid?"

She stilled, then looked up, studying him. "Why do you ask?"

He shrugged. "A bit unusual, do you not think?"

Her eyes narrowed. "How so?"

Did she really not know, or was she hedging, as he was? If so, was Helen trying to protect Margaret . . . or him?

Nathaniel hesitated. He found he was not ready to burst the little bubble he was inhabiting. He was oddly enjoying the strange secret. He was not ready to share it, for then he would have to act differently with "Nora." Guard himself. Helen would be watching. Wondering.

He feigned nonchalance. "A girl like her, clearly never in service before."

She stared at him a moment longer, then relaxed and returned her gaze to her embroidery. "I like her. I did not at first, I own. But she has proved most helpful to me."

"Has she indeed? I am glad to hear it." He paused. "So, how are plans progressing for the servants' ball?"

Helen smiled. "Very well, I think."

Knowing Helen had not initially approved of the new steward, he asked, "And how are you getting on with Hudson?"

She kept her eyes averted, but her needle stilled as she considered. Then her mouth crooked and a dimple appeared in one cheek. She echoed, "I like him. I did not at first, I own. But he has proved most helpful to me."

Nathaniel grinned. "Shall I announce the ball soon?"

"Yes. Do."

That night, Nathaniel was surprised to see "Nora" walking away from the house through the moonlit arcade. It was after ten. Why was she not in bed like every other no-doubt-exhausted maid? Was she leaving Fairbourne Hall? He followed her quietly but was relieved when she turned at the end of the arcade and started back at the same pace, apparently out for a simple stroll, like a lady of leisure. Seeing him, she started and looked about her for a place to disappear, but the narrow walkway offered little cover.

"Good evening, Nora."

She flashed him a look of surprise and alarm, clearly not expecting nor wanting him to address her.

"Sir." She dipped her head and made to skirt around him, but he halted before her.

"And what brings you outside this evening?"

"Em . . . just takin' a bit of air, sir."

He bit back a smile at her accent. "Couldn't sleep?"

"That's it, sir." Reluctantly she turned toward him, head bowed.

"I am sorry to hear it. Do you not find your life here . . . comfortable?"

"I'm not complainin', sir."

"I am surprised."

She darted a glance up at him, moonlight and confusion streaking her face.

"A life in service must be difficult," he said gently. "I understand you have not been a housemaid before?"

"No, sir."

"You had not long planned to enter service, I take it."

She shook her head.

"May I ask what you had planned for your life?"

"I . . . don't know, sir. Live independent-like, I suppose. Or marry."

"Oh? And who might the lucky man be?"

She ducked her head once more, clearly uncomfortable. "I couldn't say, sir."

Did she think he was trying to seduce her? He was making a poor job of it if he was. Still, he hated the thought of her nurturing a low opinion of his character.

"You needn't worry, Nora," he said. "I have no ungentlemanly intentions in speaking to you. Now, I will bid you good-night and hope you sleep well."

"Thank you, sir." She scurried past him, back into the refuge of Fairbourne Hall.

During morning prayers the next day, Margaret watched Nathaniel Upchurch carefully, wondering about his strange behavior of the night before. She hoped he had spoken the truth—that he had no improper intentions toward her. Then why had he taken the time to speak with her when he had rarely done so before?

Across the hall, Nathaniel capped his prayer with his usual amen, then removed his spectacles and tucked them into his pocket. He regarded the assembled servants, but instead of dismissing them, he drew his shoulders back and began, "I have an announcement. It has come to my attention that over the last two years, the Christmas and Epiphany festivities here at Fairbourne Hall have been regretfully few. Therefore we have decided—Mr. Hudson, Miss Upchurch, and I—that it is long past time for a servants' ball."

Kitchen-maid Jenny let out a whoop, then quickly threw a hand over her mouth. Craig elbowed the hall boy, Freddy, beside him.

Mr. Upchurch allowed a small grin. "I take it the plan meets with your approbation?"

Freddy gushed, "Don't know 'bout that, sir, but it sounds grand!"

Mr. Upchurch and his steward exchanged a look. Hudson chuckled. Mrs. Budgeon shook her head, but her stern expression was softened by the sparkle in her eyes.

"Miss Upchurch and Mr. Hudson are planning the affair and will no doubt keep you apprised of the details. But for now you are dismissed."

Instantly the maids began whispering and giggling amongst themselves even as the footmen and grooms laughed and teased each other. Mrs. Budgeon didn't even reprimand them, which was surprising. Margaret hoped the ball would be a success and they would all enjoy themselves. . . .

Wait. I am a servant, she thought. *She* would be attending. Her first servants' ball as a servant.

She had attended several in her youth, as the daughter of the family. Her father had insisted upon allowing their small clutch of servants an evening of frivolity and pleasure on Twelfth Night. Lime Tree Lodge was too small to have a proper servants' hall, and the basement kitchen and workrooms were too cramped for dancing. So Stephen Macy had given them use of the family dining room, pushing the table to the side to be laden with punch and victuals, and the rest of the furniture cleared away for the night. He'd hired several waiters to do the serving and cleaning up and brought in a fiddler to play the dances. When she was old enough to stay up late, she had joined in with the dancing, finding it amusing to put her small silken hands in the gardener's rough paws and be led around the room in a jig. She had felt a princess among peasants. Now she wondered if they had really looked upon her with the fond benevolence she had imagined, or if they thought her condescending and spoiled. She would not blame them.

When Margaret went to Miss Upchurch's room to dress her hair the next morning, Helen said, "I must ask you to hurry today, Nora. I'm meeting with Mr. Hudson before prayers to finalize arrangements for the ball."

Margaret nodded. Gathering the brush and pins, she said, "Would you ever consider inviting the staff of another house to join us?"

Helen looked at her in the mirror. "I had not thought of it. Why?"

Margaret began brushing Helen's hair. "I met a housemaid from Hayfield when I went to Weavering Street, and she mentioned the house has been in mourning and the servants haven't had any privileges or entertainments for over a year."

Helen pursued her lip, considering. "I like the idea. I shall see what Mr. Hudson thinks."

Margaret bit back a smile. "You have been spending a great deal of time with Mr. Hudson of late."

"Do you think so? It is only that there are so many details to attend to."

Is that all? Margaret wondered. "Perhaps a little rouge today, Miss Helen?"

"I'm not sure there's time."

Margaret traded hair brush for cosmetic brush. "Won't take a moment."

"Oh . . . very well. Why not."

Margaret deftly brushed subtle color to Helen's cheeks and dabbed just a smidge of lip rouge to her mouth. The old rouge pot was nearly empty, she noticed. She would soon need to make more. She switched to fine talcum powder and dusted Helen's nose, chin, and cheeks.

Helen said wryly, "You are skilled in altering a lady's appearance, I see. You handle that brush like an artist."

Margaret shrugged, eyes focused on Helen's cheek. "It is very like painting, actually."

"Do you enjoy painting?"

"I did, yes. Though I haven't done so in ages."

Margaret gathered Helen's hair and began to pin it up. "Miss Upchurch, I wonder. Do you remember that trunk of old gowns and things I found when I cleaned the schoolroom?"

"Yes?"

"If you haven't use for them, would you mind allowing the maids to wear them? For the servants' ball, I mean. Perhaps I could make over a few of them for the girls who haven't a stitch beyond their everyday frock to wear."

"That would be very kind of you, Nora. I am surprised you want to."

"I would enjoy it very much."

"Very well. Only don't fail in your other work. We don't want Mrs. Budgeon to find reason to dismiss you." Helen's eyes twinkled, and Margaret grinned in return.

Margaret found it funny and perplexing that Helen Upchurch still carried on the pretense, addressing her as the maid Nora, while at other times it seemed clear she knew who she really was. Was it merely a game to her or was it to keep her from becoming confused—from calling her Margaret or Miss Macy at an inopportune moment? Or was she enjoying treating her as a subservient? Margaret sensed no malice in the woman's demeanor, but there was still that reserve, that caution in her aspect, that made Margaret realize she not yet passed whatever test Nathaniel Upchurch's sister was giving her.

With Mrs. Budgeon's approval, Margaret asked several of the maids to join her in Miss Nash's room late one afternoon when their duties were done. She had one gown hanging on the dress form, two laid out on the bed, and two others spread on the worktable. She had in mind which gown would suit each woman but wanted to give them a choice in the matter.

Hester and kitchen maids Jenny and Hannah bustled in first, all giggles and eagerness, while Betty and Fiona held back, lingering in the threshold.

Hester made a beeline for one of the gowns on the bed—a sheer overgown with a silk chemise beneath, both embroidered in a lily-of-the-valley motif.

"It's gorgeous!" she enthused, holding the gown up in front of herself. It was immediately evident that the slender-cut chemise would not accommodate Hester's generous proportions. Her cheerful face fell.

Margaret hurried to one of the gowns on the worktable—a full-skirted cream-colored gown to which Margaret had added side and back panels of blue, trimmed with ribbon embroidery in cream to match the original fabric. "Hester, I thought this one, with its blues and creams, would look so well with your perfect complexion."

"Do you think so?" Hester handed the first gown to slim Hannah and took the second from Margaret, holding it to her shoulders and looking down at the ribbon trim at neckline and bodice.

Margaret said, "Let's try it on, shall we?"

She helped Hester off with her everyday frock and into the made-over ball gown. The material slid over Hester's ample bosom and hips easily. Margaret pinched an inch of loose material at the high waist. "Why, it's a tad big, Hester. I shall have to take it in for you."

Hester beamed.

"You look a picture, Hester," Jenny breathed.

"Indeed she does," Betty said. "What a pity Connor is away in London. Why, if he saw you in that gown, he shouldn't be able to take his eyes off you."

Hester blushed prettily.

Margaret noticed that Fiona had disappeared from the doorway. She tried not to let it hurt her but could not quite ignore the sting of disappointment. Her offering—rejected. She forced a smile and helped Betty into a garden frock of pale green satin with capped sleeves and a hem embellished with gold fringe. The soft green flattered Betty's coloring and dark red hair.

Fiona reappeared in the doorway several minutes later, wearing a gown of white gauze over an underslip of pink silk. "Might this do?"

Margaret stared. "Why, Fiona, it's beautiful."

The others stared as well, mouths ajar.

Fiona asked, "Ya don't think I'll look out of place—silk purse from a sow's ear and all that?"

Hannah and Jenny shook their heads vigorously.

Margaret said, "No, you look lovely."

"Really lovely," Hester echoed.

Fiona blustered, "Oh, go on with ya. Sure and ya know how to embarrass a girl."

Margaret began, "The dress is splendid. Where did you—?"

Betty pinched her elbow, and Margaret faltered. "Em . . . where have you been hiding it?"

"At the bottom of my trunk. Never thought I'd have reason to unearth it."

Margaret stifled her questions and smiled. "Well, I'm glad you did."

The servants' ball was a recurring feature
of country-house life.

—Giles Waterfield and Anne French, *Below Stairs*

Chapter 19

The date of the servants' ball arrived at last, and very little work was accomplished that day. In some ways, it was unfortunate Miss Helen had acted upon Margaret's suggestion and invited outside guests, because that news caused Mrs. Budgeon to demand the house receive a more thorough cleaning and polishing than usual. But the staff had finished that work the day before.

The servants' hall was closed once the midday meal was over, and only Mrs. Budgeon, Mr. Hudson, and the hall boy were allowed in, readying the room for the night's festivities.

Monsieur Fournier labored all day, preparing not only the family's meals, but also a lavish buffet for the ball. But he seemed happy with the extra work, grinning and humming to himself in an amusing compote of English, French, and foolishness. His hands flew about, dusting this dish with sugar, and that with sprigs of mint.

"Tonight you shall see what you have been missing! Zen tomorrow it is back to burnt sausages and gruel. *Quel dommage!*"

Margaret offered to arrange Betty's hair for the occasion, and before she knew it, she had four other women clustered around her in Miss Nash's room, begging to be next. Margaret curled, pinned, powdered, and rouged, but kept her kohl pencil well concealed. She didn't want to give anyone ideas.

Fiona wore her own gown but did accept a pair of long gloves and allowed Margaret to dress her hair with a comb of silk flowers. Betty, Hester, Jenny, and Hannah wore the made-over gowns. Margaret demurred when they insisted she should wear one of them, since she had done the work, but she did not wish to draw attention to herself. Especially since she knew Nathaniel Upchurch would be in attendance for at least the first few dances. And what of Joan? She hoped her former maid would not give her away.

Margaret donned the blue dress she had worn at the masquerade ball, but without an apron. In place of her mobcap, she wore a wide blue ribbon as a headband—for ornamentation yes, but also to assure her wig stayed in place during the dancing.

At half past six, the first carriage rattled up the drive from Hayfield, soon followed by a wagon loaded with men young and old in Sunday best. At seven, the doors to the servants' hall were thrown wide. The long room gleamed with candles dressed in ivy and strung with garlands of colored paper. Wooden boards had been laid over the stone floor for dancing. The buffet table boasted a centerpiece of colorful mums, fresh fruit, and fronds—which Margaret had helped to arrange. Surrounding it were serving dishes resplendent with roasted turkey, salads of every description, and the largest baked salmon she had ever seen swimming in a sea of shrimp sauce, mouth ajar, eyes glassy, curved at head and tail to fit on the platter. There were also delicious-looking desserts—miniature gooseberry tarts, blancmange, and syllabub in tall glasses. Knowing the attendees were likely to drink a little wine punch or ale, Miss Helen and Mr. Hudson had thought it wise to serve food throughout, instead of waiting for a late supper.

Margaret watched nervously as the guests arrived, waiting to see Joan. She hoped the harsh housekeeper had allowed her to attend.

Then, there she was, in the same blue dress Margaret remembered but without an apron. Instead of a cap, a string of beads ornamented her carefully arranged hair. Joan did not look her way. Was she ignoring her? Were they supposed to pretend they did not know one another, to avoid questions of how they had met? But Margaret longed to speak to her again, even as she feared it.

She waited while Joan greeted Mr. Hudson and Mrs. Budgeon, in the role of host and hostess for the evening. Impulsively, she poured two cups of punch and carried them to Joan, hoping her peace offering would not be rejected.

"Hello, Joan," she said tentatively, braving a smile.

Joan's eyes widened. "Miss—!"

"Nora. It's just Nora." She made no effort to disguise her voice with her former maid. "I've brought you some punch."

Joan eyed it almost warily, Margaret realized with chagrin. Had she given her so much reason to distrust her?

"Imagine that. You servin' me," Joan quipped, making no move to take the glass.

"I have some experience at it now. Though nothing to you, of course. I never realized how hard you worked until I came here."

Joan cocked her head to one side, as if gauging her sincerity. "Is that so?"

"It is."

"Then I shall have that punch and thank you." She accepted the glass at last and lifted it in a toast.

Margaret returned the gesture, and they both sipped.

Margaret said, "I was hoping you would be here."

"Were you? I figured you gave up and went home since I saw you last."

"I was tempted more than once, I can tell you. I had no idea what I was getting myself into."

Joan shook her head in wonder. "I still can't believe it. You . . . a housemaid."

Margaret nodded. "Though not a very good one."

Joan's eyes danced. "What I wouldn't have given to be a mouse in the corner the first time you had to empty the slops."

Margaret chuckled. "Don't remind me." She bit her lip, smile fading. "I've wanted to tell you how sorry I am for . . . well, everything. And to thank you for helping me."

Again Joan shook her head. "Sorry and thank you . . . I never thought to hear those two words from you."

Margaret grimaced. "I'm sorry for that too."

Tears blurred her eyes. And she was surprised when answering tears brightened Joan's eyes as well.

Her former maid gripped her fingers. "Now, that's enough of that. This is supposed to be a happy occasion."

Margaret returned her watery smile.

A voice at her elbow interrupted them.

"And who is this pretty lady you're talking to, Nora?" the second footman, Craig, asked, all eagerness. "Do introduce me."

Margaret grinned first at Joan, then Craig. "Miss Joan Hurdle, may I present Craig . . . I'm afraid I don't know your last name."

"Craig is my last name! But we already had a Thomas, didn't we?"

"Oh. Well then, may I present Mr. Thomas Craig."

"How do you do?" Joan dipped her head.

"A great deal better now you're here. Say you'll save a dance for me, Miss Joan, and I shall do better yet."

Joan smiled. "Very well."

How pretty Joan looked when she smiled. How had Margaret not noticed that before?

The fiddler arrived late—and somewhat tipsy, Margaret surmised as he began warming up his bow. On cue, Nathaniel Upchurch entered the hall, Helen on his arm. The crowd instantly quieted in awkward solemnity. Margaret had been so busy helping the other maids prepare for the ball, that she had neglected Miss Upchurch. A pity too. For her hair lay flat and severely pulled back. Her face bare. Her dress . . . What a horrid old thing. Someone had taken a ball dress at least a decade old and added a new ruffled neckline and flounces in a contrasting color and ill-suited material. Still, when Helen looked around the candlelit room and the finely turned out crowd, she smiled broadly, and with that smile she was a real beauty.

"How well you all look!" She beamed.

"Indeed," Mr. Upchurch agreed. "Now don't stop enjoying yourselves on our account." He nodded to the fiddler, who then struck up the notes of the first dance.

As expected, Nathaniel stepped before Mrs. Budgeon, bowed, and asked her for the first dance. Likewise, Mr. Hudson, as the top-ranking male servant, bowed before his mistress. Margaret wondered if sour Mr. Arnold minded the newcomer usurping this honor, but one glance told her Mr. Arnold was busy enjoying yet another cup of punch and liberal samplings of the tempting buffet.

The fiddler played a lively Scottish reel and a few other couples filled in. Margaret watched Nathaniel, surprised to see that he was a better dancer than she remembered, impressed to witness the warmth and respect with which he exchanged pleasantries with his housekeeper. She also watched Miss Upchurch as she danced with Mr. Hudson. They bounded through the steps in lively abandon. Mr. Hudson's form was a bit ungainly, but he had never seemed so young and handsome as he did while dancing with Miss Upchurch. Margaret wondered if she glimpsed admiration in Miss Helen's eyes for the house steward as well. She wished again she had taken time with Helen's hair.

Craig and Joan danced near them in a jaunty facsimile of the steps, their smiles and shy glances more evident than skill.

After the reel "Speed the Plow" was called, Mr. Upchurch escorted Mrs. Budgeon to the edge of the room, bowed, then asked whom he should lead out next. Mrs. Budgeon looked around to locate the upper housemaid, Margaret guessed, but Betty stood behind Mr. Arnold frantically gesturing to be spared.

"Ah. Betty is occupied at present," Mrs. Budgeon said. "Perhaps the newest member of our staff might receive the honor?" She gestured toward Margaret.

Why had she so blatantly been looking at Mrs. Budgeon, Margaret lamented. The woman must think she was begging a partner!

Nathaniel Upchurch looked her way. Did he hesitate? There was no smile on his face as he nodded to Mrs. Budgeon and walked toward her. Should she demur as well?

He stopped before her and she trained her gaze on his waistcoat, too nervous to look up at him.

"Might I have this dance, Nora?"

"Oh. I thought . . . I am hardly an upper servant."

"Apparently the first housemaid is avoiding me like the plague. I trust you will not reject me as well."

Reject me . . . Was it a veiled reference to her cruel rejection of his offer of marriage? She was imagining things. If he'd recognized her he would have tossed her out by now, demanded an explanation, or alerted Sterling Benton. But he had done none of these, as far as she knew.

She swallowed. "No, sir."

He led her through the steps of the dance, formed those vague half smiles of acknowledgment when they faced or passed one another, but showed little of the warmth he had displayed with Mrs. Budgeon. He had known the housekeeper for years, she reminded herself. And he knew "Nora" not at all, even if she had done him and his steward a good turn that night in London.

She thought of other long-ago nights, when they had danced together at this ball or that. Then he had looked at her with admiration, nearly adoration, in his serious, bespectacled eyes. His fingers had lingered on her hand, her waist, whenever the steps and positions of the dance brought them together. Now his eyes were distant, his closed-mouth smile false, his hand cool and quick to depart. The ballrooms had been larger then, the guests wealthier, the music finer, but if he would only smile at her—truly smile—she would rate this night with this company the more enjoyable occasion.

When the silence between them became strained, he asked politely, "Are you enjoying yourself?"

"Yes, sir."

"Is the music to your liking?"

"Yes. Very nice." What a ninny she was. Why could she not think of one appropriate thing to say?

He asked, "Are the others enjoying themselves, do you think?"

"Yes, sir. Very much."

"Is this your first servants' ball?"

"As a mai—matter of fact, yes."

"And how are you getting on in your position here?"

"Better, I think. Thank you for asking." She licked her lips and forged a question of her own. "And how fares your father, sir, if I may ask?"

"He fares well, according to his last letter. Thank *you* for asking."

Margaret was relieved when the dance ended and Mr. Upchurch escorted her to the perimeter of the room and bowed his farewell.

Helen Upchurch, she noticed, was talking to Mr. Arnold, with whom she had danced the second dance. How puffed up the under butler appeared, swaggering across the room with the lady of the house on his arm.

After the customary two dances, master and mistress took their leave of the party, thanking Mrs. Budgeon and Mr. Hudson, shaking hands, and bestowing a general farewell wave to the assembly on their way out.

Part of Margaret was disappointed they were leaving, but the others were apparently relieved, for the tension in the room faded when the two departed and a relaxed buzz of conversation and laughter rose.

One person, however, did not look happy. Monsieur Fournier. Margaret saw him leaning against the wall, empty glass dangling in his hand, watching Mrs. Budgeon's every move.

Margaret strolled nonchalantly to the housekeeper's side.

"Evening, Nora."

"Mrs. Budgeon." They watched the fiddler down another glass and wobble a bit as he asked what they wished him to play next.

Someone yelled, " 'The Roast Beef of Old England'!"

Margaret said in a low aside, "Mrs. Budgeon, I was wondering. Is it not true that in many houses, the chef is actually higher ranking than the under butler?"

She considered this. "Yes, I believe so."

"But Miss Upchurch danced with Mr. Arnold, and not Monsieur Fournier. I wonder if that is why he looks so . . . disappointed."

A small line formed between Mrs. Budgeon's brows. "But Miss Upchurch has already taken her leave."

"I know. But perhaps you might at least acknowledge the slight, or offer to dance with him yourself?"

"Me? I hardly think I'm suitable replacement. I don't imagine Monsieur even likes to dance."

"I don't know. I hate to see him looking so sad. He worked so hard for tonight. . . ."

Mrs. Budgeon looked over at the chef and found him looking at her. He quickly looked away and feigned a sip from his empty glass. How strange it was to see him in a brown tweed suit, instead of his customary white coat and hat.

The housekeeper drew herself up. "Thank you, Nora. I will at least compliment Monsieur on the success of his buffet. We don't want him to feel unappreciated."

"Good idea."

As Mrs. Budgeon crossed the room toward him, Monsieur Fournier straightened, pushing away from the wall. His expression was uncertain, as if he wasn't sure if reprimand or pleasure was coming his way.

It was really too bad of her, but she couldn't help herself. Margaret had to hear. She walked along the buffet table, plucking a grape here and a fig there as she made her way to the table's end, listening to their conversation.

"Monsieur Fournier. Good evening."

"Madame."

"I hope you are enjoying yourself?"

He shrugged.

"I must compliment you on the buffet. You have outdone yourself."

"*Merci*, madame."

Mrs. Budgeon hesitated. "I am afraid it is my fault Miss Upchurch danced the second with Mr. Arnold. An oversight, I assure you."

"No matter, madame."

"You don't care to dance, I suppose?"

He hesitated. "With you?"

Her mouth parted. She reddened. "Never mind. I thought . . . I only meant . . ."

The fiddler launched into the next tune, and the chef leaned nearer to be heard. "With you, Mrs. Budgeon, I would happily dance."

He offered his arm, and after a surprised pause, she gave a tentative smile.

Margaret smiled too. In fact, she could not stop smiling as she watched the tall, thin chef dance like a smitten, gangly youth with proper, staid Mrs. Budgeon.

But midway through the set, the fiddler, swaying and doing a little drunken jig as he played, backed into a chair, knocked his mug off the pianoforte, and crashed to the floor, out cold. Margaret was more disappointed for the chef than for anyone else that the dance should be cut short.

Mr. Arnold and Thomas carried the fiddler down the passage to the kitchen, while Betty rushed to clean up the spilled ale. After a moment's hesitation—it still wasn't second nature to Margaret to respond to such domestic crises—she hurried to Betty's aid and righted the chair.

"I am afraid that concludes our ball," Mrs. Budgeon apologized.

"Not so," Monsieur said. "Perhaps you might play for us, Mrs. Budgeon."

Again her mouth parted. She sputtered, "Me? No. I cannot play. Not really."

"Of course you can. You are very accomplished. I hear you from ze kitchen now and again."

Her face puckered, surprised and disconcerted. "But . . . I always check to make certain no one is about before I begin. And I shut the door as well."

"When you play, I leave my room and come into ze kitchen to hear you better."

She blushed like a schoolgirl. "Oh! I had no idea. I shall never play again."

He placed a hand on his chest. "Please don't say so. What a loss of pleasure for us both."

Jenny, tipsy and brazen, said, "Come on, Mrs. Budgeon. Favor us with a song or two. Something lively we can dance to."

The housekeeper wrung her hands. "But I never play for an audience. I am woefully out of practice and play very ill."

"Not at all," Monsieur insisted.

"None of us can play a note," Jenny said. "So if you blunder, we wouldn't know any better, would we?"

Mr. Hudson added gently, "You won't find a more appreciative audience."

"I would be too self-conscious with all of you listening."

"Aww. We promise not to listen too close," Craig said, his arm around Joan. "We'll be too busy dancin'."

"Oh, very well." Mrs. Budgeon relented, flustered by all the attention. "If you promise to dance and not listen for my mistakes."

Everyone clapped and cheered and found partners for the next dance.

Monsieur Fournier stayed near the pianoforte and smiled down at its fair musician. Margaret had no partner this time but watched the dancers with pleasure.

When the song ended, Joan returned to her side, breathless and grinning. "And how are you getting on with that housemaid who barely tolerates you?"

Margaret blew out a breath between puffed cheeks. "Better, I think."

Joan surveyed the crowd. "Which one is she?"

Margaret nodded toward Fiona, now dancing gracefully with a Hayfield footman. She marveled at the transformation. Fiona looked almost happy, and as elegant as a lady. "That's her. Fiona."

Joan regarded the Irishwoman thoughtfully. "I'm not surprised." She tilted her head. "For all her smiles tonight, that one's had a hard life. I can tell."

Margaret asked tentatively, "And you, Joan. How is life at Hayfield—any improvement?"

Joan shrugged. "About the same. Though having this to look forward to has helped. How surprised we were to be invited." Joan slanted her a knowing glance. "I don't suppose you had anything to do with that?"

Margaret only shrugged.

Fred, the hall boy who had been posted upstairs on door duty, ran in and found Mr. Hudson. "Thought you should know, sir. Mr. Lewis Upchurch just arrived. Wants his horses and carriage attended to."

Mr. Hudson frowned. "He was not expected. Thank you, Freddy."

He dispatched the groom, who left with a good-natured groan, promising to return in a flash.

Then Mr. Hudson laid a hand on Fred's shoulder. "You stay here and enjoy yourself, Freddy. I'll mind the door."

Fred beamed. "Awfully decent of you, sir!"

But Margaret's mind was still echoing with Fred's news. Lewis Upchurch had returned.

Then, before Hudson had even moved, there Lewis was, framed in the doorway, resplendent in evening attire, frock coat and cravat, as though he had just been dining out and not on the road for the last few hours. His valet, Connor, also well dressed, slipped in behind him.

Lewis surveyed the room. "What's all this, then? A party without me? I'm crushed." His tone was part hurt, part humor. Was he truly offended or jesting?

"Your brother knew you'd approve," Hudson soothed, handing him a glass of punch and deftly smoothing things over. "In fact, I believe he credited you with the notion."

Lewis hesitated, then lifted his chin. "Dashed right too." He took a long swallow. "Though had I planned the affair there would be real drink instead of this weak woman's punch."

"Exactly," Hudson agreed, a strange glint in his eyes.

Connor, Margaret noticed, skirted the crowd and sidled over to a beaming Hester. He took her hands, spread them wide, and surveyed her new dress with admiration.

Lewis downed the remainder of his cup and strode across the room. "Mrs. Budgeon, I wish to claim my dance as eldest son and master in my father's absence."

"I'm sorry, sir. But I am needed to play. We engaged a fiddler, but I am afraid he is, em, indisposed."

Jenny protested loudly, "Flat-out foxed, more like!"

Mrs. Budgeon offered apologetically, "Perhaps another of the staff will do?"

Once again Betty ducked behind Mr. Arnold. Lewis looked around the room, frowned at Jenny's saucy gap-toothed smile, hesitated on Joan, then landed on Nora.

His eyes narrowed as he walked toward her. "You look familiar. What's your name?"

Accent, don't fail me now! "Nora, sir. Nora Garret."

"Have we met?"

She almost said she made his bed every morning but feared he would find some unintended innuendo in that. Instead she laughed nervously and looked down at her clasped hands. "Not likely."

She was aware of Joan's wide eyes as she looked from this gentleman to her former mistress and back again. Had Joan ever seen Lewis Upchurch? It was possible she had seen him when he called at Berkeley Square once or twice early in the season. She certainly hoped Joan wouldn't say anything to expose her now. She had enough to worry about, fearing she might expose herself.

Something about the flat gleam in Lewis's eyes made Margaret wary, but when he offered his arm, she took it.

Nathaniel sat in the cozy sitting room upstairs, spent. Helen sat in an armchair near the fire, book in hand. He was glad they had decided to give the servants their ball. But it had never crossed his mind that in so doing, he might be compelled to dance with Margaret Macy again, and in his very home. He might have reconsidered had he known. His traitorous body had reacted to her nearness, the touch of her hand in his, in annoying fashion.

Hudson gave his telltale double knock and entered when bid. Nathaniel was still not used to seeing his friend in such a role. In Barbados, things had been much more informal between them.

"Good evening, Hudson. Everything all right belowstairs?"

"I . . . believe so, sir. Shall I have tea and sandwiches sent up for you here?"

"Thank you, Hudson, yes," Helen replied for them both.

Hudson hesitated. "I thought you would want to know that Mr. Lewis has just arrived."

"Lewis?" Helen's countenance brightened. "We weren't expecting him."

Nathaniel frowned and sat forward. "Where is he?"

"Last I saw him he was dancing with our new housemaid."

Nathaniel stood abruptly to his feet. Helen rose and stepped to his side, laying a hand on his arm. "Nathaniel . . . careful. Please don't fight again. Lewis means no harm to . . . anyone, I'm sure."

It was an odd reaction, he realized after his burst of anger subsided, unless she knew the true identity of the new housemaid.

"I shall just go down and welcome him home." Nathaniel patted Helen's hand, extracted himself from her grip, and quit the room. He strode down the corridor and jogged down the stairs. In the basement, the unexpected sound of the pianoforte—along with the aromas of savory meats, yeasty breads, and ale—ushered him down the narrow passageway to the servants' hall.

From the doorway, Nathaniel saw them, and his stomach clenched. Lewis, tall and handsome, hand in hand with Nora, looking self-conscious. But in a flash, he saw not Nora but Margaret. Not with black hair but with blond. Her simple frock replaced with a gown of fine white satin, jeweled ornaments in her golden curls, eyes sparkling up into the face of his dashing older brother. He felt again the sharp kick of jealousy, the iron weight of dread he had felt two years ago when he realized, *She doesn't look at me that way. . . .* And he'd tried to ignore the growing fear that he was losing her. To his very own brother. A man who would never appreciate her, never love her as he did.

Lewis danced Nora through the doorway, all but colliding with Nathaniel, jarring him from his miserable reverie.

Lewis drew up short. "Nate, ol' boy. Grand party. Well done. Wouldn't have thought it of you."

"Mr. Upchurch!" Nora blurted, face blushing. "I . . . I am glad to see you. Again."

He doubted it. She looked embarrassed. Caught.

Bemused, Lewis glanced from the girl's flushed face back to him. "A housemaid is glad to see you. And why should that be, I wonder?"

"I have no idea," Nathaniel said, avoiding her eyes. "What brings you home?"

"I must have sensed something afoot. I can smell a party forty miles off."

"Apparently."

Nora pulled her hands from Lewis's grasp and excused herself, hurrying away down the passage.

Lewis watched her go. "She reminds me of someone. . . . Who is it?"

"One of your many conquests, no doubt," he said dryly. "Well, I shall leave you to it. Just wanted to welcome you home."

Retreating into the kitchen, Margaret wrung her hands in time with the twisting of her stomach. Now Nathaniel would think the worst of her. If he still thought her simply a maid, he would now think her a flirt, a saucy light-skirt who had instigated the dance and near tête-à-tête with Lewis. And worse, if he suspected who she was, he would surely think she was up to her old tricks. Trying to woo his older brother. She paced the kitchen, fretting.

One of the hired servers looked up from the tray she was laying with tea and sandwiches. "All right, love?"

Margaret nodded. Then her eyes locked on the tray. "Is that for upstairs?"

"It is."

"May I take it up?"

The older woman shook her head. "Don't want them thinkin' I'm shirkin' my duty. Yer to be dancin'. Aren't you enjoying it?"

"I was, but . . . a certain man was becoming a bit forward."

"A footman, was it?" The woman tsked. "Always a footman."

Margaret stepped near. "May I please take it up? The sitting room is it?"

"Yes, but . . . Oh, very well. If yer set on it. Any man comes lookin' fer ya, I'll send him on his way sharp-like, all right?"

"Thank you."

Hands trembling, Margaret carried the tray upstairs and along the corridor to the sitting room. This way, she told herself, Nathaniel would see her and know she was not still with Lewis. Would not imagine the two of them alone together somewhere and believe the worst. Using her elbow, she hooked the door and pulled it open, letting herself in. Carrying the tray inside, she kept her head down to mask her anxiety.

"Ah, Nora," Helen said. "Why are you not at the ball? The hired servers were to relieve you all tonight."

"I don't mind. They were busy, so I offered."

Helen nodded, but Nathaniel watched her through narrowed eyes as she set down the tray on the table before them.

"Shall I pour, or . . . ?"

She hoped to delay her departure, though she was sure her hands would shake if she tried to pour under his scrutiny.

But Helen excused her. "Never mind, I shall pour. You go back downstairs and enjoy yourself."

"Thank you, miss." Margaret curtsied and stepped to the door, just as Lewis sailed through it.

He hesitated at seeing her. "There you are. Wondered where you'd gone to."

"Lewis!" Helen called warmly.

He turned to his sister, "Hello, Helen old girl." He walked over to kiss her upturned cheek, and Margaret made her escape.

Nathaniel wasn't sure what to think. Would "Nora" and Lewis still be dancing, or lingering alone in the dim passage, had she not been asked to bring up the tray? Or had she really offered, and if so why? She clearly had not taken advantage of a private moment to reveal her identity to Lewis, for he obviously had no idea who she was.

"A ball at Fairbourne Hall, at long last." Lewis smirked. "I take it the economizing is over?"

Nathaniel shook his head. "No. But we thought it wise to do something good for our people here, after recent . . . misunderstandings. But we still must tighten our belts or we may yet need to take more radical steps. Perhaps even sell the London house."

"Never say so." Lewis's face puckered. "Promise me you will not do . . . In fact, you cannot, without my consent, my being the eldest and all."

Nathaniel willed himself not to grow angry. "Lewis, you are perfectly welcome to stay and manage the estate if you like, but you cannot manage it from your London club."

Lewis stared at him, shaking his head. "I still don't understand why you didn't remain in Barbados. We were managing fine here on our own. Weren't we, Helen?"

Helen sipped her tea but made no answer.

Nathaniel said, "Even if that were true, it was time for me to come home."

One of Lewis's eyebrows rose. "Barbados didn't suit you?"

"It wasn't Barbados I objected to. It was slavery, as you know."

Lewis pressed, "You think we have problems now? Force Father to give up slave labor and you'll learn the meaning of financial straits."

"Money isn't everything, Lewis."

Lewis frowned. "Then why do you always ride me about it? Your lofty morals don't put you in charge, Nate. Nor do they give you the right to sit there and play potentate."

Nathaniel seethed. "Father put me in charge when you insisted on remaining in London while Fairbourne languished. Had you stayed in Barbados as he wished, I—"

Lewis leaned back and crossed his long legs. "Too dashed hot there. Too much work." He raised a brow. "Not enough beautiful women."

"Lewie . . ." Helen scolded, but affection tinged her tone.

Nathaniel inhaled deeply and moderated his voice. "So, to what do we owe the pleasure?"

Lewis shrugged. "No reason. Does a man need a reason to come to his own home?"

"Usually. Do you mean to stay, then?"

"No, not yet. I've just come down for a day or two."

"What are your plans?"

"No plans." He grinned at Helen. "Just wanted to see my favorite girl."

Even though Lewis directed the words at Helen, Nathaniel had the distinct impression she was not the "girl" he meant.

Life in service could be very regimented and dictatorial,
with little time off and the knowledge that romantic
relations between servants were forbidden in many houses.

— *Luxury and Style,* "The History of Country House Staff"

Chapter 20

In the morning, Margaret trudged downstairs beside Betty. They were both exhausted from being up so late the night before.

"Fiona looked so lovely in her gown last night," Margaret said. "I still can't imagine how she came by it. And did you see her dancing? So graceful and elegant. Almost as if she were a lady."

Betty sighed wearily, eyes distant. "She might have been once."

Margaret turned to stare at her.

"Thought she was giving up all this"—Betty lifted her housemaid's box—"but it weren't to be."

Stunned, Margaret grasped Betty's wrist to halt her progress. "What are you talking about?"

Betty winced, chagrined. "I'm tired and not thinking straight. I shouldn't have said anything."

"But you have to tell me now."

Betty shook her head. "No I don't. And don't you be askin' Fiona either, my girl. That would be foolhardy indeed. Do you hear?"

Margaret nodded. Satisfied, Betty continued down the stairs, but Margaret stood there, mind whirling.

After breakfast and prayers, Margaret set about cleaning Lewis Upchurch's bedchamber, which had been fastidiously neat until his return the night before, but which had already been marred by his presence—small clothes on the floor, bedclothes in a tangle as though he'd spent the night wrestling angels or someone more earthly, water sloshed onto the washstand, a jumble of toiletry items in disarray. And she didn't even want to think about what might await her in the chamber pot. The reality of men was certainly different than the pristine image they portrayed in a ballroom.

Where was Connor? She had not seen him since morning prayers. Even with a valet in residence, she would be expected to deliver water and empty slops first thing in the morning, and to return later to clean the room and make the bed. But the valet was responsible for his master's clothing. Was Connor down in the stillroom, becoming "reacquainted" with Hester? Margaret lofted the bedclothes high, enjoying the way they rose and billowed before settling flat. The door behind her flew open with a bang. She stifled a shriek and spun around, pillow to her chest. A shield.

Lewis Upchurch hesitated fractionally upon seeing her, and then a lazy grin spread over his face. "Well, well. Look who's here. How kind of you to pay a call after our dance last night."

He was wearing riding clothes—cutaway coat, leather breeches, Hessian boots. He looked devilishly handsome, and his light brown eyes glinted with confidence and mischief. She had always been drawn to confident men.

She dipped an awkward curtsy, pillow still in arms. "Good day, sir."

She should have gone about her work. Instead she remained motionless, thoughts racing. Was this an unfortunate coincidence or the answer to her plight? Before her stood Lewis Upchurch, the very man she had sought out with marriage in mind at the Valmores' ball, hoping to foil Sterling Benton's plan. Now, at last, she was alone with him—in broad daylight and behind closed doors. The thought made her palms perspire.

Should she tell him who she was? Dramatically remove her cap, wig, and spectacles and wait for realization to dawn? Her heart pounded, her breathing grew shallow and rapid. How would he react? Would his heart go out to her when she explained her desperate situation, or would he grimace in scandalized disgust to see Miss Macy so denigrated? Or worse, would he sneer or flee, thinking it a desperate ploy to trick him into marriage? *"By Jove, one moment I was in my bedchamber flirting harmlessly with a housemaid, and in the next, I was trapped by a spoiled hoyden demanding I rescue her reputation!"*

Lewis walked near. "Cat got your tongue?"

Margaret swallowed. So near, yet no flicker of recognition. Should she abandon the idea while she still could? If he refused her, how humiliating that would be. What would she do then—shrug, slap her wig back on, and empty his chamber pot?

In her earlier fantasies, she had imagined a thrilling scenario. The tragic heroine, standing on the dim balcony, staring up at the stars bemoaning her unjust fate, when handsome Lewis appeared. One moment, he regarded a dejected housemaid with compassion. The next, the scales fell away, and his eyes were opened.

"Of course! No wonder I thought we had met before. My soul recognized you, even if my foolish eyes did not!"

And he would put his hands on her shoulders, turning her to face him when she would look away. *"Look at me. What is the matter?"*

And she would tell him, all maidenly embarrassment and injury. And he would assure her no one would harm her. No one would touch her, except him. His hands would cradle her face.

"There you are," he would whisper, his voice growing husky, his face, his lips nearing hers. *"How I have missed you . . ."*

"You missed something."

"Hmm?" Shaken from her reverie, she found Lewis smirking at her. He pointed to a soiled stocking on the floor.

Cheeks heating, she bent to retrieve it. When she straightened, she saw him tugging off his gloves.

He glanced around the room with a frown. "Have you seen my valet recently?"

"No, sir."

He muttered something derogatory about the young man, then arched an eyebrow. "I don't suppose you would like to help me undress?"

He was probably joking, but still her body flushed in indignation. "No, Mr. Upchurch, I would not."

She turned and stalked from the room, glad she had not revealed herself to him. She was halfway down the corridor before she realized she had addressed him in her normal voice, and quite haughty in the bargain.

On her way downstairs, Margaret stopped at the housemaids' closet to gather up the lamps she had collected. She carried them down to the butler's pantry, where Craig would trim the candles and clean the lamps. On her way along the basement passage, she passed the stillroom, surprised to see its door partially closed—it was usually wide open. She glanced around the door, hoping Hester was all right.

She was more than all right, apparently. She was leaning back against her worktable, wrapped in the arms of a ginger-haired man in a dark suit of clothes. Margaret pulled back guiltily and quickly continued on her way. She had wondered where Lewis's valet was. Now she knew.

Margaret watched Mrs. Budgeon fly about the house in a flutter of nerves and preparations. Evidently, Lewis Upchurch had taken it upon himself to invite guests to dinner while he was home and they had insufficient staff to wait at table. Piers Saxby, his sister, and Miss Lyons had come to Maidstone to visit the Earl of Romney and see all the improvements to his estate. But Lewis had persuaded them to come to Fairbourne Hall first. Together with Helen, Lewis, and Nathaniel, they would be a party of six.

Mr. Arnold, Thomas, and Craig would wait at table, of course, as would the valet, Connor. But that meant they would also need to find livery to fit Freddy, the hall boy. And one of the maids would need to wait table as well. Betty was chosen, but Mrs. Budgeon informed Fiona and Nora that they would need to lend a hand as needed, both in delivering dishes from the servery warming cupboard and carrying away lids from covered dishes and plates from used courses as the dinner progressed.

Margaret was relieved she would not be required to stand behind one of the chairs, to serve the guests directly and risk Lavinia Saxby or even Miss Lyons recognizing her. If Helen was any indication, women were more likely to see through her disguise than men were. The thought of venturing into the back of the dining room to deliver and carry made her nervous enough.

At seven, the guests made their way into the dining room, lit with candelabras and decorated with towering displays of fruits and flowers, which Margaret had helped the chef arrange. Monsieur Fournier was more tense and bossy than she had ever seen him. Not harsh, but focused and exacting, aware of the pressure to perform, to please, and well represent his employers. Pressure exacerbated by the fact that they were all—from chef to scullery maid—out of practice in entertaining.

Young Freddy seemed especially nervous, decked in livery tacked up to shorten sleeves in haste, hair slicked back. Betty looked somewhat flushed herself, in black dress and white cap and apron, pressed for the occasion. Fiona, meanwhile, was cool and calm as usual. Thomas and Craig were powdered and proud in their best livery, and Mr. Arnold oozed chin-up decorum, though Margaret noticed his hand tremble when he poured the wine.

With Fiona, Margaret carried up dish after dish from kitchen to servery, now and then peeking in to catch a glimpse of the august company. There was Nathaniel, stiff yet undeniably masculine in evening dress. Lewis looked handsome as always, perfectly attired and with an air of confident ease. Piers Saxby eschewed traditional dark colors for a patterned waistcoat in apple green, his hair brushed into a high cockscomb over his brow. Fitting, Margaret thought.

Beside Helen sat Lavinia Saxby, Mr. Saxby's sister, with whom Margaret had been at school. And between Piers and Lewis sat the beautiful brunette, Miss Barbara Lyons, whom Margaret had seen with these same two men at the London masquerade ball. How Margaret's life had changed since then.

Carrying in courses and handing them off to Mr. Arnold or Thomas, Margaret heard snatches of dinner conversation. Most of it vague pleasantries—the weather, upcoming shoots and hunts, various house parties attended. But then Margaret heard her own name mentioned and nearly spilled a platter of poached pigeon.

". . . scouring all of London and beyond, but still no sign of the missing Miss Macy." Saxby swallowed a bite, then continued, "At first, the gossips predicted an elopement."

Margaret's cheeks burned. She felt someone's eyes on her and glanced over to find Helen looking her way.

Thomas stepped near and took the pigeon from her, whispering for her to next bring in the sweetbreads. In the servery she could still hear the humiliating conversation.

"But if that were the case, the family would have heard from her by now," Lavinia Saxby insisted. "And we would have heard of a missing gentleman as well."

Saxby considered. "Then perhaps she has been abducted. Or worse."

"Never say so," Lavinia protested.

Margaret returned from the servery and stood at the rear of the dining room, holding a silver serving dish of sweetbreads at the ready.

Lewis leaned back, all elegant nonchalance. "Be careful what you say about Miss Macy," he warned. "Nathaniel here was quite besotted with her once upon a time."

"Were you indeed?" Miss Lyons asked, brows arched high.

Nathaniel fidgeted. "That was a long time ago. Before I sailed for Barbados."

Saxby smirked. "Some say that was why you left the country."

"I left because my father asked me to, Mr. Saxby."

"Nate here is the dutiful son." Lewis winked. "Or was."

"I don't imagine Margaret was very happy when her mother married Sterling Benton so soon after Mr. Macy's death," Helen mused. "And even less so when Benton sold their family home."

"To give up some rural cottage for a chance to live in Berkeley

Square with Sterling Benton?" Miss Lyons scoffed. "I'd say she had not a thing to complain about."

Nathaniel's expression hardened. "Then you did not know Stephen Macy, nor Lime Tree Lodge, if you think Sterling Benton or Berkeley Square could compare favorably with either of them."

Margaret's throat tightened to hear Nathaniel say so.

"So what do you say, Nate," Saxby asked. "Has some harm befallen Miss Macy, or has she gone off on a lark?"

Nathaniel flicked a glance across the room—toward her? "Miss Macy was headstrong and impulsive when I knew her years ago. And I imagine she is headstrong and impulsive now."

Embarrassment flushed through Margaret.

Saxby goaded, "Impulsive, as in throwing you over for a chance at Lover Boy Lewie here?"

Margaret's vision blurred and she felt herself sway.

"Piers, really," Miss Lyons murmured disapprovingly.

Likely hoping to bring the subject to less volatile ground, Lavinia said quickly, "I wonder if there is any truth to the rumor that Margaret will inherit a great—"

Crash. The silver serving dish slipped from Margaret's fingers. All heads turned her way. She swiftly turned and bent to begin picking up the mess, self-conscious at having her backside taken in by so many pairs of eyes. In a moment, Fiona was on her haunches beside her, scooping up the sweetbreads and sending her an empathetic grimace.

Mr. Arnold spoke up. "I'm terribly sorry, sir."

"No matter, Arnold," Nathaniel said. "These things happen."

Face burning, Margaret retreated belowstairs.

Nathaniel glanced toward the servery door. The uncomfortable conversation continued, though its subject had disappeared from sight.

"I only met Miss Macy once," Barbara Lyons said. "At the Valmores' ball. And she did seem desperate enough to elope. For she all but begged a partner. I nearly felt sorry for her."

"If she wanted a partner," Saxby said, "she had only to turn to Marcus Benton, who was at her heel all night, like a besotted hound."

Barbara shook her head. "It was obvious to me she did not care for young Mr. Benton." She fluttered her lashes at Lewis. "She only had eyes for you, Mr. Upchurch."

Lewis leaned near the brunette beside him. "While I only had eyes for you, Miss Lyons."

"As did I," Saxby said, glaring at him.

Lewis shook his head and confessed, "I am afraid I was less than gallant with Miss Macy. For the truth was, I was smitten with another lady." He looked meaningfully at Miss Lyons. "One as far from my reach as Miss Macy is from Nate's."

Nathaniel inhaled slowly, willing anger to remain at bay.

Saxby huffed. "Oh, you are never heartbroken for long, Lewis. I seem to recall you flirting with a whole succession of females since then."

"None seriously." Lewis kept his gaze on Miss Lyons's face, coyly dipped though it was.

"I wonder you find yourself at Fairbourne Hall so much more often lately," Saxby persisted, reptilian eyes sliding to Miss Lyons before returning to Lewis.

"It's Nate here," Lewis quipped. "Has me on a short tether these days."

"Has he? I thought it might have more to do with a certain ginger-haired girl in Maidstone."

Lewis's grin faded. "I don't know what you are talking about."

"Oh, come, *Lewie*," Saxby sneered. "You forget Lavinia and I still have friends and family nearby. Local gossip does not fail to reach us."

Lewis said through clenched teeth, "The gossips have it wrong."

"Do they indeed?"

Nathaniel wondered if Saxby manufactured such a claim to put a wedge between Lewis and Miss Lyons. It was obvious both men were vying for the woman's affections.

While the question, the challenge, hung in the air, Lewis flicked a look across the room, as if checking his reflection in the window. Connor, his valet, stood behind his chair, ramrod straight.

Lewis then riveted Saxby with an icy glare. "Indeed."

"Then I stand corrected." Saxby met his glare, then relaxed back against his chair. "Or should I say, *sit* corrected." He raised his glass in a mock toast.

Nathaniel glanced at his brother's valet. Noticed Connor's jaw tighten. He supposed the young man was privy to most of Lewis's comings and goings, clandestine or otherwise. He likely knew whether Lewis—or the gossips Saxby quoted—spoke the truth. But Nathaniel knew a good valet was nothing if not discreet. Lewis's secrets would be safe.

Just as Margaret's secrets were safe with him.

Formidable in her dark silk dress, the keys to the household at her belt . . . it was often the housekeeper's duty to show visitors around the house.

—Margaret Willes, *Household Management*

Chapter 21

Even after the uncomfortable dinner party, Margaret's mind continued to drift to the mystery of Fiona's ball gown. While she and Betty scrubbed the dining room floor the next morning, Margaret daydreamed about Fiona's past, imagining several possible scenarios.

Unable to resist any longer, she slid her pail forward and asked, "*Why* can't I ask Fiona about the dress?"

Betty pulled a face. "Not this again. Just . . . don't ask."

"A gown like that must have cost a great deal of money. Too much for a housemaid to afford. And I can't imagine her mistress handing down such a gown—it's too impractical."

Betty squeezed out her cloth. "Fiona wouldn't want us talking about this."

"Do you know how she came by it?"

Betty hesitated. "Yes. But not because she told me." Betty sat back on her heels, regarded her warily. "Fiona will be vexed indeed if you pry into this—believe me."

Margaret sniffed. "Very well."

The upper housemaid studied her, a knowing glint in her blue eyes. "I see how you are, Nora. You won't let it lie, so I'll tell you. Only to keep you from askin' Fiona and makin' life difficult for us all."

Guilt pricked Margaret. "I shouldn't tempt you to gossip. I'm sorry. Listen, Betty, let's forget it."

"No, you listen. Fiona has never breathed a word to me. But my uncle is butler at Linton Grange, where Fiona last worked, and he told me."

"Does Fiona know you know?"

Betty pursed her lip. "I don't believe so. You'd think she'd wonder, knowing the butler had the Tidy surname, same as me. But she's never mentioned it."

Betty scrubbed at a stubborn stain, then paused, gathering her thoughts. "This all happened some five or six years ago. Fiona was housemaid at the Grange, as she is here. It's the old story: the young master—the only son—fell in love with her. Asked her to marry him. Even set her up in her own cottage on the estate. It was him what gave her that fine gown—and dreams of a better life in the bargain."

Betty shook her head, lips pressed in a thin line. "I don't know if he really meant to marry her, or only told her so. His parents forbade the match, as you can imagine, throwing all sorts of obstacles in their way. But Fiona was certain he would marry her eventually, or so my uncle said. But it weren't to be. The young master died in a hunting accident. His gun misfired."

"Oh no." Margaret's heart sank.

Betty nodded. "He lived long enough to beg his parents to provide for Fiona after he'd gone."

"Your uncle heard that as well?"

"Servants hear everything, Nora," Betty said shrewdly. "Haven't you figured that out yet?" Her eyes hardened. "But that young man was no sooner in his grave than they put her out. Out of the cottage, off the estate. Without a bean to her name or a character. In the end, my uncle wrote one for her on the sly. He told me, and I put in a good word for her here. Mrs. Budgeon trusted me and hired her."

"Poor Fiona."

Betty nodded and returned to her scrubbing. "I've never regretted vouching for her. She's a hard worker and has a good heart for all that. She may be slow to trust, but once she does she's very loyal. And if she is a mite bitter . . . well, maybe now you'll understand why."

Margaret shook her head. "It isn't right."

"That's life in service for many a poor girl, Nora. Mind you take care 'round men. Even them what call themselves *gentlemen*."

For a few moments, Margaret scrubbed rather aimlessly as she considered everything Betty had told her. Then she said, "I'm surprised Fiona wore that dress. She must have known we would wonder. . . ."

"Nora." Betty's voice held a warning note. "If you dare let on I told you, I'll box your ears."

"Very well. Her former life is safe with me." Margaret winced on aching knees. "I am good at keeping that sort of secret."

That afternoon Margaret clumped down the back stairs, her housemaid's box in hand. Finished with the public rooms and bedchambers, she had been asked to clean Mrs. Budgeon's parlor belowstairs. Margaret crossed the passage into the servery, heading toward the basement stairs. As she did, she heard the jingling of keys. Normally, the jangle of Mrs. Budgeon's impressive set of keys was the signal to pick up one's pace, or quit gossiping and get back to work. But today that familiar jangle was accompanied by a less common sound—Mrs. Budgeon's voice raised, not in reprimand or command, but in fine elocution worthy of a museum curator. Margaret turned back and listened from the servery door.

"Fairbourne Hall was completed in 1735 by Lambert Upchurch and his wife, Katherine Fairbourne Upchurch. A covered walkway, or arcade, was added in 1760 by his eldest son, inspired by the Italian architecture he had seen on his grand tour. . . ."

Margaret realized Mrs. Budgeon was showing the house to some travelers, likely touring the Kent countryside. She knew this was a common duty for housekeepers in fine old country estates, and she found it oddly touching to hear Mrs. Budgeon in the role, going on with such pride about the house and its ancestors as though she were part of the family. Margaret wondered how much she would receive as a perquisite for her trouble.

Margaret remained hidden within the servery and listened. Footsteps told her Mrs. Budgeon was leading the visitors across the marble-floored hall.

"There are more family portraits in the salon, but allow me to draw your attention to a few here in the hall."

A high affected voice asked, "Is it true the Upchurch family made their fortune in the West Indies sugar trade?"

"Dorcas!" came a whispered reprimand. After all, a lady did not discuss money in public.

"The Upchurches have owned a sugar plantation in Barbados for well over a hundred years," Mrs. Budgeon replied. "In fact, Mr. James Upchurch, the current head of the family, presently resides there."

"So who lives here now?" the second young woman asked.

The voice struck a chord of familiarity in Margaret. A pleasant familiarity. Emily Lathrop . . . What was she doing here?

Mrs. Budgeon answered, "His grown children—his daughter, Helen, and his sons, Lewis and Nathaniel. Though Lewis is often in London." Then the housekeeper resumed her prepared commentary.

Margaret crept from the servery and peered around the corner as Mrs. Budgeon directed the attention of her small entourage to several paintings hung in the hall. Margaret saw her old friend Emily as she solemnly attended Mrs. Budgeon's narration. A second young woman stood at Emily's side, a close-in-age cousin, Margaret thought, though she had only met her once or twice. A matronly companion Margaret did not recognize stood behind them.

"Here we have portraits of three generations of Upchurch men: Lambert, Henry, and James."

The housekeeper stepped to the side and gestured regally to two other paintings. "And here are portraits of the sons of James Upchurch: Lewis and Nathaniel. Each was commissioned to honor his twenty-first birthday."

The matronly chaperone pointed across the hall and asked timidly, "May I ask, Mrs. Budgeon, about that black urn? It is most unusual."

"Ah." Mrs. Budgeon flipped a page in her book. "That is a basalt-ware urn produced by Josiah Wedgwood. . . ."

As the older women crossed the hall to examine the urn on its pedestal, the two young ladies stayed where they were, gazing up at the likenesses of Lewis and Nathaniel Upchurch.

Emily said, "Lewis Upchurch is exceedingly handsome, is he not?"

"Which is he?" the cousin asked in her high voice.

"The one on the left, of course."

"I don't know . . ." her cousin considered. "I like the face of the other. It is a strong face. Serious. Masculine."

"Do you think so? All the women I know think Lewis the more attractive. But then again, he is the elder and heir, which no doubt adds to his appeal." Emily giggled, and her cousin smiled obligingly.

"In fact, the younger Mr. Upchurch once proposed to my friend Margaret, but she refused him, so taken was she by his elder brother."

"And did the elder brother propose?"

"No." Emily sighed. "I could have told her he would not. But she wouldn't have listened."

Margaret's stomach sank to hear her friend say so.

"Has there been any word from her?"

Emily shook her head. "Not that I know of."

Margaret was surprised her mother had not shared news of the letter Margaret had sent. She hoped her mother had received it.

"What has become of her, do you think?"

Emily shrugged her thin shoulders. "Some guessed she had eloped, but word of the marriage would have reached us by now."

The cousin smirked. "If Marcus Benton shared my house, I should have no cause to wander, I assure you. Is it true they are engaged?"

"I cannot credit it. Margaret protested not to like him."

"I think you must be right. For did you see him dancing with that horse-faced American at Almacks last week? How she ever made it past the patronesses, I shall never know."

"I'm surprised Mr. Benton went at all with Margaret missing."

"Perhaps she isn't really missing."

Emily looked over sharply. "What do you mean?"

"Perhaps she *had* to go away, if you take my meaning."

"I don't."

"To hide a certain . . . condition?"

As the implication struck Margaret, she thought she might be sick.

"Not Margaret." Emily frowned, then tilted her head to one side as she considered. "Though she was a bit of a flirt and might have got in over her head . . ."

"With Marcus Benton?"

"Not him." Emily regarded the portraits once more. "But Lewis Upchurch is a notorious rake."

"And the more time passes without word of marriage . . ."

Margaret longed to rush into the hall and set the two young women straight, but her appearance would cause more scandal than it alleviated.

Perhaps she ought to write to Emily. Did Sterling have his tentacles in the Lathrop post as he did in his own house? She had to do something. As it was, her quest to spare her virtue seemed to be laying ruin to her reputation.

When the tour moved on and the hall was empty once more, Margaret lingered, quietly crossing the marble floor. She stood before Lewis and Nathaniel Upchurch. Their portraits, at any rate. She first regarded Lewis. The artist had skillfully captured the mischievous light in his golden-brown eyes and the hint of a smirk about his full mouth, as though he possessed a secret he was eager to tell. His nose was perfect, his features so well formed that he was almost beautiful. And knew it.

She turned her head to study Nathaniel's likeness. This was the Nathaniel of old. He did not wear spectacles in the portrait, but he did wear his somber expression. His face appeared pale and his thin mouth nearly prim. The artist had not treated kindly his long, pointed nose, but had painted it in bold, unforgiving strokes. His eyes—had she ever looked so closely at his eyes before?—were a stormy bluish green. His hair, darker than Lewis's, was thick and straight, lacking the rich curl of his elder brother's. Margaret thought, of the two, only Lewis's portrait flattered its subject. Even so, Nathaniel did have a good face, she decided, agreeing with the earlier assessment of Emily's cousin. *Strong, serious, masculine.*

Glimpsing a thin cobweb in the corner of the frame, she unconsciously lifted the portrait brush from the housemaid's box still in her hand, a nearly natural extension of her arm. She flicked away the offending filament. The brush lingered, and she gently dusted Nathaniel's portrait with a feathery touch—the firm cheek, the long nose, strong jaw, and stern mouth, wishing she might once again see him smile.

The echoing approach of footsteps on marble startled her. She swiftly turned, muscles tense, then relaxed to see it was only Mr. Hudson.

"How diligent you are. Even keeping Mr. Upchurch in shipshape." His brown eyes glinted with humor. "What do you think, Nora. Does that old thing do him justice?"

She shook her head. "Not at all, sir."

"Oh?" He reared back on his heels, clearly expecting nothing more than a smile or self-conscious assent. He considered the painting once more. "You are quite right, Nora. How dour he looks in that pose."

"Mr. Upchurch rarely smiles, sir."

Hudson's brows rose as he regarded her, then he looked back at the portrait, his lower lip protruding in thought. "He used to smile more often. I particularly remember several happy occasions in Barbados. ..."

A throat cleared to their left. Both Margaret and Mr. Hudson turned their heads, and she was surprised and chagrined to find Nathaniel Upchurch standing in the library doorway.

Hudson winced. "Forgive us, sir. We meant no harm. Only deciding that this portrait doesn't do you justice. Is that not right, Nora?"

Margaret ducked her head, nodding stiffly.

Nathaniel crossed his arms. "And what do you find lacking?"

She hoped he was addressing Mr. Hudson, but glancing up, she found Nathaniel's piercing eyes riveted on her. She squirmed. "Na— nothing, sir. Only that, in reality, you are more ... That is, you have changed. ... In appearance, I mean, and ..."

He said dryly, "Are you suggesting I have improved with age?"

She swallowed. "Yes, actually." She dared add, "A smile might improve your looks all the more."

He frowned. "I have had little cause to smile of late."

Hudson looked from one to the other. "Well, we shall have to work on that, Nora, shan't we." He chuckled and blithely winked at her.

Under Nathaniel's unwavering stare, Margaret's cheeks heated. She murmured, "Yes, sir," and excused herself, fleeing to safety belowstairs.

It was after midnight when Nathaniel walked through the upstairs sitting room on his way to the balcony. He could not sleep and hoped the crisp night air would help clear his head. His mind would not stop spinning with questions. What to do about his damaged ship, his brother, his sister, his housemaid . . .

Almighty God, make clear to me my path. Help me to do your will.

He pushed open the balcony door and stepped outside. A gasp startled him, and he tensed to full alert, as though "Pirate" Preston had just leapt over the railing.

But the figure at the far end of the balcony was no criminal. A threat? Yes, she certainly was that.

"Beg pardon, sir." Nora—Margaret—ducked her head and stepped back from the railing.

He said, "No need to rush off on my account."

"But you will want your solitude. I should not be here."

He supposed that was true. But he was suddenly eager she remain. Had he so soon forgotten his determination to avoid the pain of her presence like the plague itself?

"Please stay," he said.

Apparently he had.

She hesitated, then turned and gripped the railing once more.

He was relieved she did not ask why. His only answer could have been, *"Because I am a fool."*

She looked up, at the stars he supposed, or perhaps simply to avoid his gaze.

"That's the North Star." He pointed. "The bright one there. Do you see it?"

She followed his finger. "Yes."

"How many nights I looked for her on the voyage home. A favorite lady with our sailing master."

She nodded but was silent. He assumed he had failed to engage her in conversation.

But a moment later she asked quietly, "Did you enjoy the sea, sir?"

Satisfaction. "I did, though my return was not without its losses."

He felt her gaze, and looked over to find her watching him, brows quirked in expectation. She wore her spectacles, but he noticed her customary dark fringe was missing. Instead, her cap was pulled down low, her hair tucked up in it. Even so, she looked more like herself without all that dark hair around her face.

He asked, "Do your spectacles help you see things in the distance— like those stars?"

She looked back up at the stars, then tucked her chin to look over the top of the lenses. "Yes."

"I used to wear spectacles most of the time, until I realized all I really needed them for was reading and close work."

She nodded, then asked quietly, "You spoke of losses?"

He grimaced. "We were attacked at the docks by a man we knew in Barbados. Calls himself the Poet Pirate nowadays. Wasn't terribly poetic of him to rob and burn my ship."

She shook her head in sympathy. "Mr. Hudson mentioned it. How sorry I was to hear it."

"That's why I was insensible the night Hudson drove the coach and lost his way. He'd taken me to a nearby surgeon the customs house recommended. The man dressed my wounds and was overly generous with the laudanum."

She nodded her understanding once more.

Studying her profile, he asked quietly, "And how did you lose *your* way? How did you end up near the docks, then in Maidstone?"

"Tryin' to avoid trouble, I suppose."

"What sort of trouble?"

She shrugged, clearly uncomfortable.

"Were you . . . let go, for some reason? I promise it shall not jeopardize your situation here."

"It wasn't anything like that, sir. What I mean is . . . One of the men in the house, he made things . . . difficult for me."

"Difficult, how?"

She fidgeted, then whispered, "I'd rather not say."

"Had you no recourse, no friend or relative to protect you?"

She shook her head, once again staring up at the stars. "I found myself thinkin' of Joseph. When Potiphar's wife tried to seduce him, he fled, didn't he? He ran and ran fast without thinkin' ahead to the consequences, without lookin' back."

"So that's what you did."

She nodded.

He grinned wryly. "Joseph ended up in prison, you know."

"Oh," she breathed. "I forgot that part."

"I trust Fairbourne Hall is a better fate than prison. You are treated with respect, I hope?"

"Yes, sir, that is . . ." She faltered, began again. "Everyone on staff has been very kind."

He stiffened at her hesitation. Had Lewis trifled with her? "Miss—Nora. If anyone dares . . . If anyone bothers you, you must not hesitate to tell me. At once. I will"—*kill the man*—"reprimand severely any man who mistreats you. Do you understand?"

Tears filling her eyes, she nodded, but did not speak.

Dash it. "I'm sorry. I . . . didn't mean to upset you." *What an idiot I am.*

She shook her head. "I'm fine. My hardships are little to yours. Is your ship lost completely?"

He sighed, looking up. "No, but the costs to repair it will be higher than that star."

"I'm sorry, sir." She hesitated. "Was her name . . . the *Ecclesia*?"

"Yes. How did you know?"

"It was the name on your model ship." She looked sheepish about breaking it over again.

"Ah. Yes—*Ecclesia*. Latin for 'church.' "

"Clever."

"I once thought so. But I don't think myself very clever these days."

Her profile was painfully familiar by moonlight as she gazed up at the night sky. He was tempted to reveal that he knew who she was, ask why she was hiding, and offer to help her. But would she be mortified to be discovered in such a humbling role? Would she thank him or curse him for exposing her?

He bit his tongue. Why should he want to help her? Had she not proven herself fickle and shallow? But somehow, looking at her now, he saw none of those traits. He saw a shadow of the loneliness he felt inside himself. A quiet desperation to fix something broken. He knew what was broken in his life—his family's finances, his ship, his sister's heart . . . and his own. But what was broken in Miss Macy's life, and how did running away fix it?

He decided to bide his time. "Nora. You came to our aid—Hudson's and mine—and I am grateful. If there is any way we . . . I . . . can return the favor, you need only ask."

She looked over at him, pale eyes wide and silvery in the moonlight. She opened her mouth as though to respond, to confide in him, but instead pressed her lips together. Lips he had longed to kiss for years . . . and heaven help him, still did. Warmth swept through him at the thought of the kiss they had shared, at least in his dreams.

She whispered, "Thank you, Mr. Upchurch." Once again she hesitated, then dipped her head. "And now I shall bid you good-night."

She had forgotten to use a working class accent in her final words, but he made no comment. He liked hearing her voice. Her real voice. "Good night, Nora."

In his mind, he added, *"Good night, Margaret."*

The steward supervised the duties of the entire household, hiring and firing other servants, paying their wages and controlling expenditure.

—Giles Waterfield and Anne French, *Below Stairs*

Chapter 22

In the morning, Nathaniel stopped by Hudson's office to speak to him. "I have a project for you, Hudson. If you don't mind another trip to London."

"Not at all, sir."

Nathaniel studied his friend. "That was quick. And eager. Find the life of a house steward confining, do you?"

"A bit of getting used to, sir," he said diplomatically. "Not that I'm complaining."

"I don't blame you." Nathaniel could have gone to London himself, but he was reluctant to leave Fairbourne Hall so soon after returning. *Who am I fooling?* he asked himself. It was perfectly obvious he was reluctant to leave Margaret. He pulled the door closed behind him and cleared his throat. "It's a bit of a . . . *private* project."

Hudson leaned forward, interlacing his fingers on the desk.

Nathaniel began, "I want you to find out everything you can about a Marcus Benton, and while you're at it, Sterling Benton, of Berkeley Square, Mayfair."

Hudson did not blink a lash. "The man who came here looking for his stepdaughter?"

Nathaniel nodded.

"What am I looking for, sir?"

Nathaniel inhaled deeply. "I don't know exactly. Financial situation, family relations, unexplained absences, anything . . . unusual." He took another deep breath, contemplating how much to tell the man. He trusted Hudson implicitly, but there was no reason he needed to know—not yet, at any rate—just whom he had hired in the position of housemaid.

Hudson considered the request. "Do I take it you believe the step-father has something to do with this, em . . . ?"

"Miss Macy."

"Miss Macy's disappearance?"

"It is only suspicion at present."

"What about the girl? She may have run off of her own accord. Shall I investigate her whereabouts as well?"

"I don't think that necessary."

Hudson cocked his head to one side, studying him. "May I ask, sir, how you are acquainted with Miss Macy?"

"No, Hudson. You may not."

Mrs. Budgeon kept a stack of writing paper in the servants' hall, free for anyone who wished a piece or two to write home. Margaret wondered again if she ought to write to her friend Emily. A defensive measure. When she learned that evening that Mr. Hudson was returning to London once again, she saw it as a definite sign that she should.

> *My dear Emily,*
>
> *You have no doubt heard that I have gone away. I know that you, my dearest friend, would never assume the worst. Still, I thought I should write to you, so you will not fret about me. I did*

send a letter to Mamma—did she tell you? If she has not, then I fear it may have gone astray and never made it into her hands. I hope this letter fares better.

Nothing dire has befallen me. I have not been kidnapped, nor have I eloped, nor have I been compromised—even if cruel gossips are tempted to bandy such nonsense about. (Not you, of course, dear Emily.)

The truth is that I no longer felt safe living under the same roof as Marcus Benton. You know his uncle had been pressuring us to marry, and Marcus had become quite desperate to convince me or compel me by any means necessary—with his uncle's blessing, no less. Perhaps you will not believe me, or think my estimation of my charms puffed up and my worries foolish fancy. But trust me when I tell you my fears were very real and justified.

I don't expect you to defend me to fickle society nor to the world at large, but I did want you to know, dear loyal friend, that I am well and safely hidden for now.

Yours sincerely,
Margaret Macy

"Mr. Hudson?" Margaret's heart beat fast the next morning when she stepped into the steward's office. Perhaps she ought to have asked Miss Helen to act as her intermediary again, but she didn't want to press the issue of her identity with the woman, who seemed determined to carry on the ruse for some reason of her own. She hoped Mr. Hudson would not refuse her—or worse, show the letter to Nathaniel Upchurch. He would surely recognize the name and wonder how his housemaid knew Emily Lathrop—closest friend of Margaret Macy. He might easily put two and two together and her secret would be revealed—and her safe hiding place gone with it.

"Yes, Nora?"

"I understand you are traveling to London this afternoon?"

"I am."

"I wonder if you might do something for me. I don't want to presume, but—"

"What is it, Nora?" His lips tightened a bit, perhaps anticipating an unreasonable request.

"I was hoping you could post this letter for me. From London."

"I could post it from Maidstone on my way. . . ."

"From London, if you please." She hurried to add, "It is bound for London, you see, and will arrive all the quicker."

"Ah." He held out his hand. "You do know, Nora, that whoever receives this letter will have to pay the postage."

"I know, sir." She placed the letter into his waiting palm.

He glanced down at the direction, brows furrowed, and for a moment she feared he recognized the name. Then his dark expression lifted. Had he perhaps expected a letter to a young man, and did not relish being party to some illicit communication?

He said, "I trust Miss Emily Lathrop will find the postage no hardship?"

"No hardship, sir."

"Very well, Nora."

Relief washed over her. She smiled. "Thank you, sir."

Nathaniel stepped from his room, hat and gloves in hand, and Jester at his heel. He needed to go into town to take care of a brief errand. In the corridor, he saw Helen in her bedroom doorway, speaking in low tones to Margaret, who wore bonnet and shawl. He wondered idly where she had been. He skirted the women to avoid interrupting their conversation.

Helen called him back. "Nathaniel, are you driving into Maidstone?"

He turned. "Yes."

"Good. Would you mind taking Nora to the modiste's on Bank Street?"

Nathaniel considered. He had already asked for the dogcart to be brought around, so a passenger would be no problem. He enjoyed driving the small sporting carriage, harnessed to a sturdy Cleveland bay. And Jester could ride along as well, which the dog seemed to relish. Best of all, while he was in the bank, no one would be tempted to steal a carriage with a wolfhound sitting watch.

He said, "If you like. I am headed to the county bank very near there."

"Are you?" Helen's wide eyes were all innocence. "How convenient, then."

Nathaniel slanted her a narrow glance. Was his sister up to something?

Feeling self-conscious, Margaret followed Mr. Upchurch downstairs and outside, remaining several paces behind him. A small carriage with two tall wheels waited on the drive, harnessed to a single horse.

Nathaniel said to the groom, "The housemaid is going along on an errand for Miss Upchurch."

Clive lowered the tailboard and gave her a boost up while Nathaniel climbed onto the front bench and took the reins. Jester leapt in behind Nathaniel's seat, and off they went. How strange it felt to be riding on the back of a vehicle driven by Nathaniel Upchurch.

They passed through Weavering Street and followed the road into town. Around them, men wielded scythes in lush golden fields, finishing up the harvest. Margaret tipped her face to the mild sunshine and breathed in the crisp autumn air. Behind her, Jester took in the passing countryside, tongue lolling, eyes at blissful half-mast in the brisk breeze.

Several minutes later, they rumbled into Maidstone and turned down Bank Street. In front of the ladies' shop, Margaret alighted.

Mr. Upchurch looked down from his bench. "How long do you need?"

"Not long. Perhaps . . . twenty or thirty minutes?"

He nodded. "I shall collect you here in half an hour's time."

She stepped inside the modiste's. From the shop window, she wistfully watched Nathaniel tip his hat to an elderly matron and return the wave of a passing lad as he drove off toward the bank.

Margaret made quick work of selecting the face powder and new rouge Miss Upchurch wanted. Helen had asked her to purchase the items rather than prepare them in the stillroom. She didn't want the servants speculating about her sudden interest in cosmetics.

Half an hour later, Mr. Upchurch halted the cart in front of the shop as arranged. She hopped up on the tailboard, reminding herself that a servant would not expect her master to assist her.

He glanced back to make sure she was settled, then told his horse to walk on.

She noticed he turned down an unfamiliar street—taking a different route home. A few minutes later, the road curved to follow a narrow mill leat. Accelerating around the bend, the cart wheel hit a deep hole, and Margaret suddenly felt herself thrust off the tailboard. For one second, a midair weightlessness tingled through her stomach. She gave a little shriek and landed in a bone-rattling thud on the hard road.

Jester barked a warning.

Vaguely she heard Mr. Upchurch call a "Whoa" to the horse some distance ahead. Blood roared in her ears and pain shot from hip to leg. She drew in a ragged breath as stars danced before her eyes.

Jester bounded over and licked her cheek.

Nathaniel jogged to her side. "Are you all right?" Alarm rang in his voice—more than the slight accident called for.

She looked up at him from her unladylike sprawl, gathering her skirts and parcels and trying to sit up.

"Wait. Be still. Jester, down." He frowned in concern. "Is anything broken, do you think?"

"I . . ." Mentally she surveyed her body. Hip throbbing. Palm burning. Head spinning. Though the latter might be caused by Nathaniel Upchurch's nearness.

"I've had the wind knocked out of me, that's all," she murmured. "I'm fine, really." She tried in vain to push herself to her feet.

Bending low, he took her hand and with his other cupped her elbow and pulled her gently to her feet. Her leg tingled numbly and threatened to buckle.

He wrapped his arm around her waist, steadying her. "Your ankle?"

"Just strained, I think. I'm fine." She had actually landed on her hip and bum, but wasn't about to specify that part of her anatomy.

She hobbled a step toward the cart, and suddenly his arm dipped beneath her legs and the other behind her back and she found herself swept up into his arms.

"Put your hands around my neck."

She felt her face flush, certain she was too heavy, self-conscious at having her side pressed flush to his body, his arm under her knees.

His mouth tightened and his neck beneath his cravat tensed— whether from bearing her weight or concern, she was afraid to hazard.

Reaching the cart, he set her on the tailboard. Jester barked his approval and hopped up behind her.

"Perhaps we ought to have the surgeon or at least the apothecary take a look at that ankle."

"No, sir. Really, I'm fine."

He lifted a hand toward her dangling limb. "The left one I believe . . . May I?"

She felt her mouth form an O, but no sound came.

He cupped the heel of her slipper and lifted it gently. His other hand grasped the toe, gingerly rotating her ankle. "Does that hurt?"

She swallowed and shook her head. Actually, it felt heavenly.

His gloved hand worked its way up her stocking-swathed ankle in a series of tentative squeezes. "All right?"

She nodded.

"Let's see your hands."

She held them forth for inspection like a grotty waif. Both were dirty, but she'd scraped the left one as well, trying to stop her fall.

Mr. Upchurch withdrew a clean handkerchief from his pocket. "Stay here."

He strode to the lazily flowing mill leat, dipped the handkerchief into the water and returned, squeezing it out as he neared. Again he held her left palm, and with his other hand dabbed at the dirt and scrape. The cool water felt wonderful on her raw, burning skin.

She felt like a child and yet like a cherished woman at the same time. *Foolish girl,* she told herself. *He is only being kind.*

He wiped the dirt from her other palm, then looked into her face. "You, em . . ." He cleared his throat. "You might want to, em, tidy your hair. Your . . . cap is a bit askew."

Dread rippled through her. *Oh no.* Had her wig slipped? Was any blond hair showing? He appeared self-conscious at pointing it out but not shocked or suspicious.

"Thank you," she murmured, reaching up to pull down her cap, and hopefully her wig with it.

He turned his back as she did so, stepped a few feet away, and sank to his haunches, studying a series of gouges in the road large enough to bury a cat.

"I attended a commissioners' meeting, where repairs to this road were approved and funds allocated. Progress is not what it should be. I shall have to speak to the town council." He rose. "Nora, do sit up front for the rest of the trip. I don't want to see you knocked off again."

Her nerves pulsed a warning—*too close.* "That's all right, sir. I don't mind."

"Please. I insist." He gestured toward the front bench, high over the cart's tall wheels.

Uncomfortable at the thought, she said, "Sir. Um. I don't know that I should be sitting up there. That is, when we reach Fairbourne Hall. I . . . think I would rather walk the rest of the way."

"But your ankle."

"It's fine, sir, truly. Please."

He gave her a knowing look. "It would not go well for you below-stairs if you were seen riding beside Mr. Upchurch. Is that it?"

"Something like that."

"I see. Very well. But do take care with that ankle."

"I will, sir. Thank you."

As he climbed up and drove on, Margaret wondered if he would have been as kind and attentive had Betty or Fiona fallen from his cart. Probably, she thought.

But she hoped not.

When she reached Fairbourne Hall and delivered the powder and rouge, Helen asked how the errand had gone.

"Fine." Margaret answered vaguely.

Helen's eyes sparkled with mischief. "Did Mr. Upchurch . . . notice you?"

Is that what Helen hoped would happen? "Not especially. But he was very kind."

Helen lifted one eyebrow. "Was he?"

Margaret felt her cheeks heat under Helen's watchful gaze but did not elaborate further.

A few days later, Nathaniel sat in the library, reviewing sketches for a proposed new row of laborer cottages. But he had difficulty concentrating. His mind kept wondering, replaying the scenes from the last weeks. Dancing with Miss Macy at the servants' ball. Standing near her on the balcony, staring up at the stars. Strolling with her along the moonlit arcade. Carrying her in his arms. . . .

A knock roused Nathaniel from his reverie. He looked up, feeling almost guilty, as if caught doing something he ought not. He was surprised to see Robert Hudson in the threshold.

"Hudson, hello. I didn't expect you back so soon."

"Is this a good time, sir?"

"Yes, of course." Nathaniel straightened and cleared his throat. "How did it go?"

"Very well, I think."

Nathaniel gestured toward the chair before the desk. "What did you find out?"

"Several interesting things." Hudson sat and pulled a small leather-bound notebook from his coat pocket. "First, Sterling Benton is indeed in financial straits, over head and ears in debt, according to a talkative banker."

"You were discreet in your inquiries, I trust?"

"Sir." Hudson tucked his chin, mouth down-turned, offended he even needed ask.

Nathaniel rotated his hand, gesturing for his steward to continue.

"Sterling Benton has borrowed too much, spent too much, and gambled too much, and refuses to retrench. Evidently very keen on keeping up appearances."

Nathaniel was reminded of Lewis's spend-all ways. "Go on."

"Marcus Benton is Sterling's nephew and apparent heir—assuming Sterling's marriage to the forty-something Macy widow results in no offspring." He opened the leather cover and consulted his notes. "Marcus is three and twenty years of age and is the son of Sterling Benton's younger brother—a law clerk—who resides in Greenwich. Apparently Sterling sponsored his nephew through Oxford, where he read the law. Marcus has no profession at present and lives the life of a gentleman supported by his uncle's generosity."

"Generosity that may be coming to an end."

Hudson nodded. "So it seems. Marcus has lately come to reside with his uncle and new wife in Mayfair. The wife has three children, but the eldest daughter had been the only one residing at Berkeley Square regularly. Except at school vacations, Caroline Macy boards at a girls' seminary and Gilbert Macy is at Eton."

Hudson hesitated. "I know you did not ask me to investigate the missing Margaret Macy, but I did learn something during my inquiries that bears on the situation."

Nathaniel steeled himself, fearing he might hear something unsavory about Miss Macy's conduct.

"Go on."

"Apparently, she will come into a good deal of money from a great-aunt who left her fortune in a trust, which is set to mature at Miss Macy's twenty-fifth birthday on . . ." Again Hudson consulted his notes.

"November the twenty-ninth," Nathaniel murmured, lost in thought. He became aware of the high arch of Hudson's eyebrows but ignored his expectant expression.

"Might explain why an eligible nephew has come to stay," Hudson said.

Nathaniel screwed up his face in thought. "I wonder why this inheritance has been such a secret before now. I never heard it mentioned before—by her or the gossipmongers."

"Perhaps she hoped to avoid—what is the term?—fortune hunters. Not that I include you in that lot, sir."

"Thank you," he said dryly. "Does she even know of the trust, do you think?"

"I did not gather it was unknown by her, but rather that she and her parents made a point of keeping it secret from society at large."

"I wonder if Benton knew before he married into the family."

Hudson coughed. "Do you mind a little hearsay along with the facts?"

"I suppose not."

"I gather there was quite a row in the Benton house when Sterling learned the details of the trust. From the tenor of the argument, it seemed evident that he thought *his wife* was the one inheriting the money."

Nathaniel stared at his steward, incredulous. "How on earth did you learn the details of an argument between man and wife in their own home?"

"My dear Nathaniel"—Hudson gave him a tolerant smile, reverting to Christian names as they had used in Barbados—"if one wishes to learn what really goes on in a house, one need only sweet-talk the right housemaid."

Sweet-talk the right housemaid . . . Nathaniel mused. He wondered if he ought to give it a try. And he had just the right housemaid in mind.

Despite his intentions, Nathaniel didn't manage to see Margaret all day.

That evening, he and Helen had just sat down to dinner when the second footman opened the dining room door and announced their brother. Lewis strode unceremoniously past the young man, and flopped into a chair.

"Lewis," Nathaniel said. "We did not expect you back so soon."

"Not that we aren't glad to see you," Helen added quickly.

"Hello, old girl. You are looking well, I must say."

Helen self-consciously touched her curled and styled hair. "Thank you."

Nathaniel gestured to the under butler. "Another place setting, Arnold."

"Right away, sir." Arnold signaled to the first footman, who languidly turned to do his bidding. Arnold, meanwhile, set several glasses before Lewis and poured wine.

Lewis took a long drink, then said, "I had to come and tell you the news."

"Oh?"

"I saw Sterling Benton in town. You remember him—married the Macy widow?"

Nathaniel felt Helen's quick look but kept his focus on Lewis. "Yes, what of him?"

"I spent a most diverting evening at White's, I can tell you. I won several guineas off an obliging solicitor-friend of mine. Well, not *friend* exactly, but a useful acquaintance."

Nathaniel frowned at the thought of Lewis gambling away family money—money needed for the estate, but he bit back a reprimand. "I thought you were going to tell us something about Benton?"

"I'm getting to that. Be patient." Lewis took another drink and gestured for a refill. "I was in a generous mood, having won for once, so I bought this solicitor-friend several rounds. Don't scold—a wise investment, as it turns out."

Nathaniel felt his jaw tighten. "How is that?"

"Well, he was well in his cups when Sterling Benton comes in, puffed up and slicked down as usual, that pup of a nephew at his heels."

Lewis took a long swallow of burgundy. "My friend takes one look at the haughty pair of them, then leans near and tells me he has a few ideas about why the Macy girl went missing."

Lewis had Nathaniel's full attention at last.

His brother's eyes glinted. "He hinted that Miss Macy has quite a tidy fortune coming to her on her next birthday. She's to be quite the little heiress."

Helen's eyebrows rose. "Really? I had no idea."

"Nor I," Lewis said, turning to him. "Did you know?"

Nathaniel hedged, "She never said a word to me."

So, Nathaniel thought, *the once-secret inheritance is becoming generally known.* He supposed Margaret's disappearance had loosened the tongues of the few who knew about it, whoever they were.

Lewis returned to his tale. "At all events, I called Sterling Benton over, ignoring the sharp kicks my companion delivered under the table, and asked after Miss Macy. Benton feigned such fatherly concern, but I could tell it was balderdash. So I told him he need not worry about her."

Helen's brow furrowed. "What? But how . . . ?"

Lewis grinned. "I believe I *may* have hinted that I knew where she was . . . and planned to elope with her or some such. I don't remember exactly, for I had kept pace with that solicitor in all those drinks, sorry to say."

"Lewisss . . ." Helen scolded.

Lewis waved away the lecture before she could begin. "I'd wager he doesn't care a whit about the girl, just wants to keep the money in the family. Stab me, I'm half tempted to find the chit and marry her myself. I wouldn't have to live on the meager allowance Nate wants to leash me to—"

"Don't." Nathaniel bit out the single syllable.

Lewis regarded him, one brow raised. "Why not? Want a second shot at her yourself, do you?"

Helen laid a hand on Nathaniel's forearm. Had she not been there, Nathaniel knew he would probably have lost control and punched his brother again.

Instead he gritted his teeth and warned, "Don't trifle with Sterling Benton, Lewis. The man is financially desperate. Far more so than we are. There's no telling what he might do if he thinks you stand between him and a fortune."

Early the next morning, Margaret began her duties in the drawing room, glad it was Fiona's day to carry the water and slops. As she opened the shutters, she thought back to Nathaniel Upchurch's kind attention when she'd fallen from the cart, and to their conversation on the moonlit balcony. His vow to defend her should any man mistreat her. His intense, earnest eyes had captured hers, and she had felt powerless to look away . . . to breathe. Tears had come from nowhere, burning her throat and filling her eyes. Oh, to have a man like Nathaniel Upchurch protect her. Love her.

Click. Somewhere nearby, a door latch opened. That was odd.

Pulse accelerating, she tiptoed to the threshold of the adjoining conservatory and peered around the doorjamb. By dawn's light seeping through the many panes of glass, she saw a figure— a man with his back to her—gingerly close the terrace door behind him. That door should have been locked. The man turned and crept across the room. For a rash second, she feared it was that pirate Nathaniel had mentioned. But then she recognized the man's profile. It was Lewis, coming in at dawn, his cravat untied and in need of a shave. He had obviously been out all night again. She wondered with whom.

He pulled up short at seeing her in the doorway but only lifted a finger to his lips and continued past her without a second glance. Apparently too tired—or sated—to bother flirting with her.

Margaret felt a dull stab of disappointment. Disappointment at his behavior, not at his disinterest in her. She had given up all thought of Lewis Upchurch, at least romantically. She hoped the poor girl, whoever she was, knew what she was doing.

Margaret sighed and returned to her work. The carpets were not going to brush themselves.

The masquerade . . . became the entertainment
of the century par excellence, not just with the upper
classes but much lower down the social scale.

—Giles Waterfield and Anne French, *Below Stairs*

Chapter 23

A round midday, Nathaniel read the staid *Times* before turning to the livelier of the London newspapers, the *Morning
Post*. He skimmed quickly through the social columns, the
who had been seen with whom, the engagements, births, and scandals.
Suddenly he stopped, heart lurching painfully against his breastbone.
His gaze flew back to the top of the column, and he read the lines
again, temples pounding with each word.

> *Young woman found drowned in the Thames. The body has*
> *not yet been officially identified, pending coroner inquisition*
> *and family notification, but an anonymous source reports*
> *that authorities speculate the deceased might be 24-year-old*
> *Margaret Macy of Berkeley Square, Mayfair, who has been miss-*
> *ing since . . .*

What in the world? Was Margaret not somewhere in his house at
that very moment? He searched his memory. When had he last seen

her? Come to think of it, he had not seen her that morning. Nor had he found her on the balcony last night as he'd hoped. Had he seen her yesterday? He scoured his brain. Yesterday had been quite busy—a review of the account books with Lewis, a tedious hour with the under butler as he reported in minute detail on the inventory of the cellar, and a meeting with the council at town hall. But he believed he had seen Margaret the day before yesterday. Surely she did not have time to return to London and drown? This was mere speculation, surely. Irresponsible reporting. That was all.

He threw down the paper and rose, knowing he would have no peace until he made certain. Where would she be this time of day? In the past, he'd had no knowledge of what his mostly invisible maids did when. But since recognizing "Nora," he had found himself keenly aware of her movements, where he might catch a glimpse of her during her daily rounds. He consulted his pocket watch and winced in thought, trying to recall where she would be at this time. Belowstairs, he believed. He did not like to intrude into the servants' domain, but he could not wait.

From the library, he walked across the hall past the main staircase, then slipped through the servery and trotted down the basement stairs. Passing the butler's pantry, he turned and followed the dim passage past the kitchen and stillroom, neck craning for any glimpse of her as he went. It was quiet belowstairs. The kitchen was empty. Where on earth was everyone? He pushed open the door to the servants' hall, door banging off the wall like gunshot, startling the seated occupants within. Heads jerked around the table, and many pairs of wide eyes darted up at him. Ah, the servants' dinner time—he had forgotten it was so early. His eyes raked over the faces gaping at him and snagged on a certain pair of pale blue eyes, as startled as the rest. He resisted the urge to go to her. Take her hand. Feel her pulse. Relief swept over him. He realized he had thrown a hand over his chest and was clutching at his ragged heart.

Hudson rose, as did Arnold.

"Is everything all right, sir?" Hudson asked in concern.

Nathaniel held out a placating palm. "Sit. Please. I am sorry to disturb your dinner."

From the foot of the table, Mrs. Budgeon asked, "Is there something you needed, sir?"

He inhaled deeply, realizing he was out of breath. He laid his eyes on Margaret once more, satisfying himself.

"No, em, never mind. Everything is fine."

He formed an awkward smile, gestured for them to continue, and backed from the room, closing the door behind him. He was embarrassed, but relieved. *Everything is fine,* he repeated to himself. *Margaret is fine.*

He wondered who the anonymous source had been and if the report was really pure conjecture. Or had someone a motive for wanting Margaret Macy declared dead?

Nathaniel knew Lewis was somewhere about the place but decided not to seek him out. Instead, he went upstairs and knocked on Helen's door. He was nearly relieved when she did not answer. He didn't trust his ability to appear disinterested should he show her the news in person. What would he say? *"The* Morning Post *reports that Miss Macy's body may have been found—drowned in the Thames. Poor creature. Can you imagine?"*

Besides, he had the sneaking suspicion his sister knew very well who Nora was—perhaps had known long before he did.

He settled for circling the column of type with a stroke of blue ink and leaving the newspaper on the writing desk in her room. Closing the door behind him, he wondered where she was. During the early days of his return, Helen had rarely ventured farther than the sitting room, except for meals and Sunday services. But since the servants' ball, she had begun walking out-of-doors and involving herself in church charity work, and had even accepted an invitation to dinner from the vicar's wife.

At least someone's lot had improved since his return. He had a sneaking suspicion, however, that his sister's renewed interest in life had less to do with him than his steward, Robert Hudson. And he still wasn't quite certain how he felt about that.

Half an hour later, Helen burst into the library, cheeks flushed and out of breath, brandishing the folded newspaper like a weapon. "Did you leave this in my room?"

Nathaniel fought to keep his face impassive. He glanced up at the newspaper as though to remind himself. "Ah, yes. I thought you might be interested. You were some acquainted with her, as I recall."

"*I* was acquainted with her?" His sister's eyes pierced him, and he nearly quailed.

He found himself murmuring the lame lines he had practiced before. "Poor creature. Can you imagine?"

Helen narrowed her eyes, weighing his sincerity. Did she know? Did she know he knew? Or perhaps she merely studied him to see if he was more devastated by the possibility of Miss Macy's death than he was willing to let on.

"It is only speculation," Helen said. "You know the *Morning Post* is more gossip than fact. I would not worry if I were you."

"I am not worried."

One brow rose. "Are you not?"

He shrugged. "Are you?"

She stared at him, and he forced himself to meet her gaze blankly. She asked, "Have you shown this to Lewis?"

"No."

"Shall I?"

Nathaniel shrugged. "If you like. It makes no difference to me."

Helen frowned, studying him for several moments longer. Finally, she turned on her heel with a huff and swept from the room.

Apparently, acting disinterested had not earned him any points with his sister.

Margaret and Fiona were carrying baskets of laundry down the back stairs when Helen Upchurch called from the top of the stairs, "Nora, I need to speak with you. Alone."

Fiona gave her a hard look that asked, *"What have you done now?"* She took Margaret's basket atop her own and jerked her head to send her on her way.

Nervously, Margaret followed Miss Upchurch upstairs and into her apartment. Afternoon sunlight spilled warmly through the window and onto Helen Upchurch as she seated herself at her writing desk. Standing before her, Margaret gripped her hands together. Hard.

Helen handed her a newspaper. "My brother Nathaniel gave this to me. I thought you should see it."

Margaret accepted the folded paper and began reading the circled print. She felt disoriented, confused as the words swam before her, making no sense. She blinked, and read again.

"I don't understand," Margaret whispered, nerves flaring.

"Nor do I."

"Mr. Upchurch showed this to you?"

Helen hesitated. "Yes." She considered. "I cannot say he seemed terribly upset about it."

A flash of hurt stung Margaret. What was wrong with her? The *Morning Post* was speculating about her death, and she was disappointed Nathaniel Upchurch wasn't more affected by the news?

She skimmed the article again . . . *the body not yet officially identified . . . anonymous source . . . authorities speculate . . . deceased might be . . .*

Dear God in heaven, whose body?

Was the report mere speculation, based on the fact that she had yet to be found, alive or otherwise? Clearly, Sterling had reported her disappearance to the authorities. Had he done more than that? Had he resorted to violence? Or simply made convenient use of some other poor girl's death to suggest, anonymously, that the body was that of his missing stepdaughter?

Margaret! she scolded herself. *You're being ridiculous. Melodramatic.* Certainly Sterling Benton would not stoop so low, would not carry out such a desperate act.

Yet who would receive Margaret's inheritance if Margaret was dead or officially declared so? Her mother, or her sister? Either way, the Benton men were sure to profit.

"Thank you for showing me," Margaret murmured.

Helen's eyes widened with sympathetic concern. "What will you do?"

Margaret slowly shook her head. "I have no idea."

The next morning, a cloud of dread and uncertainly hovered over Margaret. She plodded through her duties, thoughts heavy with the news of her death and what, if anything, she should do about it.

After Margaret dressed Helen's hair, Miss Upchurch turned from the mirror to face her. "I have been giving it a great deal of thought and have decided you and Nathaniel are right. I have shunned society for too long."

"I . . . am relieved to hear it," Margaret said, though in truth her mind remained on the more pressing matter of news of her own demise. "Will you begin paying calls, then?" Margaret hoped she wouldn't be expected to accompany her.

"Something better. I have decided we should host a party here. It has been far too long since the Upchurches have entertained."

Here? They would be inviting a houseful of guests—some of whom Margaret was sure to have met, since they had acquaintances in common—to Fairbourne Hall, her hideaway?

She asked hopefully, "A small party with local friends . . . ?"

"A big party with local friends and friends from town. Many have quit London for their country estates, but a fair number live near enough to attend. I am thinking of a ball—as I so enjoyed my two dances at the servants' ball. Perhaps even a masquerade, since that was the last event I attended before . . ."

"A ball . . . ?" Margaret's mind was a whirl of worry and worse-case scenarios—London friends, perhaps Sterling Benton and her mother, or even Marcus Benton. She might be asked to serve them, or stand ready in the ladies' dressing room to assist female guests with their wraps or with using the chamber commode. Surely her mother would recognize her.

Helen frowned at her. "You don't approve?"

Margaret hesitated. "No, I . . ." What if someone saw through her disguise? The thought abruptly stilled her. *Disguise* . . .

She drew in a long breath. "I think you are absolutely right, Miss Helen. A masquerade ball is the perfect idea."

At breakfast, Lewis piled sausages on his plate and grinned at his brother and sister. "A masquerade ball, you say? Delightful notion! Why, I shall help plan the soiree myself. Do be sure to include Miss Barbara Lyons on the guest list. You know she is a favorite of mine."

"And with your friend Mr. Saxby, I believe," Nathaniel said dryly.

Lewis pulled a face. "Oh, a little friendly rivalry never hurt anybody."

Nathaniel's gut twisted. His brother's rivalry had hurt him a great deal two years ago. He avoided Helen's gaze and said evenly, "At all events, I don't think we should expect many of our London friends to come down. Besides, where would we put them all?"

"Never fear," Lewis said. "Miss Lyons has relatives nearby and might stay with them." He shrugged. "Or she could have my bed."

"Lewisss . . ." Helen reprimanded, drawing out his name as was her habit when vexed.

"Only a jest, old girl. Don't go getting all holier-than-Nate. One killjoy in the family is ample sufficient!"

Lewis stayed another night to help plan the ball. Then he returned to London with his valet in tow but promised to return for the masquerade to act the part of host for the evening.

Once he had taken his leave, Helen solicited Mr. Hudson's help. Since the two of them had made such a formidable team in planning the servants' ball, she saw no reason why they should not once again join forces to plan this one.

Even Nathaniel was pressed into duty one afternoon, in helping to write out the many invitations when he returned from his rounds of the estate.

When Helen took herself to her own room for more ink, Hudson watched her go, then turned to Nathaniel.

"Sir, uh, I wonder . . ."

Noticing Hudson's uncharacteristic unease, Nathaniel braced himself. "What?"

"You know I am . . . fond . . . of your sister," he faltered. "How would you . . . How would you feel about . . . about my . . ." He grimaced and muttered, "Arrr. Never mind. Foolish notion. A lady like her and a nobody like me."

Nathaniel looked at his friend, felt a combination of protectiveness for his sister, and true fondness and empathy for his smitten friend. No, Robert Hudson was not his sister's social equal. But he was a good man. A worthy man. He wondered how Helen would react. Had she any idea how obvious it was that she . . . well, at least, enjoyed the man's company? Was there more to it than that, or would she be offended at the notion of a match between them?

Nathaniel asked carefully, "Has my sister given you any indication she reciprocates your feelings?"

Hudson sighed. "I think so. But it's dashed hard to tell with women, isn't it? She'd be polite to the ratcatcher. But I believe it's more than politeness. And I think, maybe . . ." He sighed again. "Or maybe it's only wishful thinking on my part."

Nathaniel said, "Well, I cannot speak for her, but nor will I stand in your way."

"Do you mean it, sir?"

"I suppose I do. Though you shall have to lay off with the 'sir' bit."

Hudson grinned. "That I will, Nate. That I will."

Several days later, while Margaret put away the hairbrush and extra pins and tidied the dressing table, Helen sat at her writing desk. She picked up the first letter atop the thick pile of the morning's post.

She opened the missive and read. "Well, this is something of a surprise."

"What is?"

"We have received the first reply to our invitations. The Bentons have accepted."

Margaret's heart thudded. "Have they? All of them?"

Helen scanned the text. "Mr. and Mrs. Sterling Benton, Mr. Marcus Benton, and Miss Caroline Macy."

Gilbert was still too young and—at least Margaret hoped—too busy at Eton to attend. She fervently prayed Sterling had not made good on his threat to pull Gilbert from the institution.

The girls' seminary Caroline attended was located between Maidstone and London, so perhaps it was not so surprising her sister would attend. Perhaps their mother arranged to visit her daughter and attend the ball in the same journey to better justify the distance. Or perhaps Sterling had his own reasons for wanting to visit Fairbourne Hall once more.

Helen said, "I suppose we can conclude that the Benton family does not believe the speculation about Miss Macy's death. For they would not accept an invitation if they were in mourning."

Any mourning the Benton men observed on her account, Margaret thought, would be only for show. Though, of course, her mother and siblings would be devastated.

Helen picked up the next reply in the stack. "Let us see who else is coming to our little soiree. It's going to be quite an interesting night, I think. Most revealing."

Masquerade balls were sometimes set as a game among the guests. The masked guests were supposedly dressed so as to be unidentifiable. This would create a type of game to see if a guest could determine each other's identities.

—The Jane Austen Centre

Chapter 24

As the date of the masquerade ball approached, Margaret's nerves and fears escalated. Not only would Sterling Benton again be under the same roof, but also Marcus, as well as her mother and sister. She prayed everything would go according to plan.

Helen had actually ordered a new evening gown for the occasion—light blue with a low round neckline edged in gathered white lace. This, plus a high belt of white ribbon, accentuated Helen's figure admirably. Puffed white lace sleeves peeked out from slashed cap oversleeves of blue. The gown was simple yet elegant, and both Helen and Margaret liked it immensely.

On the night of the masquerade, Margaret helped Helen dress and arranged her hair. She had rolled Helen's hair with pomade and paper curls the night before and now she piled Helen's curly hair high, leaving tendrils loose at her temples to soften her face and downplay her ears. She then decorated the coif with a white ostrich feather. Margaret applied a light dusting of powder, a hint of rouge to Helen's cheeks and lips, and the slightest bit of kohl around her eyes. It was after all, a masquerade. She also helped Helen on with a pearl necklace and earrings.

"You look beautiful, Miss Helen," Margaret said sincerely. "It is a shame you plan to wear a mask."

"Only for the first half of the ball, remember. But thank you." She turned this way and that in the looking glass. "I must say I hardly recognize myself."

A knock on the door sounded, and Helen called out, "Enter."

Nathaniel stepped in, and Margaret caught her breath. How stunningly handsome he looked in full evening attire—black tailcoat, patterned ivory waistcoat, and cravat. His dark hair swept back on the sides but for a tasseled lock across his forehead.

Nathaniel, for his part, stared at his sister. "Helen . . ." He expelled a breath of astonishment. "I don't know what to say. You look lovely."

Helen grinned. "Thank you. I regret you find the notion so shocking."

"I didn't mean—"

"Never mind, Nate. I was only teasing."

"Ah. I came to tell you we have a few early arrivals. I am afraid I need to summon you to your hostess duties ahead of schedule. Lewis is already in the salon."

"No matter. I am ready." Helen pulled on long kid gloves and picked up a sandalwood fan.

"Your mask, miss," Margaret reminded, and stepped forward to tie the narrow mask over Helen's eyes.

"Thank you."

Nathaniel tied on his own mask, then offered Helen his arm. When the two reached the door, Helen raised a "wait a moment" finger and hurried back to Margaret.

She whispered, "I have asked Mrs. Budgeon to excuse you from any other duties tonight. I told her I might need you to attend me later, to refresh my hair or whatnot."

"Oh. Yes, I see," Margaret agreed, taking her hint. Nora would remain out of sight in Helen's bedchamber.

But Margaret Macy would not.

As soon as Helen left, Margaret put her plan into action, palms sweating and heart thumping, afraid to be caught before she even began. She put on the fine, if outdated, gown of silvery white silk—the only gown she had located in the schoolroom trunk which she could easily get into without help. She had brought it in earlier with the laundry and hidden it at the back of Miss Helen's wardrobe. She then removed her dark wig and—having no time to properly dress her own hair—pulled on the high Cadogan wig she had also found in the attic. It was a lofty creation with long flaxen curls at the shoulders— very Marie Antoinette. The fair blond wig shone nearly white in the fashion of the previous decade, among men and women. Though somewhat lighter than her natural color, it made her look more like herself—her old self—than did the black wig.

She bundled up her usual wig, spectacles, and everyday frock and tucked these into the back of Helen's wardrobe. It would not do for her to change in the attic. Someone might see her coming down from the servants' quarters dressed like a lady and make the connection.

For a moment, she sat at Helen's dressing table, feeling guilty for presuming to use it. But other emotions weighed more heavily than guilt—fear and dread. She worried that rumors and speculation of her death would go unchallenged and her inheritance fall into greedy hands that cared nothing about Gilbert's education or her sister's happiness, let alone her own.

This was her chance. She mustn't waste it.

Hands trembling, she powdered her face and applied rouge to her cheeks and lips. She wiped away the dark pencil from her eyebrows, restoring them to their golden hue. Then she tied the mask she had fashioned—from scraps of material from Miss Nash's room—over her eyes and around the back of the wig. The mask was not much wider than Helen's and disguised her identity somewhat but not completely. If only she could disguise her trembling hands!

Margaret regarded her reflection in the glass. The mask covered her face from just beneath her eyebrows to the tops of her cheekbones. She didn't look like Nora, but not exactly like Margaret either. Perhaps that was for the best. There were only a few in particular she wished to recognize her. She hoped none of the serving staff, the footmen, or Mr. Arnold would recognize her as Nora playing dress-up. That would never do, since she would need to slide back into that role later tonight.

Using her handkerchief, Margaret dabbed at the nervous perspiration collecting at the back of her neck. Which route should she take to descend to the long salon and adjoining drawing room where the ball was being held? She was tempted to use the back stairs. But what if one of the housemaids came upon her? Dared she use the main stairway, where she was sure to attract the notice of Mr. Arnold standing ready at the front doors, not far from the bottom of the stairs?

She waited until the ball was in full swing, hoping the hosts and servants would be too busy to notice one more guest slipping down the stairs to join the fray. Pulse pounding in her ears, hands and knees trembling, she lifted her hem daintily and stepped as regally as she could down the main stairway. She could hear the swell of music, laughter, and conversation below. Joyous sounds. Why then did she feel as though she were on her way to her own execution? Suddenly the Marie Antoinette wig seemed a very poor choice indeed.

When she neared the bottom of the staircase, Mr. Arnold looked up from his post beside the door, but if he was surprised to see her descending, his impassive face revealed nothing.

She said in a voice of great hauteur, "I seek the ladies' dressing room."

"The morning room is reserved for ladies this evening." He gestured across the hall. "First door on the left."

She inclined her head but did not reply, keeping her chin high and not looking directly at the servant, as had been her habit in the past.

There was no flicker of recognition in Mr. Arnold's eyes. But would she even know if he did recognize her? The man was a consummate professional. She might have come down in her shift and he would have reacted to her with the same impassive demeanor.

To avoid rousing his suspicion, she made her way to the morning room. Inside she found two giggling debutantes and an older woman being fussed over by her lady's maid, trying to straighten a wig very like Margaret's, which threatened to topple. Then Margaret faltered at the sight of Barbara Lyons, standing before one of three cheval looking glasses, deep in conversation with another woman Margaret did not recognize.

"He didn't!" the woman hissed. "*He* broke it off with *you*?" Her voice rose in incredulity.

Barbara nodded.

Margaret stepped to another looking glass, placed there that afternoon for this purpose and polished by her own hand, and made a pretense of checking her own reflection.

"But why?" the woman whispered. "Because of *you know who*?"

Barbara shrugged, adjusting the silk flower in her hair. "I told Piers I was only flirting with Lewis and didn't mean anything by it. But nothing I said would sway him."

Interesting, Margaret thought. Did that mean Miss Lyons was not the woman Lewis had been out with all night?

Margaret adjusted her mask once more, tugged her gloves a bit higher, took a deep breath, and let herself back into the hall. She crossed the marble floor, keeping her face averted from Mr. Arnold, and followed the rise and fall of music to the salon.

A damp muzzle nudged her hand. Startled, Margaret looked down, surprised to see Jester in the hall, gazing up at her with adoring eyes. "No. Shoo," she whispered. Would the dog follow her into the ball? That was no way to enter unobtrusively.

"Go away," she urged. But Jester only wagged his tail.

Craig appeared, in full livery and powdered wig, and grabbed the dog's collar. "Beg pardon, madam." As he led the dog away, she heard him grumble, "You're to be kept belowstairs tonight. When I find that Fred . . ."

Relieved at Craig's interference, Margaret made a mental note to be nicer to the young man in future and continued to the salon. At one of its double doors, she lingered, getting a lay of the land. Two older gentlemen stood in front of her, taking turns speaking loudly into one another's ears to be heard over the music. She hovered a few feet behind them, using the men as a sort of shield as she took in her surroundings. At one end of the room, a five-piece orchestra played. At the other, a punch table stood ready to offer refreshment. In the center of the room, twelve couples danced. She spied her sister, Caroline, among the dancers. Her partner: Marcus Benton.

Her heart soured to see sweet Caroline in his arms. Caroline smiled as she reached her hands forward to Marcus, who caught them with a grin of his own as the ladies and gentlemen changed sides in the dance. Obviously Caroline did not know what sort of man Marcus really was. She saw only his good looks and charm. As had Margaret, initially. Thank goodness her little sister had no fortune to tempt the man—at least, not into marriage. Would Caroline even heed a warning if Margaret managed to get close enough to impart the words?

She had to try.

She waited until the set ended and Marcus escorted Caroline back to their mother. Oh! Margaret's heart pricked with a sudden needle of homesickness at seeing her mother's graceful form. But then Sterling Benton appeared at her mother's side, handing her a glass of punch, and Margaret's heart dulled. She would never have the courage to approach Caroline or her mother while they were standing with him. She wished Caroline might excuse herself in search of the ladies' dressing room, where Margaret might speak to her in private, but for several minutes her sister just stood there, smiling and talking with the Bentons and her mother.

Glancing about nervously, Margaret saw Piers Saxby and Lewis Upchurch talking with Miss Lyons. Margaret had been surprised to hear Saxby had broken things off with the beautiful brunette. He and Lewis were once again costumed as pirates, while most of the other guests had settled for dominos, or simple masks with traditional evening clothes.

Margaret fidgeted. How long dared she stand there, lurking?

Finally, she had her chance. Caroline walked across the room to speak to a girl near her own age, perhaps a school friend. When the music started and that girl's partner came to claim her, Caroline was left alone. Margaret walked quickly over to her, doing her best to keep her face averted and her back to the side of the room where Sterling stood. She did not wish him to recognize her. Not yet, at any rate.

"Hello, my dear," she began in an affected voice, should anyone be listening. "Will you not join me in the ladies' dressing room? I have not seen you in an age!"

Caroline's mouth dropped open. "Margaret?"

"Not here, my dear," she said breezily, taking her arm. "Let us speak in private."

She managed to lead her sister toward one of the doors before Caroline pulled her to a stop and faced her. "Margaret! I knew it. I knew you could not be dead."

"Hush, Caroline." Margaret looked about, but no one seemed to be paying them any heed. "I cannot stay long. I only wanted you to know I was well and to warn you. I—"

"But Mother and Sterling are here!" Caroline began pulling *her* arm, in the direction they had come. "We must tell them. How relieved they shall be."

Margaret resisted, grasping her sister by both arms. Everything within Margaret warned her that if Sterling got her alone, it would all be over. He and Marcus would take her arms in a steely grip and escort her from the house before she knew what had happened. "You may tell them later. Caroline, listen to me. You must be on your guard with Marcus Benton."

Her sister's face clouded. "We were only dancing. I thought you didn't like him, so I didn't see the harm in—"

"I know he seems charming, Caroline," Margaret interrupted. "I thought so too at first, but he pressured me to marry him in a most ungentlemanlike manner. For the inheritance. That is why I left."

Caroline shook her head. "But I have no inheritance."

Margaret closed her eyes and asked for patience. "Money isn't the only thing men want." Suddenly she sensed someone watching her from the side of the room.

She glanced over and saw Nathaniel Upchurch staring at her from behind his mask, looking as though he had seen a ghost. Did he see a woman he once knew? Or was he stunned for another reason—did he see "Nora" masquerading as a lady in a blond wig?

Were his eyes playing tricks on him—was this a figment of his imagination? For there stood Margaret Macy in all her fair glory. A mass of white-gold hair crowning her head, curls on delicate bare shoulders. Her gown shimmered white and seemed somehow familiar. The small mask she wore did little to disguise the blue eyes, the high cheekbones, the arch of golden brows, the sensible nose, the wide, shapely mouth he had memorized and dreamt about.

How could he be certain? She was wearing a mask, after all. Was it wishful thinking on his part? He knew himself fallible in recognizing women who'd changed their hair color. But, no. It was her. He knew it.

A rush of emotions swamped him. Curiosity. Concern. Why was she revealing herself here and now, when the men she had ostensibly been hiding from were in attendance that very moment? Did she not know? Should he warn her?

Nathaniel watched surreptitiously as Margaret spoke earnestly with a younger girl—her sister, he believed. When she turned and would have hailed the Bentons, Margaret gripped her arms and stayed the gesture. Clearly Margaret wanted to talk to her sister alone, likely to assure her she was all right.

Margaret glanced over her shoulder, and Nathaniel followed the direction of her gaze. Sterling Benton suddenly straightened, eyes alert. Nathaniel straightened as well.

He could stand back and watch or he could do something to help her. He did not know exactly what she was after or what she was up against, but he knew she was eager to avoid Sterling Benton. The look of fear on her face made his decision for him.

Pulling off his mask, Nathaniel strode over to her, reaching Margaret just ahead of Sterling. Margaret whirled, prepared to take flight, but Nathaniel blocked her way.

Jaw clenched, he offered his arm. "My waltz, I believe."

She stared up at him, mouth slack. He was oddly tempted to strum his thumb over her protruding lower lip.

Instead Nathaniel took her hand, tucked it beneath his arm, and all but pulled her onto the dance floor. Behind him he heard the low rumble of Benton's voice, peppering the sister with terse questions.

What am I doing? Nathaniel berated himself. How did asking Margaret Macy to dance jibe with his determination to avoid her? How would feeling the warmth of her hand spread up his arm and into his chest help him forget her?

He bowed to her, and she, belatedly, curtsied. For a moment he feared the tall wig would topple from her head.

"Mr. Upchurch?" she whispered, breathless before the dance had even begun.

"Yes, Miss . . . ?" He lifted his brows expectedly.

She frowned. "Miss Macy. Margaret Macy."

He lifted his chin. "Ah. I thought so, but I was not certain I was supposed to recognize you."

Her brow furrowed.

"With your mask, I mean."

"Oh!" She blushed and reached up to touch her mask, as though she had forgotten she wore one.

The music passed the introductory notes and swelled into tempo. Nathaniel grew increasingly disquieted by the direct stare of her blue eyes. He looked instead down at her waist, more disquieting yet, and placed his hands there. *Oh, not helping at all.*

She reached up and placed her hands on his forearms.

Quite the opposite. One tug and she would be in his arms, snug against him. He grimaced, attempting to banish the thought.

Her eyes widened. "Did I step on your foot? I am sorry if I did."

"Not at all."

She lifted her chin. "You needn't dance with me if you don't wish to."

He glanced over and glimpsed the Benton party gaping at them. Lewis and Saxby as well. "I thought you might appreciate the . . . diversion."

He tightened his grip on her waist and whirled her around, too preoccupied to recall the various positions of the German and French waltz. She seemed preoccupied as well, craning her neck to look over his shoulder, keeping an eye on the Bentons as she spun past.

"All of London speaks of you. Of your disappearance," he said, as they repeated the basic step and turns.

"Do they?"

"Is that why you came? To prove you are alive and well?"

A worry line appeared between her brows above the mask. "In part, yes."

"Then why not remove your mask and show the world who you really are?"

"It is a masquerade, Mr. Upchurch."

"Ah. I see. And you are the queen of disguises."

She darted a look up at him, unsure of his meaning.

Lewis appeared beside them, roguish grin on his handsome face. "Miss Macy, as I live and breathe! How I have longed to see you again. Do say you'll dance with me. Nate won't mind if I cut in. Will you, ol' boy?"

Nathaniel felt the old stab of jealousy. He glanced from his brother's face—perfectly confident she would agree—to Margaret's.

She looked at Lewis squarely and said, "Actually, I would prefer to dance with your brother."

Lewis's mouth parted in disbelief.

Heart lifting, Nathaniel whirled Margaret away from his stunned brother. It was likely the first time a woman had turned him down for anything.

His fleeting feeling of victory faded, for Margaret suddenly looked quite distressed.

"Mr. Upchurch," she fumbled. "I . . . I must take my leave directly. But before I go, allow me to say how sorry I am for the callous way I treated you in the past. I regret it most keenly."

His heart squeezed even as he felt his brows rise. "Do you?"

She swallowed. "I was wrong about you. I was wrong about a great many things."

He stared at her. From the corner of his eye, he glimpsed Sterling Benton striding purposely around the perimeter of the room in their direction. Their time was nearly up.

"I fear Mr. Benton may try to cut in next," he said. Lewis had likely put the idea into his head.

She paled.

Nathaniel looked toward the main doors, where Hudson hovered. When their eyes met he lifted his chin. His steward instantly straightened to attention. Nathaniel nodded toward Benton with a pointed look, then lifted one finger at half mast and tapped his lips—a signal devised after working many auctions together, buying supplies and selling sugar.

Hudson followed his gaze and nodded.

As the music ended, Nathaniel whirled Margaret toward the second pair of doors and bowed over her hand. "I think, Miss Macy, you had better go the way you came and quickly."

"Oh . . ." she murmured, breathless. "Thank *you*." She held his gaze a moment longer, the emphasis on the *you* plucking a taut chord in his chest, pleasure and pain. It seemed clear she was thanking him for more than the dance.

She turned and hurried from the room.

Nathaniel glanced over and saw Sterling Benton making a beeline for the main doors. Hudson stepped directly into his path, and the two men collided shoulder to chest. Hudson was broader than elegant Sterling Benton, and the impact stunned the slender man momentarily.

He snarled, "I say, have a care."

Margaret rushed from the room, Cendrillon fleeing the ball, the clock striking midnight and her ruse nearly up. Shivering in icy anticipation, she expected any moment for Sterling to grip her shoulder from behind. But, miraculously, she entered the hall alone.

She looked right and left and, seeing no one about, rushed across the hall and down the far corridor to the back stairs. She prayed she would not be turned away by one of the servants. As she reached the stairs, she nearly collided with Craig coming down, but he leapt aside, murmuring, "Pardon me, madam."

Hurrying up the steps, she hoped Sterling would not ask Craig if he'd seen a lady matching her description.

In the upstairs corridor, she looked ahead and saw Betty—*Betty!*—scurrying along carrying an extra blanket. Betty would recognize her if anyone would. Margaret ducked her head, feigning an interest in her sleeve, but when she risked a glance, she saw Betty with her nose pressed to the wall.

How strange to see Betty become "invisible" in her presence. Years of practice and exhortations had made the action second nature, like a turtle retreating into its shell at the first sign of danger. Margaret felt amusement mixed with chagrin that Betty should face the wall for *her*. How she would chafe if she knew. But there was no time to waste now. She needed to slip into Miss Helen's bedchamber and change back into her customary attire.

Margaret decided that enough people had seen and recognized her to quash the rumors of her death. Dancing around the room in full view of everyone had been brazen but effective. She wouldn't have risked it had Nathaniel not all but pulled her onto the floor. Now she was glad he had. She was glad, too, to have that chance, though brief, to speak to Nathaniel as herself. She had very much wished to say something to melt the icy wall between them—her fault. But with Sterling Benton breathing down her neck, she had fumbled to find the words.

She hoped he'd understood.

"A thousand pardons, sir," Hudson said to Sterling Benton, all meekness as he made a show of straightening the man's coat. "I am terribly sorry. Please excuse me."

Nathaniel stepped out into the hall, in time to hear retreating footfalls hurry not to the outside doors, nor up the main stairs, but rather down an interior passage—one that led to the servants' stairs. He walked casually toward the front doors.

She had been right not to take the formal stairway that rose from the hall, for she never would have ascended from sight in time.

Sterling Benton rushed into the hall, looking this way and that. Seeing him, Sterling said, "Upchurch. The lady you were dancing with, is she . . . ?"

"Gone. You just missed her. Her carriage was ready and waiting."

"What? Where was she going? Do you know?"

"I don't." He glanced at his steward behind Sterling. "Do you, Hudson?"

"I am afraid not, sir."

Sterling fidgeted. "Did you . . . recognize her?"

"Yes. Did you?"

"I . . . did not have the opportunity to speak with her. Caroline said it was Margaret. I wanted to believe her, but I thought perhaps she was mistaken—wishful thinking, you know."

Nathaniel placed a hand on the man's shoulder, ostensibly in comfort, but in reality, to make sure he did not rush upstairs and begin searching the house. "What a relief it must be to know Miss Macy is alive and well. Those rumors put to bed."

"Yes," Sterling murmured. "Yes, of course."

"She did seem determined to avoid you tonight. Any idea why?"

The man's blue eyes glinted, ice cold. "No. None at all."

The Bentons took their leave soon after, perhaps to ride off in search of the fleeing Margaret, or possibly to avoid the resulting questions and rumors her appearance had caused. They were a grim-faced lot, each for his or her own reason, no doubt. Nathaniel was not sorry to see them go.

He returned to the ball. He had been so distracted by the unexpected appearance of Margaret Macy that he had nearly forgotten the reason for the ball in the first place—to reintroduce Helen to society and society to Helen. He was glad the near-confrontation between Margaret and the Bentons had not marred the occasion for her. He hoped his sister was enjoying herself. He knew she was realistic enough about her age and moderate beauty not to expect to cause a stir among the single gentlemen or anything as fancifully romantic as that. But he did hope she was becoming reacquainted with her female friends and their husbands.

He had seen Helen dance with Lewis earlier—an act which had raised Nathaniel's esteem and affection for his sometimes thoughtless brother. Now Nathaniel planned to claim Helen for a second dance. There was no reason she should sit along the sidelines of her very own ball.

He looked for her among the chattering clutch of matrons seated together beyond the punch table, fanning themselves, but did not find her. He looked through to the adjoining drawing room, where gentlemen congregated around card tables, but saw no sign of her there either. Was she off in the dining room, overseeing final preparations for the midnight supper? She ought to leave that to Mrs. Budgeon.

Couples dancing a reel gave a vigorous "Hey!" as they spun and stepped lively to the jaunty tune. Surveying the dancers, he saw several couples he knew well and a few less familiar or masked.

He stopped midstride. There she was. *Good gracious.* He had almost not recognized his own sister. What a ninny he was. But with her fashionable gown, flushed, smiling face, energetic steps, and youthful partner, he had mistaken her for a much younger woman. A younger, beautiful woman. What sort of magic had Margaret worked on his sister?

He glanced around, and there against the wall stood Robert Hudson. Apparently, the magic had worked on him as well. For the man's face held a sorrowful longing Nathaniel easily recognized as unrequited love. It was a look—and a feeling—he remembered far too well.

Our party went off extremely well. There were many solicitudes, alarms & vexations beforehand, of course, but at last everything was quite right. The rooms were dressed up with flowers & looked very pretty.

—Jane Austen, in a letter to her sister, 1811

Chapter 25

The ball had continued until well after two in the morning and Nathaniel did not have opportunity to speak to Helen alone. He hoped she'd enjoyed herself.

At breakfast the next morning, she came in late, looking tired. Lewis's friend Piers Saxby had stayed the night in one of the guest rooms but had not made an appearance. Nor had Lewis.

Nathaniel smiled. "Why, if it isn't the belle of the ball. Good morning, Helen."

She flashed a quick self-conscious grin. "I was rather, wasn't I?"

She poured herself a coffee from the spigot urn on the sideboard. "No sign of Mr. Saxby yet this morning?"

"Not yet. He played cards until nearly two, and lost badly by the looks of it."

"And Lewis?"

"I have not seen him since early last night. He disappeared shortly after he danced with you."

"Did he? I suppose I was too busy dancing to notice much of anything."

He winked. "So I saw."

Arnold came in, carrying the morning post on a silver salver. Nathaniel took the single letter—soiled parchment, addressed to him in a flamboyant hand. He pried open the seal and unfolded the letter. It contained only four lines.

> *Such shy profits the chest contained*
> *Where is the rest, I wonder?*
> *Must I visit Fairbourne Hall*
> *And rent the place asunder?*

Stunned anger flushed through him. A chill followed when he recalled Abel Preston's threat. *"Your place. When you least expect it."*

"Anything interesting?" Helen asked.

He considered not telling her but reminded himself that she was a grown woman. "A threat from the man who robbed my ship. In rhyme no less. Apparently he's figured out he didn't steal all our profits after all. Here, read it for—"

Suddenly, from somewhere in the house, came a great tumult of slamming doors and a keening wail. Running feet and shouts. Nathaniel and Helen swung their heads around to stare at each other, then both lunged for the door.

"Stay here," he ordered.

"I will not."

Nathaniel ran out into the hall, looking this way and that for the source of the mayhem. Nothing. *Dear God in heaven . . . tell me that scapegrace has not come here already.*

Nathaniel ran toward the back stairs. One of the footmen ran from the basement through the servery and nearly bowled him over.

"Thank God, sir. I was come to find you." In his obvious distress, the young man didn't even apologize for knocking into him.

"What's happened?"

"It's Mr. Lewis, sir. He's been shot."

"Shot?" Nathaniel's nerves went into full alarm mode. *God, no. Please.*

Behind him, Helen gasped, both hands pressed to her mouth.

"Is he alive?" Nathaniel asked. "Where is he?"

"Yes, sir, he breathes. They've got him laid out in the stillroom. Mr. Hudson's sent Clive for the surgeon."

He hoped the groom had taken their fastest horse.

Nathaniel ran down the stairs, Helen at his heels.

Clusters of agitated servants, talking to one another behind their hands, shrunk into the wall to allow them to pass. Monsieur Fournier crossed himself. Nathaniel found the metallic smell of blood mingling with the scents of cinnamon and pastry nauseating.

Inside the stillroom, Hudson bent over Lewis's prone form, pressing a handkerchief to his chest. "Another cloth, please, Mrs. Budgeon," Hudson asked, polite even in his anxiety.

Lewis lay still, limp limbs dangling off the worktable, his face and jaw slack and unnaturally grey.

Hudson glanced up at their entrance. "Sir. Miss Upchurch."

"What happened?" Nathaniel asked.

"I don't know. His valet and a local farmer, a Mr. Jones, brought him home in the farmer's wagon. Something about a duel."

Nathaniel winced. "How bad is it?"

Hudson glanced up once more, skirting Helen's face to square on his. "Bad."

At closer range, Nathaniel could see that someone had ripped open Lewis's waistcoat and shirt, exposing his chest, though most was covered by Hudson's large hands and the blood-soaked handkerchief.

Mrs. Budgeon handed Hudson a clean cloth. Hudson hesitated before handing the soiled one to the housekeeper, but she stoically took it from him and set it into a nearby basin.

Hudson said to her, "Make sure someone leads that surgeon here without delay."

She nodded and briskly strode from the room. Only then did Nathaniel notice the young valet huddled in the corner of the still-room, white-faced and dazed, his cravat bloodstained. A plump maid held his hand.

"What can I do?" Nathaniel asked.

"And I?" Helen added.

Hudson checked the new cloth, saw it rapidly soaking up blood, before he looked from one to the other. "Pray."

Three hours later, the surgeon Mr. White had come and gone—bullet removed, wound cleaned, dressing applied, and little hope given.

They carefully moved Lewis, still insensible, up one flight of stairs to the library, which Mrs. Budgeon had quickly outfitted as a sickroom while the surgeon finished bandaging the wound. They dared not jostle him more than necessary nor risk carrying him up additional flights of stairs. The surgeon, bloodstained and weary, said he would send a seasoned chamber nurse to tend Lewis, even though Helen insisted she would sit with her brother all night.

Mr. White promised to return in the morning and told them to send for him if there was any change, though the offer was made with little enthusiasm. Would Lewis even live through the night? Nathaniel's soul heaved at the thought. He and his brother had not been close in years, but the thought of losing him grieved his heart.

Nathaniel sat next to Helen at Lewis's bedside in the library-turned-sickroom. He was torn between wanting to remain at his brother's side, to share his final hours on earth, if final they were, and wanting to discover what had happened and who was to blame. Was Lewis the challenger, or the challenged? Had he chosen the weapons to be used, in this case, apparently pistols? It seemed possible, as Lewis had never been good with a sword. Too much dashed work, he'd always complained.

Who had acted as his second—Saxby? Or perhaps Lewis's valet.

Nathaniel thought back to his brief glimpse of the young man below-stairs. He had looked ashen and shaken from the ordeal. Nathaniel would need to talk with him soon but would first allow the man time to get over the worst of the shock.

Mrs. Budgeon knocked softly on the open door. Nathaniel rose and crossed the room to speak to her.

"Pardon me, sir. But when we were bundling up Mr. Upchurch's clothes to take to the laundry—those which could be salvaged, that is—we found a few things in his pockets and thought you would want to have them."

She held forth a rosewood tray. Servants were taught not to hand small objects directly to their betters, to avoid the accidental brush of hands—a practice that seemed incredibly trivial in the circumstances.

For some reason, Nathaniel felt the need to reach out and lay his hand on hers. "Thank you, Mrs. Budgeon. For everything."

She seemed taken aback but did not pull away. "You're welcome, sir. And we shall all be praying for your brother's recovery."

Again he thanked her, carried the paltry collection to Helen, and reclaimed his seat beside Lewis's sickbed.

He watched as Helen tearfully fingered through the items: a pocket watch, several coins, a length of blue ribbon, and a folded scrap of paper, stained with blood. Eyes wide, Helen handed the note to him. Nathaniel unfolded it and read.

I demand satisfaction, Mr. Upchurch. And I demand it now. Penenden Heath tomorrow at half past seven.

P.

Could it be? If Preston had written it, then had this letter truly been meant for Lewis, or for him? What could Abel Preston have against Lewis? The two men had likely met while both resided in Barbados, but Nathaniel didn't recall any mention of strife between them. Preston had made no secret of his grudge against *him*, but Nathaniel had never heard him speak a word against Lewis. Nathaniel's stomach roiled. Had Lewis taken a bullet meant for him?

Nathaniel went to look for Lewis's friend Saxby but could not find him. Nor had any of the servants seen him. So he returned to the library. The vicar arrived and led them in prayer at Lewis's bedside, beseeching God for his life. Afterward, Nathaniel left his brother for a time in the capable hands of his sister and the chamber nurse.

He asked Hudson to send Lewis's valet to him in the morning room and paced until the young man knocked at the open door.

"Connor. Come in."

The young man stepped inside and stood before him, hands behind his back. His face looked pale beneath his red hair, but he held himself erect and met Nathaniel's gaze directly.

"I want to know what happened," Nathaniel said. "Everything. Spare no detail or my feelings."

"Very well, sir." The young man's Adam's apple bobbed. "It was awful. . . ."

Nathaniel braced himself. "Start at the beginning. There was mention of a duel. Had you known of it beforehand?"

"I only learned of it this morning."

"Had it something to do with the reason Lewis left the ball early last night?"

Connor frowned. "Did he? I didn't know it, sir. I didn't see him from the time he dressed for the ball until he returned to his room about three in the morning. He asked me to wake him only a few hours later—at six. You know he was never one to rise early, sir, so that surprised me, but he didn't tell me why, and neither did I ask."

No servant would ask. "Go on."

"When I woke him, he bid me to help him dress and to prepare myself for going out. He also told me to bring his dueling pistols." Connor swallowed. "I asked if I should wake the coachman and call for a carriage, but he said we would ride. So I roused the groom to saddle two horses.

"I asked if I should pack an overnight case for him, but he said only the pistols in the saddle bag." His Adam's apple rose and fell. "I confess I was nervous."

Nathaniel nodded. "Go on."

"When we neared Penenden Heath, he told me he needed me to act as his second."

Nathaniel wondered why Lewis had not asked his friend Saxby to act for him. Unless . . . might Piers Saxby have been the challenger? "Had you acted for him before?"

Connor ducked his head. Duels were illegal, and Nathaniel didn't blame the young man for not wanting to implicate himself or his master.

Nathaniel said, "Now is not the time to worry about protecting anyone's honor. Just tell me."

Connor nodded. "Once before, sir. But neither man was hurt that time. Both were so foxed that neither hit his mark. Though one old ewe did die."

"And this time?"

"Both men sober as Quakers."

"Who was it?"

"I . . ." The valet hesitated. "I could not say, sir."

"Why not?"

"I don't believe I knew the man."

"Don't *believe* you knew him?"

"That's right, sir. I didn't recognize him. He wore a mask."

Nathaniel reared back. "A mask?"

Connor nodded briskly. "Yes, sir. Never did I see the like."

Fury seethed through Nathaniel like overfermented ale. The man was a coward, whoever he was. He asked, "Did Lewis call him by name?"

Connor shook his head. "I heard no names spoken, sir. Only insults."

"What insults?"

Connor's eyes flashed. "Mr. Lewis said the man was no gentleman—that I did hear."

Nathaniel clenched his jaw. "Did this man even follow the rules?"

Illegal though dueling was, gentlemanly conduct was expected. He continued, "Was no apology solicited? Did his second not offer you a chance to reconcile your masters before a shot was fired?"

The young man frowned in confusion. "I . . . No, sir. Not that I know of."

"Did you not recognize his second either?"

"No, sir."

Nathaniel scoffed. "Was he masked too?"

"No, sir."

Nathaniel crossed his arms. "He did have a second?"

"Of course. But I didn't know him. Never saw him before."

"How had Lewis offended the man's honor?" Nathaniel realized he assumed Lewis had been the one to cause offense. Guilt plagued him at thinking ill of his poor brother.

Connor squirmed. A valet was expected to be discreet, to keep his master's secrets. "I don't exactly know, sir. Something about a woman, I believe."

Yes, that would be it. Nathaniel flopped into a chair. "Tell me what happened next."

"The other second and I inspected the weapons. Then they paced off and—"

"Not very many paces, by the looks of it. The surgeon said the shot was made at close range, judging by the wound."

"I did try to negotiate for more than twelve paces, but the man was adamant. And Mr. Upchurch too proud to insist."

"Was the duel fought to first blood?"

Connor paled further. "Yes."

There were two other options, normally negotiated by the seconds— until one man could no longer stand, or to the death. "What then?"

"Well, like I said, the men paced off, turned, and shot. Mr. Upchurch fell."

"At the first shot?"

"Yes."

"And you watched to make sure nothing dishonorable happened?"

Connor pressed his lips together. Nathaniel feared the young man might retch. "Yes. I watched."

"And the other man. Was he injured?"

"No, I don't think so, sir."

Dash it.

"In any case, he and his second rode away. And when I saw how bad Mr. Upchurch was, I ran to the road and hailed the first wagon that passed."

"And I thank you for doing so." Nathaniel inhaled deeply. "You didn't recognize the man, but do you have any guesses? Know of anyone with a grudge against my brother?"

"I don't know, sir." Connor's face puckered in thought. "I'm not thinking very clearly at the moment."

Nathaniel sighed. "Of course you're not. Sorry to push you so." He stood. "Very well, Connor. That will be all for now. If you think of anything else, do let me know."

"Yes, sir. I am sorry, sir."

"So am I. But don't despair; he may yet recover."

"There is hope, then?"

"There is always hope, with God. Though the surgeon holds out little. I have sent for a physician, a friend of my father's. Until he arrives, we can do little but pray."

Killing in a duel had long been outlawed by the
beginning of the 1800s, but the practice of dueling continued
to be found through the late 19th century, though by
this time duels were rarely fought to the death.

—Caliburn Fencing Club

Chapter 26

Nathaniel had not seen Mr. Saxby all day. But he did join
Nathaniel and Helen for a somber dinner that night.
Nathaniel asked him nothing during the meal, but when
Helen excused herself to return to the sickroom, Nathaniel lingered
in the dining room while Lewis's friend sipped his port.

"Do you know anything about the duel?" Nathaniel asked.

Saxby's eyes were steely. "What should I know about it?"

"Did you see Lewis last night after he left the ball?"

"No."

"Where did he go, do you know?"

Saxby shrugged. "The only thing that would draw Lewis from a
room full of ladies is a female more fair—or more willing—somewhere else."

Nathaniel's anger flared, and Saxby must have seen it. "Come, take
no offense, Nate. You know your brother as well as I do. There is no
need to saint him while he yet breathes."

"Do you know the identity of this *fair* lady?"

Saxby sipped. "Never said she was a lady."

Nathaniel fisted his hand. "Then we are not speaking of Miss Lyons?"

The man's eyes flashed anger of his own. "No, we are not. Not that Lewis hasn't tried his charms in that direction. But that lady prefers a more . . . sophisticated gentleman."

"Meaning yourself."

He shrugged and flicked a piece of invisible lint from his coat sleeve. "A gentleman does not like to brag."

"Then who? Who was she?"

"I don't know her name. Some local chit, I gather."

Was it really some other woman, or was Saxby trying to cover for Miss Lyons? To save face by not admitting his lover had left the ball—alone at night—with Lewis?

Knowing he might very well say something he regretted if he stayed longer, Nathaniel excused himself and went to join Helen in the sickroom.

Before dawn the next morning, Nathaniel trudged downstairs in his dressing gown to check on Lewis. The chamber nurse, Mrs. Welch, reclined on the settee in the corner, softly snoring. Helen sat on a chair near the foot of the bed. She was bent forward at the waist, her arms folded on the bed, her head on her arms. Asleep. Poor thing had sat there all night.

Lewis lay, unmoving. Yet beneath the bedclothes his bandaged chest rose and fell. His breaths were shallow, but he was still alive. Nathaniel thanked God.

He gently touched his sister's shoulder. "Helen?" he whispered.

"Hmm?" she murmured, eyes flickering open, then widening when she saw him. She pushed up from the bed, her gaze flying to Lewis's face. "Is he . . . ?"

"He's breathing. Go up to bed. I shall get dressed and then sit with him while you sleep."

"I did sleep," she protested.

Nathaniel was reminded of when they were children. Helen, small for her age, had always been determined to prove herself as strong and capable as both her older and younger brother. Now, seeing the imprint Helen's sleeve had left on her cheek, he felt tenderness for her tighten his heart.

"Go on," he gently urged. "Besides, you need your beauty sleep." He winked. "I shall be down directly. In the meantime, Mrs. Welch will tend him." He turned his head and said more loudly, "Won't you, Mrs. Welch?"

The older woman sputtered awake, straightening on the settee. "I was only resting me eyes."

Brother and sister shared wobbly grins.

Nathaniel returned to his room and set about washing and dressing. A knock sounded at his door.

"Enter."

Connor stepped inside. "I was wonderin', sir."

"Yes?"

"Would you like a shave? With Mr. Lewis abed, I would consider it an honor to valet for you."

Nathaniel ran a hand over his bristly jaw. "Very well. Thank you."

"Don't thank me, sir. I wish there was more I could do."

A few minutes later, Nathaniel sat before his dressing mirror, face lathered and a white cloth tied at his neck to shroud his clothes. Connor stood, wielding the razor far more deftly than Arnold ever had. The valet tilted Nathaniel's jaw and stroked the straight razor across his whiskered cheek, pausing between strokes to swish the blade in the basin of water.

Connor began, "You told me, sir, to tell you if I thought of anything. . . ."

"About?"

"About the man who shot Mr. Lewis."

Nathaniel's eyes flashed upward, catching the young man's face in the mirror. "Yes?"

"There is something. I don't like to speak out of turn. . . ."

"Go on."

"You asked if I knew of anybody who had something against your brother."

"Yes?"

"I wonder, sir. How well acquainted are you with Mr. Saxby?"

Nathaniel felt his pulse begin to accelerate. "Fairly well. But don't let that hinder you."

"It's only . . . I do know those two gentlemen argued over a certain lady. A lady they both admired."

"Miss Lyons?"

"I . . . believe so, sir. Though one tries not to attend to every detail of personal conversations."

"Of course. Did you hear Saxby threaten Lewis?"

"I wouldn't say threaten exactly. But he did warn him to stay away from her."

"I see. Are you suggesting the man at Penenden Heath might have been Mr. Saxby?"

"I'm not suggesting anything, sir. It isn't my place. I just thought I should mention it."

"But you said you didn't recognize his second. You have met Mr. Saxby's valet, I trust, while he's been here?"

"I have, sir. And no, he wasn't the second. I didn't recognize the man."

"What did the second look like?"

Connor shrugged. "Average looking. Slight. Dark hair. Maybe twenty or a few years older."

No one came to mind. "And the masked man—what you could see of him?"

"He was well-dressed, sir. A gentleman—that I did notice. Medium build. Brown hair. Perhaps five and thirty years of age."

Nathaniel considered. Such a description might fit Saxby. Perhaps even Preston, though he was closer to forty. But it wasn't enough to act upon. Nathaniel asked, "Are there other women . . . other jealous suitors or offended fathers I should know about?"

The young man reddened. "I couldn't say, sir."

"Couldn't or won't?"

"I don't like to speak ill of Mr. Lewis. Not when he's laid low."

"I'm not asking you to gossip, Connor. Only to tell me anything that might help me identify the man who shot my brother." A thought struck Nathaniel. "Can I ask you something? The masked man—would you recognize his voice should you hear it again?"

The valet hesitated, frowning. "His voice . . . ? I don't know."

"He didn't happen to speak in a certain, say . . . accent . . . perhaps an upper crust accent, or poetical speech?" He didn't like to lead Connor but didn't know how else to pull the information from him. He wanted to know. If Preston had shot his brother, Nathaniel would not rest until he had found him and demanded satisfaction of his own.

"Poetical, you say?" In the mirror, Connor's face puckered. "You're not suggesting that Poet Pirate might have done it?"

"The thought did cross my mind."

Connor hesitated, considering. "They say he looks and dresses every inch the gentleman, don't they?"

"Yes. I know the man, and it is true."

The valet's eyes widened. "Do you indeed, sir?"

"I'm afraid so. Dashed fiend torched my ship."

The razor hovered midair as Connor winced in concentration. "He . . . may have spoken a bit pompous-like. But poetical? I'm not sure. I shall have to think about that, sir. See what I might remember."

"You do that."

Connor wiped the lingering soap from Nathaniel's cheek and smoothed on a spicy-smelling balm. "Would you mind, sir, if I looked in on Mr. Lewis myself? I could bring down fresh nightshirts and help the nurse bathe him. Maybe even shave him if she thinks it wouldn't hurt him."

"You certainly may." Nathaniel felt the slightest flicker of wistfulness. Perhaps he ought to have hired his own valet years ago. "Your thoughtfulness does you credit."

Connor shook his head, sheepish. "I just want to do *something*."

Nathaniel nodded. "I understand exactly how you feel."

Margaret went through her early morning duties in a haze. She couldn't believe it. She felt ill at the thought. Who would shoot Lewis Upchurch? Lewis was a flirt, but she could not imagine him challenging anyone to a duel. So what had he done to cause another man to rise up in defense of his honor? Had Lewis insulted the wrong man . . . or the wrong man's wife, sister, or lover? That she could imagine. Still, she shuddered to think of him hovering near death.

Margaret went upstairs in hopes of offering Helen some comfort, but when she reached Helen's room, Betty was just coming out, lips pursed.

"She's not there. And her bed hasn't been slept in either. Spent the night in the sickroom, I'd wager. Poor lamb."

Margaret had no appetite, so instead of the servants' hall for breakfast, she stopped in the stillroom, hoping to talk with cheerful and level-headed Hester. She found Hester bent over her worktable, both hands gripping a scrub brush, bucket of soapy, steamy water nearby. She bent from the waist, using her entire body to push the brush over the surface with grim-lipped vigor, cheeks ruddy from the effort, breath heaving, forearms bulging.

"Hester . . . ?"

Hester glanced up but did not cease her motions. "No matter how many times I scrub it, with salt, lye, soap . . . It makes no difference. I can't get it clean."

Margaret had never seen Hester upset before. She touched her shoulder. "Let me have a go. You're exhausted."

Hester nodded gratefully, wiping the heel of her hand over her brow. She leaned against the sideboard while Margaret picked up the brush and resumed scrubbing.

"Between you and me," Hester said, "I'll never be able to roll dough on this table again. I shall always have to cover it with parchment or a tray. No matter how hard I scrub, I still see his blood. Smell it too."

"I'm so sorry, Hester. It's awful, isn't it?"

"Awful. Never saw the like before and pray I never do again."

"Is there anything else I can do to help?"

"Just having you to chat with has helped already, Nora. I don't care what the others say, you're a bit of sunshine to me."

Chagrined, Margaret scrubbed the worktable for a quarter of an hour, then rinsed away the soap and dried it with a clean towel. "Spotless," she announced.

"Better," Hester amended.

Margaret squeezed Hester's hand and took her leave, realizing it was almost time for morning prayers. She stepped into the passage and nearly ran into Connor, who was just coming into the stillroom. "Oh! Excuse me."

He nodded dully and stepped aside, face pale. He looked as low over the tragedy as Hester herself. But of course he would, witnessing it firsthand, having to drag Mr. Upchurch's body into a wagon.

Margaret paused in the passage, listening curiously as Hester greeted the young man in low, comforting tones. "How are you holding up there, Connor?"

His voice rumbled in low reply, almost a groan.

"There now. It wasn't your fault. You mustn't blame yourself so."

Another low reply.

"Now, don't you worry. Mr. Lewis may yet recover. You just see if he don't."

Clearly, Margaret was not the only person who sought out Hester for comfort.

After prayers that morning, Nathaniel followed Clive back out to the stables to speak with him in private. When he returned several minutes later, he sought out Mr. Saxby. He found him in the guest room, overseeing his valet's efforts in packing too many articles of clothing into too few valises.

"Give us a moment, will you?" Nathaniel said to the valet.

With a glance at his master, the slight man bowed and departed.

When the door closed, Nathaniel said, "I spoke with our groom just now. He verified the approximate time Lewis left the house yesterday morning, his valet with him. He also mentioned that you called for your horse soon after."

Saxby shrugged. "So? I was restless and went for a ride."

"So early? It isn't like you."

Saxby smirked. "You have no idea what I'm like. But if you must know, I tried to follow Lewis. He called me a liar when I suggested he was seeing a local girl. I thought I would follow him, catch the two together, and prove *him* the liar. But I never caught up with him."

"Then where were you all day yesterday?"

Saxby's eyes flashed irritation. "I rode over to Hunton to see my cousin George. I didn't realize I needed to report my every move to you."

Nathaniel studied the man's heated expression. Yes, there was defensiveness there, but guilt? He did not know.

Mr. Saxby took his leave later that morning. He stayed long enough to visit Lewis in the sickroom, emerging pale and stricken. He asked to be kept apprised of Lewis's condition, then bent over Helen's hand and gave Nathaniel a somber bow.

"You have my sympathies."

From the hall windows, Nathaniel and Helen watched the man walk across the drive and step inside his carriage.

Staring out the window, Helen said, "Tell me he is going to live."

Nathaniel swallowed as he reached over and squeezed his sister's hand. "He's going to live." To himself he added, *Lord willing.*

Dr. Drummond, a longtime family friend, had been away attending at a birth, but he came that afternoon. He examined Lewis, not only the wound itself, but the rest of Lewis as well. Afterward, he redressed the wound and then took Nathaniel and Helen aside and gave his report.

"I see no sign of infection setting in. His internal organs—heart and lungs—seem to be functioning normally, which, considering how near the bullet came to damaging both, is a miracle in my book. If you believe in such things."

"I do," Nathaniel replied.

The physician nodded. "He did sustain a knock to the head when the shot felled him—I found a raised lump, nothing alarming, but a concussion might account for his insensibility. That and, of course, the laudanum Mr. White administered when he removed the bullet. I wouldn't give him any more laudanum unless he displays signs of distress or discomfort. It is important he lie still to allow his wound to heal, so his insensible state has its benefits. It is sometimes a body's way of coping with shock and trauma."

Before he took his leave, Dr. Drummond left instructions for Nurse Welch, said he would return on the morrow, and asked to be advised if there was any change in Lewis's condition.

Nathaniel sat with Helen at Lewis's bedside that evening, trying to read an agricultural journal but mostly staring at the taper as it burned and guttered. "Did Lewis say anything to you about a woman?"

"Barbara Lyons, do you mean?"

He shrugged, knew he was grasping at straws. "Saxby suggested a local woman. But according to the valet, Lewis and Saxby argued over Miss Lyons."

Helen lifted her hands. "Lewis made no secret of admiring her. Why do you mention it?"

He held up the blue ribbon Mrs. Budgeon had found in Lewis's pocket. "This piece of feminine frippery has me thinking. And Lewis's valet said he thought the duel was fought over a woman's honor."

A maid entered, head bowed as she maneuvered a tray through the door. She glanced up, and he saw it was Margaret.

With no pause in conversation, Helen gestured her forward. "But Mr. Saxby is not even engaged to Miss Lyons."

Nathaniel watched Margaret approach. "But a gentleman could feel his honor offended should a friend seduce the woman he loves." Nathaniel thought back to how Lewis had suddenly begun showering Miss Macy with attention after *he* had begun courting her. Lewis seemed to find other men's ladies irresistible.

Margaret set down the tea tray and quietly departed.

"Lewis would nev—" Helen stopped abruptly, chuckling without mirth. "I was about to say Lewis would never do such a thing, but of course I know better. Still it shames me to say so while he lies so near death." She choked back a sob. "How I love him."

"Of course you do. And so do I. That needn't mean we are blind to his faults, nor take no recourse against his assailant."

"But if it was a duel, fought honorably, a jury isn't likely to convict the gentleman."

"Duels are illegal, and more than one man has hanged for killing another, duel or no." Nathaniel added, "There's something else. I spoke with the groom. He mentioned that Saxby called for his horse just after Lewis left that morning."

Helen stared at him. "Are you saying you think Mr. Saxby shot Lewis?"

"No . . . I don't know. He said he tried to follow Lewis but couldn't find him so instead rode to Hunton."

Nathaniel ran a hand over his face. "The valet says the man wore a mask, dressed like a gentleman, and spoke in a pompous accent. So I suppose it *might* have been Saxby, but I find myself wondering whether the man who robbed the *Ecclesia* might have shot Lewis."

Helen's eyes widened. "No."

Nathaniel shrugged. "He did threaten to come here and 'rend the place asunder.'"

"The duel was held only a few hours after our masquerade ball, remember," Helen said. "Any number of gentlemen might have worn a mask."

"I know."

"Why would that Preston fellow shoot Lewis? And if he did, why bother with a mask?"

"I don't know," Nathaniel repeated, exasperated. He expelled a deep breath. "I don't know what to think."

Helen said gently, "Until we know more, please don't report Lewis's part in this. I don't want him to face prosecution if . . ." Her voice broke. "Oh, God, I pray he lives."

Nathaniel squeezed her hand. "Eventually I shall have to report this to someone in authority, as will Dr. Drummond, most likely. But I shall be careful."

If only Lewis would wake up. He could name the man and save them all the trouble. If only Lewis would live, this suffocating dread might lift and Nathaniel could breathe easily again. *Dear Lord, please let him live.*

Mrs. Budgeon had assigned Nora the added duty of attending the sickroom, keeping it tidy, serving meals to the chamber nurse, and delivering trays to the family, who now spent so much time there.

That night, Margaret reached her bedchamber in the attic before she realized she had forgotten to collect the tea things she had delivered to the sickroom a few hours before. She sighed wearily and made her way back downstairs.

On the ground floor, she quietly tiptoed from the stairwell. When she reached the hall, she glanced across it to the library-turned-sickroom. The door was closed. She wondered if Helen and Nathaniel still kept their vigil or if the chamber nurse, Mrs. Welch, had arrived to relieve them. The door opened, and Margaret paused, stepping back into the shadows behind the grand staircase to let the family pass.

A man stepped out and closed the door quietly behind him. In a shaft of moonlight, Margaret saw that it was only Connor, Lewis's valet, toilet case in hand. Her heart squeezed to see the young man tending his master.

When she stepped into the hall, Connor flinched. "Nora. You startled me."

"Sorry." She smiled apologetically, then whispered, "How is he?"

He shook his head. "Still hasn't woken."

She pressed his forearm. "You are kind to check on him."

"That nurse is in there as well. You needn't bother."

"I forgot to collect the tea things earlier."

"Oh." He nodded his understanding. "I should have done that for you."

"Isn't your job. Now get some sleep."

"I'll try. Good night, Nora."

"Good night."

She quietly unlatched the door. She was no longer shocked to be entering the room where Lewis Upchurch slept—only shocked that it was now a sickroom.

The elderly chamber nurse looked up at her entrance and smiled. Mrs. Welch had a kind, wrinkled face framed by a floppy mobcap.

"How is he?" Nora whispered.

"The same, my dear. No better, no worse."

Margaret picked up the tray. "May I bring you anything before I go to bed?"

"How kind you are to offer, but I have everything I need."

"Good night, then." She paused a moment, looking down at Lewis. She hated to see him so pale and still.

She recalled what she'd overheard Helen and Nathaniel discussing earlier when she'd delivered the tray. Nathaniel apparently thought Mr. Saxby might have challenged Lewis to a duel over Miss Lyons. But Miss Lyons had told her friend that Mr. Saxby had broken things off with her before the ball. Should she tell Nathaniel? She hated the thought of him falsely accusing Lewis's friend.

After she returned the tray to the kitchen, Margaret went upstairs to the balcony. She hoped to see Mr. Upchurch, to offer her condolences, and perhaps mention what she knew about Mr. Saxby and Miss Lyons.

Instead, she stared at the North Star alone. Still, she somehow felt closer to Nathaniel on the balcony, empty though it was. There, she prayed for Lewis to live. She prayed for peace for Helen and Nathaniel. She prayed for safety for her family—her mother, sister, and brother.

She found herself remembering her father's final hours. The Reverend Mr. Macy had been struck by a runaway coach-and-four when he'd stopped to help a fellow traveler on the road. The surgeon had been summoned, but there was little he could do for such severe internal injuries. Her father lingered a few hours, insensible, before slipping into eternity. Knowing him, he had been ready to meet his Maker. But she had not been ready to lose him.

"I miss you, Papa," she whispered, blinking back tears anew.

A Briton knows . . .
That souls have no discriminating hue,
Alike important in their Maker's view;
That none are free from blemish since the fall,
And love divine has paid one price for all.

—William Cowper, "Charity," 1782

Chapter 27

H ere it is, sir. That's all of it."
Nathaniel had asked Connor to go through all the pockets of Lewis's many coats as well as his other belongings, looking for more clues for the identity of the man, or the woman, behind the duel. After morning prayers the next day, the valet delivered the things he'd found. Nathaniel thanked the young man and dismissed him.

Sitting at the small morning room table, Nathaniel fingered through the pile of club receipts, opera ticket stubs, and one of Lewis's own calling cards bearing a "kiss"—the imprint of full lips in red rouge.

What was he to do with that? Take it about the county and ask all the women he met to pucker until he found a match? Useless.

He unfolded a piece of paper, a small sheet of stationery, and read.

> *Ye cruel, vain, blasted louse*
> *Detested by all in my house*
> *How dare ye set yer hands upon her*
> *Such a sweet innocent girl*
> *Go somewhere else to seek yer pleasure*
> *With some other poor pearl.*

Light flashed behind his eyes. His stomach clenched. He wanted to tear the paper to shreds as though the author himself. What shoddy rhyme. What a shoddy waste of paper and ink.

He read the note again. The words spoke of heartfelt injury. Yet he doubted this "poet" had a heart. One phrase snagged his attention: "*a sweet innocent girl . . .*" Could it be—had Lewis met and seduced one of Preston's daughters when he lived in Barbados? Nathaniel shook his head. It didn't make sense. Lewis had left Barbados more than two years ago. Why now? Yet here was proof before his eyes, if proof it was. He squeezed them shut. He had lost all objectivity in his determination to identify the man who shot Lewis. He hated feeling helpless, unable to do even this for his poor brother.

He decided he would show the poem to Helen. Perhaps she could make sense of it.

Someone scratched at the morning room door. He looked up as it inched open and Margaret's face appeared.

"Pardon me, Mr. Upchurch?"

His pulse quickened. "Yes, Nora?"

She swallowed. "May I speak with you a moment?"

He hesitated, conflicting emotions coursing through him. His determination to keep his distance warring against the irrational longing to be near her. "Very well. Come in."

She shut the door behind her and stepped forward. "Please excuse me, but I couldn't help overhearing a little of your conversation with your sister last night. About Mr. Saxby."

He stared at her. Realized she had forgotten to use her accent.

"I felt I should say something." She clasped her hands before her. "While I cannot speak to his character, I think you are wrong to accuse him of challenging your brother to a duel over Miss Lyons."

"Oh? Why?"

"I happen to know Mr. Saxby broke things off with Miss Lyons before the . . . incident."

"And how would you know that?"

She swallowed. "I overheard her tell a friend he had done so."

"When was this?"

"The evening of the masquerade ball. In the ladies' dressing room."

He considered this. "He might have changed his mind."

She faltered, "Do men . . . change their minds once they deem a woman unworthy?"

He studied her, pondered her words. "Not easily."

She looked down.

"Perhaps Saxby was only upset with Miss Lyons but still loves her." He added in a low voice, "Any man might be angry, to think the woman he loved preferred Lewis."

She met his gaze. "She does not."

He regarded her closely. "Doesn't she?" Was she speaking for Miss Lyons or for herself?

She shook her head. "If she once did, she does no longer."

He blinked, pulling his stubborn gaze from hers. "And have you a better theory? A more likely suspect?"

"I am afraid not."

"Well—" he rose—"thank you for telling me."

She nodded. "May I ask how your brother fares this morning?"

"There is no improvement, I fear."

"We are all of us praying belowstairs." She reached for the door latch, then turned back. "I am so sorry this happened. For all your sakes."

How wide her blue eyes, how appealing her tremulous lips. It was all he could do not to take her in his arms. What a comfort that would be. What a torment.

Instead he remained where he was. "Thank you."

After Margaret left, Nathaniel gathered the poem he had just found in Lewis's things, the duel challenge note, and Preston's "must I visit Fairbourne Hall" threat, and took all three up to the sitting room to show Helen.

He first handed her the new "How dare ye set yer hands upon her, blasted louse" poem.

She read it and breathed, "Good heavens."

Nathaniel jabbed a finger toward the note. "This points to Preston. The man calls himself the Poet Pirate, after all. Yet I had no idea his vendetta encompassed Lewis as well."

Helen held out her palm. "Let me see the poem he wrote threatening to come here for the rest of the profits."

He handed it to her, and she compared the two poems. "The handwriting is completely different."

Nathaniel looked over her shoulder. "You're right. Why would he disguise his hand, yet write in his signature poetry?"

"I don't know."

He handed her the third letter he'd brought upstairs. "Here's the note challenging Lewis to a duel in the first place."

Helen compared the brief challenge note to the latest poem. "These two were written by the same person."

Nathaniel grimaced. "Are you saying Preston wrote only the first letter, threatening to come here, and the other two were written by a different person?"

Helen nodded.

"Two poets?" Nathaniel said, incredulous. "One threatening me, the other threatening Lewis?"

Helen nodded. "I agree it seems highly unlikely." She frowned over the latest poem and read it aloud. " 'Ye cruel, vain, blasted louse. Detested by all in my house. How dare ye set yer hands upon her. Such a sweet innocent girl. Go somewhere else to seek yer pleasure.

With some other poor pearl.'" She shook her head. "I feel as though I have read this before. . . ."

Nathaniel agreed. "It is very like the Burns poem 'To a Louse.'"

Helen's eyes lit in recognition. "Ah. So it is."

Abel Preston specialized in manufacturing poetry to suit the occasion. But two poets? Nathaniel's head hurt. He felt more confused than before.

On her way to the servants' hall for dinner, Margaret peeked into the stillroom and glimpsed a flash of deep red—the back of Connor's auburn head. She supposed he was talking with Hester again. But was talking all they were doing? Margaret hoped Mrs. Budgeon wouldn't catch them. Staff romances were deeply frowned upon, she knew.

But when Margaret reached the servants' hall, there was Hester, cheerfully helping Jenny lay out the servants' dinner.

"Oh." Margaret drew up short. "I thought you were in the stillroom."

Hester set down a tray of savory biscuits and looked up. "Now, why would you think that?"

Margaret waited until Jenny had returned to the kitchen and then said, "I saw Connor in there."

Hester's face lit up. "Did you? Wonder what he needs." She winked. "Besides me, a'course."

Seeing the fondness shining in Hester's eyes, Margaret felt oddly envious of the stillroom maid. Oh, to be loved and to have that love reciprocated. She thought back to her last conversation with Nathaniel. It was almost as if his words had carried latent meaning for her—Margaret. *"Any man might be angry, to think the woman he loved preferred Lewis."* And the way he had looked at her . . .

But no, she was reading too much into his looks and the words he'd spoken to a housemaid named Nora.

Dr. Drummond returned that afternoon as promised. Again he examined Lewis but found no change in his condition. After the physician took his leave, Nathaniel sat at the library desk with the newspapers, while Helen sat nearby at Lewis's bedside.

Several minutes later, Nathaniel tossed the *Times* onto the library desk and laid his head in his hands. *What next?*

Helen looked over at him, alarmed. "What is it?"

"News from Barbados. A slave revolt."

"No!" She pressed a hand to her mouth, eyes wide.

He nodded. "Estates damaged. Cane fields burned, property destroyed. By the time soldiers crushed the revolt, a quarter of the island's sugar crop had gone up in smoke."

"Our estate?"

"It is not mentioned. Thank God we got our harvest in early."

"What else does it say?"

He picked up the *Times* once more. "'Approximately four hundred slaves, men and women both, armed with pitchforks and a few muskets fought against the well-armed militia and regulars. Hundreds of rebels were killed.'" He shook his head as images of Upchurch slaves flashed before his mind's eye. Tuma, Jonah, Cuffey . . . *Please, no.*

He forced himself to continue, "'Hundreds more were captured and will be executed or sold elsewhere.'"

Nathaniel had warned his father what might happen if planters rejected the registry bill. But even he had not predicted such a grisly outcome.

Helen asked, "Were any planters killed?"

He shot her a look, surprised she was concerned only for the white owners. But he couldn't really blame her. She had never met an enslaved person. Did not know dozens, as he did. He shook his head. "Only two soldiers apparently, one white and one black soldier from the West India Regiment."

"That's a relief. I mean . . . that Papa and his neighbors are all right."

He bit back a bitter retort. It wasn't Helen's fault. "I shall write

338

to Father directly to make certain. But no doubt we will hear from him any day now."

Helen nodded. "In the meantime, I shall pray for his safety."

Nathaniel thought, *And I shall pray for theirs.*

Margaret carried an armload of yellow chrysanthemums and purple verbena into the stillroom. It was late in the season, and these were the only flowers she could find to brighten the sickroom.

She drew up short at seeing Connor standing again at the worktable—Hester's domain. "Oh. Hello, Connor. Where's Hester?"

"She'll be in the servants' hall about now, I expect."

He was in shirtsleeves, wearing a black bib-apron to protect his clothing.

Margaret nodded, then hesitated, wondering what he was doing. A mortar and pestle stood on the worktable before him, a jar of something beside it, a bit of powder spread about. "Making something for Mr. Upchurch, are you?"

He looked up at her. "What do you mean?"

She shrugged easily. "Some elixir or restorative, I imagine."

He glanced at her, then back to the worktable. "I am not an apothecary, Nora."

She smiled at him. "Hester says you prepare your own shaving soap and hair tonic. Don't be so modest."

He shook his head. "I am only grinding a bit of tooth powder."

"Then I shall leave you to it." Margaret turned to the sideboard and set about trimming and arranging the flowers in a green glass vase.

The silence between them as they worked felt uncomfortable. Sensing Connor was not completely at ease sharing the close quarters with a maid other than Hester, Margaret didn't tarry over her task. As soon as she had cleaned up after herself, she lost no time in carrying the arrangement to the library upstairs.

That night, Connor did not appear for supper. After grumbling about his absence, Mr. Arnold determined they would eat without him, with Mr. Hudson's approval, of course.

"As you like," the steward said, in his mild-mannered way.

Margaret wondered why Connor was missing the meal—it was unlikely Monsieur Fournier would save him a plate, though she guessed Hester might very well do so in secret. Margaret hoped nothing had happened—that Lewis had not taken a turn for the worse. She decided to check on him as soon as she had finished eating.

After the upper servants excused themselves to take their dessert and port in Mrs. Budgeon's parlor, leaving the rest of the servants to partake of a simple bread pudding in the servants' hall, Margaret excused herself. This brought a raised-brow glance from Fiona, who knew how very fond of sweets Nora was.

"Shall I eat yars, then?"

"Please do."

Margaret hurried up the passage, pausing to glance into the stillroom. Finding it empty, she continued on her way upstairs and across the hall to the sickroom.

She quietly inched open the door, slowly revealing the library—fire crackling in the hearth, oil lamp burning low on the side table beside the flowers she'd brought, Lewis's prone figure on the bed, and Connor standing over him. It was as she thought, he was missing his supper to check on his master.

The door creaked.

Connor whirled, dropping something from his hand. "Dash it, Nora, you startled me."

"I'm sorry," she whispered. "I didn't mean to. I only wanted to check on you."

"Check on me?"

"When you didn't come down for supper, I grew worried. I thought perhaps Mr. Upchurch had taken a turn for the worse."

The valet lifted his chin in understanding, then turned to regard Lewis. "He does seem a bit worse to me. I was worried myself. That's why I came to sit with him."

"Where is Mrs. Welch?"

"She excused herself to use the necessary."

"Oh."

"It was good of you to check on me, Nora. But why don't you return to your supper?"

"I've already eaten. The others are finishing their pudding. If you hurry, I imagine Hester and Jenny will put together a plate for you."

"I'm not hungry."

Both stood awkwardly, looking down at Lewis Upchurch. His color seemed a little better to her, though she was no judge.

Margaret said, "It is kind of you to be so concerned for him, Connor. But you should eat something."

Connor shrugged. "He is my responsibility, isn't he?"

His ragged tone tugged at her heart. Had she ever inspired such loyalty in a servant? Would she? Gently, she said, "I'll ask Hester to save your supper on the stillroom stove, shall I?"

"Thank you."

Margaret turned to go, but then hesitated. "I think I made you drop something when I came in and startled you. Shall I help you find it?"

Connor looked about him. "Did I? Perhaps something from the toilet case. I'll take a look after you leave."

"I don't mind helping."

"Thank you. But I don't think you want me lifting Mr. Upchurch's bedclothes to search for it in your presence."

Her neck heated at the thought. "You're right. Well, see you later."

Nathaniel stood in his bedchamber, eyeing his bed with longing. He was exhausted and wanted nothing more than to undress, climb under the bedclothes, and sleep for hours. But his spirit was troubled. He felt drawn to pray at his brother's bedside first. Leaving his room, he quietly descended the stairs.

At the half landing, he paused. A figure stood in the shadows, just outside the sickroom door. For a moment, panic seized him. Had Saxby or Preston come to finish the job? But then he realized the figure was feminine. A girl in an apron. Mobcap askew atop dark curls. Margaret—keeping a nighttime vigil. Such devotion. His heart ached to see it. She'd declared she no longer had feelings for Lewis, and he wanted to believe her.

If only he could ignore the evidence of his eyes.

*They formed a small investigative unit named the
Bow Street Runners. These were private citizens not paid
by public funds but rather permitted to accept rewards.*

—John S. Dempsey, "Introduction to Private Security"

Chapter 28

D r. Drummond called again the next day. He seemed perplexed as to why Lewis had yet to regain his senses. But
he did say he was pleased with how well the wound was
healing. The physician gave credit to the surgeon, even though Mr.
White had seemed certain Lewis would not survive the first night. Apparently he had taken the time to do his best work anyway. Nathaniel
decided he would send the surgeon his gratitude and perhaps a gratu-
ity as soon as he had opportunity.

When the physician had taken his leave, Robert Hudson entered
the library.

"Sir? A man was here while you were busy with Dr. Drummond.
A Mr. Tompkins. He was asking questions about the shooting."

"Did the sheriff of Kent send him?"

"That was my first guess. But he isn't a local man. He's from London."

"London? Why would a London man stray so far?"

"He's a runner, sir. Engaged to look into the matter."

"Engaged by whom?"

"He would not say, beyond 'a private citizen.' Someone acquainted with your brother, I gather, who wants to see justice done."

Nathaniel frowned. "I want that more than anyone. Still, I find it irksome that someone should be investigating the matter without involving me."

Hudson cleared his throat. "If you don't mind my saying, sir, I deduced from the man's questions that you are one of his chief suspects."

"Me?"

"Did not many people witness the fight between you and your brother at that London ball?"

Nathaniel groaned.

"Perhaps whoever hired the runner fears justice will not be done if you are overseeing the inquiry—or if local officials are in the pocket of the influential Upchurch family."

In one sense that was true. Because Helen had urged him not to involve the local magistrates, Nathaniel had gone to see the current sheriff of Kent privately to inform him of the matter. The sheriff was an appointed official with affairs of his own to manage. He was not likely to spend much time looking into the situation, especially when the family was not urging him to do so. He was also an old friend of their father's and understood Nathaniel's request to keep the duel quiet, so as not to endanger Lewis should he recover. Should Lewis die, then that would be another matter entirely.

A thought struck Nathaniel. "Might the man who shot Lewis have hired the runner to keep abreast of Lewis's condition—to discover if we know his identity so he might flee if necessary to avoid arrest?"

Hudson screwed up his face in thought. "It's possible, I suppose. But I wouldn't think he'd want to link himself to the duel for fear of drawing suspicion to himself."

"Unless he means to divert suspicion by assuming the role of avenger." Nathaniel ran an agitated hand through his hair. "In any case, we need to find out who is paying this runner."

"Shall I take it on, sir?" Hudson asked, eyes alight.

Nathaniel studied him. "So eager for any assignment that relieves you of your house steward duties?"

He tucked his chin. "You know me too well."

Margaret couldn't sleep. Tired of tossing and turning, she pulled on her wrapper and shawl and tucked her hair into her mobcap, just in case. She walked downstairs and out onto the balcony, but it was empty, as was the arcade below. Restless, she took herself down to the main level and across the dark, echoing hall.

She entered the sickroom on the pretense of seeing if the nurse needed anything, only to find Mrs. Welch asleep. Margaret sat in a chair near the door, oddly comforted by Lewis's regular breathing and even by the elderly nurse's soft snoring from the settee across the room. An oil lamp burned atop the mantel. Embers glowed in the hearth. This room was warmer than her own, and Margaret felt comfortable in her nightclothes and shawl. She didn't expect to see anyone at this hour except Mrs. Welch, who wouldn't mind her state of dress—especially as she slept on, undisturbed by her presence.

The tall case clock struck midnight, but sleep felt far away. Margaret's spirit was troubled. For Lewis's sake, for Helen's, for Nathaniel's, even for her own, she thanked God Lewis still lived. But something wasn't right, beyond the fact that Lewis Upchurch had been shot in the first place. It had been three days and he had yet to wake.

Margaret found herself thinking of all those nights her dear papa had been called away—or had gone on his own initiative—to sit at the bedside of an ailing or dying parishioner. She felt somehow closer to her father, keeping vigil in Lewis Upchurch's sickroom.

A creaking door startled her.

A man whispered, "How devoted she is, sitting by his bedside like a loyal hound."

"Mr. Upchurch . . ." she breathed, rising to her feet. Nathaniel lounged against the doorjamb fully dressed, arms crossed. He did not look pleased to see her there.

She tiptoed to stand near him. She spoke in an accent, and a whisper to avoid waking Mrs. Welch. "I had only come to check on him."

"And where is the nurse? Or are you assuming that role as well?"

"Of course not." She gestured toward the settee, where the woman lay on her side, a lap rug over her middle. "I couldn't sleep, while Mrs. Welch clearly does not share that problem."

She tentatively grinned, but he did not return the gesture.

"I hope, Nora, that you do not cherish any . . . romantic notions about my brother."

Margaret frowned in surprise. "Why would you say that, sir?" As Nora, she had not knowingly flirted with anyone. Yet Nathaniel had seen them together at the servants' ball. . . .

"You would not be the first to do so, nor the last. . . ." He winced. "God willing, not the last."

"You needn't worry, sir. I don't think of him that way."

His gaze pierced hers in the lamplight. "Do you not?"

Why did she feel like he was asking *her*, and not Nora the housemaid? She shook her head. "I do not. Besides," she faltered. "Your brother is . . . That is, I believe another woman has already captured his heart."

"Are we speaking of Miss Lyons again?"

"No, sir. Not a London lady."

"What makes you think so?"

She hesitated. For Lewis's *heart* might have had nothing to do with those late-night rendezvous. She felt her cheeks heat at the thought. "I . . . It's just that . . ."

"You needn't protect him, Nora. I am familiar with my brother's . . . proclivities. But I want to find out who did this." He gestured toward the unnaturally still figure in the bed. "Anything you can tell me about Lewis's affairs, so to speak, might be important."

She nodded. "It is only that I have seen him come in very early in the morning."

"An early ride, perhaps."

"No, sir. I mean very early. Five or six o'clock in the morning. As though he'd been out all night."

"And what are you doing up so early . . . beyond spying on my brother?"

"Spying?" She pulled a face. "You forget, sir. While you are still abed, I am up by five thirty, opening shutters and polishing grates."

He slowly shook his head. "How you must hate it, having to rise before noon."

She lifted her chin. "I have never slept so late, sir. Even before I . . . came here. What must you think of me!"

His gaze roved her eyes, her face, her cap. "I don't know what to think of you."

Did he look at her with approval or disapproval? It was difficult to tell in the dim light.

He drew himself up. "It proves nothing. How do you know he had been out all night?"

"He wears the same rumpled clothes and is in need of a shave."

His eyes glinted. "How closely you regard him, to notice such detail." He paused. "Still, he might have been out with friends, playing cards or some such."

"I don't think so."

"Based on what?"

How awkward this was. How did one describe the subtle things— not the obvious smell of perfume, nor lip rouge on his cravat. But his warm, tousled look. His smirk of satisfaction. His lack of interest in trifling with her . . .

"Let us just say feminine intuition."

He quirked a brow. "I don't suppose your feminine intuition can conjure the name of this theoretical female friend?"

She shook her head. "No, but he comes home on foot through the side door, so she cannot live too far away. Weavering Street, I would suppose. Or Maidstone."

He studied her. "And are you jealous of this phantom woman, whoever she is?"

"Not at all."

His eyes narrowed. "I hope you speak the truth."

A snort interrupted them. On the settee, Mrs. Welch smacked her lips and muttered something under her breath. The wooden frame creaked as she struggled to sit up.

Nathaniel shook his head and, with an empathetic grimace, slipped from the room. Margaret guessed he hoped to spare the woman the embarrassment of being found asleep on duty. She hesitated, surprised to realize she thought so charitably, so highly, of Nathaniel Upchurch now. Had he changed since her arrival, or had she?

"What? Who's there?" Mrs. Welch murmured. "I was only restin' me eyes."

"It's all right, Mrs. Welch. It's only me, Nora."

"Ohhh." The old woman exhaled in relief. "Forget the tea tray again, did you?"

Margaret smiled to herself. "That's it. Good night."

Hudson left early the next morning to return to London. In his absence, Nathaniel made the rounds of the estate on his own, but he did not tarry, unwilling to leave his brother for too long. Later, Nathaniel sat at the desk in the library reading correspondence and scouring newspapers for further reports on the slave revolt and its aftermath. Helen had yet to join him.

Now and again he looked across the room at his brother lying so still in the transplanted sickbed. He liked to be near Lewis. Keep him company in this way, even if Lewis was unaware of his presence. Four days and he still hadn't wakened.

The under butler, Arnold, appeared in the doorway and coughed. "Sir, there is a Mr. Tompkins to see you. I've put him in the morning room."

Tompkins? Was that not the name of the runner who had already questioned Hudson?

Nathaniel rose. "I'll see him there."

"Very good, sir."

The man who stood when Nathaniel entered the morning room was short, slight, and bald. He was perhaps thirty or five and thirty, not old enough to have lost all his hair naturally. Nathaniel fleetingly wondered if he shaved his head and why he would do so. The skin of his face was smooth, his brows giving evidence of hair that would be brown, had he any to show.

"Mr. Nathaniel Upchurch, I presume."

"Yes."

"John Tompkins." The man offered neither hand nor bow. "I have a few questions to put to you, sir, if you don't mind."

"And if I do?"

"Well, sir"—his eyes glinted—"then I might think you had something to hide. And we wouldn't want that, would we?"

Nathaniel crossed his arms. "I have nothing to hide, personally, but nor do I want my family's business bandied about the county. Who sent you?"

"I am not at liberty to say."

Nathaniel was tempted to refuse to answer the man's questions but tried another tack. "A pity, for I would be happy to share your employer's expense. For you see, I too am very interested to learn who shot my brother."

"You assume that's why I am here, sir?"

Nathaniel frowned. "My steward told me you were here yesterday asking about it."

"Ah." Tompkins nodded his understanding.

Nathaniel regarded him. "Perhaps I might hire you to reveal the name of the person employing you?"

Tompkins grinned. "Ah. That's a good one, sir. But I'm afraid I've got my hands full at present."

Nathaniel said, "One wonders how the matter came to the attention of someone in London—where I assume whoever hired you lives, you being a Bow Street man."

The small man regarded him, eyes alight. "Perhaps you ought to consider a career in detection, sir. You have a gift for it."

Nathaniel shrugged.

"Have you any idea who might have done it?" Tompkins asked.

"What, me do your job for you?" Nathaniel smirked. "Actually, I do have several ideas."

"Thought you might," the man said wryly.

Nathaniel had been thinking about what Margaret had told him, but he was not ready to dismiss Saxby as a suspect yet. He said, "I don't like to malign anyone without proof, but I have heard from several sources that the fight was over a woman."

"Usually is. Who are these 'sources,' if I may ask?"

"A friend of Lewis's, a housemaid who saw him returning after being out all night, and his own valet."

"Might that friend be Piers Saxby, sir?"

Nathaniel hesitated, surprised. It had crossed his mind that Saxby might have hired Tompkins, but would the runner name him if he had? In either case, Nathaniel felt no obligation to protect Saxby. "Yes, as a matter of fact, it is."

Tompkins shrugged. "I have already spoken to Mr. Saxby about . . . well, several items."

"What *items*?"

"Oh, you know," Tompkins said casually, with a dismissive wave of his hand. "About that brawl between you and your brother in Mayfair, which he witnessed, as did so many shocked ladies and gents. Such threats. Such violence. But then you know all about that, so I won't bore you."

Nathaniel gritted his teeth. "If you have spoken to Saxby, then I trust he told you all about his feud with Lewis over one Miss Lyons?"

"Miss Lyons?" The man's endless brow furrowed. "I don't recall him mentioning that lady by name. Though several others did enter the conversation, including a Miss Macy."

Nathaniel stilled. Knowing Tompkins was watching him carefully, he attempted to retain a neutral expression, though inwardly alarm bells sounded. *Miss Macy—what has she to do with it?*

"Did you and your brother not 'feud' over that young lady at one time?"

Is that what he was getting at? Nathaniel wondered. "That was years ago."

"Still, resentments left to fester often lead to violence in the end."

Nathaniel clenched his jaw. "I did not shoot my brother, Mr. Tompkins. I was here, in the house, when they brought him in by wagon."

"So your Mr. Hudson said."

"You don't believe him? Then ask my sister. Besides, do you not think Lewis's valet would have recognized me, masked or not, had I been the man?"

"Recognized maybe. Reported? Not likely. Servants—and sisters for that matter—are so dashed loyal, I find. Makes ferreting out the truth, as well as other hidden . . . things, quite difficult."

Nathaniel felt his temper rising but held his tongue.

"Any other ideas?" Tompkins asked, clearly humoring him.

"You have heard, I trust, of the thief who calls himself the Poet Pirate?"

"Indeed I have, sir. There is quite a reward offered for his capture."

"I know." Nathaniel said dryly. "I am the man who offers that reward."

Tompkins appeared skeptical, nearly amused. "You don't expect me to believe the Poet Pirate did this?"

"Why not? The man's real name by the way is Abel Preston. He burnt my ship and stole from me—why not shoot my brother?"

He felt the man's amused condescension. How desperate to throw off suspicion he must appear. He thought of mentioning Sterling Benton—how Lewis had provoked the man by threatening to elope with his moneyed stepdaughter. But he decided against it.

Tompkins shook his head. "I shall take it under advisement, sir. But while I'm here, I would like to speak to the valet and that housemaid you mentioned. What was her name?"

Nathaniel wished he had never mentioned her, but refusing to name her now would only make them both seem suspect. "Her name is Nora, though I doubt she can tell you any more than I have." He frowned at the man. "I am surprised you did not speak to Lewis's valet during your first call. As he is the only known witness to the events of that morning, I would have thought interviewing him your first priority."

For the first time, the implacable man looked ill at ease. "I . . . take your point, sir. An oversight I shall redress promptly, if you would be so good as to arrange such an interview."

"Very well, I shall send him in directly." Nathaniel turned. Inwardly, he breathed a sigh of relief, hoping he had successfully diverted Mr. Tompkins's attention from a certain housemaid. At the door, he turned back. "If you learn the identity of my brother's assailant, I should very much like to know."

The man's eyes glinted. "I am sure you would, sir."

His knowing smirk irritated Nathaniel, but he thought it wiser not to display the temper that had already made him a suspect in someone's eyes.

Margaret came in the servants' entrance with Fiona. The Irishwoman carried a basket of fresh laundry from the washhouse, while Margaret carried a bundle of chrysanthemums—the last of the season, Mr. Sackett had said.

"Nora."

Margaret looked up. Connor stood there in the passage, his skin pale and glazed with sweat.

She stopped where she was. "What is it?"

"There's a man wants to speak to you. In the morning room."

"Who?"

"A Mr. Tompkins. He's looking into Mr. Lewis's . . . situation."

Confusion snaked through her. "Does Mr. Upchurch know?"

He nodded. "He's the one who sent for me. Tompkins said he wanted to speak with me first, then you."

She knew Nathaniel was eager to learn the identity of the other man involved. But even so she was surprised he thought she had any information to offer.

She placed a hand on Connor's arm. "I am sorry you had to go through that again."

He nodded, eyes downcast, and took his leave.

Fiona shifted the basket to one hip and held out her hand for the flowers. "I'll take them to the stillroom and put them in water for ya."

"Thank you, Fiona."

Margaret walked upstairs, through the servery, and past the dining room toward the front of the house. She felt her hands perspiring and wiped them on her apron. She had no reason to be nervous, she told herself. But her accelerating pulse paid her no heed.

She stepped inside the morning room, hands clasped before her. The man sat at the modest table, bald head dipped over the tea someone had brought him. Betty or Mrs. Budgeon most likely.

He looked up, and her nerves gave a little start. Did she know him? Or was it just the surprise of his youthful unlined face beneath the incongruous bald head?

He set down his cup and rose. "Nora, is it?"

She nodded.

He gestured toward one of the other chairs around the table. "Won't you be seated?"

She sat primly on the edge of the chair across the table from his, posture erect, hands clasped in her lap. If he looked familiar to her, might she look familiar to him?

He resumed his seat. "And what is your surname, if I may ask?"

"Garret."

With a stubby drawing pencil, he jotted her name in a small notebook. "Nora Garret. And how long have you been in service here?"

"A few months now."

One sable eyebrow rose. "A newcomer, then. Have there been any other new arrivals to the house?"

"Besides Mr. Hudson, you mean?"

He nodded, adding, "And not necessarily among the servant ranks."

She shook her head. "Only me, sir."

"And where were you before that?"

She shifted on her chair and primed her tongue to deliver her best working-class accent. "London, sir. But wha' has that to do with Mr. Lewis? Is that not why you've come?"

"Who told you that?"

"Why, Connor, sir."

He crossed his arms and leaned back in his chair, regarding her. "London, you say? Perhaps that is why you seem familiar. I may have seen you there."

She swallowed. "Perhaps. Though London is an awful big place."

He nodded vaguely. "So, working behind the scenes here, I imagine you've learnt quite a lot about the Upchurch family. Their comings and goings. Their affections and arguments. What they are capable of."

"A bit. Though maids don't mix with the family much, do they?"

"Don't they? You tell me."

"I did see Lewis Upchurch coming in a few times early of a morning, as though he'd been out all night. That's why I thought maybe he had a lady friend nearby. I assume Mr. Upchurch mentioned it and that's why you've asked to see me?"

He studied her through narrowed eyes. "I'm not really certain anymore."

Keeping his focus on her, he withdrew something from his coat pocket and laid it on the table beside his saucer.

She felt her gaze drawn to it, and her heart lurched. It was a framed miniature portrait—her portrait. The very one Sterling had shown to the staff weeks ago. She schooled her expression, hoping her anxiety was not as apparent as it felt. She lifted her gaze from the portrait to the man's face, forcing her features into placid unconcern.

He looked away first but not before she remembered where she had seen the man before. He had been at Emily Lathrop's house when she'd gone there with Joan. The runner who'd ridden up and spoken to Sterling and Mr. Lathrop on the stoop.

He said, "You have heard, perhaps, that Nathaniel Upchurch once courted a certain young lady, only to have her spurn him in favor of his elder brother?"

She swallowed. "I may have heard somethin'. But that was long afore I come."

He glanced down at the miniature. "Many a man would fall for such a beauty. Would fight for her. Even kill for her."

Margaret frowned. "Wha' are ya sayin'? That Mr. Nathaniel tried to kill his own brother, over some vain chit wha' knew no better? If you think that, then you don't know Nathaniel Upchurch. He would never do such a thing. He's an honorable, God-fearing man."

One side of the man's mouth quirked into a wry grin. "But you don't mix much with the family, you say?"

She felt her cheeks burn. "We servants see things, sir—know things."

He slid the miniature across the table toward her. Wiping her hands once more on the apron spread over her knees, Margaret picked it up. Looked at it without really seeing, heart pounding in her ears.

"Have you seen her? Has she been here?"

She took a deep breath and called upon every ounce of acting ability she possessed. "I 'ave seen her."

He sat up straight. "Have you? Where?"

She handed the portrait back. "A man come here some weeks back. Showin' off this pretty picture. One isn't like to forget such a face."

He looked from the portrait to her. The mantel clock ticked once, twice, three times. "No. One is not."

Nathaniel sat in the library near Lewis's bed, telling Helen about Mr. Tompkins's inquiries. The door opened, and Lewis's valet entered, toilet case in hand.

"Connor, there you are. How did it go with that Mr. Tompkins? He wasn't too hard on you, I hope."

The young man ducked his head. "No, sir. Fine, sir. He's talking to Nora now."

"Nora?"

The young valet looked up, surprised. "He said you knew. Told me you'd suggested he do so."

Nathaniel's heart began pounding dully. He didn't like the thought of that man alone with Margaret. That man seeking *hidden things.* "I . . . did, yes. Still, I didn't think he would need to speak with her after speaking with you."

"And why's that, sir?"

"Because you were there, of course, while she was not." He turned to his sister. "Helen, might you come with me a moment?"

She set down her needlework and rose, unconcerned. "Am I to be questioned next?"

He took her hand and pulled her along with him out the door and across the hall.

"Nate, what is it?"

"Probably nothing, but I don't trust the man." *Or whoever hired him.*

He burst into the morning room without knocking. Margaret stood at the table poised to flee. Mr. Tompkins sat opposite, tucking something into his pocket as they entered.

"Sorry to interrupt," Nathaniel began, not sounding at all apologetic.

Margaret turned to them, face flushed, eyes unnaturally bright. "Perfect timing. I was just leaving."

Mr. Tompkins rose. Nathaniel noticed his sister look from Nora to the bald man, and back again.

"I should hope so," Helen said, mock-imperious. "You have neglected your work long enough, Nora. Really, Mr. Tompkins, we don't pay our people to have tea with callers."

The man sputtered, "I-I'm not . . ."

"Sorry, Miss Upchurch." Margaret dipped a quick curtsy, flashed a look of gratitude at Helen, and scurried from the room.

Nathaniel watched the exchange with interest, and then said, "This is my sister, Miss Helen Upchurch. I brought her in . . ." He hesitated. He couldn't say, *"as an excuse to see what you were up to with Margaret."* So instead he said, "To ask her to verify my whereabouts the morning Lewis was shot."

Tompkins raised one brow, barely glancing at Helen. "How . . .

convenient. But I already told you how little I value the word of sisters and servants."

Nathaniel seethed. "If you dare question my sister's honesty, her honor, I shall—"

The runner lifted a hand. "Ah! The famous Upchurch temper raises its fierce head once again. I wonder your brother survived as many years as he did."

Nathaniel clenched his fist and prepared to charge.

Helen laid a staying hand on his arm and said almost sweetly, "If you do not leave this very moment, Mr. Tompkins, I fear it is you who will not survive much longer."

*Bonnet was a sugar planter who knew nothing
about sailing. He started his piracies by buying an
armed sloop on Barbados and recruiting a
pirate crew, possibly to escape from his wife.*

—The Pirate Encyclopedia

Chapter 29

Margaret retreated belowstairs, her pulse still tripping at an alarming rate after her disconcerting interview with Mr. Tompkins. Did he leave satisfied, believing she was Nora Garret, or would he be back? Margaret wondered if she should tell Helen or even Nathaniel about the strange interview. If he had been there to discover Lewis's assailant, why did he carry her portrait?

Pondering all of this, Margaret arranged the flowers in a vase with trembling fingers, then carried them up to the sickroom. She entered quietly, expecting Helen and perhaps Nathaniel to be inside, but the room was empty except for Lewis Upchurch. Approaching the bed, she reached out to set the vase on the bedside table and nearly dropped it.

Lewis's eyes were open.

"Margaret . . . ?" he breathed, hoarse and confused. His eyes drifted closed once more.

"Thank God," Margaret whispered.

Interview forgotten, she ran from the room to find Helen and Nathaniel.

Pacing the arcade, Nathaniel replayed the scenes with Tompkins in his mind—the unexpected questions the man had asked, the expected questions he'd failed to ask. The hints and taunts about *him* being the man who shot Lewis. But they were taunts without substance, without judgment, as though he didn't really believe it. It was almost as if he had merely tried to provoke him.

Nathaniel wanted to speak with Margaret. Assure himself she was all right. Find out what the man had asked her and why she looked so shaken when he and Helen had interrupted their meeting.

He found Margaret where he'd feared he would. Just leaving Lewis's room. She had said she no longer held romantic notions about Lewis. Had that been Nora speaking or Margaret? He hoped it was true for them both.

"I was just coming to find you." She beamed up at him. "Lewis opened his eyes just now."

Energy surged through his body; the stranglehold around his neck and chest loosened. "Thank God."

Other thoughts fleeing, he strode past her into the sickroom. Margaret followed but stayed in the background as he approached the bed and gently grasped his brother's arm.

"Lewis? Lewis, it's Nate. Can you hear me?"

Lewis's eyes fluttered opened, then closed once more.

"Lewis?"

Lewis winced. "Stop . . . shouting."

Nathaniel's heart leapt to hear a voice he'd feared silenced forever. "Lewis, you've been hurt. Who did this to you?"

But Lewis turned his face to the wall and responded no further to his entreaties.

Miss Macy stepped to his side and whispered, "Still, that is a good sign, is it not?"

"Yes." His heart buoyed. "I've got to tell Helen."

Margaret was about to offer to summon Helen for him, but Nathaniel had already bolted from the room, a boy eager to share a great surprise with his sister. From the hall, Margaret heard him call to someone, "He's coming around. Is that not good news?"

A moment later, Connor stepped inside, toilet case in hand. He asked in disbelief, "Is he awake?"

She shook her head. "Only for a few moments."

"Did he say anything?"

"Just muttered a little nonsense."

He looked at her. "What nonsense?"

My name, she thought, but said only, "He told Mr. Upchurch to stop shouting." Margaret grinned at the memory, but Connor only sighed.

"I wish I had been here."

He set the case on the bedside table. "I would have attended him earlier, but you would hang about. And now I am late in giving him his wash and shave."

"I'm sorry. I only meant to bring in some flowers, but then I—"

"Have you no other work? Perhaps I ought to mention it to Mrs. Budgeon."

She was stunned by his cutting words. "She's the one who asked me to tend this room. You might have come in while I was here."

"I could not very well see to his personal needs in a woman's presence, now could I?"

"You could have asked me to leave."

"I'm asking now."

His face flushed, a shade lighter than his hair. A pulse ticked in his jaw.

"Very well, Connor," she said softly. "You needn't be nasty about it."

His expression crumbled, sheepish. Pained. "I'm sorry, Nora. Just please go."

Margaret took herself belowstairs to see her cheerful friend Hester. But Hester did not smile when she entered the stillroom.

"Hello, Hester. Did you hear Mr. Lewis is coming around? Is that not good news?"

The stillroom maid scooped up the corner of her apron and snatched a copper pot from the hearth, setting it atop the worktable with a bang.

"Hester? What is it?"

She took up a utensil and began mashing whatever was in that pot with righteous indignation.

Margaret's stomach dropped. What had she done now? Was she to lose her only real friend belowstairs? "Hester? Did I do something?"

Hester struck the utensil's handle against the side of the pot to dislodge its contents. *Clang, clang, clang.* "Not to me, you didn't. But you are making Connor's life difficult."

"Am I?" Margaret was sincerely surprised. She knew he had been distracted and even a little surly of late but had no idea it was her doing. She thought of his recent tirade, but Hester could not yet know about that. "What have I done?"

"Sticking your nose in where it don't belong. He says you have no place flittin' in and out of the master's room. Isn't right."

Margaret was incredulous. "I'm in his room every day to make his bed and dump the slops."

"But not in the sickroom. Connor sees that as *his* place."

"I had no intention of usurping—"

"Of what?"

"Of taking over his responsibilities, as he sees them."

"Then what are you doing hanging about the sickroom at all hours?"

"Mrs. Budgeon asked me to keep the room tidy and serve the chamber nurse. But, yes . . . I own I nip in now and again to check on Mr. Lewis, or take in some flowers. I didn't realize I was getting in the way." *Until just now,* she added to herself.

Hester glanced up at her with narrow eyes, shaking her head without ceasing her work. "You're a fool if you've taken a liking to Lewis Upchurch. Mind you, you wouldn't be the first girl to break her heart over the handsome devil. Her heart . . . and worse."

Hester worked in choppy, agitated movements, dumping the contents of the pot onto a marble board and rolling the lump flat.

Margaret asked tentatively, "You?"

"Me?" Hester scoffed. "I'm no fool. Connor warned me about him long ago. Said that man could charm a nun out of her convent and a bride from her wedding trip."

Margaret bit back a grin at the colorful and rather accurate description.

Hester frowned. "You think it's funny when a young girl is ruined by such a rake, is that it?"

Margaret sobered immediately. "Not in the least. It's why I left my last place. To avoid that very fate."

Hester stilled a moment, studying her as though to gauge her sincerity. Apparently satisfied, she nodded. "Then you understand. I know Connor and his brothers are terrible careful about their young sister. Have you a brother, Nora?"

Margaret hesitated, confused by the jump in topic. "Yes."

"Could he not protect you from the man threatening you?"

Oh. "He is much younger than I. Only a boy."

Hester nodded. "A pity. And your father?"

"Passed on."

Hester glanced up from her work. "Sorry to hear it."

Margaret was sorry as well. She found herself missing both Gilbert and her father very much at that moment.

The next day Nathaniel paced the library, agitated. Lewis had not again regained his senses. He had so hoped his brief waking had been a sign that he was coming around. Improving. Had it been a fluke? He sat at the desk and tried to calm himself by reading from the Psalms, but his anxious mind kept wandering.

A double knock sounded on the door, signaling Hudson's return. Nathaniel rose to shake his hand. "How glad I am to see you. That was a quick trip. What did you find out?"

Hudson hung his head. "I'm sorry, sir. But I am afraid I didn't learn who hired Mr. Tompkins to investigate the duel."

"Dash it." Nathaniel ran a hand over his face, then took in Hudson's hangdog expression. "Don't look so low, man. It isn't your fault."

Hudson said, "I did learn something that will interest you. It seems our poetical friend Preston is becoming less mythical and more genuine pestilence."

"Oh?"

"His crimes are mounting, and with it his infamy. Word around London and the admiralty is that he stole a shipment of Royal Navy prize money bound for Portsmouth. At least he is being credited with the deed. The navy has added to the reward you've already offered."

"The insolence of the man. When was this?"

"The fifth of November. Which means, if true, Preston could not have shot your brother. He was eighty miles away in Portsmouth, robbing the navy."

Nathaniel frowned. "Why is that not a comforting thought?"

"Because that means we still don't know who did it."

Nathaniel shook his head. "If not him, if not Saxby, if not me, then who?"

Away from home, the valet waited on [his master]
at table and loaded his shotguns.

—Upstairs and Downstairs, Life in an English Country House

Chapter 30

He has come to finish what he started, Margaret thought, standing frozen in the shadowy sickroom, unable to move or cry out as a man tried to force Lewis Upchurch to swallow some poisonous weed. But Lewis was asleep and could not chew. The weed wouldn't go down Lewis's throat, no matter how the man stuffed it in his mouth.

The man looked over at her, and with a start she realized it was Sterling Benton.

"You can't marry Lewis if he's dead," Sterling said, his face a grimace of effort as he jammed his fingers into Lewis's slack mouth. "Now you shall have to marry Marcus. . . ."

Margaret's eyes flew open, startled awake. The disturbing images lingered along the edges of her mind, and she shuddered. How relieved she was to realize it was only a dream. An unsettling dream. *Lewis is all right*, she told herself. No one—not Sterling, nor masked man, nor pirate—had come to finish him off.

Still, an eerie sense of fear prickled through her limbs and needled her stomach. There would be no falling back asleep now. Giving up, she threw back her covers and climbed from bed. She pulled on her wrapper, slid her feet into slippers, and let herself from her room. The attic was perfectly quiet. Yet the eerie feeling did not diminish; if anything, it coiled and grew.

She crept down the first set of stairs and paused to listen. Had she heard something? She wasn't certain. She padded down the back stairs to the ground floor. How still and museum-like the soaring hall felt in mottled moonlight, filtering through the high half-circle transoms. Nothing but the ticking of a tall case clock to disturb the silence, mark time, match her stride and heartbeat.

Her feet took her past the main stairway and Hudson's office and across the marble floor to the library. There should be only two people inside at this time of night. Lewis and his nurse. Why did she feel they were not alone? Why this sense of imminent danger?

Nathaniel sat on a bench outside, leaning his back against a low-bending willow. From where he sat, he had a clear view of the moonlit arcade and gardens beyond. He hoped Margaret might venture out tonight and join him.

Unfortunately, thoughts of Lewis, and of Preston's threat to come calling, kept impinging on more pleasant thoughts of Miss Macy. Even if the scoundrel had robbed the navy in Portsmouth five days ago, he could easily have returned to Kent by now. At the thought, he idly ran his finger over the hilt of the sword at his side. Ever since Lewis had been shot, he'd kept it near at hand.

Footsteps sounded on the flagstones of the arcade. He swiveled his head, but it was not Margaret emerging from the house. It was a man emerging from the shadows, wearing a long, many-caped coat.

And a tricorn hat.

Nathaniel rose and crept to the arcade. Though his blood boiled, he managed a cool façade. "Good evening."

Abel Preston started. Surprise widened his eyes and slackened his mouth. But just that quickly, his eyes hardened, his lip curled. "Hello, Nate. Are you the welcome party?"

Nathaniel drew his sword. "If this is the welcome you had in mind."

The man sighed. "I had hoped to find the rest of that money first. I know there's more."

Nathaniel glanced beyond the man, alert to the possibility of accomplices. "Where are your partners in crime?"

"Oh, they don't like to venture so far from the sea. Besides, I assured them I could handle this small errand myself. I don't suppose you would give me leave to do so, if I promise to return afterward and die like a gentleman?"

"You are no gentleman, sir."

"There's no call to be rude, Nate. I didn't take your life when I had the chance, did I? But I will kill you now if you dare stand in my way."

"I dare." Nathaniel raised his sword.

Again the man sighed in a longsuffering manner and drew his own sword. The blade suddenly flashed and Nathaniel barely dodged in time. Thunder and turf, the man was fast. Again and again Preston advanced. Nathaniel parried, losing ground, barely keeping out of range of the man's flashing blade.

He soon realized the former army major was still the better swordsman, regardless of his hours of practice with Hudson. He would not be able to withstand him much longer. *Gracious God, your will be done....*

It was only a feeling, Margaret told herself. Not strong enough nor certain enough to justify rousing Mr. Hudson or some other ally to accompany her. Was she foolish to venture into the library on her own? A chill crept up her spine at the thought. She remembered what Hudson and Nathaniel had said about the pirate with a grudge. What if he had shot Lewis and returned tonight to finish him off? Or what if Sterling was in there, as in her dream? Lying in wait for her after that runner reported she was hiding in Fairbourne Hall as a housemaid. Would Sterling kill a man to keep her from marrying anyone other than Marcus? She shivered. Margaret detested the man, but she did not believe him that evil.

She gingerly lifted the latch and inched open the door.

Dim lamplight and stillness. As the arc of the door widened, she saw first the nurse, Mrs. Welch, slumped in the settee in the corner, mouth ajar, snore noticeably absent. She opened the door farther, revealing the bed, Lewis's still form, and a man bent over him, pressing a pillow to his face. . . .

Hoping to distract his foe, Nathaniel panted, "What, no poetry tonight?"

They circled each other, catching their breaths.

"I didn't think you appreciated my poetry."

"True."

"Still, I might try, if you insist. . . ."

For a fleeting second Preston's focus shifted, and Nathaniel kicked, catching his opponent off guard and knocking his feet out from under him. Preston *oof*ed to the ground, but still managed to raise his sword to block Nathaniel's attack.

A voice rang out, "Lay down your weapon."

Nathaniel whirled. Robert Hudson trained a pistol on the man on the ground.

Glancing from Hudson's resolute expression to his steady pistol, Preston laid down his sword and slowly got to his feet, arms raised in apparent surrender. "Well, well. If it isn't Robbie Hudson, my former clerk. Surely you wouldn't shoot your old master."

"If I have to."

"Thou shalt not kill, remember."

"You have killed plenty. How many slaves died at your hands?"

Preston flinched. "I left that life behind."

Hudson's lip curled. "And your wife and children in the bargain."

Keeping his eyes on Preston, Hudson said to Nathaniel, "Should we send the coachman for the sheriff?"

Suddenly, Preston leapt and in one continuous blur of motion, shoved Hudson and yanked a small pistol from his boot. Hudson's arms windmilled as he careened back, fighting to keep his balance, barely managing to keep to his feet.

"No prison for me, thank you," Preston said, pointing his pistol at Hudson's chest.

Nathaniel cried out, "Nooooo!"

A shot rang out, and a man fell.

Icy terror sliced through Nathaniel's veins. If Hudson had been killed, he would never forgive himself. He blinked. Looked about him.

Hudson still stood, expression dazed. The Poet Pirate lay sprawled on his back, coat spread wide, blood blossoming from his shirt.

Nathaniel whirled about. If Hudson had not shot him, who had? There stood his answer.

In the steely form of bald Mr. Tompkins, arm stretched before him, pistol still smoking.

Margaret blinked and the scene before her changed. Perhaps it was due to her nightmare, or the fact that she'd read too many gothic novels, but for a moment she'd thought she'd seen a man bent over the bed, pressing a pillow to Lewis's face. In reality, the man sat on the bed. He was neither masked man, pirate, nor Sterling Benton. By the light of the lamp burning on the side table, she recognized the familiar figure of Connor. The young valet sat, stoop-shouldered, on the edge of his master's bed, head bowed, pillow on his lap. Defeated. Had she only imagined him trying to suffocate Lewis?

She darted a look back to Lewis's face, then to his chest. Was there any rise and fall there? Was she too late?

"Nora?" Connor looked up at her, face bleak, eyes bleary. Had he gotten drunk for courage?

"Connor." She licked suddenly dry lips. "What are you doing with that pillow?"

He looked down at it as if only then realizing he held it in his arms. "Nothing, as it turns out," he whispered, more to the pillow—to himself—than to her.

"Is Mr. Upchurch . . . ?"

"Alive and well," he muttered darkly.

Relief filled her. She amended, "Not exactly *well*."

"He will be. Dr. Drummond said as much."

Margaret felt her brow pucker. "Said what?"

"That Mr. Lewis would recover. Was quite sure of it. And you heard him talking. Coming around. It is only a matter of time."

Realization prickled through her. "Is that why you are here?"

As if in a stupor, he nodded. "But in the end I couldn't do it."

Worriedly, she glanced at Mrs. Welch, unnaturally still on the settee. "Connor, why is Mrs. Welch still asleep?"

He shrugged. "A little laudanum in her tea is all."

Is that why the woman slept so heavily? "This isn't the first time, is it?"

He shook his head. "Didn't want her to see me giving him the stuff. She might have said something. I only meant to keep him quiet until he passed on."

"Is that what you were doing when I walked in on you a couple of days ago?"

"You made me drop the stuff. It's not cheap either." Connor rubbed his brow. "Mr. White was so certain he wouldn't survive. I thought I could bide my time, but he lived on and on."

"But it was you, wasn't it? You shot him in the duel?"

He uttered a desolate laugh. "There was no duel."

"But, Miss Upchurch mentioned a challenge letter—"

"I wrote that letter and slid it under Mr. Lewis's door the night of the ball. When he finally returned to his room and read it, he believed Mr. Saxby had called him out over Miss Lyons. How he blustered and paced. I feared he would back out. He decided he would meet Saxby but hoped to dissuade the man from the duel. Said he planned to apologize instead."

"But still he brought the dueling pistols?"

"I brought them. I had cleaned and loaded them enough times to know how it was done."

Now that he was talking, it seemed Connor wished to confess all. Margaret wished she was not alone in hearing it.

"When we arrived at Penenden Heath, we tied our horses and

Lewis looked for his challenger. I gave Mr. Upchurch one of the pistols, and said I was he. I told him to face me man to man, but he refused. 'Dueling is only for *gentlemen*,' he says." Connor spit out the word like a vile thing. "And apparently as a valet, I am barely even a man, let alone a gentleman. And Laura's honor not worth risking his life over, not worth anything at all, beyond the few trinkets he'd given her."

"Who is Laura?" Margaret whispered, fearing she already knew the answer.

"My little sister. Dearest creature God ever made. Only sixteen." Margaret did not know which act sickened her more.

"To see his smirking face, when he spoke of sweet Laura. It was beyond me to endure. . . . I pointed the gun and told him to stop laughing, but he would not stop. He said he knew I could not shoot him, that *I* knew I could not shoot him."

White-faced, Connor swallowed and whispered, "He was wrong."

Margaret slowly, gingerly pulled the pillow from his grasp, as though a loaded pistol. "Did you intend to kill him?"

He inhaled deeply. "I was angry. I wanted to stop him. To punish him for hurting her, using her. I didn't think past that. But later . . . Later I saw how stupid I had been. I tried to throw suspicion on Saxby, even that Poet Pirate fellow. No one suspected me. But Lewis knew. If he lived . . . I would hang."

She asked gently, "You shot him but could not suffocate him?"

Connor shook his head, expression bleak. "I would do anything to save Laura. But not, it seems, to save myself."

If you have a bad servant
part with him, a diseased sheep
spoils a whole flock.

—Joseph Florance, celebrated French chef, 1827

Chapter 31

Nathaniel and Helen sat in chairs pulled near Lewis's bed in his own room at last. Lewis sat propped up with pillows. Though still weak, he had quickly regained his senses once Connor wasn't there to administer large amounts of laudanum.

Helen raised the teacup to his lips, recalling the doctor's admonition to give him plenty of liquids.

Lewis sipped, then shook his head. "To think I trusted him."

Helen bit her lip, then whispered, "As his sister trusted you?"

He glanced at her, then away. "She wasn't complaining."

"She is *sixteen*, Lewis. You must have seemed a god to her. Wealthy and handsome. And old enough to know better."

He slanted her another glance, then looked at Nate. "So what have you done with him? Has he gone to prison?"

"Connor is on a ship bound for Barbados as we speak."

Lewis frowned. "What?"

"Nathaniel and Mr. Hudson procured a place for him with an acquaintance returning to the West Indies," Helen explained.

"But he shot me, tried to—"

Nathaniel cut off his protests before Lewis could work himself into a lather. "Prison means a trial, Lewis. A trial in which your part would be made quite public. In Connor's mind it was a duel for his sister's honor. In all truth, I cannot say I completely blame him. If someone treated Helen the way you treated that poor girl"—Nathaniel's voice shook—"I might very well have done the same."

Disgust filled him, but he would not lash out at his brother when he was still so weak. He inhaled deeply to calm himself. "Even so, we thought you might sleep better knowing the young man was out of the country."

Their stillroom maid had begged to go with Connor and would soon be his wife, but Nathaniel did not think Lewis would appreciate the concession and didn't mention it.

Lewis said nothing for several ticks of the clock, staring at his hands. "And what of the sister?"

With a glance at Nathaniel, Helen said quietly, "She has been settled with relatives. Far away."

Lewis nodded, lifting his gaze to stare at the striped wallpaper. "Fine by me. She'd grown tiresome of late."

Inwardly Nathaniel's anger turned to pity and prayer. Would his brother never change his ways?

Helen offered Lewis more tea, but he waved the cup away, eyes distant. "Still, I shall find her again if I decide to. See if I don't."

Pain flashed in Helen's eyes. Pain and disappointment. "I do see." She opened her mouth to say more, hesitated, and then instead turned to Nathaniel.

"When you returned from Barbados, I was less than kind to you. I misjudged you, and I apologize. I see now that your motivations were honorable. Your actions meant to protect our family. Thank you."

Nathaniel's heart squeezed.

She turned back to their older brother, expression tight. "Lewis, for all your charm and good looks, you are . . ." She broke off, and tears flowed in place of the unspoken words. Her voice thick, she whispered, "But I never could hear a word against you."

Later that day, Nathaniel sat with his steward and his sister in the library, thankful for the fact that it no longer served double duty as sickroom. Nathaniel enjoyed having the private use of the library once more, though Helen still spent more time there than she had before. As did Hudson.

Robert Hudson rubbed his palms together. "What shall we take on next, sir? New plans for drainage? Expanding the orchards? Another trip to London?"

Before he could answer, Mrs. Budgeon knocked on the open doorjamb.

"Mr. Hudson, sorry to disturb you, but the candidates are here. Should you like to sit in on the interviews?"

Hudson pulled a face. "Mrs. Budgeon, I have every confidence in your ability to hire a suitable stillroom maid."

"Thank you, Mr. Hudson. And please do remember the annual inspection of linens and livery is at three."

"How could I forget?" He smiled wryly, and the housekeeper departed.

Helen watched the exchange with interest. "Forgive me for saying so, Mr. Hudson, but life in service doesn't seem to suit you."

Hurt and defensiveness crossed his face. "I am sorry if I've disappointed you."

"Not at all. But it is clear to me you are ambitious and capable of a much more self-directed life."

He narrowed his eyes. "That almost sounds like a compliment, Miss Helen."

"It is. Good heavens, have I been such a shrew you don't recognize praise from me when you hear it?"

"No, miss. But nor do I take praise from your lips lightly."

She inclined her head. "I think you could accomplish anything you set your mind to."

He looked at her significantly. "Anything?"

She blushed. "I refer to business, of course."

Arnold came in with a special delivery on a tray. Nathaniel's heart surged to see the familiar handwriting. The much-anticipated letter.

He waved it to gain Helen's attention. "A letter from Father."

Helen pressed a hand to her chest. "What does he say?"

Hudson, Nathaniel noticed, gave Helen's arm a discreet, comforting squeeze.

Nathaniel unfolded the letter and read the first line. "He assures us he is well."

Helen pressed her eyes closed and sighed. "Thank God."

He continued to read. Paused. Blinked his eyes, then read the words again. Stunned, he handed the letter to his sister.

For several moments Helen read silently, frowned, then stared up at him, eyes wide. "Good heavens. I have never known him to be so . . . Apparently he was quite shaken by the revolt, the brutality of the soldiers, the confessions of the implicated slaves. . . ."

"Does he say what I think he says?"

She nodded slowly. "I believe so. He says . . . he says you were right, Nathaniel. And he vows to put into motion your plans to extricate our family from any involvement with slavery."

Nathaniel released a long exhale. "I was afraid to believe my eyes."

His heart lifted. Sitting there with his sister and friend, and knowing that his father and brother were safe, Nathaniel had a sudden longing to see another quite dear to him.

Margaret dusted the desk in Nathaniel's bedchamber, careful not to knock over the candle lamp nor break anything else of his. The door opened behind her, and she turned, startled. It was Nathaniel himself.

She backed up a step, disconcerted by the look in his eye.

He stepped forward.

"What is it?" she asked. She held the feather duster before her like a sword.

He advanced, eyes riveted on hers. "Seeing you puts me in mind of a piece of French chocolate."

She swallowed and took another step backward.

"If one wants to discover what is inside, one must first remove the foreign wrapping."

The odd light in his eyes both mesmerized and frightened her. She wanted to run; she wanted to stay. Her body, nerves tingling, mind whirling, refused to move. Like a hare cornered by a fox about to pounce, she could only stare, eyes wide. Frozen.

He was only a foot away from her now.

He lifted both hands toward her face. She leaned her head back to evade his reach, but her head came to rest against the wall.

He touched not her face, but her spectacles, gently unhooking them from her ears and lifting them from her nose. "You don't really need these, do you," he murmured.

"I do, actually," she whispered, but he continued on, setting the spectacles on the desk.

He returned his gaze to her face. A gaze too penetrating for comfort. She was torn between wanting to look away and wanting to sink into those intense sea-storm eyes.

He tilted his head to one side, regarding her. "I hope you don't think me rude for mentioning it, but you have a little something on your face." He withdrew his handkerchief, dipped it into the pitcher and came forward with it. She tipped her head back, but he grasped her chin in his long fingers, gently but firmly, and wiped first at one eyebrow, then the other.

"A bit of soot, perhaps," he said and tossed the handkerchief aside. "From your work with the grates, no doubt."

"I . . ." she faltered but could form no further words, because now both his hands touched her skin. His fingertips slid over her cheeks and jaw, cupping her face, while his thumbs reached up to rub arcs over each eyebrow, the fine hairs bristling to life under his touch.

Her heart thudded. He knew. He had to know. Was he not surprised to find blond brows beneath the dark? He did not appear surprised.

Emotions crossed his features like lightning dancing across the sky, sparking behind his eyes. "And this cap doesn't suit you. I'm sorry to say something so ungallant, but there it is. Do you mind?"

She licked her lips. A tremor passed through her, of anticipation, of fear, of hope. If he didn't know, if he had merely removed her spectacles to see her face more clearly, to ease his way toward—her chest ached to even think the phrase—*kissing her.* If he really had mistaken her darkened brows for soot . . .

But beneath her cap lay a wig. A wig could be mistaken for nothing but disguise, unless she were bald beneath! No, he must know.

He raised his hands when she would have happily endured them on her face far longer. He peeled off the cap and tossed it on the desk. Again he regarded her. "I am afraid, miss, that your hair, if hair it can be called, does not suit you either. May I?"

Yes, he definitely knew. He did not seem angry, as she would have guessed. Or was he so self-possessed that it did not show? How in control of himself, of the situation, of her, he seemed.

He gave a gentle pull, but the wig caught at its anchor pins, stinging her scalp.

"Pins," she murmured and managed to reach up and pull them from behind each ear. She was helping him? Yes, she was, she realized. She suddenly wanted very much to stand before him as herself, with no more guise or lies between them. Her hands hesitated, then lowered to her sides. Heart hammering, and more self-conscious than ever, she waited. Waited for him to bare her hair. Her identity.

Slowly, carefully, he pulled the wig from her head. He asked, bemused, "You just happened to have this lying about?"

"I meant to wear it for a masquerade."

He chuckled, deep in his throat. An intimate sound that warmed her. "And you certainly did. The longest masquerade in history."

He set the wig aside, his eyes lingering on her face, her hair. He reached up, stroking a tendril at her temple that had come free when he'd pulled the wig away.

Then Nathaniel cupped the sides of her face once more. He leaned near, lowering his face toward hers, tipping her chin one way, angling his the other. His eyes roamed her cheeks, her eyes, her lips.

She felt warm and flushed, as though she had sipped orange wine. He leaned nearer yet, and she could smell his sweet peppermint breath and shaving soap.

Her voice sounding young and nearly giddy in her ears, she asked, "Are you certain, sir, you ought to kiss a housemaid?"

No answering chuckle. "I have never been more certain of anything in my life," he whispered, his breath tickling her upper lip with each syllable.

He was going to kiss her. Sweet heaven. Nathaniel Upchurch was going to kiss her. Her knees suddenly felt weak, her heart shot through with electricity.

His head dipped and his lips touched hers, softly, faintly. Too faintly. She couldn't help it. She leaned up on her tiptoes and pressed her mouth more tightly to his. In a second, his arms were around her, molding her body to his in an embrace that stole what was left of her breath. *Is this what love is? Oh, what I have been missing!*

He pulled his mouth away, grasped her shoulders firmly and took a half step back. "Forgive me, I should not. Not so . . ."

He cleared his throat. If Nathaniel had lost his self-control for one moment, now by painful degrees he mastered it again. He removed his hands, and she felt bereft, nearly chastised, for she had been as overcome with passion as he. For a moment she feared he regretted the kiss, but he leaned forward and kissed her cheek, chasing those doubts away. He then placed his fingertip where his lips had been, tracing the hollow beneath her cheekbone.

She asked, "How long have you known?"

"Ever since I saw you coming from your bath with a towel around your head."

"So long! And you never said a word?"

"At first I thought I must be imagining things. Then I feared you would be mortified to be discovered in such a role. Finally, I decided

I needed to learn what was going on—why you were here, and what you were running from—before I tipped my hand."

"And have you?"

"I learnt of your coming inheritance and of Sterling Benton's desperate financial situation. That coupled with the installation of his favorite nephew under his roof led me to believe he was pressuring the two of you to marry. The pressure must have been strong indeed to cause you to run away. To"—he gestured vaguely toward her discarded wig and feather duster—"drive you to this."

She nodded. "You're right."

His gaze roved her face. "I am glad you came to Fairbourne Hall."

She glanced at him, uncertain. "Are you?"

"Yes," he said, mouth quirked in a lopsided grin. "We needed a new maid."

He leaned in for another kiss.

Voices in the corridor brought them both up short. This was not the best manner nor place to end her charade. She quickly slicked back her hair and pulled the wig into position. He tugged on her cap for her and crossed to the door while she replaced her spectacles.

Fiona pushed open the door and started at seeing Nathaniel just inside. "Pardon me, sir."

"No matter, I was just leaving."

Fiona gaped at Margaret, brows high. Margaret hoped Fiona didn't notice her eyebrows, or lack thereof.

In return, Margaret shrugged and gave Fiona a bewildered look. It was no doubt convincing.

For she *was* bewildered.

Nathaniel took himself back down to the library, whistling as he went.

Helen looked up at him from the novel she was reading. "What has you so happy?"

His only answer was a grin.

Hudson, standing near the library window, gave the old globe on its stand an idle twirl, running his finger along the equator as it spun.

Helen watched him. "How much of the world have you seen, Mr. Hudson?"

"Oh, I saw many places in my younger days. The Cape of Africa, Trinidad, Tobago, Antigua. . . . I traveled with a merchant for several years before I decided to stay on in Barbados." He looked over at her. "And you, Miss Helen?"

"Me? I have been nowhere, save London. Do you miss traveling?"

With a glance toward Nathaniel, he said apologetically, "I admit to a growing restlessness, being indoors so much of the time, and being so far from the sea. I was raised along the coast, you know. And later in Barbados, I was never far from the sea."

She nodded thoughtfully.

"I don't suppose, Miss Helen . . ." he began cautiously, as if he dreaded her answer. "I don't suppose you can imagine life anywhere besides Fairbourne Hall?"

She looked up at the ceiling in thought. "Actually, Mr. Hudson, after my years of self-imposed seclusion, I find myself longing for a change. I don't know if you are aware, but my first love was a sea captain. I looked forward to life on the coast, perhaps even traveling with him from time to time."

Hudson's eyes dulled. "I am sorry for your loss."

She nodded. "I felt sorry for myself too. For a long while. Too long. It was a blow at the time, but it is in the past. I am ready to leave it there."

Hudson studied her closely. "I am glad to hear it."

"Which part?"

He grinned. "All of the above."

Nathaniel was glad to hear it as well.

Arnold appeared in the open doorway. "That Mr. Tompkins is here to see you again, sir."

Nathaniel pursed his lips in surprise. "Is he? Very well, I shall see him in the morning room."

Hudson stepped toward the door. "Shall I go with you?"

"No thank you. I will see him myself."

"Then I suppose I shall return to my duties," Hudson said with little relish.

Helen looked over at him. "I have a few things to discuss with you, Mr. Hudson, if you wouldn't mind staying a little longer?"

Hudson stilled. "Of course, miss."

Helen turned toward Nathaniel. "Unless you wish me to go in with you again, like the last time . . . ?"

Ever the big sister. "No need; stay as you are."

Leaving Helen and Hudson in quiet conversation, Nathaniel crossed the hall. When he entered the morning room, the bald man stood, chimney-pot hat in hand. Did he not trust the under butler with it?

Nathaniel said, "Well, Tompkins. I am surprised to see you. I thought you would be celebrating your capture of the poetic Preston and spending your reward by now."

The man smiled, but the gesture did not reach his eyes. "I have, sir. But there is still one outstanding piece of business between us."

"If it relates to my brother, perhaps you have not heard. He has regained his senses and told the sheriff of Kent all about the ill-advised duel. The challenger has left the country, and considering what Lewis has suffered already, the sheriff has decided not to pursue legal action."

"I had heard that, yes, sir."

"Then why are you here? Sorry not to claim that reward as well, from the man who hired you?"

"Finding your brother's assailant wasn't what he commissioned me to do."

"No?" Anger and alarm wrestled within Nathaniel, but he clenched his jaw and waited to hear the man out.

"No." Tompkins's high forehead creased into many furrows. "Sorry, sir. A convenient subterfuge."

Nathaniel guessed the answer, but still asked, "Why were you here, then?"

"I think you know, sir."

Nathaniel merely stared at him, jaw ticking.

"I came here to find Miss Margaret Macy. Quite a reward was offered me for her return too, should I succeed." He glanced up at Nathaniel, expectant.

Nathaniel clenched his fist at his side, torn between wanting to pummel the man and wanting to bolt from the room and find Margaret.

He said, "I take it, then, that Sterling Benton hired you?"

"Oh, not exactly *hired*. But he did put up the reward."

"Too bad you failed to find her."

One brow rose. "Oh, but I did not fail."

Nathaniel clenched both fists now. "Oh?"

"Come, sir. We are men of the world, the both of us. And I see how it is. I would have taken her too, had Preston not shown up here the very night I meant to snag Miss Macy. And as your reward was twice Benton's, and as I never cared for the man, I took my leave of Kent without her, wishing the both of you happy."

Nathaniel stared at the man, stunned.

"I only returned to tell you." He sighed dramatically. "I needed someone to know I'd succeeded, even if I can't tell anybody else."

Nathaniel stepped forward, offering his hand. "Thank you, Tompkins."

The man shook his hand firmly and smiled at last. "Thank you, sir."

Nathaniel hesitated. "May I offer you something for your kindness?"

Pursing his lips, Tompkins shook his head. "No need. With my new reputation as the thief-taker who brought in the Poet Pirate, I'm set for life."

Abruptly, Tompkins dug into his coat pocket. "By the way, sir. I've brought you some news from London. Hasn't reached you here yet, I'd wager. I'll leave it to you to do with it what you will." He handed Nathaniel a torn and folded piece of newsprint.

Glancing at the torn page and seeing only a portion of the society section, Nathaniel tucked it into his pocket to read later.

No sooner had Mr. Tompkins taken his leave than Dr. Drummond arrived to pay a final call on his patient. Walking upstairs with the physician, Nathaniel quite forgot about the news smoldering in his pocket.

Endeavour to serve with such good will
and attention to the interest of your employers,
that they know they are blessed in having gotten
such a good servant, one who serves, not with
eye-service as a man-pleaser, but in
simplicity of heart as a Christian.

—Samuel and Sarah Adams, *The Complete Servant*

Chapter 32

D r. Drummond took his leave, quite satisfied with Lewis's recovery, and Nathaniel walked him out. On his way back through the hall, Hudson called him into his office to discuss the latest repair estimates and the progress of the new tenant cottages. Before Nathaniel knew it, it was time to dress for dinner.

When he entered the dining room at seven, he noticed that Helen wore a pretty blue evening gown he didn't recall seeing before.

"You look lovely," he said.

She lifted her chin. "Yes, I do." She gave a saucy grin. "Thank you for noticing."

As they began the first course, Helen asked, "How did it go with Mr. Tompkins?"

"Fine."

"You explained the situation?"

She referred to Lewis and the "duel," he knew. Aware of the listening ears of Arnold and the footmen, he decided to wait and tell her the real reason for the man's visit another time.

"He went away satisfied, yes."

"Good." Helen expelled a relieved breath, and their conversation moved on to other pleasantries in no danger of being repeated in the servants' hall.

It wasn't until later that night, when Nathaniel returned to his room, that he recalled the newspaper in the pocket of the coat he'd worn earlier that day. Expecting nothing more than an article about Mr. Tompkins's success with the Poet Pirate, or some piece of gossip about Sterling Benton, he pulled it out and unfolded it by the light of a candle lamp.

As he read the words, surprise, relief, and concern washed over him in waves. But at the thought of telling Margaret, his stomach soured. He was tempted to put it off until the next day, or the next. Instead, he forced his feet along the corridor and up the back stairs.

Nathaniel felt self-conscious, as he always did, standing in the attic passageway. Thankfully, his dog had kindly shown him which room was hers weeks before. He would not like to have to go knocking on every maid's room to find her.

Had she really been a maid, he would have summoned her downstairs, but he was not overly concerned with preserving the good name of "Nora Garret." Glancing around and seeing no one, he quietly knocked on Margaret's door.

"Who's there?" came Margaret's wary whisper.

"It's Nathaniel. I am sorry to disturb you, but I have news. . . ."

The latch clicked, and the door opened several inches, revealing the figure and face of Margaret Macy in her nightclothes. His heart banged, his lips parted. Of course he knew it was her, but somehow speaking with her as Nora had been easier. Now here she stood, in nightdress and wrapper, golden blond hair uncovered, coiling down one shoulder in a long plait, highlights of white gold flickering by the light of the bedside candle. No frumpy cap, no dark wig and drawn-on brows, no apron. Just her. He relished the sight.

She looked down at herself, self-conscious. "I'm sorry, but I was just going to bed."

"That's all right. It's only a surprise to see you like this."

She ducked her head, nervously twirling the end of her plait.

He could not help himself. He reached forward and caught her hand, gently capturing the blond plait inches from her collarbone.

"I had almost forgotten how fair your hair is."

Liar, he silently admonished. He wished he might untie the ribbon, unwind the plait, and run his fingers through the silky weight of it. He swallowed.

Down the passage a door slammed, and both of them jumped.

"Perhaps you ought to step inside a moment," she whispered.

He hesitated, but being so near to her, common sense and propriety fled. He stepped inside, closed the door behind him, and stood there staring at her like an idiot.

"You have news?" she prompted.

Had he? It had flown from his mind. It was all he could do not to lean close, pull her into his arms, and kiss her. He saw a tremor pass over her body and became aware of his own gooseflesh.

"It is chilly up here," he said. Forcing his gaze from her, he looked instead around the small, plain chamber. "How strange to find Miss Macy living in such humble surroundings."

"I don't mind."

"I almost believe you." His eyes returned to her face, savoring her features. "How you have changed."

She shivered again.

"You're cold." He slid his hands over her shoulders, slowly sliding his palms down her arms, over the sleeves of her wrapper. He took one of her hands, then the other, rubbing each between his larger, warmer hands. "That should warm you."

She inhaled. "Indeed."

His hands stilled but continued to hold hers. She made no move to step back or pull her hands away. He hoped it meant she felt as he did. Or did she feel she was in his debt, afraid of losing her hiding place should she refuse? That thought dampened his ardor, and he suddenly remembered why he'd sought her out at this hour in the first place.

He cleared his throat and released her. "I've just read a startling piece of news."

"Oh?" She became instantly alert, eyes widening and body stiffening in anticipation. He still dreaded telling her, though he knew he must. He was afraid of what she might do.

Margaret steeled herself for the news.

He pulled something from his pocket and began, "It's an engagement announcement."

Margaret inwardly quailed. *Oh no.* Had Sterling puffed off the news of an engagement between her and Marcus, hoping to force her hand?

Nathaniel continued, "The engagement of Marcus Benton and Miss Caroline Macy."

Shock rippled through Margaret. Her heart banged painfully against her ribs. "*Caroline* Macy? Are you certain?"

"Yes." He handed her the paper and waited while she read it by the light of the bedside candle. He said, "I don't suppose this is good news."

"How could it be?"

"Well, a man you did not wish to marry is now engaged to someone else."

"That someone else is my sister! Who is barely seventeen. Far too young and far too innocent for a lecher like Marcus Benton."

He expelled a breath. "That is what I feared."

Margaret's head began to pound, and her stomach roiled. Did Marcus really intend to marry Caroline, or was Sterling hoping to flush Margaret out with the news? Margaret remembered how happy Caroline had looked in Marcus's arms at the ball. Yes, a girl not yet out of the schoolroom could have her head turned by Marcus Benton quite easily. And by the time Caroline realized the character of the man she had married, it would be too late.

Margaret turned and paced the small room.

Nathaniel said, "Allow me to help."

She kept pacing. "What can you do?"

"I can marry you."

She whirled, incredulous. "Marry me?"

He flinched as though she'd slapped him. "I know it was Lewis you wanted. If that is still the case, I will do everything in my power to convince him. In fact, he may be more amenable, now he knows of your inheritance."

She frowned. "I don't want to marry Lewis. How would marrying anybody help my sister?"

"If Marcus has proposed to your sister to force you from hiding . . . and still hopes to marry you for your inheritance . . ."

"My birthday is only two weeks away. If I can remain unwed until I receive my inheritance I will grant Caroline a generous dowry and she can marry someone worthy of her. And I can marry, or not, as I wish."

He shook his head. "You have been living under our roof for months now, Margaret. A gentleman in such a situation, unusual as this one is, has a certain duty, a certain obligation."

A chill ran through her. She lifted her chin. "I assure you there is no obligation, Mr. Upchurch. You and your brother did not know I was here, though I suspect your sister knew all along. You need not worry. You are under no compunction to uphold my honor, such as it is after all this."

"It would be no burden, Miss Macy, I promise you." He took a step nearer, a grin touching his mouth. "In fact, I can think of no other woman I would rather be shackled to."

She stiffened, anger flaring. "I don't want you to be *shackled* to me. I don't want *anyone* to have to marry me. Not Marcus Benton, not Lewis, and not you."

"Margaret, I was only joking. Don't—"

She whipped opened the door and whispered harshly, "Now I must ask you to leave, sir, this very moment."

Nathaniel hesitated. Then, with a look of pained regret, he complied.

She closed the door behind him, then lay on her bed and wept, sorrow and confusion muddling her thoughts. Surely a marriage of convenience to a good man was not the only alternative to marrying a despicable man. Had Nathaniel offered only out of duty as she'd accused him? Or did he really wish to marry her? He had never said he loved her. She remembered his kiss. He certainly wanted her physically. But did he love her? Was he, like Lewis, only willing to overlook her faults and give her a second chance now that she came with the added attraction of an inheritance?

She detested the thought of giving in to the Bentons, especially now that her birthday was a mere fortnight away. She was so close to reaching her independence. But if she waited to save her money—herself—might her sister be lost?

But Margaret also knew the Upchurches needed money. If she gave up her inheritance to buy Caroline's freedom, would she be giving up her chance with Nathaniel Upchurch all over again?

What a mess he had made of it. He never should have suggested he was *willing* to marry her to protect her reputation. How condescending he must have sounded. He *wanted* to marry Margaret with every ounce of his being. He fought the urge to wallow in the sense of rejection that hovered over him like a wet wool blanket, foul and suffocating. But was he fooling himself? Had he not all but begged her to marry him as he had two years before only to be rejected again?

He tried to imagine himself in her situation. But it was difficult to guess what a woman might be thinking on the best of days, let alone in the midst of the strange muddle Margaret Macy had created for herself.

Nathaniel ran frustrated fingers over his face. Who could understand women? Perhaps another woman, he realized. He would ask his sister. But it was late and Helen had already gone to bed. He would ask her first thing in the morning.

Nathaniel awoke early. Perhaps one of the maids delivering hot water had awoken him, though he saw no one about. More likely, it was his eagerness to right last night's debacle that spurred him from bed. He couldn't wait until breakfast. He wanted to talk to his sister now and figure out what to do about Margaret.

Helen answered his knock and invited him in with a sleepy smile, sitting up in bed. "Well, well. You haven't come to my room this early since we were children. What is it?"

"It's Margaret, uh, Nora, um . . ."

"It's all right, I know. I've known all along. Well, practically."

"I wondered if you did. You always were the cleverest of our lot."

She frowned. "Tell me she hasn't thrown you over for Lewis again— that was my biggest fear. If she has, I promise I shall brain her."

"No, it isn't that."

"Then what is it? Tell me everything."

So he told her. Everything. Well, not quite everything. He didn't exactly mention that kiss in his room. . . .

Helen listened soberly to his recounting of events and his last conversation with Margaret. When he finished, she asked, "Did you tell her?"

"Tell her what?"

"That you love her?"

Nathaniel felt his cheeks heat to be speaking of such things with Helen. What had he been thinking to confess to her what had transpired between him and Margaret? But then her words penetrated his self-conscious embarrassment and echoed in his mind.

Had he? He racked his brain. *She must know.* All the things he *had* said. The way he had looked at her, touched her, offered to marry her . . . But had he ever said it?

"Not in so many words," he admitted. What an imbecile he was.

Helen rolled her eyes, looking heavenward for patience. "Nathaniel Aaron Upchurch. What am I going to do with you?"

"I suppose you would have me write her a sonnet or some flowery nonsense."

She shook her head. "Actually, I don't care for poetry. Just tell her how you feel. Tell her the truth."

He nodded, thinking of all he should have said.

"Well?" she asked, brows arched high.

Nathaniel hesitated. "Well, what?"

Helen chucked a pillow at him. "Go and tell her!"

Dodging it, Nathaniel turned toward the door.

"Oh," Helen began, "and tell her I need her to . . ."

Nathaniel paused, hand on the latch.

Helen sighed. "I suppose I shall have to give her up in that regard. Such a pity. My hair has never looked so good."

She winked and shooed him from the room.

Nathaniel first went downstairs and looked in the public rooms where Margaret usually worked that time of day but did not see her. So he mounted the taboo back stairs to the attic once more. If she wasn't there, he would have to brave the servants' hall.

Reaching her room, he knocked, but no one answered. The door creaked open from the pressure of his knuckles. She'd left it unlatched.

He gingerly pushed the door wide. "Margaret? It's me."

Silence.

He stepped inside and his heart plummeted. The bed had been stripped bare. No hand towel hung on the washstand, no spare apron on its peg. The room was empty. Lifeless.

She was gone.

He trudged back downstairs, then increased his pace, hoping he might yet catch her belowstairs.

Hudson hailed him as he crossed the passage toward the servery, his face lined with concern. "I was just coming to find you, sir. I have a note for you. From Nora."

Hudson handed Nathaniel the sealed paper. "It was inside her letter to Mrs. Budgeon and me. Giving notice."

"Dash it," Nathaniel muttered and squeezed his eyes shut. He took the letter into the library to read it in private.

Dear Mr. Upchurch,

I hereby give you notice that I am leaving Fairbourne Hall and returning to London. I know this may confuse you after our recent conversations, but I hope, should you hear news of me that surprises you, that you will not think the worst of me.

I want to thank you for allowing me to stay under your roof even after you knew I had no business being there. I learned a great deal from the experience. I learned that my long list of faults includes the tendency to judge people by first appearances and to judge wrongly. I learned much more as well. I learned to love your sister and understand your brother and, dare I say it, to admire you. It was a foolish, shallow girl who turned down your offer two years ago, and a wiser young woman who has learned the meaning of regret. There is nothing to be done about that mistake, nor that regret now, but I did want you to know.

I wish the best of health and happiness to all your family.

M.E.M.

P.S. Your Mr. Hudson is a gem. I hope you will give him and Miss Helen your blessing.

His heart beat hard. Erratic. What had she gone and done? What had he done, in not making his feelings and hopes clear? In not promising to do all in his power to help her, so she would not think she had to face Sterling Benton on her own?

He felt someone's scrutiny and glanced up to find Robert Hudson hovering on the threshold, eyeing him cautiously.

Hudson held a second letter in his hand. He raised it as though he were bidding at an auction. "In her letter to me, she wrote that Betty Tidy deserves a rise in wages." He glanced down at the lines. "And that I should hire a Joan Hurdle from Hayfield to replace her." Hudson looked up at him once more. "What did she tell you?"

Nathaniel blinked. "That I ought to allow you to marry my sister."

Hudson's eyebrows rose high. "Did she indeed?"

"Indeed."

Nathaniel wanted nothing more than to call for his horse and give chase immediately, but he could not leave. Not yet.

Lord, please protect her from Benton. And don't let her do anything foolish before I can get there.

He who is not a good servant
will not be a good master.

—Plato

Chapter 33

Taking the first wages she had earned in her life, Nora Garret walked into Maidstone's Star Hotel and purchased coach fare for London. In the small women's lounge off the hotel's dining parlor, she shed her apron, wig, and cap, and carefully tucked her father's spectacles into her carpetbag.

Several minutes later, Margaret Elinor Macy emerged in a plain but serviceable blue dress, shawl, bonnet, and gloves, her blond hair pinned simply to the crown of her head. How light and free she felt without the wig and cap. How strangely vulnerable.

Soon her coach was called and Margaret went out to meet it. The guard handed her in, and she settled herself on the bench opposite an old cleric and his wife. She smiled politely but then closed her eyes to avoid conversation. She needed to think.

She spent the trip in catnaps and self debate, wondering if she had done the right thing in leaving Fairbourne Hall, and if she had any hope of preventing Caroline's nuptials. She was determined to offer Sterling the majority of her inheritance if he would forbid Marcus to marry Caroline. If he refused, she would even offer to marry the mongrel herself, in her sister's stead, hopefully with a reasonable marriage settlement. Though she prayed it would not come to that.

When the stagecoach reached London several hours later, the route ended at an inn some distance from Berkeley Square.

Margaret hired a hack to take her to Emily Lathrop's house first. She wondered if the runner she had met—or someone like him—would be loitering about the place, watching for her. But all was quiet. She might have thought Sterling had given up, if not for that recent engagement announcement. Paying runners had likely grown too expensive and he had simply changed his methods.

The Lathrops' footman admitted her, but before he could even announce her, Emily ran out into the hall.

"Margaret, what a relief! I despaired of ever seeing you again." Emily embraced her warmly and led her into the drawing room. "I was so glad to receive your letter. I shared it with your family as well. I had no choice, really. Father mentioned it to Sterling, and he insisted on seeing it."

"I suppose he denied everything?"

"Yes." Her friend hesitated. "And considering recent events . . ."

"Recent events" meaning Marcus's engagement to her sister, no doubt. So much for the man's "desperate" determination to marry Margaret, as she had described in her letter.

Margaret didn't stay long—only long enough to assure her old friend she was well and to assure herself that someone knew she was returning to Berkeley Square. As irrational as the thought might be, she didn't want Sterling to be tempted to make her "disappear" all over again, this time permanently, to get his hands on her inheritance at last.

Emily offered to go with her. Margaret thanked her but refused. She felt she must face him alone.

"Well, I insist on sending you the rest of the way in our carriage, at least." Emily said, asking the footman to alert the groom and coachman.

While they waited, Emily took Margaret's hand and asked cautiously, "So . . . you have heard the news about Marcus Benton?"

Margaret nodded.

"Good. I was afraid you had changed your mind and come back for him."

Margaret shook her head. "No." She had not come back *for* him. Not in that sense. Though she did hope to end his engagement to Caroline. But that sounded too incredible to say out loud, and she hadn't the energy for long explanations. She simply squeezed her friend's hand and took her leave.

When Margaret arrived at Berkeley Square, the butler opened the door, his normally implacable expression cracking with surprise.

"Miss Macy! You're . . . We were not expecting you. Uh . . . welcome. Welcome home."

It still wasn't home. Never would be. But she smiled at the man. "Thank you, Murdoch."

She felt the weariness creeping into her bones, leaching her strength. She thought facetiously, *My inheritance for a bath and a full night's sleep . . .*

Murdoch took her shawl and bonnet.

She asked, "Is my mother at home?"

"No, miss. She's gone out. Only the master is in at present. Shall I announce you?"

"Not just yet, please. I'd like to change first. Is there someone who might help me?"

"Of course, miss. Right away."

The footman, Theo, who once made a nuisance of himself following her whenever she dared leave Berkeley Square, now became a godsend as he brought in the tub and carried up pail after pail of hot water with the help of a new housemaid.

Miss Durand, her mother's lady's maid, bustled in, praising God in rapid-fire French for Margaret's safe return and lamenting the state of her hair, complexion, and hands. She added rose-scented bath salts to the water and helped Margaret undress, unpin her hair, and step into the tub. Margaret was too tired to object.

Miss Durand scrubbed her back and washed Margaret's hair.

Heavenly. Her scalp felt tingly clean, her skin warm and soft. She began to feel like her old self again. *Is that a good thing?* she wondered.

Miss Durand helped her into clean underthings, traditional long stays, which took her breath away, and an evening gown of pink and cream silk. Then she curled and dressed her hair. As the lady's maid powdered Margaret's nose, she lamented the slight pink tone. "Mademoiselle has been in ze sun, n'est-ce pas? On ze continent were you? Or ze coast?"

She hadn't the heart to tell the woman she had forsaken a bonnet simply to gather flowers as a housemaid in a Kent garden. "I shall never tell," Margaret said mysteriously.

The lady's maid's eyes lit with the glow of new tales to share in the housekeeper's parlor.

"Well, it is ze Gowland's Lotion for you, miss," she said, prescribing the popular remedy for a whole host of ladies' complexion complaints.

Miss Durand's accent brought Monsieur Fournier to mind, and Margaret found herself smiling wistfully. She would miss the man— his desserts as well.

Margaret regarded herself in the looking glass. She had not looked as pretty in months. She had no wish to be vain, but she did want to feel as confident as she could before facing Sterling Benton.

She fingered the neckline of the gown, wishing she might wear the cameo necklace her father had given her. She blinked back tears. *Ah well.*

Rising, Margaret took a deep breath, steeling her resolve. It was now or never.

In rose satin slippers she skimmed down the stairs and into the drawing room. Sterling sat slumped in a high-backed chair near the fire, glass of brandy in his hand, staring at the flames.

He didn't look over but must have heard her enter. Likely Murdoch had already shared the "good news" of her return.

"Come to gloat, have you?" he asked.

She frowned. "No." She glanced around the empty room. "Mother is still out?"

"Apparently."

She steeled herself. "Where is Marcus?"

He turned his head and frowned at her, eyes bleary, cheeks flushed. "Do you really not know, or are you merely pouring salt in the wound?"

"Know what? Where is he?"

"On his wedding trip about now, I should imagine."

Wedding trip—so soon? Her stomach knotted. She was too late!

"I can't believe it." Her mind reeled. She had missed her own sister's wedding. Margaret found herself murmuring to no one in particular, "I did not even know . . . or attend her . . ."

Sterling's lip curled. "We couldn't exactly send you an engraved invitation, could we? Unless we sent it . . . what, in care of Fairbourne Hall?" He slumped back in his chair. "Surprised you'd care anyway. Didn't know you were even acquainted with"—he said the name with distaste—"Miss Jane Jackson."

"Jackson?"

"I know. I couldn't believe it either. To marry an American, whose father is in trade?" He snorted. "Though Mr. Jackson is highly successful by all accounts. All Marcus had to do was marry the horse-faced daughter and he becomes instant partner." Sterling snapped his fingers. "Furthermore, he shall inherit the lot of it through his wife when the old man dies." He shook his head. "The fool has gone against my express wishes and ruined all my plans."

Margaret blinked hard to clear away the dreadful images of sweet Caroline bound forever to Sterling's puppet-nephew. How stunning to discover Marcus had shed his uncle's influence and developed gumption while she'd been gone. "I'd think you'd be happy. You wanted him to marry a rich woman and he has." And thank God that rich woman would not be her.

Sterling grimaced. "And he shall be rich. In America, not here."

Ah . . . where Sterling could not wheedle his way into his nephew's purse. She lifted her chin. "Well, good for him. And Caroline?"

"Gone back to her precious seminary, I believe."

What a relief.

Benton rose and swayed. His cravat listed, askew. His face was less handsome when mottled and slack. "Now, Margaret. You're a good girl. I know you will do your duty by your family. You don't want to see us all starve, do you? I'm sure we can come to some amicable arrangement. With your money and my able management, we'll deal very well together."

Margaret leaned away from his foul breath and squared her shoulders. "I will help my mother, and provide for my brother and sister. But you, Sterling, will not see a farthing. I heard what you told Marcus to do to me." She shook her head and forced a gentle tone. "If I were you, I would retrench and learn to live within my means. But if you are unwilling or too proud, then you can starve if you like. I have far more important things to do with my inheritance."

Margaret went back upstairs to her room to await her mother's return. Her relief over Caroline's escape was tempered by the nagging thought that she had left Fairbourne Hall in vain. And without proper notice in the bargain. She rolled her eyes at herself—still thinking like a responsible servant. Worse yet, in her panic to try and save her sister—an unnecessary intervention as it turned out—she had once again refused an offer of marriage from Nathaniel Upchurch. A man she loved. Would he ever forgive her? She feared she had hurt him irreparably, that he would never ask a third time. How impulsive she had been. Again.

What should she do now? She could not return to Fairbourne Hall as a maid, nor could she return as herself—an uninvited guest. How brazen that would be. She could pay a call on Helen, she supposed. But Helen would guess her real motivation for the visit. And how could she face the servants as herself? How strange that would be.

She could write Nathaniel a letter . . . though correspondence between unmarried ladies and gentlemen was considered improper by many. Of course such a minor indiscretion paled in comparison to her other recent acts. Even if she dared write, what would she say? *"Em . . . sorry about running off like that. All for nothing it turns out. Would you care to repeat your proposal?"*

She consoled herself with the fact that at least she had left word where she was going. He knew where she was if he wished to contact her. She would wait.

Wait for what? To reach her twenty-fifth birthday, gain her inheritance . . . and then what? Yes, she still looked forward to providing for her brother and sister. But her mother? She was less certain that relationship could be restored. Margaret felt betrayed—disappointed that her mother had fallen in with Sterling's schemes. On the other hand, her mother might very well be disappointed in her, for endangering herself and the family's reputation by running away.

A soft knock interrupted her reverie. Her heart lurched until she reminded herself that Marcus Benton was on a ship bound for America.

"Come in."

The door opened slowly, and her mother appeared, expression cautious, still clad in walking dress and pelisse, from whatever errand had taken her out that afternoon.

"Margaret," she breathed. "How glad I am to see you, safe and sound."

Joanna Macy Benton hesitated at the door, making no move to embrace her daughter, perhaps unsure of her reception.

"I want to apologize, Margaret," she said. "I am so sorry you did not feel safe under our roof. That you felt you had no choice but to flee. I don't know what I could have done, but I should have done something to make certain Marcus paid you no improper attention."

"Why didn't you?"

Her mother winced. "You can't have lived with me this last year and not know why. It's no excuse, but you saw how Sterling was, how disapproving and critical. I have tried to work out what I did wrong to lose his good opinion. I've done everything I could think of to win back his approval, his admiration, to no avail."

"I know."

"He is my husband, Margaret. But there comes a point when a woman must protect her children even in the face of her husband's displeasure. I did not stand up to him when that point came, and I am sorry. I hope someday you will forgive me."

What could Margaret say? *"You did nothing wrong, Mamma, beyond marrying him in the first place. Beyond failing to make it clear your modest marriage settlement would remain modest, that any rumored inheritance from Aunt Josephine would not end in his pockets."* But Margaret could not come out and say Sterling had only married her for money, money that would never come. It would be too cruel.

Her mother clasped her hands together. "I am relieved neither you nor Caroline has married someone who would not love you for yourself."

Margaret nodded. The poor woman knew too well what that felt like. "How is Caroline?" she asked.

"Heartbroken. Disillusioned. Angry with Marcus, with us. But she is young, and she will recover."

"I was so relieved to hear the news."

"As was I. My introduction of Miss Jackson turned out to be quite propitious."

"*Your* introduction?"

Mrs. Macy-Benton sighed. "Yes. I introduced her to Marcus, Mr. Jackson being an old acquaintance of your father's. I was almost sorry to do so. But I saw Marcus's marriage to her as the lesser of two evils. And if I don't miss my guess, Miss Jackson will keep him on a short tether from now on."

Margaret stared at her, impressed.

Her mother retrieved something from her reticule. "This is the card of the solicitor handling Aunt Josephine's estate. The time has come for you to make your wishes known to someone outside our family. You are a grown woman now, Margaret, and there is no need for Sterling or me to act as your guardian any longer."

She twiddled the card in her fingers. "I went to see Mr. Ford myself this afternoon and made him aware that, regardless of what my husband has told him in the past, Sterling is no disinterested party who will objectively advise you. Mr. Ford and his partner will be happy to fill that role."

How careful, how nearly timid she was. It smote Margaret's conscience.

She reached out to take the card from her mother, gently grasping her outstretched hand. Her mother looked up in surprise.

"Thank you, Mamma."

Tears brightened her mother's eyes, and Margaret felt her own fill in reply.

"I forgive you," Margaret whispered. "And I hope you will forgive me for not sending word sooner, for worrying you."

"Oh, Margaret." Her mother held out her arms, and Margaret entered the long-missed embrace.

Margaret went to see the solicitor the very next day.

The grey-haired, bespectacled man rose when she entered. "Ah, Miss Macy. What a pleasure to see you. You gave us all a scare, disappearing the way you did."

"I am alive and well, as you see."

He regarded her with small, kind eyes. "I have not seen you since the reading of your great-aunt's will. You have changed, my dear, if you will allow me to say so. You look very well indeed."

"Thank you, Mr. Ford."

They spoke for half an hour about the inheritance, investment options, and the necessary steps to set up a trust for Gilbert and a dowry for Caroline.

"If you would be so good as to return on your birthday to sign the paper work," he said, "I will have all I need to deposit the funds into an account in your name at the bank of your choice."

"Thank you. I would be happy to return on the twenty-ninth. Would two o'clock suit?"

"Perfectly."

She rose and pulled on her gloves.

He stood as well. "In the meantime, is there anything else I can do for you?"

She looked up at him, bit her lip, and considered. "There is one thing. . . ."

When she returned to Berkeley Square, Margaret asked Murdoch if there was anything for her in the post.

"Yes, miss. Three letters."

She shuffled through them, mood sinking. None from Maidstone.

Murdoch cleared his throat. "And several gentlemen have called for you as well. I told them you were out, but one insisted on waiting. I've put him in the morning room."

Margaret's heart leapt. "Who is it?"

He handed her several calling cards on a silver salver. She flipped through them, her elation fading. She wasn't interested in any of these men. None were Nathaniel Upchurch.

Serve one another in love.

—Galatians 5:13

Chapter 34

Margaret and her mother planned a simple evening party for Margaret's upcoming birthday. She didn't want anything lavish, nor many guests. Just her family and Emily Lathrop. Gilbert would remain at school until Christmas, but Caroline had come home for good. She was as educated and finished as Miss Hightower could make her, apparently. Margaret was glad to have her under the same roof once more.

Margaret returned to Mr. Ford's offices on the afternoon of her birthday. She was relieved the waiting was over but was not as thrilled about the fortune as she had expected. This was partly due to all the unwanted attention she was receiving over it from would-be suitors. And partly due to the complete lack of attention from the only suitor she wanted.

Mr. Ford greeted her warmly but with a reserve that told her the news about her special request was not good.

"I looked into the matter as you requested. But I am afraid I was unsuccessful. Ironically, Lime Tree Lodge has recently been for sale. Several interested parties placed bids, including a new clergyman determined to acquire it as his vicarage. The sale was finalized before I could enter a bid on your behalf. I am sorry."

So close. Tears pricked her eyes. "Well. Thank you for trying, Mr. Ford."

"I wish I had better news on your birthday."

She smiled bravely, the gesture pushing the tears down her cheeks.

He asked, "I don't suppose there are any other properties you would be interested in?"

She shook her head. "Not at present."

For the next few minutes, he showed her where to sign the rest of the paper work and told her he would let her know as soon as the money was deposited in her name. As she prepared to depart, he congratulated her and wished her every happiness.

"From your lips to God's ears," she said, over the lump in her throat.

Upon her return to Berkeley Square, Murdoch met her with yet another salver of calling cards and invitations.

Removing her bonnet, she asked, "Any from Maidstone?"

"I'm afraid not, miss."

She sighed. "Please tell the gentlemen I am not at home to callers today. I find rejecting them so unpleasant and have no wish to do so on my birthday."

"Very good, miss. I understand."

She thanked him and went upstairs without looking at a single card.

Margaret knocked softly on Caroline's door and entered when bid. Caroline sat at her dressing table, the new maid brushing her hair.

Margaret held out her hand. "Please, allow me."

The maid handed over the brush, curtsied, and turned to go.

"Thank goodness," Caroline huffed. "That girl is inept."

The housemaid faltered, then scurried from the room.

"Caroline . . ." Margaret gently admonished. "People in service are still people. She's young, but she'll learn. Be kind."

"Oh, don't fuss at me, Margaret. I doubt she even understood what I said."

"I don't know. . . . Appearances can be deceiving." She added in a lower voice, "As you and I have both learned."

Caroline hung her head. She sat quietly for several moments, then whispered, "I was deceived. I thought Marcus loved me, but he only pretended. He confessed he only asked me to marry him to please his uncle. Sterling was certain it would bring you home."

"And he was right." Margaret twisted and pinned Caroline's hair. "You won't believe me now, but it is a blessing Marcus ended the engagement. He would have broken your heart a thousand times over. Better to know it was all an act before the vows were said."

"I know you're right. But it still hurts."

"I know, my love. I know."

Margaret went into her own room. She ought to summon Miss Durand to help her dress for dinner. Instead she stood at her window feeling listless and let down. She had so hoped for some word from him.

She glanced out the window at the Berkeley Square garden below and told herself to cheer up. She saw a traveling coach waiting across the street and wondered who had called. With a start, she recognized the coachman on the bench and the young groom climbing up beside him. Clive! It was the Upchurch coach. Nathaniel must have come to call while she was in Caroline's room. The coachman lifted the reins, and the horses began to move off.

Leaving? Had Murdoch turned away Mr. Upchurch as well?

She flew from her room, drummed down the many stairs and across the hall, heedless of decorum. Flinging open the door, she prayed she would reach him in time. She leapt the stoop and dashed into the street, but the carriage was already turning the corner.

She was too late. The Upchurch coach disappeared from view.

Tears filled her eyes. If only she had not refused to see callers today, of all days. She had only herself to blame, for she had told Murdoch to send all gentlemen away. Foolish girl!

Margaret wiped her cheeks with the back of her hand, gave a deep shuddering sigh, and turned toward the house.

She stopped short, breath catching. For there on the front stoop stood Nathaniel Upchurch.

"Mr. Upchurch," she breathed.

He wore a dark green coat, buff breeches, and tall boots. He did not smile. He only looked at her, his expression inscrutable. "Miss Macy," he said dryly. "I was told you were not at home."

Chagrined, she hurried to explain. "I am sorry. I have had a great many callers of late, and I—"

"Suitors, I suppose?"

"I'm afraid so. All desperate fortune hunters, the lot of them."

His brows rose.

"Oh! Not that I include you among them, Mr. Upchurch. I didn't mean that." Now that he stood before her at last, she rambled on like a schoolroom miss. She swallowed and gestured vaguely toward the street. "I'm afraid your carriage has left without you."

He nodded. "I told them to go on. I was determined to wait as long as necessary. Your butler was testy until I told him I had come a long way to see you. For some reason, at the mention of Maidstone he became much more welcoming."

Her cheeks heated. "Oh."

He tilted his head to the side. "Where do you tell people you've been?"

"I . . . don't. I say only that I was staying with friends. At least . . . I hope that is true . . . that we are friends?"

He narrowed his eyes. "Is that what you want?"

"Of course."

He stepped from the stoop and walked toward her, studying her as he neared.

Unnerved under his scrutiny, she rushed on, "I am glad you've come. I've been thinking about y—Uh . . . H-how is Lewis?"

"He is doing well."

"I am glad to hear it." She hesitated, then gestured toward the house behind him. "Would you like to come in . . . again?"

He winced up at the house, then looked over her shoulder. "How about a turn in the garden instead?"

The day was chilly and the garden spent. But she said, "Of course. Just give me a moment to collect my shawl." She stepped past him toward the door.

Murdoch, as if sensing her intention—or eavesdropping—hurried out with her shawl and draped it around her shoulders.

"You ran out before I could announce him," he whispered. "Did I do right in allowing him to wait?"

"You most certainly did. Thank you."

He leaned near. "From Maidstone, miss?"

She nodded, quaking with nerves and excitement.

The butler bestowed a rare smile.

Together Margaret and Nathaniel crossed the street and entered the long oval garden at the center of the square. Walking beneath a canopy of autumn-red maples, they crushed dry leaves with each step.

Nathaniel abruptly began, "You know you nearly killed me, don't you?"

Margaret gaped up at him. "Killed you? How?"

He clasped his hands behind his back. "You were barely gone a day when we heard Marcus Benton had changed course and married a different lady."

She nodded. "An American heiress."

"I know that now. Hudson and I have our ways. But you gave me a few dashed miserable days, I can tell you."

Her heart tingled at the thought. "I'm sorry. I thought of writing . . . but, well . . ." Her words trailed away.

He nodded. "You don't know how I thanked God when I learned the truth."

He gestured toward a park bench, and she sat down.

He crossed his arms and remained standing. "Will you ever be able to come back to Fairbourne Hall, do you think? I imagine it could be somewhat awkward for you."

Come back? How did he mean? As maid, friend, wife? She decided to tell the truth, hoping it wouldn't spoil her chances. "It would be awkward, I'm afraid."

"Even for a visit, perhaps?"

A visit . . . Then he was not thinking of asking her to marry him. Disheartened, she murmured, "Perhaps a short visit." She would, after all, like to see Helen again.

Sitting there surrounded by late autumn color, Margaret breathed in great draughts of crisp November air and breathed out a prayer. *Be thankful*, she told herself. *Nathaniel is here. . . . There is hope.*

"I would have come sooner," he said. "But I had something very particular to attend to first."

"Oh. I see." She didn't see but hoped he would explain.

"As soon as that was taken care of, I came." He sank onto the bench beside her. "And of course, I had to see you today, on your birthday."

"You remembered?"

He turned to her, expression earnest. "I remember everything about you, Miss Macy. Every moment between us—the good and the bad." He chuckled dryly. "Though I prefer to linger on more recent pleasant moments."

She tilted her head to look at him. "When I was in your employ, you mean?"

He nodded. "I found I quite enjoyed having you under the same roof. Being able to see you, hear your voice many times a day. I miss that." His eyes locked on hers. "I miss you."

Margaret's heart pounded. *Can this really be happening?*

A hint of a smile, tentative and hopeful, lifted Margaret's lips, and it was all Nathaniel could do not to kiss her then and there in front of every busybody in Mayfair.

Instead, he fished a box from his pocket. "You left something at Fairbourne Hall that belongs to you."

"Oh?"

My heart, he thought, but didn't say it, only handed her the flat rectangular box.

Her eyes flashed up at him, then back down at the box. She opened it eagerly.

Inside lay the cameo necklace he had seen the new housemaid pawn at a shop in Weavering Street.

"You bought it back for me," she breathed, eyes shining. "You have no idea what this means—it was a gift from my father."

He nodded. "There is more."

She looked inside the box again. Under the cameo lay a piece of thick paper. She extracted it and handed him the box to hold. She turned the paper over, revealing the small watercolor of Lime Tree Lodge. Her brow puckered. "Thank you, but you might have kept it. I wouldn't have minded."

He tucked his chin as though offended, and insisted, "I spent a great deal of money on it."

"On this?" She raised her fair brows, incredulous.

"Not on the painting. On Lime Tree Lodge itself."

She stared at him, stunned. "You didn't . . ."

"I did."

"But . . . my solicitor told me some vicar was very keen on buying it."

"He was. But I was keener."

"How did you . . . Forgive me, but I know you needed every shilling for Fairbourne Hall and to repair your ship."

"True."

"Then, how?"

"I sold my ship. The damage did not lower its value as much as I had feared, and it brought a good price. Besides, I have no need of it any longer."

"I thought you needed it to transport sugar from Barbados?"

He shook his head. "My father has decided to sell the plantation at last. To my great relief. If all goes well, he shall be returning to England next year, his new bride with him."

She shook her head in surprise. "A new mistress at Fairbourne Hall? What will Helen do?"

"Oh, she and Hudson have plans of their own."

One corner of her mouth quirked. "Have they indeed?"

"Yes. And once my father returns, I will no longer be needed at Fairbourne Hall. I plan to invest in a new venture Hudson has in mind. We are still hammering out the details, but I look forward to it. I can think of no more capable business partner."

"Congratulations," she murmured.

He expelled a pent-up breath. "Margaret . . ." He reached over and took her hands in his. He studied and stroked her bare fingers. She had run outside without gloves. "How rough your hands still are."

Embarrassed, she made to pull them away, but he held them fast. "Yet never have I longed to kiss any woman's hands as I long to kiss these."

Looking into her eyes, he brought first one hand to his mouth, then the other.

"I love you, Margaret Macy. And there is something I need to ask you. Something I've asked twice before and am nearly afraid to ask again. The Scriptures say let our yes be yes and our no be no, but I pray, in your case, your no may have changed . . . ?"

Margaret leaned forward and kissed him firmly, warmly, on the lips. Then she smiled at him, her eyes brimming with tears. "Yes, it most definitely has."

Author's Note

I would like to thank Susan Rabson, whom I met at the Pennsylvania bookstore where she works, helpfully recommending books to wandering readers—or in my case, a wandering parent looking for books to bring home for her sons. I was instantly drawn to her friendly smile and beautiful accent. Turns out Sue is not only passionate about books but is also a native of Maidstone, Kent, where I had already planned to set this book. She generously offered to pick up information for me on her next visit home, which she did, sending me several books and pamphlets about Maidstone and its history. Thanks so much, Sue!

I would also like to thank author Anne Elisabeth Stengl and her husband, Rohan de Silva, for their gracious help with the fencing scenes. (Any errors about either Maidstone or fencing are mine alone.)

I enjoyed the research for this book and learning about servant life. I attended a class through the Beau Monde chapter of Romance Writers of America, read many books on the subject (the sources of many of the epigraphs in the novel), and toured the belowstairs world and attic servants' quarters of several country houses and town houses in England. (For example, Lanhydrock in Cornwall, Number One Royal Crescent in Bath, The Georgian House in Bristol, and Tredegar House in Newport, Wales.)

As interesting as the research was, I found writing about servant life somewhat daunting. A great deal of information is available, but some of it conflicts. Different houses had different rules, schedules, and ways of doing things. For my purposes, I have simplified the servant routines and duties. And really, how much do you want to read about polishing brass and emptying chamber pots? Also, the staff of Fairbourne Hall is fairly skeletal compared to the number of servants a large country house would have actually needed to operate smoothly in the early 1800s. But I didn't want to give you *too* many characters to keep track of! I hope those more expert than I will forgive the liberties taken for fiction's sake.

On another historical note, the Barbados slave revolt mentioned was an actual event which began on Good Friday (April 14) 1816.

Also, the plaque quoted in chapter 7 was an actual plaque in the servants' hall of the manor in Lower Slaughter, one of my husband's favorite Cotswold villages.

As always, I would like to thank my husband and sons for their love and support. My first reader, Cari Weber, for her honest and helpful feedback. My diligent editor Karen Schurrer, as well as the entire family at Bethany House Publishers, for whom my love and gratitude know no bounds.

Discussion Questions

1. How would you like to have a servant (or servants) living in your basement, attic, or guest room? Would the help be worth the loss of privacy to you?

2. If you lived a few hundred years ago, do you think it more likely you'd employ servants or be a servant? Why? If a servant, what type of work would you do best?

3. Did anything surprise you about the life of servants in the early 1800s? How well do you think you would cope if you found yourself in service in Regency England tomorrow?

4. Why do you think the author chose the opening quotation "Judge not according to the appearance"? How might that relate to the story?

5. Does Margaret change during the course of the novel, and if so, how?

6. Other than that of Nathaniel and Margaret, what relationship in the story intrigued you the most? How so?

7. If you could choose one character from the book to have over for dinner, which would you choose? What did you like about him or her?

8. Which characters, if any, would you like to know more about? What would you like to see occur in their lives after the story's end?

9. If this book were ever made into a movie, which actors could you see in the leading roles?

10. If you had to choose one, would you prefer to live in a large country manor like Fairbourne Hall, a charming cottage like Lime Tree Lodge, or a posh London town house?

JULIE KLASSEN loves all things Jane—
Jane Eyre and Jane Austen. A graduate of the
University of Illinois, Julie worked in publishing
for sixteen years and now writes full time. Two of
her books, *The Silent Governess* (2010) and *The
Girl in the Gatehouse* (2011), won the Christy
Award for Historical Romance. *The Girl in the
Gatehouse* also won the Midwest Book Award for
Genre Fiction. Julie and her husband have two
sons and live in a suburb of St. Paul, Minnesota.

For more information, visit *www.julieklassen.com.*

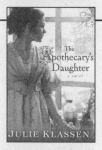